W9-AEC-848
F. S. Talcott.
Buffalo,
N. Y.
1907.
WITHDRAWN

"THE UNVEILED DANCERS CAME AND WENT"

THE WEAVERS

A TALE OF ENGLAND AND EGYPT
OF FIFTY YEARS AGO

BY

GILBERT PARKER

AUTHOR OF
"THE RIGHT OF WAY" "THE SEATS OF THE MIGHTY"
ETC. ETC.

er. Weavers
d Claridge, a sturdy English Quaker carries
new civilization of the West to the
tian East. He becomes counsellor and
ident of Prince Kaid and fights battles
him. The story is a reenactment of the
rors of Shadrach,Meshach and Abednego in
e fiery furnace; for David,invincible in the
ght of truth,is unharmed by the firewhich is
consuming traditional and superstitional
athenism.

NEW YORK AND LONDON
HARPER & BROTHERS PUBLISHERS
MCMVII

BOOKS BY THE SAME AUTHOR

NOVELS AND STORIES

PIERRE AND HIS PEOPLE
MRS. FALCHION
THE TRESPASSER
THE TRANSLATION OF A SAVAGE
THE TRAIL OF THE SWORD
WHEN VALMOND CAME TO PONTIAC
AN ADVENTURER OF THE NORTH
THE SEATS OF THE MIGHTY
THE POMP OF THE LAVILETTES
THE BATTLE OF THE STRONG
THE LANE THAT HAD NO TURNING
THE RIGHT OF WAY
DONOVAN PASHA
A LADDER OF SWORDS

HISTORY

OLD QUEBEC. (In collaboration with C. G. Bryan.)

TRAVEL

ROUND THE COMPASS IN AUSTRALIA

POETRY

A LOVER'S DIARY

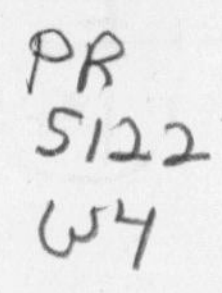

Published September, 1907.

H2

BEAUTIFUL AND BELOVED

THIS

TO

YOU

CONTENTS

BOOK I

BOOK II

BOOK III

CONTENTS

BOOK IV

BOOK V

BOOK VI

ILLUSTRATIONS

NOTE

This book is not intended to be an historical novel, nor are its characters meant to be identified with well-known persons connected with the history of England or of Egypt; but all that is essential in the tale is based upon, and drawn from the life of both countries. Though Egypt has greatly changed during the past generation, away from Cairo and the commercial centres the wheels of social progress have turned but slowly, and much remains as it was in the days of which this book is a record—in the spirit of the life at least.

G. P.

"Dost thou spread the sail, throw the spear, swing the axe, lay thy hand upon the plough, attend the furnace door, shepherd the sheep upon the hills, gather corn from the field, or smite the rock in the quarry? Yet whatever thy task, thou art even as one who twists the thread and throws the shuttle, weaving the web of Life. Ye are all weavers, and Allah the Merciful, does He not watch beside the loom?"

BOOK I

THE WEAVERS

I

AS THE SPIRIT MOVED

THE village lay in a valley which had been the bed of a great river in the far-off days when Ireland, Wales and Brittany were joined together, and the Thames flowed into the Seine. The place had never known turmoil or stir. For generations it had lived serenely.

Three buildings in the village stood out insistently, more by the authority of their appearance and position than by their size. One was a square, red-brick mansion in the centre of the village, surrounded by a high, red-brick wall enclosing a garden. Another was a big, low, graceful building with wings. It had once been a monastery. It was covered with ivy, which grew thick and hungry upon it, and was called the Cloistered House. The last of the three was of wood, and of no great size —a severely plain but dignified structure, looking like some council-hall of a past era. Its heavy oak doors and windows with diamond panes, and its air of order, cleanliness, and serenity, gave it a commanding influence in the picture. It was the key to the history of the village—a Quaker Meeting-house.

Involuntarily the village had built itself in such a way that it made a wide avenue from the common at one end to the Meeting-house on the gorse-grown upland at the other. With a demure resistance to the will of its makers the village had made itself decorative. The people were unconscious of any attractiveness in themselves or in their village. There were, however, a few who felt the beauty stirring round them. These few, for their knowledge and for the pleasure which it brought, paid the accustomed price. The records of their lives were the only notable history of the place since the days when their forefathers suffered for the faith.

One of these was a girl—for she was still but a child when she died; and she had lived in the Red Mansion with the tall porch, the wide garden behind, and the wall of apricots and peaches and clustering grapes. Her story was not to cease when she was laid away in the stiff graveyard behind the Meeting-house. It was to go on in the life of her son, whom to bring into the world she had suffered undeserved, and loved with a passion more in keeping with the beauty of the vale in which she lived than with the piety found on the high-backed seats in the Quaker Meeting-house. The name given her upon the register of death was Mercy Claridge, and a line beneath said that she was the daughter of Luke Claridge, that her age at passing was nineteen years, and that "her soul was with the Lord."

Another whose life had given pages to the village history was one of noble birth, the Earl of Eglington. He had died twenty years after the time when Luke Claridge, against the custom of the Quakers, set up a tombstone to Mercy Claridge's memory behind the Meeting-house. Only thrice in those twenty years had he slept in a room of the Cloistered House. One of those occasions was the day on which Luke Claridge put up the gray stone in the graveyard, three years after his daughter's death. On the night of that day these two men met face to face in the garden of the Cloistered House. It was said by a passer-by, who had involuntarily overheard, that Luke

Claridge had used harsh and profane words to Lord Eglington, though he had no inkling of the subject of the bitter talk. He supposed, however, that Luke had gone to reprove the other for a wasteful and wandering existence; for desertion of that Quaker religion to which his grandfather, the third Earl of Eglington, had turned in the second half of his life, never visiting his estates in Ireland, and residing here among his new friends to his last day. This listener—John Fairley was his name—kept his own counsel.

On two other occasions had Lord Eglington visited the Cloistered House in the years that passed, and remained many months. Once he brought his wife and child. The former was a cold, blue-eyed Saxon of an old family, who smiled distantly upon the Quaker village; the latter, a round-headed, warm-faced youth, with a bold menacing eye, who probed into this and that, rushed here and there as did his father, now built a miniature mill, now experimented at some peril in the laboratory which had been arranged in the Cloistered House for his scientific experiments; now shot partridges in the fields where partridges had not been shot for years; and was as little in the picture as his adventurous father, though he wore a broad-brimmed hat, smiling the while at the pain it gave to the simple folk around him.

And yet once more the owner of the Cloistered House returned alone. The blue-eyed lady was gone to her grave; the youth was abroad. This time he came to die. He was found lying on the floor of his laboratory with a broken retort in fragments beside him. With his servant, Luke Claridge was the first to look upon him lying in the wreck of his last experiment, a spirit-lamp still burning above him, in the gray light of a winter's morning. Luke Claridge closed the eyes, straightened the body, and crossed the hands over the breast which had been the laboratory of many conflicting passions of life.

The dead man had left instructions that his body should be buried in the Quaker graveyard, but Luke Claridge and the Elders prevented that—he had no right to the privileges of a Friend; and, as the only son was afar, and no near relatives pressed the late Earl's wishes, the ancient family tomb in Ireland received all that was left of the owner of the Cloistered House, which, with the estates in Ireland and the title, passed to the wandering son.

II

THE GATES OF THE WORLD

STILLNESS in the Meeting-house, save for the light swish of one graveyard-tree against the window-pane, and the slow breathing of the Quaker folk who filled every corner. On the long bench at the upper end of the room the Elders sat motionless, their hands on their knees, wearing their hats; the women in their poke-bonnets kept their gaze upon their laps. The heads of all save three were averted, and they were Luke Claridge, his only living daughter, called Faith, and his dead daughter's son David, who kept his eyes fixed on the window where the twig flicked against the pane. The eyes of Faith, who sat on a bench at one side, travelled from David to her father constantly; and if, once or twice, the plain rebuke of Luke Claridge's look compelled her eyes upon her folded hands, still she was watchful and waiting, and seemed demurely to defy the convention of unblinking silence. As time went on, others of her sex stole glances at Mercy's son from the depths of their bonnets; and at last, after over an hour, they and all were drawn to look steadily at the young man upon whose business this Meeting of Discipline had been called. The air grew warmer and warmer, but no one became restless; all seemed as cool of face and body as the gray gowns and coats with gray steel buttons which they wore.

At last a shrill voice broke the stillness. Raising his

head, one of the Elders said, "Thee will stand up, friend." He looked at David.

With a slight gesture of relief the young man stood up. He was good to look at—clean-shaven, broad of brow, fine of figure, composed of carriage, though it was not the composure of the people by whom he was surrounded. They were dignified, he was graceful; they were consistently slow of movement, but at times his quick gestures showed that he had not been able to train his spirit to that passiveness by which he lived surrounded. Their eyes were slow and quiet, more meditative than observant; his were changeful in expression, now abstracted, now dark and shining as though some inner fire was burning. The head, too, had a habit of coming up quickly with an almost wilful gesture, and with an air which, in others, might have been called pride.

"What is thy name?" said another owl-like Elder to him.

A gentle, half-amused smile flickered at the young man's lips for an instant, then, "David Claridge—still," he answered.

His last word stirred the meeting. A sort of ruffle went through the atmosphere, and now every eye was fixed and inquiring. The word was ominous. He was there on his trial, and for discipline; and it was thought by all that, as many days had passed since his offence was committed, meditation and prayer should have done their work. Now, however, in the tone of his voice, as it clothed the last word, there was something of defiance. On the ear of his grandfather, Luke Claridge, it fell heavily. The old man's lips closed tightly; he clasped his hands between his knees with apparent self-repression.

The second Elder who had spoken was he who had once heard Luke Claridge use profane words in the Cloistered House. Feeling trouble ahead, and liking the young man and his brother Elder, Luke Claridge, John Fairley sought now to take the case into his own hands.

"Thee shall never find a better name, David," he said, "if thee live a hundred years. It hath served well in England. This thee didst do. While the young Earl of Eglington was being brought home, with noise and brawling after his return to Parliament, thee mingled among the brawlers; and because some evil words were said of thy hat and thy apparel, thee laid about thee, bringing one to the dust, so that his life was in peril for some hours to come. Jasper Kimber was his name."

"Were it not that the smitten man forgave thee, thee would now be in a prison cell," shrilly piped the Elder who had asked his name.

"The fight was fair," was the young man's reply. "Though I am a Friend, the man was English."

"Thee was that day a son of Belial," rejoined the shrill Elder. "Thee did use thy hands like any heathen sailor—is it not the truth?"

"I struck the man. I punished him—why enlarge?"

"Thee is guilty?"

"I did the thing."

"That is one charge against thee. There are others. Thee was seen to drink of spirits in a public-house at Heddington that day. Twice—thrice, like any drunken collier."

"Twice," was the prompt correction.

There was a moment's pause, in which some women sighed, and others folded and unfolded their hands on their laps; the men frowned.

"Thee has been a dark deceiver," said the shrill Elder again, and with a ring of acrid triumph; "thee has hid these things from our eyes many years, but in one day thee has uncovered all. Thee—"

"Thee is charged," interposed Elder Fairley, "with

visiting a play this same day, and with seeing a dance of Spain following upon it."

"I did not disdain the music," said the young man dryly; "the flute, of all instruments, has a mellow sound." Suddenly his eyes darkened, he became abstracted, and gazed at the window where the twig flicked softly against the pane, and the heat of summer palpitated in the air. "It has good grace to my ear," he added slowly.

Luke Claridge looked at him intently. He began to realize that there were forces stirring in his grandson which had no beginning in Claridge blood, and were not nurtured in the garden with the fruited wall. He was not used to problems; he had only a code, which he had rigidly kept. He had now a glimmer of something beyond code or creed.

He saw that the shrill Elder was going to speak. He intervened. "Thee is charged, David," he said coldly, "with kissing a woman—a stranger and a wanton—where the four roads meet 'twixt here and yonder town." He motioned towards the hills.

"In the open day," added the shrill Elder, a red spot burning on each withered cheek.

"The woman was comely," said the young man, with a tone of irony, recovering an impassive look.

A strange silence fell, the women looked down; yet they seemed not so confounded as the men. After a moment they watched the young man with quicker flashes of the eye.

"The answer is shameless," said the shrill Elder. "Thy life has been that of a carnal hypocrite."

The young man said nothing. His face had become very pale, his lips were set, and presently he sat down and folded his arms.

"Thee is guilty of all?" asked John Fairley.

His kindly eye was troubled, for he had spent numberless hours in this young man's company, and together they had read books of travel and history, and even the plays of Shakespeare and Marlowe, though drama was anathema to the Society of Friends—they did not realize it in the life around them. That which was drama was either the visitation of God or the dark deeds of man, from which they must avert their eyes. Their own tragedies they hid beneath their gray coats and bodices; their dirty linen they never washed in public, save in the scandal such as this where the Society must intervene. Then the linen was not only washed, but duly starched, sprinkled, and ironed.

"I have answered all. Judge by my words," said David gravely.

"Has repentance come to thee? Is it thy will to suffer that which we may decide for thy correction?" It was Elder Fairley who spoke. He was determined to control the meeting and to influence its judgment. He loved the young man.

David made no reply; he seemed lost in thought.

"Let the discipline proceed—he hath an evil spirit," said the shrill Elder.

"His childhood lacked in much," said Elder Fairley patiently.

To most minds present the words carried home—to every woman who had a child, to every man who had lost a wife and had a motherless son. This much they knew of David's real history, that Mercy Claridge, his mother, on a visit to the house of an uncle at Portsmouth, her mother's brother, had eloped with and was duly married to the captain of a merchant ship. They also knew that, after some months, Luke Claridge had brought her home; and that before her child was born news came that the ship her husband sailed had gone down with all on board. They knew likewise that she had died soon after David came, and that her father, Luke Claridge, buried her in her maiden name, and brought the boy up as his son, not with his father's name, but bearing that name so long honored in England, and even in the far places of the earth—for had not Benn Claridge, Luke's brother, been a great carpet-merchant, traveller, and explorer in Asia Minor, Egypt, and the Soudan—Benn Claridge of the whimsical speech, the pious life? All this they knew; but none of them, to his or her knowledge, had ever seen David's father. He was legendary; though there was full proof that the girl had been duly married. That had been laid before the Elders by Luke Claridge on an occasion when Benn Claridge, his brother, was come among them again from the East.

At this moment of trial David was thinking of his uncle, Benn Claridge, and of his last words fifteen years before when going once again to the East, accompanied by the Muslim chief Ebn Ezra, who had come with him to England on the business of his country. These were Benn Claridge's words: "Love God before all, love thy fellow-man, and thy conscience will bring thee safe home, lad."

"If he will not repent, there is but one way," said the shrill Elder.

"Let there be no haste," said Luke Claridge, in a voice that shook a little in his struggle for self-control.

Another heretofore silent Elder, sitting beside John Fairley, exchanged words in a whisper with him, and then addressed them. He was a very small man with a very high stock and spreading collar, a thin face and large, wide eyes. He kept his chin down in his collar, but spoke at the ceiling like one blind, though his eyes were sharp enough on occasion. His name was Meacham.

"It is meet there shall be time for sorrow and repentance," he said. "This, I pray you all, be our will: that for three months David live apart, even in the hut where lived the drunken chairmaker ere he disappeared and died, as rumor saith—it hath no tenant. Let it be that after to-morrow night at sunset none shall speak to him till that time be come, the first day of winter. Till that day he shall speak to no man, and shall be despised of the world, and—pray God—of himself. Upon the first day of winter let it be that he come hither again and speak with us."

On the long stillness of assent that followed there came a voice across the room, from within a gray and white bonnet, which shadowed a delicate face shining with the flame of the spirit within. It was the face of Faith Claridge, the sister of the woman in the graveyard, whose soul was "with the Lord," though she was but one year older and looked much younger than her nephew, David.

"Speak, David," she said softly. "Speak now. Doth not the spirit move thee?"

She gave him his cue, for he had of purpose held his peace till all had been said; and he had come to say some things which had been churning in his mind too long. He caught the faint, cool sarcasm in her tone, and smiled unconsciously at her last words. She, at least, must have reasons for her faith in him, must have grounds for his defence in painful days to come; for painful they must be, whether he stayed to do their will, or went into the fighting world where Quakers were few and life composite of things they never knew in Hamley.

He got to his feet and clasped his hands behind his back. After an instant he broke silence.

"All those things of which I am accused, I did; and for them is asked repentance. Before that day on which I did these things was there complaint, or cause for it? Was my life evil? Did I think in secret that which might not be done openly? Well, some things I did secretly. Ye shall hear of them. I read where I might, and after my taste, many plays, and found in them beauty and the soul of deep things. Tales I have read, but a few, and John Milton, and Chaucer, and Bacon, and Montaigne, and Arab poets also, whose books my uncle sent me. Was this sin in me?"

"It drove to a day of shame for thee," said the shrill Elder.

He took no heed, but continued. "When I was a child I listened to the lark as it rose from the meadow; and I hid myself in the hedge that, unseen, I might hear it sing; and at night I waited till I could hear the nightingale. I have heard the river singing, and the music of the trees. At first I thought that this must be sin, since ye condemn the human voice that sings, but I could feel no guilt. I heard men and women sing upon the village green, and I sang also. I heard bands of music. One instrument seemed to me more than all the rest. I bought one like it, and learned to play. It was the flute—its note so soft and pleasant. I learned to play it—years ago—in the woods of Beedon beyond the hill, and I have felt no guilt from then till now. For these things I have no repentance."

"Thee has had good practice in deceit," said the shrill Elder.

Suddenly David's manner changed. His voice became deeper; his eyes took on that look of brilliance and heat which had given Luke Claridge anxious thoughts.

"I did, indeed, as the spirit moved me, even as ye have done."

"Blasphemer, did the spirit move thee to brawl and fight, to drink and curse, to kiss a wanton in the open road? What hath come upon thee?" Again it was the voice of the shrill Elder.

"Judge me by the truth I speak," he answered. "Save in these things my life has been an unclasped book for all to read."

"Speak to the charge of brawling and drink, David,"

rejoined the little Elder Meacham with the high collar and gaze upon the ceiling.

"Shall I not speak when I am moved? Ye have struck swiftly; I will draw the arrow slowly from the wound. But, in truth, ye had good right to wound. Naught but kindness have I had among you all; and I will answer. Straightly have I lived since my birth. Yet betimes a torturing unrest of mind was used to come upon me as I watched the world around us. I saw men generous to their kind, industrious and brave, beloved by their fellows; and I have seen these same men drink and dance and give themselves to coarse, rough play like young dogs in a kennel. Yet, too, I have seen dark things done in drink—the cheerful made morose, the gentle violent. What was the temptation? What the secret? Was it but the low craving of the flesh, or was it some primitive unrest, or craving of the soul, which, clouded and baffled by time and labor and the wear of life, by this means was given the witched medicament—a false freedom, a thrilling forgetfulness? In ancient days the high, the humane, in search of cure for poison, poisoned themselves, and then applied the antidote. He hath little knowledge and less pity for sin who has never sinned. The day came when all these things which other men did in my sight I did—openly. I drank with them in the taverns—twice I drank. I met a lass in the way. I kissed her. I sat beside her at the roadside and she told me her brief, sad, evil story. One she had loved had left her. She was going to London. I gave her what money I had—"

"And thy watch," said a whispering voice from the Elders' bench.

"Even so. And at the cross-roads I bade her good-by with sorrow."

"There were those who saw," said the shrill voice from the bench.

"They saw what I have said—no more. I had never tasted spirits in my life. I had never kissed a woman's lips. Till then I had never struck my fellow-man; but before the sun went down I fought the man who drove the lass in sorrow into the homeless world. I did not choose to fight; but when I begged the man Jasper Kimber for the girl's sake to follow and bring her back, and he railed at me and made to fight me, I took off my hat, and there I laid him in the dust."

"No thanks to thee that he did not lie in his grave," observed the shrill Elder.

"In truth I hit hard," was the quiet reply.

"How came thee expert with thy fists?" said Elder Fairley, with the shadow of a smile.

"A book I bought from London, a sack of corn, a hollow leather ball, and an hour betimes with the drunken chairmaker in the hut by the lime-kiln on the hill. He was once a sailor, and a fighting man."

A look of blank surprise ran slowly along the faces of the Elders. They were in a fog of misunderstanding and reprobation.

"While yet my father"—he looked at Luke Claridge, whom he had ever been taught to call his father—"shared the great business at Heddington, and the ships came from Smyrna and Alexandria, I had some small duties, as is well known. But that ceased, and there was little to do. Sports are forbidden among us here, and my body grew sick because the mind had no labor. The world of work has thickened round us beyond the hills. The great chimneys rise in a circle as far as eye can see on yonder crests; but we slumber and sleep."

"Enough, enough," said a voice from among the women. "Thee has a friend gone to London—thee knows the way. It leads from the cross-roads!"

Faith Claridge, who had listened to David's speech, her heart panting, her clear gray eyes—she had her mother's eyes—fixed benignly on him, turned to the quarter whence the voice came. Seeing who it was—a widow who, with no demureness, had tried without avail to bring Luke Claridge to her—her lips pressed together in a bitter smile, and she said to her nephew clearly,—

"Patience Spielman hath little hope of thee, David. Hope hath died in her."

A faint, prim smile passed across the faces of all present, for all knew Faith's allusion, and it relieved the tension of the past half-hour. From the first moment David began to speak he had commanded his hearers. His voice was low and even; but it had also a power which, when put to sudden quiet use, compelled the hearer to an almost breathless silence, not so much to the meaning of the words, but to the tone itself, to the man behind it. His personal force was remarkable. Quiet and pale ordinarily, his clear russet-brown hair falling in a wave over his forehead, when roused, he seemed like some delicate engine made to do great labors. As Faith said to him once, "David, thee looks as though thee could lift great weights lightly." When roused, his eyes lighted like a lamp, the whole man seemed to pulsate. He had shocked, awed, and troubled his listeners. Yet he had held them in his power, and was master of their minds. The interjections had but given him new means to defend himself. After Faith had spoken he looked slowly round.

"I am charged with being profane," he said. "I do not remember. But is there none among you who has not secretly used profane words and, neither in secret nor openly, has repented? I am charged with drinking. On one day of my life I drank openly. I did it because something in me kept crying out, 'Taste and see!' I tasted and saw, and know; and I know that oblivion, that brief pitiful respite from trouble, which this evil tincture gives. I drank to know; and I found it lure me into a new careless joy. The sun seemed brighter, men's faces seemed happier, the world sang about me, the blood ran swiftly, thoughts swarmed in my brain. My feet were on the mountains, my hands were on the sails of great ships—I was a conqueror. I understood the drunkard in the first withdrawal begotten of this false stimulant. I drank to know. Is there none among you who has, though it be but once, drunk secretly as I drank openly? If there be none, then I am condemned."

"Amen," said Elder Fairley's voice from the bench.

"In the open way by the cross-roads I saw a woman. I saw she was in sorrow. I spoke to her. Tears came to her eyes. I took her hand, and we sat down together. Of the rest I have told you. I kissed her—a stranger. She was comely. And this I know, that the matter ended by the cross-roads, and that by and forbidden paths have easy travel. I kissed the woman openly—is there none among you who has kissed secretly, and has kept the matter hidden? For him I struck and injured, it was fair. Shall a man be beaten like a dog? Kimber would have beaten me."

"Wherein has it all profited?" asked the shrill Elder querulously.

"I have knowledge. None shall do these things hereafter but I shall understand. None shall go venturing, exploring, but I shall pray for him."

"Thee will break thy heart and thy life exploring," said Luke Claridge bitterly. Experiment in life he did not understand, and even Benn Claridge's emigration to far lands had ever seemed to him a monstrous and amazing thing, though it ended in the making of a great business in which he himself had prospered, and from which he had now retired. He suddenly realized that a day of trouble was at hand with this youth on whom his heart doted, and it tortured him that he could not understand.

"By none of these things shall I break my life," was David's answer now.

For a moment he stood still and silent, then all at once he stretched out his hands to them. "All these things I did were against our faith. I desire forgiveness. I did them out of my own will; I will take up your judgment. If there be no more to say, I will make ready to go to old Soolsby's hut on the hill till the set time be passed."

There was a long silence. Even the shrill Elder's head was buried in his breast. They were little likely to forego his penalty. There was a gentle inflexibility in their natures born of long restraint and practised determination. He must go out into blank silence and banishment until the first day of winter. Yet recalcitrant as they held him, their secret hearts were with him, for there was none of them but had had happy commerce with him; and they could think of no more bitter punishment than to be cut off from their own society for three months. They were satisfied he was being trained back to happiness and honor.

A new turn was given to events, however. The little wizened Elder Meacham said, "The flute, friend—is it here?"

"I have it here," David answered.

"Let us have music, then."

"To what end?" interjected the shrill Elder.

"He hath averred he can play," dryly replied the other. "Let us judge whether vanity breeds untruth in him."

The furtive brightening of the eyes in the women was represented in the men by an assumed look of abstraction in most; in others by a bland assumption of judicial calm. A few, however, frowned, and would have opposed the suggestion, but that curiosity mastered them. These watched with darkening interest the flute, in three pieces, drawn from an inner pocket and put together swiftly.

David raised the instrument to his lips, blew one low note, and then a little run of notes, all smooth and soft. Mellowness and a sober sweetness were in the tone. He paused a moment after this, and seemed questioning what to play. And as he stood, the flute in his hands, his thoughts took flight to his Uncle Benn, whose kindly, shrewd face and sharp brown eyes were as present to him, and more real, than those of Luke Claridge, whom he saw every day. Of late when he had thought of his uncle, however, alternate depression and lightness of spirit had possessed him. Night after night he had had troubled sleep, and he had dreamed again and again that his uncle knocked at his door, or came and stood beside his bed and spoke to him. He had wakened suddenly and said "Yes" to a voice which seemed to call to him.

Always his dreams and imaginings settled round his Uncle Benn, until he had found himself trying to speak to the little brown man across the thousand leagues of land and sea. He had found, too, in the past that when he seemed to be really speaking to his uncle, when it seemed as though the distance between them had been annihilated, that soon afterwards there came a letter from him. Yet there had not been more than two or three a year. They had been, however, like books of many pages, closely written, in Arabic, in a crabbed, characteristic hand, and full of the sorrow and grandeur and misery of the East. How many books on the East David had read he would hardly have been able to say; but something of the East had entered into him, something of the philosophy of Mahomet and Buddha, and the beauty of Omar Khayyám had given a touch of color and intellect to the narrow faith in which he had been schooled. He had found himself replying to a question asked of him in Heddington, as to how he knew that there was a God, in the words of a Muslim quoted by his uncle:

"RAISING THE FLUTE TO HIS LIPS, HE BEGAN TO PLAY"

"As I know by the tracks in the sand whether a Man or Beast has passed there, so the heaven with its stars, the earth with its fruits, show me that God has passed." Again, in reply to the same question, the reply of the same Arab sprang to his lips—"Does the Morning want a Light to see it by?"

As he stood with his flute—his fingers now and then caressingly rising and falling upon its little caverns, his mind travelled far to those regions he had never seen, where his uncle traded, and explored. Suddenly, the call he had heard in his sleep now came to him in this waking reverie. His eyes withdrew from the tree at the window, as if startled, and he almost called aloud in reply; but he realized where he was. At last, raising the flute to his lips, as the eyes of Luke Claridge closed with very trouble, he began to play.

Out in the woods of Beedon he had attuned his flute to the stir of leaves, the murmur of streams, the song of birds, the boom and burden of storm; and it was soft and deep as the throat of the bell-bird of Australian wilds. Now it was mastered by the dreams he had dreamed of the East, the desert skies, high and clear and burning, the desert sunsets, plaintive and peaceful and unvaried—one lovely diffusion, in which day dies without splendor and in a glow of pain. The long, velvety tread of the camel, the song of the camel-driver, the monotonous chant of the river-man, with fingers mechanically falling on his little drum, the cry of the eagle of the Libyan Hills, the lap of the heavy waters of the Dead Sea down by Jericho, the battle-call of the Druses beyond Damascus, the lonely gigantic figures at the mouth of the temple of Abou Simbel, looking out with the eternal question to the unanswering desert, the delicate ruins of moonlit Baalbec, with the snow mountains hovering above, the green oases, and the deep wells where the caravans lay down in peace—all these were pouring their influences on his mind in the little Quaker village of Hamley where life was so bare, so grave.

The music he played was all his own, was instinctively translated from all other influences into that which they who listened to him could understand. Yet that sensuous beauty which the Quaker Society was so concerned to banish from any part in their life was playing upon them now, making the hearts of the women beat fast, thrilling them, turning meditation into dreams, and giving the sight of the eyes far visions of pleasure. So powerful was this influence that the shrill Elder twice essayed to speak in protest, but was prevented by the wizened Elder Meacham. When it seemed as if the aching, throbbing sweetness must surely bring denunciation, David changed the music to a slow, mourning cadence. It was a wail of sorrow, a march to the grave, a benediction, a soft sound of farewell, floating through the room and dying away into the midday sun.

There came a long silence after, and in it David sat with unmoving look upon the distant prospect through the window. A woman's sob broke the air. Faith's handkerchief was at her eyes. Only one quick sob, but it had been wrung from her by the premonition suddenly come that the brother—he was brother more than nephew—over whom her heart had yearned, that he had, indeed, come to the cross-roads, and that their ways would henceforth divide. The punishment or banishment now to be meted out to him was as nothing. It meant a few weeks of disgrace, of ban, of what, in effect, was self-immolation, of that commanding justice of the Society which no one yet save the late Earl of Eglington had defied. David could refuse to bear punishment, but such a possibility had never occurred to her or to any one present. She saw him taking his punishment as surely as though the law of the land had him in its grasp. It was not that which she was fearing. But she saw him moving out of her life. To her this music was the prelude of her tragedy.

A moment afterwards Luke Claridge arose and spoke to David in austere tones: "It is our will that thee begone to the chairmaker's hut upon the hill till three months be passed, and that none have speech with thee after sunset to-morrow even."

"Amen," said all the Elders.

"Amen," said David, and put his flute into his pocket, and rose to go.

3

III

BANISHED

The chairmaker's hut lay upon the north hillside about half-way between the Meeting-house at one end of the village and the common at the other end. It commanded the valley, had no house near it, and was sheltered from the north wind by the hilltop which rose up behind it a hundred feet or more. No road led to it—only a path up from the green of the village, winding past a gulley and the deep cuts of old rivulets now overgrown by grass or bracken. It got the sun abundantly, and it was protected from the full sweep of any storm. It had but two rooms, the floor was of sanded earth, but it had windows on three sides, east, west, and south, and the door looked south. Its furniture was a plank bed, a few shelves, a bench, two chairs, some utensils, a fireplace of stone, a picture of the Virgin and Child, and of a Cardinal of the Church of Rome with a red hat—for the chairmaker had been a Roman Catholic, the only one of that communion in Hamley. Had he been a Protestant his vices would have made him anathema, but, being what he was, his fellow-villagers had treated him with kindness.

After the half-day in which he was permitted to make due preparations, lay in store of provisions, and purchase a few sheep and hens, hither came David Claridge. Here, too, came Faith, who was permitted one hour with him before he began his life of willing isolation. Little was said as they made the journey up the hill, driving the sheep before them, four strong lads following with necessaries—flour, rice, potatoes, and such like.

Arrived, the goods were deposited inside the hut, the lads were dismissed, and David and Faith were left alone. David looked at his watch. They had still a handful of minutes before the parting. These flew fast, and yet, seated inside the door and looking down at the village which the sun was bathing in the last glow of evening, they remained silent. Each knew that a great change had come in their hitherto unchanging life, and it was difficult to separate premonition from substantial fact. The present fact did not represent all they felt, though it represented all on which they might speak together now.

Looking round the room, at last Faith said: "Thee hast all thee needs, David? Thee is sure?"

He nodded. "I know not yet how little man may need. I have lived in plenty."

At that moment her eyes rested on the Cloistered House. "The Earl of Eglington would not call it plenty."

A shade passed over David's face. "I know not how he would measure. Is his own field so wide?"

"The spread of a peacock's feather."

"What does thee know of him?" David asked the question absently.

"I have eyes to see, Davy." The shadows from that seeing were in her eyes as she spoke, but he did not observe them.

"Thee sees but with half an eye," she continued. "With both mine I have seen horses and carriages, and tall footmen, and wine and silver, and gilded furniture, and fine pictures, and rolls of new carpet—of Uncle Benn's best carpets, Davy—and a billiard-table, and much else."

A cloud slowly gathered over David's face, and he turned to her with an almost troubled surprise. "Thee has seen these things—and how?"

"One day—thee was in Devon—one of the women was taken sick. They sent for me because the woman asked it. She was a Papist; but she begged that I should go with her to the hospital, as there was no time to send to Heddington for a nurse. She had seen me once in the house of the toll-gate keeper. Ill as she was, I could have laughed, for, as we went in the Earl's carriage to the hospital,—thirty miles it was—she said she felt at home with me, my dress being so like a nun's. It was then I saw the Cloistered House within, and learned what was afoot."

"In the Earl's carriage indeed—and the Earl?"

"He was in Ireland, burrowing among those tarnished baubles, his titles, and stripping the Irish Peter to clothe the English Paul."

"He means to make Hamley his home? From Ireland these furnishings come?"

"So it seems. Henceforth the Cloistered House will have its doors flung wide. London and all the folk of Parliament will flutter along the dunes of Hamley."

"Then the bailiff will sit yonder within a year, for he is but a starved Irish peer."

"He lives to-day as though he would be rich to-morrow. He bids for fame and fortune, Davy."

"'Tis as though a shirtless man should wear a broadcloth coat over a cotton vest."

"The world sees only the broadcloth coat. For the rest—"

"For the rest, Faith?"

"They see the man's face—and—"

His eyes were embarrassed. A thought had flashed into his mind which he considered unworthy, for this girl beside him was little likely to dwell upon the face of a renegade peer, whose living among them was a constant reminder of his father's apostasy. She was too fine, dwelt in such high spheres, that he could not think of her being touched by the glittering adventures of this daring young member of Parliament, whose book of travels had been published, only to herald his understood determination to have office in the government, not in due time, but in his own time. What could there be in common between the sophisticated Eglington and this sweet, primitively wholesome Quaker girl?

Faith read what was passing in his mind. She flushed—slowly flushed until her face and eyes were one soft glow, then she laid a hand upon his arm and said: "Davy, I feel the truth about him—no more. Nothing of him is for thee or me. His ways are not our ways." She paused, and then said solemnly, "He hath a devil. That I feel. But he hath also a mind, and a cruel will. He will hew a path, or make others hew it for him. He will make or break. Nothing will stand in his way, neither man nor thing, those he loves nor those he hates. He will go on—and to go on, all means, so they be not criminal, will be his. Men will prophesy great things for him—they do so now. But nothing they prophesy, Davy, keeps pace with his resolve."

"How does thee know these things?"

His question was one of wonder and surprise. He had never before seen in her this sharp discernment and criticism.

"How know I, Davy? I know him by studying thee. What thee is not, he is. What he is, thee is not."

The last beams of the sun sent a sudden glint of yellow to the green at their feet from the western hills, rising far over and above the lower hills of the village, making a wide ocean of light, at the bottom of which lay the Meeting-house and the Cloistered House, and the Red Mansion with the fruited wall, and all the others, like dwellings at the bottom of a golden sea. David's eyes were on the distance, and the far-seeing look was in his face which had so deeply impressed Faith in the Meeting-house; by which she had read his future.

"And shall I not also go on?" he asked.

"How far, who can tell?"

There was a plaintive note in her voice—the unavailing and sad protest of the maternal spirit, of the keeper of the nest, who sees the brood fly safely away, looking not back.

"What does thee see for me afar, Faith?" His look was eager.

"The will of God, which shall be done," she said with a sudden resolution, and stood up. Her hands were lightly clasped before her like those of Titian's Mater Dolorosa among the Rubens and Tintorettos of Madrid, a lonely figure, whose lot it was to spend her life for others. Even as she already had done; for thrice she had refused marriages suitable and possible to her. In each case she had steeled her heart against loving, that she might be all in all to her sister's child and to her father. There is no habit so powerful as the habit of care of others. In Faith it came as near being a passion as passion could have a place in her even-flowing blood, under that cool flesh, governed by a heart as fair as the apricot blossoms on the wall in her father's garden. She had been bitterly hurt in the Meeting-house; as bitterly as is many a woman when her lover has deceived her. David had acknowledged before them all that he had played the flute secretly for years! That he should have played it was nothing; that she should not have shared his secret, and so shared his culpability before them all, was a wound which would take long to heal.

She laid her hand upon his shoulder suddenly with a nervous little motion.

"And the will of God thee shall do to His honor, though thee is outcast to-day. . . . But, Davy, the music—thee kept it from me."

He looked up at her steadily; he read what was in her mind.

"I hid it so, because I would not have thy conscience troubled. Thee would go far to smother it for me; and I was not so ungrateful to thee. I did it for good to thee."

A smile passed across her lips. Never was woman so grateful, never wound so quickly healed. She shook her head sadly at him, and stilling the proud throbbing of her heart, she said:

"But thee played so well, Davy!"

He got up and turned his head away, lest he should laugh outright. Her reasoning — though he was not worldly enough to call it feminine, and though it scarce tallied with her argument— seemed to him quite her own.

"How long have we?" he said over his shoulder.

"The sun is yet five minutes up, or more," she said, a little breathlessly, for she saw his hand inside his coat, and guessed his purpose.

"But thee will not dare to play—thee will not dare," she said, but more as an invitation than a rebuke.

"Speech was denied me here, but not my music. I find no sin in it."

She eagerly watched him adjust the flute. Suddenly she drew to him the chair from the doorway, and beckoned him to sit down. She sat where she could see the sunset.

The music floated through the room and down the hillside, a searching sweetness.

She kept her face ever on the far hills. It went on and on. At last it stopped. David roused himself, as from a dream. "But it is dark!" he said startled. "It is past the time thee should be with me. My banishment began at sunset."

"Are all the sins to be thine?" she asked calmly.

She had purposely let him play beyond the time set for their being together. "Good-night, Davy." She kissed him on the cheek.

"I will keep the music for the sin's remembrance," she added, and went out into the night.

IV

THE CALL

"England is in one of those passions so creditable to her moral sense, so illustrative of her unregulated virtues. We are living in the first excitement and horror of the news of the massacre of Christians at Damascus. We are full of righteous and passionate indignation. 'Punish—restore the honor of the Christian nations' is the proud appeal of prelate, prig, and philanthropist, because some hundreds of Christians who knew their danger, yet chose to take up their abode in a fanatical Muslim city of the East, have suffered death."

The meeting had been called in answer to an appeal from Exeter Hall. Lord Eglington had been asked to speak, and these were among his closing words.

He had seen, as he thought, an opportunity for sensation. Politicians of both sides, the press on all hands, were thundering denunciations upon the city of Damascus, sitting insolent and satiated in its exquisite bloom of pear and nectarine, and the deed itself was fading into that blank past of Eastern life where "there are no birds in last year's nest." If he voyaged with the crowd, his pennant would be lost in the clustering sails! So he would move against the tide, and would startle, even if he did not convince.

"Let us not translate an inflamed religious emotion into a war," he continued. "To what good? Would it restore one single life in Damascus? Would it bind one broken heart? Would it give light to one darkened home? Let us have care lest we be called a nation of hypocrites. I will neither support nor oppose the resolution presented; I will content myself with pointing the way to a greater national self-respect."

Mechanically a few people who had scarcely apprehended the full force of his remarks began to applaud; but there came cries of "*'Sh! 'Sh!*" and the clapping of hands suddenly stopped. For a moment there was absolute silence, in which the chairman adjusted his glasses and fumbled with the agenda paper in his confusion, scarcely knowing what to do. The speaker had been expected to second the resolution, and had not done so. There was an awkward silence. Then, in a loud whisper, some one said:

"David, David, do thee speak."

It was the voice of Faith Claridge. Perturbed and anxious, she had come to the meeting with her father. They had not slept for nights, for the last news they had had of Benn Claridge was from the city of Damascus, and they were full of painful apprehensions.

It was the eve of the first day of winter, and David's banishment was over. Faith had seen David often at a distance—how often had she stood in her window and looked up over the apricot-wall to the chairmaker's hut on the hill! According to his penalty David had never come to Hamley village, but had lived alone, speaking to no one, avoided by all, working out his punishment. Only the day before the meeting he had read of the massacre at Damascus from a newspaper which had been left on his doorstep overnight. Elder Fairley had so far broken the covenant of ostracism and boycott, knowing David's love for his Uncle Benn. All that night David paced the hillside in anxiety and agitation, and saw the sun rise upon a new world—a world of freedom, of home-returning, yet a world which during the past four months had changed so greatly that it would never seem the same again.

The sun was scarce two hours high when Faith and her father mounted the hill to bring him home again. He had, however, gone to Heddington to learn further news of the massacre. He was thinking of his Uncle Benn—all else could wait. His anxiety was infinitely greater than that of Luke Claridge, for his mind had been disturbed by frequent premonitions; and those sudden calls in his sleep—his uncle's voice—ever seemed to be waking him at night. He had not meant to speak at the meeting, but the last words of the speaker decided him; he was in a flame of indignation. He heard the voice of Faith whisper over the heads of the people, "David, David, do thee speak." Turning he met her eyes, then rose to his feet, came steadily to the platform, and raised a finger towards the chairman.

A great whispering ran through the audience. Very many recognized him, and all had heard of him—the history of his late banishment and self-approving punishment were familiar to them. He climbed the steps of the platform alertly, and the chairman welcomed him with nervous pleasure. Any word from a Quaker, friendly to the feeling of national indignation, would give the meeting the new direction which all desired.

Something in the face of the young man grown thin and very pale during the period of long thought and little food in the lonely and meditative life he had led; something human and mysterious in the strange tale of his one day's mad doings fascinated them. They had heard of the liquor he had drunk, of the woman he had kissed at the cross-roads, of the man he had fought, of his discipline and sentence. His clean, shapely figure, and the soft austerity of the neat gray suit he wore, his broad-brimmed hat pushed a little back, showing well a square white forehead—all conspired to send a wave of feeling through the audience, which presently broke into cheering.

Beginning with the usual formality, he said: "I am obliged to differ from nearly every sentiment expressed by the Earl of Eglington, the member for Levizes, who has just taken his seat."

There was an instant's pause, the audience cheered, and cries of delight came from all parts of the house. "All good counsel has its sting," he continued, "but the good counsel of him who has just spoken is a sting in a wound deeper than the skin. The noble Earl has bidden us to be consistent and reasonable. I have risen here to speak for that to which mere consistency and reason may do cruel violence. I am a man of peace, I am the enemy of war—it is my faith and creed; yet I repudiate the principle put forward by the Earl of Eglington, that you shall not clench your hand for the cause which is your heart's cause, because, if you smite, the smiting must be paid for."

He was interrupted by cheers and laughter, for the late event in his own life came to them to point his argument.

"The nation that declines war may be refusing to inflict that just punishment, which alone can set the wrongdoers on the better course. It is not the faith of that society to which I belong to decline correction lest it may seem like war."

The point went home significantly, and cheering followed. "The high wall of Tibet, a stark refusal to open the door to the wayfarer, I can understand; but, friend" —he turned to the young peer—"friend, I cannot understand a defence of him who opens the door, upon terms of mutual hospitality, and then, in the red blood of him who has so contracted, blots out the just terms upon which they have agreed. Is that thy faith, friend?"

The repetition of the word *friend* was almost like a gibe,

though it was not intended as such. There was none present, however, but knew of the defection of the Earl's father from the Society of Friends, and they chose to interpret the reference to a direct challenge. It was a difficult moment for the young Earl, but he only smiled, and cherished anger in his heart.

For some minutes David spoke with force and power, and he ended with passionate solemnity. His voice rang out: "The smoke of this burning rises to Heaven, the winds that wail over scattered and homeless dust bear a message to us. In the name of Mahomet, whose teaching condemns treachery and murder, in the name of the Prince of Peace, who taught that justice which makes for peace, I say it is England's duty to lay the iron hand of punishment upon this evil city and on the government in whose orbit it shines with so deathly a light. I fear it is that one of my family and of my humble village lies beaten to death in Damascus. Yet not because of that do I raise my voice here to-day. These many years Benn Claridge carried his life in his hands, and in a good cause it was held like the song of a bird, to be blown from his lips in the day of the Lord. I speak only as an Englishman. I ask you to close your minds against the words of this brilliant politician, who would have you settle a bill of costs written in Christian blood, by a promise to pay, got through a mockery of armed display in those waters on which once looked the eyes of the Captain of our faith. Humanity has been put in the witness-box of the world; let humanity give evidence."

Women wept. Men waved their hats and cheered, the whole meeting rose to its feet and gave vent to its feelings.

For some moments the tumult lasted, Eglington looking on with face unmoved. As David turned to leave the table, however, he murmured, "Peacemaker! Peacemaker!" and smiled sarcastically.

As the audience resumed their seats two people were observed making their way to the platform. One was Elder Fairley leading the way to a tall figure in a black robe covering another colored robe, and wearing a large white turban. Not seeing the newcomers, the chairman was about to put the resolution, but a protesting hand from John Fairley stopped him, and in a strange silence the two newcomers mounted the platform. David rose and advanced to meet them. There flashed into his mind that this stranger in Eastern garb was Ebn Ezra Bey, the old friend of Benn Claridge, of whom his uncle had spoken and written so much. The same instinct drew Ebn Ezra Bey to him—he saw the uncle's look in the nephew's face. In a breathless stillness the Oriental said in perfect English, with a voice monotonously musical:

"I came to thy house and found thee not. I have a message for thee from the land where thine uncle sojourned with me."

He took from a wallet a piece of paper and passed it to David, adding: "I was thine uncle's friend. He hath put off his sandals and walketh with bare feet!"

David read eagerly.

"*It is time to go, Davy,*" the paper said. "*All that I have is thine. Go to Egypt, and thee shall find it so. Ebn Ezra Bey will bring thee. Trust him as I have done. He is a true man, though the Koran be his faith. They took me from behind, Davy, so that I was spared temptation—I die as I lived, a man of peace. It is too late to think how it might have gone had we met face to face; but the will of God worketh not according to our will. I can write no more. Luke, Faith, and Davy—dear Davy, the night has come, and all's well. Good-morrow, Davy. Can you not hear me call? I have called thee so often of late! Good-morrow! Good-morrow! . . . I doff my hat, Davy—at last—to God!*"

David's face whitened. All his visions had been true visions, his dreams true dreams. Brave Benn Claridge had called to him at his door—"*Good-morrow! Good-morrow! Good-morrow!*" Had he not heard the knocking and the voice? Now all was made clear. His path lay open before him—a far land called him, his quiet past was infinite leagues away. Already the staff was in his hands and the cross-roads were sinking into the distance behind. He was dimly conscious of the wan, shocked face of Faith in the crowd beneath him, which seemed blurred and swaying, of the bowed head of Luke Claridge, who, standing up, had taken off his hat in the presence of this news of his brother's death which he saw written in David's face. David stood for a moment before the great throng, numb and speechless.

"It is a message from Damascus," he said at last, and could say no more.

Ebn Ezra Bey turned a grave face upon the audience.

"Will you hear me?" he said. "I am an Arab."

"Speak—speak!" came from every side.

"The Turk hath done his evil work in Damascus," he said. "All the Christians are dead—save one; he hath turned Muslim—and is safe." His voice had a note of scorn. "It fell sudden and swift like a storm in summer. There were no paths to safety. Soldiers and those who led them shared in the slaying. As he and I who had travelled far together these many years sojourned there in the way of business, I felt the air grow colder, I saw the cloud gathering. I entreated, but he would not go. If trouble must come, then he would be with the Christians in their peril. At last he saw with me the truth. He had a plan of escape. There was a Christian weaver with his wife in a far quarter—against my entreaty he went to warn them. The storm broke. He was the first to fall, smitten in 'that street called Straight.' I found him soon after. Thus did he speak to me—even in these words: 'The blood of women and children shed here to-day shall cry from the ground. Unprovoked, the host has turned wickedly upon his guest. The storm has been sown, and the whirlwind must be reaped. Out of this evil good shall come. Shall not the Judge of all the earth do right?' These were his last words to me then. As his life ebbed out, he wrote a letter which I have brought hither to one"—he turned to David—"whom he loved. At the last he took off his hat, and lay with it in his hands, and died. . . . I am a Muslim, but the God of pity, of justice, and of right is my God; and in His name be it said that this crime was a crime of Sheitan the accursed."

In a low voice the chairman put the resolution. The Earl of Eglington voted in its favor.

Walking the hills homeward with Ebn Ezra Bey, Luke, Faith, and John Fairley, David kept saying over to himself the words of Benn Claridge: "*I have called thee so often of late. Good-morrow! Good-morrow! Good-morrow! Can you not hear me call?*"

BOOK II

4

V

THE WIDER WAY

SOME months later the following letter came to David Claridge in Cairo from Faith Claridge in Hamley:

"David, I write thee from the village and the land and the people thee did once love so well. Does thee love them still? They gave thee sour bread to eat ere thy going, but yet thee didst grind the flour for the baking. Thee didst frighten all who knew thee with thy doings that mad midsummer time. The tavern, the theatre, the cross-roads, and the cockpit—was ever such a day!

"Now, Davy, I must tell of a strange thing. But first, a moment. Thee remembers the man Kimber smitten by thee at the public-house on *that* day? What think thee has happened? He followed to London the lass kissed by thee, and besought her to return and marry him. This she refused at first with anger; but afterwards she said that, if in three years he was of the same mind, and stayed sober and hard-working meanwhile, she would give him an answer, she would consider. Her head was high. She has become maid to a lady of degree, who has well befriended her.

"How do I know these things? Even from Jasper Kimber, who, on his return from London, was taken to his bed with fever. Because of the hard blows dealt him by thee, I went to make amends. He welcomed me, and soon opened his whole mind. That mind has generous moments, David, for he took to being thankful for thy knocks.

"Now for the strange thing I hinted. After visiting Jasper Kimber at Heddington, as I came back over the hill by the path we all took that day after the Meeting—Ebn Ezra Bey, my father, Elder Fairley, and thee and me—I drew near the chairmaker's hut where thee lived alone all those sad months. It was late evening; the sun had set. Yet I felt that I must needs go and lay my hand in love upon the door of the empty hut which had been ever as thee left it. So I came down the little path swiftly, and then round the great rock, and up towards the door. But, as I did so, my heart stood still, for I heard voices. The door was open, but I could see no one. Yet there the voices sounded, one sharp and peevish with anger, the other low and rough. I could not hear what was said. At last a figure came from the door and went quickly down the hillside. Who, think thee, was it? Even 'neighbor Eglington.' I knew the walk and the forward thrust of the head. Inside the hut all was still. I drew near with a kind of fear, but yet I came to the door and looked in

"As I looked into the dusk my limbs trembled under me, for who should be sitting there, a half-finished chair between his knees, but Soolsby the old chairmaker! Yes, it was he. There he sat, looking at me with his staring blue eyes and shock of red-gray hair.

"'Soolsby! Soolsby!' said I, my heart hammering at my breast, for was not Soolsby dead and buried? His eyes stared at me in fright. 'Why do you come?' he said in a hoarse whisper. 'Is he dead, then? Has harm come to him?'

"By now I had recovered myself, for it was no ghost I saw, but a human being more distraught than was myself.

"'Do you not know me, Soolsby?' I asked.

"'You are Mercy Claridge—from beyond—beyond and away!' he answered dazedly.

"'I am Faith Claridge, Soolsby,' answered I. He started, peered forward at me, and for a moment he did not speak; then the fear went from his face. 'Ay, Faith Claridge, as I said,' he answered with apparent understanding, his stark mood passing. 'No, thee said Mercy Claridge, Soolsby,' said I, 'and she has been asleep these many years.' 'Ay, she has slept soundly, thanks be to God!' he replied, and crossed himself. 'Why should thee call me by her name?' I inquired. 'Ay, is not her tomb in the churchyard?' he answered, and added quickly, 'Luke Claridge and I are of an age to a day—which, think you, will go first?'

"He stopped weaving, and peered over at me with his staring blue eyes, and I felt a sudden quickening of the heart. For, at the question, curtains seemed to drop from all around me, and leave me in the midst of pains and miseries, in a chill air that froze me to the marrow. I saw myself alone—thee in Egypt and I here, and none of our blood and name beside me. For we are the last, Davy, the last of the Claridges. But I said coldly, and with what was near to anger, that he should link his name and fate with that of Luke Claridge, 'Which of ye two goes first is God's will, and according to His wisdom. Which, think thee,' added I—and now I cannot forgive myself for saying it—'which, think thee, would do least harm in going?' 'I know which would do most good,' he answered, with a harsh laugh in his throat. Yet his blue eyes looked kindly at me, and now he began to nod pleasantly. I thought him a little mad, but yet his speech had seemed not without dark meaning.

"'Thee has had a visitor,' I said to him presently. He laughed in a snarling way that made me shrink, and answered: 'He wanted this and he wanted that—his high-handed, second-best lordship! Ay, and he would have it because it pleased him to have it—like his father before him. A poor sparrow on a tree-top, if you tell him he must not have it, he will hunt it down the world till it is his, as though it was a bird of paradise. And when he's seen it fall at last, he'll remember but the fun of the chase; and the bird may get to its tree-top again —if it can—if it can—if it can, my lord! That is what his father was, the last Earl, and that is what he is who left my door but now. He came to snatch old Soolsby's palace, his nest on the hill, to use it for a telescope, or such whimsies. He has scientific tricks like his father before him. Now it is astronomy, and now chemistry, and such like; and always it is the Eglington mind, which let God A'mighty make it as a favor. He would have old Soolsby's palace for his spy-glass, would he then? It scared him, as though I was the devil himself, to find me here. I had but come back in time—a day later, and he would have sat here and seen me in the Pit below before giving way. Possession's nine points were with me; and here I sat and faced him; and here he stormed, and would do this and should do that; and I went on with my work. Then he would buy my Colisyum, and I wouldn't sell it for all his puff-ball lordship might offer. Isn't the house of the snail as much to him as the turtle's shell to the turtle? I'll have no upstart spilling his chemicals here, or devilling the stars from a seat on my roof.'

"'Last autumn,' said I, 'David Claridge was housed here. Thy palace was a prison then.'

"'I know well of that. Haven't I found his records here? And do you think his makeshift lordship did not remind me?'

"'Records? What records Soolsby?' asked I, most curious.

"'Writings of his thoughts which he forgot—food for mind and body left in the cupboard.' 'Give them to me—upon this instant, Soolsby,' said I. 'All but one,' said he, 'and that is my own, for it was his mind upon Soolsby the drunken chairmaker. God save him from the heathen sword that slew his uncle. Two better men never sat upon a chair!'

"He placed the papers in my hand, all save that one which spoke of him. Ah, David, what with the flute and the pen, banishment was no pain to thee! . . . He placed the papers, save that one, in my hands, and I, womanlike, asked again for all. 'Some day,' said he, 'come, and I will read it to you. Nay, I will give you a taste of it now,' he added as he brought forth the writing. 'Thus it reads.'

"Here are thy words, Davy. What think thee of them now?

"'As I dwell in this house I know Soolsby as I never knew him when he lived, and though, up here, I spent many an hour with him. Men leave their impressions on all around them. The walls which have felt their look and their breath, the floor which has taken their footsteps, the chairs in which they have sat, have something of their presence. I feel Soolsby here at times so sharply that it would seem he came again and was in this room, though he is dead and gone. I ask him how it came he lived here alone; how it came that he made chairs, he, with brains enough to build great houses or great bridges; how it was that drink and he were such friends; and how he, a Catholic, lived here among us Quakers, so singular, uncompanionable, and severe. I think it true, and sadly true, that a man with a vice which he is able to satisfy easily and habitually, even as another satisfies a virtue, may give up the wider actions of the world and the possibilities of his life for the pleasure which his one vice gives him, and neither miss nor desire those greater chances of virtue or ambition which he has lost. The simplicity of a vice may be as real as the simplicity of a virtue.'

"Ah, David, David, I know not what to think of those strange words; but old Soolsby seemed well to understand thee, and he called thee 'a first-best gentleman.' Is my story long? Well, it was so strange, and it fixed itself upon my mind so deeply, and thy writings at the hut have been so much in my hands and in my mind, that I have put it all down here. When I asked Soolsby how it came he had been rumored dead, he said that he himself had been the cause of it; but for what purpose he would not say, save that he was going a long voyage, and had made up his mind to return no more. 'I had a friend,' he said, 'and I was set to go and see that friend again. . . . But the years go on, and friends have an end. Life spills faster than the years,' he said. And he would say no more, but would walk with me even to my father's door. 'May the Blessed Virgin and all the Saints be with you,' he said at parting, 'if you will have a blessing from them. And tell him who is beyond and away in Egypt that old Soolsby's busy making a chair for him to sit in when the scarlet cloth is spread, and the East and West come to salaam before him. Tell him the old man says his fluting will be heard!'

"And now, David, I have told thee all, nearly. Remains to say that thy one letter did our hearts good. My father reads it over and over, and shakes his head sadly, for, truth is, he has a fear that the world may lay its hand upon thee. One thing I do observe, his heart is hard set against Lord Eglington. In degree it has ever been so; but now it is like a constant frown upon his forehead. I see him at his window looking out towards the Cloistered House; and if our neighbor come forth—perhaps upon his hunter, or now in his cart, or again with his dogs, he draws his hat down upon his eyes and whispers to himself. I think he is ever setting thee off against Lord Eglington; and that is foolish, for Eglington is but a man of the earth earthy. His is the soul of the adventurer.

"Now what more is there to say? I must ask thee

how is thy friend Ebn Ezra Bey? I am glad thee did find all he said was true, and that in Damascus thee was able to set a mark by my uncle's grave. But that the Prince Pasha of Egypt has set up a claim against my uncle's property is evil news; though, thanks be to God, as my father says, we have enough to keep us fed and clothed and housed! But do thee keep enough of thy inheritance to bring thee safe home again to those who love thee. England is ever gray, Davy, but without thee it is grizzled—all one 'Quaker drab,' as says the Philistine. But it is a comely and a good land, and here we wait for thee.

"In love and remembrance,

"I am thy mother's sister, thy most loving friend,

"FAITH."

David received this letter as he was mounting a huge white Syrian donkey to ride to the Mokattam Hills, which rise sharply behind Cairo, burning and lonely and large. The cities of the dead Khalifas and Mamelukes separated them from the living city where the fellah toiled, and Arab, Bedouin, Copt, strove together to intercept the fruits of his toiling, as it passed in the form of taxes to the Palace of the Prince Pasha; while in the dark corners crouched, waiting, the cormorant usurers—Greeks, Armenians, and Syrians, a hideous salvage corps, who saved the house of a man that they might at last walk off with his shirt and the cloth under which he was carried to his grave. In a thousand narrow streets and lanes, in the warm glow of the bazaars, in earth-damp huts, by blistering quays, on the myriad ghiassas on the river, from long before sunrise till the sunset-gun boomed from the citadel rising beside the great mosque whose pinnacles seem to touch the blue, the slaves of the city of Prince Kaïd ground out their lives like corn between the millstones.

David had been long enough in Egypt to know what sort of toiling it was. A man's labor was not his own. The fellah gave labor and taxes and *backsheesh* and life to the state, and to the long line of tyrants above him, under the sting of the *kourbash;* and the high officials gave backsheesh to the Prince Pasha, or to his *Mouffetish*, or to his Chief Eunuch, or to his barber, or to some slave who had his ear.

But all the time the bright, unclouded sun looked down on a smiling land, and in Cairo streets the din of the hammers, the voices of the boys driving heavily laden donkeys, the call of the camel-drivers leading their caravans into the great squares, the clang of the brasses of the sherbet-sellers, the song of the vender of sweetmeats, the drone of the merchant praising his wares, went on amid scenes of wealth and luxury, and the city glowed with color and gleamed with light. Dark faces grinned over the steaming pot at the door of the cafés, idlers on the benches smoked hasheesh; female street dancers bared their faces shamelessly to the men, and indolent musicians beat on their tiny drums, and sang the song of "*O Seyyid*," or of "*Antar*"; and the reciter gave his singsong tale from a bench above his fellows. Here a devout Muslim, indifferent to the presence of strangers, turned his face to the East, touched his forehead to the ground, and said his prayers. There, hung to a tree by a deserted mosque near by, the body of one who was with them all an hour before, and who had paid the penalty for some real or imaginary crime; while his fellows blessed Allah that the storm had passed them by. Guilt or innocence did not weigh with them; and the dead criminal, if such he were, who had drunk his glass of water and prayed to Allah, was in their sight only fortunate and not disgraced, and had "gone to the bosom of Allah." Now the *Muezzin* from a minaret called to prayer, and the fellah in his cotton shirt and *yelek* heard, laid his load aside, and yielded himself to his one dear illusion, which would enable him to meet with apathy his end—it might be to-morrow!—and go forth to that plenteous heaven where wives without number awaited him, where fields would yield harvests without labor, where rich food in gold dishes would be ever at his hand. This was his faith.

David had now been in the country six months, rapidly perfecting his knowledge of Arabic, speaking it always to his servant, Mahommed Hassan, whom he had picked from the streets. Ebn Ezra Bey had gone upon his own business to Fazougli, the tropical Siberia of Egypt, to liberate by order of Prince Kaïd,—and at a high price—a relative banished there. David had not yet been fortunate with his own business—the settlement of his Uncle Benn's estate—though the last stages of negotiation with the Prince Pasha seemed to have been reached. When he had brought the influence of the British Consulate to bear, promises were made, doors were opened wide, and pasha and bey offered him coffee and talked to him sympathetically. They had respect for him more than for most Franks, because the Prince Pasha had honored him with especial favor. Perhaps because David wore his hat always and the long coat with high collar like a Turk, or because Prince Kaïd was an acute judge of human nature, and also because honesty was a thing he greatly desired—in others—and never found near his own person; however it was, he had set David high in his esteem at once. This esteem gave greater certainty, that any backsheesh coming from the estate of Benn Claridge would not be sifted through many hands on its way to himself. Of Benn Claridge Prince Kaïd had scarcely even heard until he died; and, indeed, it was only within the past few years that the Quaker merchant had extended his business to Egypt and had made his headquarters at Assiout, up the river.

David's donkey now picked its way carefully through the narrow streets of the *Mousky*. Arabs and fellahs squatting at street corners looked at him with furtive interest. A foreigner of this character they had never before seen, with coat buttoned up like an Egyptian official in the presence of his superior, and this wide, droll hat on his head. David knew that he ran risks, that his confidence invited the occasional madness of a fanatical mind, which makes murder of the infidel a passport to heaven; but, as a man, he took his chances, and as a Christian he believed he would suffer no mortal hurt till his appointed time. He was more Oriental, more fatalist, than he knew. He had also learned early in his life that an honest smile begets confidence; and his face, grave and even a little austere in outline, was usually lighted by a smile.

From the Mokattam Hills, where he read Faith's letter again, his back against one of the forts which Napoleon had built in his Egyptian days, he scanned the distance. At his feet lay the great mosque and the citadel, whose guns controlled the city, could pour into it a lava stream of shot and shell. The Nile wound its way through the green plains, stretching as far to the north as eye could see between the opal and mauve and gold of the Libyan Hills. Far over in the western vista a long line of trees, twining through an oasis flanking the city, led out to a point where the desert abruptly raised its hills of yellow sand. Here, enormous, lonely, and cynical, the pyramids which Cheops had built, the stone sphinx of Ghizeh, kept faith with the desert in the glow of a rainless land—reminders ever that the East, the mother of knowledge, will by knowledge prevail; that

"The thousand years of thy insolence,
The thousand years of thy faith,
Will be paid in fiery recompense,
And a thousand years of bitter death."

"The sword—forever the sword," David said to himself, as he looked. "Rameses and David and Mahomet and Constantine, and how many conquests have been made in the name of God! But after other conquests there have been peace and order and law. Here in Egypt it is ever the sword—the survival of the strongest."

As he made his way down the hillside again he fell to thinking upon all Faith had written. The return of the drunken chairmaker made a deep impression on him—almost as deep as the waking dreams he had had of his uncle calling him.

"Soolsby and I—what is there between Soolsby and me?" he asked himself now as he made his way past the tombs of the Mamelukes. "He and I are as far apart as the poles, and yet it comes to me now, with a strange conviction, that somehow my life will be linked with that of the drunken Romish chairmaker. To what end?" Then he fell to thinking of his Uncle Benn. The East was calling him. "Something works within me to hold me here—a work to do," he murmured.

From the ramparts of the citadel he watched the sun go down, bathing the pyramids in a purple and golden light, throwing a glamour over all the Western plain, and making heavenly the far hills with a plaintive color, which spoke of peace and rest, but not of hope. As he stood watching, he was conscious of people approaching. Voices mingled, there was light laughter, little bursts of admiration, then lower tones, and then he was roused by a voice calling. He turned round. A group of people were moving towards the exit from the ramparts, and near himself stood a man waving an adieu.

"Well, give my love to the girls!" said the man cheerily.

Merry faces looked back and nodded, and in a moment they were gone. The man turned round and looked at David; then he jerked his head in a friendly sort of way, and motioned towards the sunset.

"Good enough, eh?"

"Surely," answered David. On the instant he liked the red, wholesome face, and the keen, round, blue eyes, the rather opulent figure, the shrewd, whimsical smile, all aglow now with beaming sentimentality, which had from its softest corner called out, "Well, give my love to the girls!"

"Quaker, or I never saw Germantown and Philadelphy," he continued with a friendly manner quite without offence. "I put my money on Quakers every time."

"But not from Germantown or Philadelphia," answered David, declining a cigar which his new acquaintance offered.

"Bet you, I know that all right. But I never saw Quakers anywhere else, and I meant the tribe and not the tent. English, I bet? Of course, or you wouldn't be talking the English language—though I've heard they talk it better in Boston than they do in England, and in Chicago they're making new English every day and improving on the patent. If Chicago can't have the newest thing, she won't have anything. 'High hopes that burn like stars sublime,' has Chicago. She won't let Shakespeare or Milton be standards much longer. She won't have it—simply won't have England swaggering over the English language. Oh, she's dizzy, is Chicago—simply dizzy. I was born there. Parents, one Philadelphy, one New York, one Pawtucket—the Pawtucket one was the stepmother. Father liked his wives from the original States; but I was born in Chicago. My name is Lacey—Thomas Tilman Lacey, of Chicago."

"I thank thee," said David.

"And you, sir?"

"David Claridge."

"Of—?"

"Of Hamley."

"Mr. Claridge, of Hamley. Mr. Claridge, I am glad to meet you." They shook hands. "Been here long, Mr. Claridge?"

"A few months only."

"Queer place—gilt-edged dust-bin; get anything you like here, from a fresh gutter-snipe to old Haroun-al-Raschid. It's the biggest jack-pot on earth. Barnum's the man for this place — P. T. Barnum. Golly, how the whole thing glitters and stews! Out at Shoobra his High Jinks Pasha kennels with his lions and lives with his cellars of gold, as if he was going to take them with him where he's going—and he's going fast. Here —down here, the people, the real people, sweat and drudge between a cake of *dourha*, an onion, and a *balass* of water at one end of the day, and a hemp collar and their feet off the ground at the other."

"You have seen much of Egypt?" asked David, feeling a strange confidence in the garrulous man, whose frankness was united to shrewdness and a quick, observant eye.

"How much of *Egypt* I've seen, the Egypt where more men get lost, strayed, and stolen than die in their beds every day, the Egypt where a eunuch is more powerful than a minister, where an official will toss away a life as I'd toss this cigar down there where the last Mameluke captain made his great jump, where women — Lord A'mighty!—where women are divorced by one evil husband by the dozen for nothing they ever did or left undone, and yet 'd be cut to pieces by their own fathers if they learned that 'To step aside is human—' Mr. Claridge, of that Egypt I don't know much more'n would entitle me to say, How d'ye do. But it's enough for me. You've seen something—eh?"

"A little. It is not civilized life here. Yet—yet a few strong, patriotic men—"

Lacey looked quizzically at David. "Say," he said, "I thought that about Mexico once. I said *Mañana*—this *Mañana* is the curse of Mexico. It's always to-morrow—to-morrow—to-morrow! Let's teach 'em to do things to-day. Let's show 'em what *business* means. Two million dollars went into that experiment, but *Mañana* won. We had good hands, but it had the joker! After five years I left—with a bald head at twenty-nine, and a little book of noble thoughts—'Tips for the Tired, or Things you can say To-day on what you can do To-morrow.' I lost my hair worrying, but I learnt to be patient. The Dagos wanted to live in their own way, and they did. It's one thing to be a missionary and say the little word in season; it's another to run your soft red head against a hard stone wall. I went to Mexico a *conquistador*, I left it a child of time, who had learned to smile; and I left some millions behind me, too. I said to an old padre down there that I knew—we used to meet in the Café Manriqué and drink chocolate—I said to him, 'Padre, the Lord's Prayer is a mistake down here.' '*Si, señor*,' he said, and smiled his far-away smile at me. 'Yes,' said I, 'for you say in the Lord's Prayer, "Give us this day our daily bread."' '*Si, señor*,' he says, 'but we do not expect it till to-morrow!' The Padre knew from the start, but I learned at great expense, and went out of business—closed up shop forever, with a bald head and my 'Tips for the Tired.' Well, I've had more out of it all, I guess, than if I'd trebled the millions and wiped *Mañana* off the Mexican coat of arms."

"You think it would be like that here?" David asked abstractedly.

Lacey whistled. "There the government was all right and the people all wrong. Here the people are all right and the government all wrong. Say, it makes my eyes water sometimes to see the fellah slogging away. He's a Jim-dandy—works all day and half the night, and if the tax-gatherer isn't at the door, wakes up laughing. I saw one"—his light-blue eyes took on a sudden hardness—"laughing on the other side of his mouth one morning. They were 'kourbashing' his feet; I landed on them as the soles came away. I hit out." His face became grave, he turned the cigar round in his mouth. "It made me feel better, but I had a close call. Lucky for me that in Mexico I got into the habit of carrying a pop-gun. It saved me then. But it isn't any use going on these special missions. We Americans think a lot of ourselves. We want every land to do as we do; and we want to make 'em do it. But a strong man here at the head, with a sword in his hand, peace in his heart, who'd be just and poor—how can you make officials honest when you take all you can get yourself!—But, no, I guess it's no good. This is a rotten cotton show."

Lacey had talked so much, not because he was garrulous only, but because the inquiry in David's eyes was an encouragement to talk. Whatever his misfortunes in Mexico had been, his forty years sat lightly on him, and his expansive temperament, his childlike sentimentality, gave him an appearance of beaming, sophisticated youth. David was slowly apprehending these things as he talked—subconsciously, as it were; for he was seeing pictures of the things he himself had observed through the lens of another mind, as primitive in some regards as his own, but influenced by different experiences.

"Say, you're the best listener I ever saw," added Lacey with a laugh.

David held out his hand. "Thee sees things clearly," he answered. Lacey grasped his hand.

At that moment an orderly advanced towards them.

"He's after us—one of the Palace cavalry," said Lacey.

"*Effendi*—the Effendi Claridge! May his grave be not made till the *karadh*-gatherers return," said the orderly to David.

"My name is Claridge," answered David.

"To the hotel, effendi, first, then to the Mokattam Hills after thee, then here—from the Effendina, on whom be God's peace! this letter for thee."

David took the letter. As he read it, Lacey said to the orderly in Arabic, "How didst thou know he was here?"

The orderly grinned wickedly. "Always it is known what place the effendi honors. It is not dark where he uncovers his face."

Lacey gave a low whistle.

"Say, you've got a pull in this show," he said, as David folded up the letter and put it in his pocket. "In Egypt, if the master smiles on you, the servant puts his nose in the dust."

"The Prince Pasha bids me to dinner at the Palace to-night. I have no clothes for such affairs. Yet—"

His mind was asking itself if this was a door opening which he had no right to shut with his own hand. There was no reason why he should not go; therefore there might be a reason why he should go. It might be, it no doubt was, in the way of facilitating his business. He dismissed the orderly with an affirmative and ceremonial message to Prince Kaïd—and a piece of gold.

"You've learned the custom of the place," said Lacey, as he saw the gold piece glitter in the brown palm of the orderly.

"I suppose the man's only pay is in such service," rejoined David. "It is a land of backsheesh. The fault is not with the people; it is with the rulers. I do not lament sharing my goods with the poor."

"You'll have a big going concern here in no time," observed Lacey. "Now if I had those millions I left in Mexico—" Suddenly he stopped. "Is it you that's trying to settle up an estate here—up at Assiout—belonged to an uncle—same persuasion?"

David inclined his head.

"They say that you and Prince Kaïd are doing the thing yourselves, and that the pashas and judges and all the high-mogul sharks of the *Medjidie* think that the end of the world has come. Is that so?"

"It is so, if not completely so. There are the poor men and humble—the pashas and judges and the others of the Medjidie, as thee said, are not poor. But such as the orderly yonder—" He paused meditatively.

Lacey looked at David with profound respect. "You make the poorest your partners, your friends. I see, I see. Jerusalem, that's masterly! I admire you. It's a new way in this country." Then, after a moment: "It 'll do—by golly! it 'll do! Not a bit more costly, and you do some good with it. Yes—it—will—do."

"I have given no man money save in charity and for proper service done openly," said David, a little severely.

"Say—of course. And that's just what isn't done here. Everything goes to him who hath, and from him who hath not is taken away even that which he hath. One does the work and another gets paid—that's the way here. But you, Mr. Claridge, you clinch with the strong man at the top, and, down below, you've got as your partners the poor man, whose name is Legion. If you get a fall out of the man at the top, you're solid with the Legion. And if the man at the top gets up again and salaams and strokes your hand, and says, 'Be my brother,' then it's a full Nile, and the fig-tree putteth forth its tender branches, and the date-palm flourisheth, and at the village pond the Thanksgiving turkey gobbles and is glad. Selah!"

The sunset-gun boomed out from the citadel. David turned to go, and Lacey added:

"I'm waiting for a pasha who's taking toll of the officers inside there—Achmet Pasha. They call him the Rope-maker because so many pass through his hands to the Nile. The Old Muslin I call him because he's so diaphanous. Thinks nobody can see through him, and there's nobody that can't. If you stay long in Egypt, you'll find that Achmet is the worst, and Nahoum, the Armenian, the deepest pasha in all this sickening land. Achmet is cruel as a tiger to any one that stands in his way; Nahoum, the whale, only opens out to swallow now and then; but when Nahoum does open out, down goes Jonah, and never comes up again. He's a deep one, and a great artist, is Nahoum. I'll bet a dollar you'll see them both to-night at the Palace—if Kaïd doesn't throw them to the lions for their dinner before yours is served. Here one shark is swallowed by another bigger, till at last the only and original sea serpent swallows 'em all."

As David wound his way down the hill, Lacey waved a hand after him.

"Well, give my love to the girls!" he said.

VI

"HAST THOU NEVER KILLED A MAN?"

"Claridge Effendi!"

As David moved forward, his mind was embarrassed by many impressions. He was not confused, but the glitter and splendor, the Oriental gorgeousness of the picture into which he stepped, excited his eye, roused some new sense in him. He was a curious figure in those surroundings. The consuls and agents of all the nations save one were in brilliant uniform, and pashas, generals, and great officials were splendid in gold braid and lace, and wore flashing orders on their breasts. David had been asked for half-past eight o'clock, and he was there on the instant; yet here was every one assembled, the Prince Pasha included. As he walked up the room he suddenly realized this fact, and, for a moment, he thought he had made a mistake; but again he remembered distinctly that the letter said half-past eight, and he wondered now if this had been arranged by the Prince—for what purpose? To afford amusement to the assembled company? He drew himself up with dignity, his face became graver. He had come in a Quaker suit of black broadcloth, with gray steel buttons, and a plain white stock; and he wore his broadbrimmed hat—to the consternation of the British Consul-General and the Europeans present, to the amazement of the Turkish and native officials, who eyed him keenly. They themselves wore red *tarbooshes*, as did the Prince; yet all of them knew that the European custom of showing respect was by doffing the hat. The Prince Pasha had settled that with David, however, at their first meeting, when David had kept on his hat and offered Kaïd his hand.

Now, with amusement in his eyes, Prince Kaïd watched David coming up the great hall. What his object was in summoning David for an hour when all the court and all the official Europeans should be already present, remained to be seen. As David entered, Kaïd was busy receiving salaams and returning greeting, but with an eye to the singularly boyish yet gallant figure approaching. By the time David had reached the group, the Prince Pasha was ready to receive him.

"Friend, I am glad to welcome thee," said the Effendina, sly humor lurking at the corner of his eye. Conscious of the amazement of all present, he held out his hand to David.

"May thy coming be as the morning dew, friend," he added, taking David's willing hand.

"And thy feet, Kaïd, walk in goodly paths, by the grace of God the compassionate and merciful."

As a wind unfelt stirs the leaves of a forest, making it rustle delicately, a whisper swept through the room. Official Egypt was dumfounded. Many had heard of David, a few had seen him, and all now eyed with inquisitive interest one who defied so many of the customs of his countrymen; who kept on his hat; who used a Mahommedan salutation like a true believer; whom the Effendina honored—and presently honored in an unusual degree by seating him at table opposite himself, where his Chief Chamberlain was used to sit.

During dinner Kaïd addressed his conversation again and again to David, asking questions put to disconcert the consuls and other official folk present, confident in the naïve reply which would be returned. For there was a keen truthfulness in the young man's words, which, however suave and carefully balanced, however gravely simple and tactful, left no doubt as to their meaning. There was nothing in them which could be challenged, could be construed into active criticism of men or things; and yet much he said was horrifying. It made Achmet Pasha sit up aghast, and Nahoum Pasha, the astute Armenian, for a long time past the confidant and favorite of the Prince Pasha, laugh in his throat; for, if there was a man in Egypt who enjoyed the thrust of a word or the bite of a phrase, it was Nahoum. Christian though he was, he was, nevertheless, Oriental to his furthermost corner, and had the culture of a French savant. He had also the primitive view of life, and the morals of a race who, in the clash of East and West, set against Western character and directness and loyalty to the terms of a bargain the demoralized cunning of the desert folk; the circuitous tactics of those who believed that no man spoke the truth directly, that it must ever be found beneath devious and misleading words, to be tracked like a panther, as an antipodean bushman once said, "through the sinuosities of the underbrush." Nahoum Pasha had also a rich sense of grim humor. Perhaps that was why he had lived so near the person of the Prince, had held office so long. There were no grand viziers in Egypt; but he was as much like one as possible, and he had one uncommon virtue, he was greatly generous. If he took with his right hand he gave with his left; and Mahommedan as well as Copt and Armenian, and beggars of every race and creed, hung about his doors each morning to receive the food and alms he gave freely.

After one of David's answers to Kaïd, which had had the effect of causing his Highness to turn a sharp corner of conversation by addressing himself to the French Consul, Nahoum said, suavely:

"And so, monsieur, you think that we hold life lightly

in the East—that it is a characteristic of civilization to make life more sacred, to cherish it more fondly?"

He was sitting beside David, and though he asked the question casually, and with apparent intention only of keeping talk going, there was a lurking inquisition in his eye. He had seen enough to-night to make him sure that Kaïd had once more got the idea of making an European his confidant and adviser; to introduce to his court one of those mad Englishmen who cared nothing for gold—only for power; who loved administration for the sake of administration and the foolish joy of labor. He was now set to see what sort of match this intellect could play, when faced by the inherent contradictions present in all truths or the solutions of all problems.

"It is one of the characteristics of that which lies behind civilization, as thee and me have been taught," answered David.

Nahoum was quick in strategy, but he was unprepared for David's knowledge that he was an Armenian Christian, and he had looked for another answer.

But he kept his head and rose to the occasion. "Ah, it is high, it is noble, to save life—it is so easy to destroy it," he answered. "I saw his Highness put his life in danger once to save a dog from drowning. To cherish the lives of others, and to be careless of our own; to give that of great value as though it were of no worth—is it not the Great Lesson?" He said it with such an air of sincerity, with such dissimulation, that, for the moment, David was deceived. There was, however, on the face of the listening Kaïd a curious, cynical smile. He had heard all, and he knew the sardonic meaning behind Nahoum's words.

Fat Higli Pasha, the Chief Chamberlain, the corrupt and corruptible, intervened. "It is not so hard to be careless when care would be useless," he said, with a chuckle. "When the *khamsin* blows the dust-storms upon the caravan, the camel-driver hath no care for his camels. '*Malaish!*' he says, and buries his face in his yelek."

"Life is beautiful and so difficult—to save," observed Nahoum, in a tone meant to tempt David on one hand, and to reach the ears of the notorious Achmet Pasha, whose extortions, cruelties, and taxations had built his master's palaces, bribed his harem, given him money to pay the interest on his European loans, and made himself the richest man in Egypt, whose spies were everywhere, whose shadow was across every man's path. Kaïd might slay, might toss a pasha or a slave into the Nile now and then, might invite a bey to visit him, and stroke his beard and call him brother and put diamond-dust in the coffee he drank, so that he died before two suns came and went again, "of inflammation and a natural death"; but he, Achmet Pasha, was the dark Inquisitor who tortured every day, for whose death all men prayed, and whom some would have slain, but that another worse than himself might succeed him.

At Nahoum's words the dusky brown of Achmet's face turned as black as the sudden dilation of the pupil of an eye deepens its hue, and he said with a guttural accent:

"Every man hath a time to die."

"But not his own time," answered Nahoum maliciously.

"It would appear that in Egypt he hath not always the choice of the fashion or the time," remarked David calmly. He had read the malice behind their words, and there had flashed into his own mind tales told him, with every circumstance of accuracy, of deaths within and without the Palace. Also he was now aware that Nahoum had mocked him. He was concerned to make it clear that he was not wholly beguiled.

"Is there, then, choice of fashion or time in England, effendi?" asked Nahoum, with assumed innocence.

"In England it is a matter between the Giver and Taker of life and himself—save where murder does its work," said David.

"And here it is between man and man—is it that you would say?" asked Nahoum.

"There seem wider privileges here," answered David dryly.

"Accidents will happen, privileges or no," rejoined Nahoum, with lowering eyelids.

The Prince intervened. "Thy own faith forbids the sword, forbids war, or—punishment."

"The Prophet I follow was called the Prince of Peace, friend," answered David, bowing gravely across the table.

"Didst thou never kill a man?" asked Kaïd, with interest in his eyes. He asked the question as a man might ask another if he had never visited Paris.

"By the goodness of God, never," answered David.

"Neither in punishment nor in battle?"

"I am neither judge nor soldier, friend."

"*Inshallah*—thou hast yet far to go! Thou art young yet. Who can tell?"

"I have never so far to go as that, friend Kaïd," said David, in a voice that rang a little.

"To-morrow is no man's gift."

David was about to answer, but chancing to raise his eyes above the Prince Pasha's head, his glance was arrested and startled by seeing a face—the face of a woman—looking out of a panel in a *mooshrabieh* screen in a gallery above. He would not have dwelt upon the incident, he would have set it down to the curiosity of a woman of the harem, but that the face looking out was that of an English girl, and leering over her shoulder was the dark, handsome face of an Egyptian or a Turk.

Self-control was the habit of his life, the training of his faith, and, as a rule, his face gave little evidence of inner excitement. Demonstration was discouraged, if not forbidden, among the Quakers, and if, to others, it gave a cold and austere manner, in David it tempered to a warm stillness the powerful impulses in him, the rivers of feeling which sometimes roared through his veins.

Only Nahoum Pasha had noticed his arrested look, so motionless did he sit; and now, without replying, he bowed gravely and deferentially to Kaïd, who rose from the table. He followed with the rest. Presently the Prince sent Higli Pasha to ask his nearer presence.

The Prince made a motion of his hand, and the circle withdrew. He waved David to a seat.

"To-morrow thy business shall be settled," said the Prince, suavely, "and on such terms as will not startle. Death-tribute is no new thing in the East. It is fortunate for thee that the tribute is from thy hand to my hand, and not through many others to mine."

"I am conscious I have been treated with favor, friend," said David. "I would that I might show thee kindness. Though how may a man of no account make return to a great prince?"

"By the beard of my father, it is easily done, if thy kindness is a real thing, and not that which makes me poorer the more I have of it—as though one should be given a herd of horses which must not be sold but still must be fed."

"I have given thee truth. Is not truth cheaper than falsehood?"

"It is the most expensive thing in Egypt; so that I despair of buying thee. Yet I would buy thee to remain here—here at my court; here by my hand which will give thee the labor thou lovest, and will defend thee if defence be needed. Thou hast not greed, thou hast no thirst for honor, yet thou hast wisdom beyond thy years. Kaïd has never besought men, but he beseeches thee. Once there was in Egypt, Joseph, a wise youth, who served a

Pharaoh, and was his chief counsellor, and it was well with the land. Thy name is a good name; well-being may follow thee. The ages have gone, and the rest of the world has changed, but Egypt is the same Egypt, the Nile rises and falls, and the old lean years and fat years come and go. Though I am in truth a Turk, and those who serve and rob me here are Turks, yet the fellah is the same as he was five thousand years ago. What Joseph the Israelite did, thou canst do; for I am no more unjust than was that Rameses whom Joseph served. Wilt thou stay with me?"

David looked at Kaïd as though he would read in his face the reply that he must make, but he did not see Kaïd; he saw, rather, the face of one he had loved more than Jonathan had been loved by the young shepherd-prince of Israel. In his ears he heard the voice that had called him in his sleep—the voice of Benn Claridge; and at the same instant there flashed into his mind a picture of himself fighting outside the tavern beyond Hamley and bidding farewell to the girl at the cross-roads.

"Friend, I cannot answer thee now," he said, in a troubled voice.

Kaïd rose. "I will give thee an hour to think upon it. Come with me." He stepped forward.

"To-morrow I will answer thee, Kaïd."

"To-morrow there is work for thee to do. Come." David followed him.

The eyes that followed the Prince and the Quaker were not friendly. What Kaïd had long foreshadowed seemed at hand: the coming of a European counsellor and confidant. They realized that in the man who had just left the room with Kaïd there were characteristics unlike those they had ever met before in Europeans.

"A madman," whispered Higli Pasha to Achmet the Rope-maker.

"Then his will be the fate of the swine of Gadarene," said Nahoum Pasha, who had heard.

"At least one need not argue with a madman." The face of Achmet the Rope-maker was not more pleasant than his dark words.

"It is not the madman with whom you have to deal, but his keeper," rejoined Nahoum.

Nahoum's face was heavier than usual. Going to weight, he was still muscular and well groomed. His light-brown beard and hair and blue eyes gave him a look almost Saxon, and bland power spoke in his face and in every gesture.

He was seldom without the string of beads so many Orientals love to carry, and, Armenian Christian as he was, the act seemed almost religious. It was to him, however, like a ground-wire in telegraphy—it carried off the nervous force tingling in him and driving him to impulsive action, while his reputation called for a constant outward urbanity, a philosophical apathy. He had had his great fight for place and power, alien as he was in religion, though he had lived in Egypt since a child. Bar to progress as his religion had been at first, it had been an advantage afterwards; for, through it, he could exclude himself from complications with the Wakfs, the religious court of the Muslim creed, which had lands to administer, and controlled the laws of marriage and inheritance. He could shrug his shoulders and play with his beads, and urbanely explain his own helplessness and ineligiblity when his influence was summoned, or it was sought to entangle him in warring interests. Oriental through and through, the basis of his creed was similar to that of a Muslim: Mahomet was a prophet and Christ was a prophet. It was a case of rival prophets—all else was obscured into a legend, and he saw the strife of race in the difference of creed. For the rest, he flourished the salutations and language of the Arab as though they were his own, and he spoke Arabic as perfectly as he did French and English.

He was the second son of his father. The first son, who was but a year older, and was as dark as he was fair, had inherited—had seized—all his father's wealth. He had lived abroad for some years in France and England. In the latter place he had been one of the Turkish Embassy, and, being a Christian, and having none of the outward characteristics of the Turk, and in appearance more of a Spaniard than an Oriental, he had, by his gifts, his address and personal appearance, won the good-will of the Duchess of Middlesex, and had had that success all too flattering to the soul of a libertine. It had, however, been the means of his premature retirement from England, for his chief at the Embassy had a preference for an Oriental *entourage*. He was called Foorgat Bey.

Sitting at table, Nahoum alone of all present had caught David's arrested look, and glancing up, had seen the girl's face at the panel of mooshrabieh, and had seen also over her shoulder the face of his brother, Foorgat Bey. He had been even more astonished than David, and far more disturbed. He knew his brother's abilities; he knew his insinuating address—had he not influenced their father to give him wealth while he was yet alive? He was aware also that his brother had visited the Palace often of late. It would seem as though the Prince Pasha was ready to make him, as well as David, a favorite. But the face of the girl—it was an English face! Familiar with the Palace, and bribing when it was necessary to bribe, Foorgat Bey had evidently brought her to see the function, there where all women were forbidden. He could little imagine Foorgat Bey doing this from mere courtesy; he could not imagine any woman, save one wholly sophisticated, or one entirely innocent, trusting herself with him—and in such a place. The girl's face, though not that of one in her teens, had seemed to him a very flower of innocence.

But, as he stood telling his beads, abstractedly listening to the scandal talked by Achmet and Higli, he was not thinking of his brother, but of the two who had just left the room. He was speculating as to which room they were likely to enter. They had not gone by the door convenient to passage to Kaïd's own apartments. He would give much to hear the conversation between Kaïd and the stranger; he was all too conscious of its purport. As he stood thinking, Kaïd returned. After looking round the room for a moment, the Prince came slowly over to Nahoum, and, stretching out a hand, stroked his beard.

"Oh, brother of all the wise, may thy sun never pass its noon!" said Kaïd, in a slow, friendly voice.

Despite his will, a shudder passed through Nahoum Pasha's frame. How often in Egypt this gesture and such words were the prelude to assassination, from which there was no escape save by death itself. Into Nahoum's mind there flashed the words of an Arab teacher, "There is no refuge from God but God Himself," and he found himself blindly wondering, even as he felt Kaïd's hand upon his beard and listened to the honeyed words, what manner of death was now preparing for him, and what death of his own contriving should intervene. Escape, he knew, there was none, if his death was determined on; for spies were everywhere, and slaves in the pay of Kaïd were everywhere, and such as were not could be bought or compelled, even if he took refuge in the house of a foreign consul. The lean, invisible, ghastly arm of death could find him, if Kaïd willed, though he delved in the bowels of the Cairene earth, or climbed to an eagle's eyrie in the Libyan Hills. Whether it was diamond-dust or Achmet's thin thong that stopped the breath, it mattered not; it was sure.

Yet he was not of the breed to tremble under the descending sword, and he had long accustomed himself to the chance of "sudden demise." It had been chief among the chances he had taken when he entered the high and perilous service of Kaïd. Now, as he felt the secret joy of these dark spirits surrounding him—Achmet, and Higli Pasha, who kept saying beneath his breath in thankfulness that it was not his turn, Praise be to God!—as he felt their secret self-gratulations, and their evil joy over his prospective downfall, he settled himself steadily, made a low salutation to Kaïd, and calmly awaited further speech. It came soon enough.

"It is written upon a cucumber leaf—does not the world read it?—that Nahoum Pasha's form shall cast a longer shadow than the trees; so that every man in Egypt shall, thinking on him, be as covetous as Ashaah, who knew but one thing more covetous than himself—the sheep that mistook the rainbow for a rope of hay and, jumping for it, broke his neck."

Kaïd laughed softly at his own words. With his eye meeting Kaïd's again, after a low salaam, Nahoum made answer:

"I would that the lance of my fame might sheathe itself in the breasts of thy enemies, Effendina."

"Thy tongue does that office well," was the reply. Once more Kaïd laid a gentle hand upon Nahoum's beard. Then with a gesture towards the consuls and the Europeans, he said to them in French, "If I might but beg your presence for yet a little time!" Then he turned and walked away. He left by a door leading to his own apartments.

When he had gone, Nahoum swung slowly round and faced the agitated groups.

"He who sleeps with one eye open sees the sun rise first," he said, with a sarcastic laugh. "He who goes blindfold never sees it set."

Then, with a complacent look upon them all, he slowly left the room by the door out of which David and Kaïd had first passed.

Outside the room his face did not change. His manner had not been bravado. It was as natural to him as David's manner was to himself. Each had trained himself in his own way to the mastery of his will, and the will in each was stronger than any passion of emotion in them. So far at least it had been so. In David it was the outcome of his faith, in Nahoum it was the outcome of his philosophy, a simple, fearless fatalism.

David had been left by Kaïd in a small room, little more than an alcove, next to a larger room richly furnished. Both rooms belonged to a spacious suite which lay between the harem and the major portion of the Palace. It had its own entrance and exits from the Palace, opening on the square at the front, at the back opening on its own garden, which also had its own exits to the public road. The quarters of the Chief Eunuch separated the suite from the harem, and Mizraim, the present Chief Eunuch, was a man of power in the Palace, knew more secrets, was more courted, and was richer than some of the princes. Nahoum had an office in the Palace, also, which gave him the freedom of the place, and brought him often in touch with the Chief Eunuch. He had made Mizraim a fast friend ever since the day he had, by an able device, saved the Chief Eunuch from determined robbery by the former Prince Pasha, with whom he had suddenly come out of favor.

When Nahoum left the great salon, he directed his steps towards the quarters of the Chief Eunuch, thinking of David with a vague desire for pursuit and conflict. He was too much of a philosopher to seek to do David physical injury—a futile act; for it could do him no good in the end, could not mend his own fortunes; and, merciless as he could be on occasion, he had no love of bloodshed. Besides, the game afoot was not of his making, and he was ready to await the finish, the more so because he was sure that to-morrow would bring forth momentous things. There was a crisis in the Soudan, there was trouble in the army, there was dark conspiracy of which he knew the heart, and anything might happen to-morrow! He had yet some cards to play, and Achmet and Higli—and another very high and great—might be delivered over to Kaïd's deadly purposes rather than himself to-morrow. What he knew, Kaïd did not know. He had not meant to act yet; but new facts faced him, and he must make one struggle for his life. But as he went towards Mizraim's quarters he saw no sure escape from the stage of those untoward events save by the exit which is for all in some appointed hour.

He was not, however, more perplexed and troubled than David, who, in the little room where he had been brought and left alone with coffee and cigarettes, served by a slave from some distant portion of the Palace, sat facing his future.

David looked round the little room. Upon the walls hung weapons of every kind—from a polished dagger of Toledo to a Damascus blade, suits of chain armor, long-handled, two-edged Arab swords, pistols which had been used in the Syrian wars of Ibrahim, lances which had been taken from the Druses at Palmyra, rude battle-axes from the tribes of the Soudan, and *neboots* of dom-wood which had done service aga nst Napo'eon at Damietta. The cushions among which he sat had come from Constantinople, the rug at his feet from Tiflis, the prayer-rug on the wall from Mecca.

All that he saw was as unlike what he had known in past years as though he had come to Mars or Jupiter. All that he had heard recalled to him his first readings in the Old Testament—the story of Nebuchadnezzar, of Belshazzar, of Ahasuerus—of Ahasuerus! He suddenly remembered the face he had seen looking down at the Prince's table from the panel of mooshrabieh. That English face—where was it? Why was it there? Who was the man with her? Whose the dark face peering scornfully over her shoulder? The face of an English girl in that place dedicated to sombre intrigue, to the dark effacement of women, to the darker effacement of life, as he well knew, all too often! In looking at this prospect for good work in the cause of civilization, he was not deceived, he was not allured. He knew into what subterranean ways he must walk, through what mazes of treachery and falsehood he must find his way; and though he did not know to the full the corruption which it was his duty to Kaïd to turn to incorruption, he knew enough to give his spirit pause. What would be—what could be—the end? Would he not prove to be as much out of place as was the face of that English girl! The English girl! England rushed back upon him—the love of those at home; of his father, the only father he had ever known; of Faith, the only mother or sister he had ever known; of old Elder Fairley; the love of the woods and the hills where he had wandered came upon him. There was work to do in England, work too little done—the memory of the great meeting at Heddington flashed upon him. Could his labor and his skill, if he had any, not be used there? Ah, the green fields, the soft, gray skies, the quiet vale, the brave, self-respecting, toiling millions, the beautiful sense of law and order and goodness! Could his gifts and labors not be used there? Could not—

He was suddenly startled by a smothered cry, then a call of distress. It was the voice of a woman!

He started up. The voice seemed to come from a room at his right; not that from which he had entered.

but one still beyond this where he was. He sprang towards the wall and examined it swiftly. Finding a division in the tapestry, he ran his fingers quickly and heavily down the crack between. It came upon the button of a spring. He pressed it, the door yielded, and, throwing it back, he stepped into the room—to see a woman struggling to resist the embraces and kisses of a man. The face was that of the girl who had looked out of the panel in the mooshrabieh screen. Then it was beautiful in its mirth and animation; now it was pale and terror-stricken, as with one free hand she fiercely beat the face pressed to hers.

The girl only had seen David enter. The man was not conscious of his presence till he was seized and flung against the wall. The violence of the impact brought down at his feet two weapons from the wall above him. He seized one—a dagger—and sprang to his feet. Before he could move forward or raise his arm, however, David struck him a blow in the neck which flung him upon a square marble pedestal intended for a statue. In falling his head struck violently a sharp corner of the pedestal. He lurched, rolled over on the floor, and lay still.

The girl gave a choking cry. David quickly stooped and turned the body over. There was a cut where the hair met the temple. He opened the waistcoat and thrust his hand inside the shirt. Then he felt the pulse of the limp wrist.

For a moment he looked at the face steadily, almost contemplatively it might have seemed, and then drew both arms close to the body.

Foorgat Bey, the brother of Nahoum Pasha, was dead.

Rising, David turned, as if in a dream, to the girl. He made a motion of the hand towards the body. She understood. Dismay was in her face, but the look of horror and desperation was gone. She seemed not to realize, as did David, the awful position in which they were placed, the deed which David had done, the significance of the thing that lay at their feet.

"Where are your people?" said David. "Come, we will go to them."

"I have no people here," she said, in a whisper.

"Who brought thee?"

She made a motion behind her towards the body. David glanced down. The eyes of the dead man were open. He stooped and closed them gently. The collar and tie were disarranged; he straightened them, then turned again to her.

"I must take thee away," he said, calmly. "But it must be secretly." He looked around, perplexed.

"We came secretly. My maid is outside the garden—in a carriage. Oh, come, let us go, let us escape. They will kill you—!" Terror came into her face again.

"Thee, not me, is in danger—name, goodness, future, all. . . . Which way did thee come?"

"Here—through many rooms—" She made a gesture to curtains beyond. "But we first entered through doors with sphinxes on either side, with a room where was a statue of Mehemet Ali."

It was the room through which David had come with Kaïd. He took her hand. "Come quickly. I know the way. It is here," he said, pointing to the panel-door by which he had entered.

Holding her hand still, as though she were a child, he led her quickly from the room, and shut the panel behind them. As they passed through, a hand drew aside the curtains on the other side of the room which they were leaving.

Presently the face of Nahoum Pasha followed the hand. A swift glance to the floor, then he ran forward, stooped down, and laid a hand on his brother's breast. The slight wound on the forehead answered his rapid scrutiny. He realized the situation as plainly as if it had been written down for him—he knew his brother well.

Noiselessly he moved forward and touched the spring of the door through which the two had gone. It yielded, and he passed through, closed the door again and stealthily listened, then stole a look into the further chamber. It was empty. He heard the outer doors close. For a moment he listened, then went forward and passed through into the hall. Softly turning the handle of the big wooden doors which faced him, he opened them an inch or so, and listened. He could hear swiftly retreating footsteps. Presently he heard the faint noise of a gate shutting. He nodded his head, and was about to close the doors and turn away, when his quick ear detected footsteps again in the garden. Some one—the man, of course—was returning.

"May the fire burn his eyes forever! He would talk with Kaïd, then go again among them all, and so pass out unsuspected and safe. For who but I—who but I could say he did it? And I—what is my proof? Only the words which I speak."

A scornful, fateful smile passed over his face. "'Hast thou never killed a man?' said Kaïd. 'Never,' said he, 'by the goodness of God, never!' The voice of Him of Galilee, the hand of Cain, the craft of Jael. But God is with the patient."

He went hastily and noiselessly—his footfall was light for so heavy a man—through the large room to the farther side from that by which David and Kaïd had first entered. Drawing behind a clump of palms near a door opening to a passage leading to Mizraim's quarters, he waited. He saw David enter quickly, yet without any air of secrecy, and pass into the little room where Kaïd had left him.

For a long time there was silence.

The reasons were clear in Nahoum's mind why he

should not act yet. A new factor had changed the equation which had presented itself a short half-hour ago.

A new factor had also entered into the equation which had been presented to David by Kaïd with so flattering an insistence. He sat in the place where Kaïd had left him, his face drawn and white, his eyes burning, but with no other sign of agitation. He was frozen and still. His look was fastened now upon the door by which the Prince Pasha would enter, now upon the door through which he had passed to the rescue of the English girl, whom he had seen drive off safely with her maid. In their swift passage from the Palace to the carriage, a thing had been done of even greater moment than the killing of the sensualist in the next room. In the journey to the gateway the girl David served had begged him to escape with her. This he had almost sharply declined; it would be no escape, he had said. She had urged that no one knew. He had replied that Kaïd would come again for him, and suspicion would be roused if he were gone.

"Thee has safety," he had said. "I will go back. I will say that I killed him. I have taken a life, I will pay for it as is the law."

Excited as she was, she had seen the inflexibility of his purpose. She had seen the issue also clearly. He would give himself up, and the whole story would be the scandal of Europe.

"You have no right to save me only to kill me," she had said, desperately. "You would give your life, but you would destroy that which is more than life to me. You did not intend to kill him. It was no murder, it was punishment." Her voice had got harder. "He would have killed my life because he was evil. Will you kill it because you are good? Will you be brave, Quixotic, but not pitiful.... No, no, no," she had said, as his hand was upon the gate, "I will not go unless you promise that you will hide the truth, if you can." She had laid her hand upon his shoulder with an agonized impulse. "You will hide it for a girl who will bless your memory her whole life long. Ah—God bless you!"

She had felt that she conquered before he spoke—as, indeed, he did not speak, but nodded his head and murmured something indistinctly. But that did not matter, for she had won; she had a feeling that all would be well. Then he had placed her in her carriage, and she was driven swiftly away, saying to herself half hysterically, "I am safe, I am safe. He will keep his word!"

Her safety and his promise were the new factor which changed the equation for which Kaïd would presently ask the satisfaction. David's life had suddenly come upon problems for which his whole past was no preparation. Conscience, which had been his guide in every situation, was now disarmed, disabled, and routed. It had come to terms.

In going quickly through the room, they had disarranged a table. The girl's cloak had swept over it, and a piece of bric-à-brac had been thrown upon the floor. He got up and replaced it with an attentive air. He rearranged the other pieces on the table mechanically, seeing, feeling, another scene, another inanimate thing which must be forever and forever a picture burning in his memory. Yet he appeared to be casually doing a trivial and necessary act. He did not definitely realize his actions; but long afterwards he could have drawn an accurate plan of the table, could have reproduced upon it each article in its exact place as correctly as though it had been photographed. There were one or two spots of dust or dirt on the floor, brought in by his boots from the garden. He flicked them aside with his handkerchief.

How still it was! Or was it his life which had become so still? It seemed as if the world must be noiseless, for not a sound of the life in other parts of the Palace came to him, not an echo or vibration of the city which stirred beyond the great gateway. Was it the chilly hand of death passing over everything and smothering all the activities? His pulses, which, but a few minutes past, were throbbing and pounding like drums in his ears, seemed now to flow and beat in very quiet. Was this, then, the way that murderers felt, that men felt who took human life—so frozen, so little a part of their surroundings? Did they move as dead men among the living, devitalized, vacuous, calm?

His life had been suddenly twisted out of recognition. All that his habit, his code, his morals, his religion had imposed upon him had been overturned in one moment. To take a human life, even in battle, was against the code by which he had ever been governed, yet he had taken life secretly; and was hiding it from the world.

Accident? Had it been necessary to strike at all? His presence alone would have been enough to save the girl from further molestation; but he had thrown himself upon the man like a tiger! Yet somehow he felt no sorrow for that. He knew that if again and yet again he were placed in the same position he would do even as he had done—even as he had done with the man Kimber by the Fox and Goose tavern beyond Hamley. He knew that the blow he had given then was inevitable, and he had never felt real repentance. Thinking of that blow, he saw its sequel in the blow he had given now. Thus was that day linked with the present, thus had a blow struck in punishment of the wrong done the woman at the cross-roads been repeated in the wrong done the girl who had just left him.

A sound now broke the stillness. It was a door shutting not far off. Kaïd was coming. David turned his face towards the room where Foorgat Bey was lying dead. He lifted his arms with a sudden passionate gesture. The blood came rushing through his veins again. His life, which had seemed suspended, was set free; and an exaltation of sorrow, of pain, of action, possessed him.

"I have taken a life, O my God!" he murmured. "Accept mine in service for this land. What I have done in secret, let me atone for in secret, for this land—for this poor land, for Christ's sake!"

Footsteps were approaching quickly. With a great effort of the will he ruled himself to quietness again. Kaïd entered, and stood before him in silence. David rose. He looked Kaïd steadily in the eyes.

"Well?" said Kaïd placidly.

"I will serve thee for Egypt's sake," was the reply.

He held out his hand. Kaïd took it, but said, in smiling comment on the action, "As the Viceroy's servant, there is another way!"

"I will salaam to-morrow, Kaïd," answered David.

"It is the only custom of the place I will require of thee, effendi. Come."

A few moments later they were standing among the consuls and officials in the salon.

"Where is Nahoum?" asked Kaïd, looking round on the agitated throng.

No one answered. Smiling, Kaïd whispered in David's ear.

VII

THE COMPACT

One by one the lights went out in the Palace. The excited guests were now knocking at the doors of Cairene notables, bent upon gossip of the night's events, or were scouring the bazaars for ears into which to pour the tale of how David was exalted and Nahoum was brought low; how, before them all, Kaïd had commanded Nahoum to appear at the Palace in the morning at eleven, and the *Inglesi*, as they had named David, at ten. But they declared to all who crowded upon their words that the Inglesi left the Palace with a face frozen white, as though it was he that had met *débâcle*, while Nahoum had been as urbane and cynical as though he had come to the fulness of his power.

Some, on hearing this, said, "Beware Nahoum!" But those who had been at the Palace said, "Beware the Inglesi!" This still Quaker, with the white, shining face and pontifical hat, with his address of "thee" and "thou," and his forms of speech almost Oriental in their imagery and simplicity, himself an archaism, had impressed them with a sense of power. He had prompted old Diaz Pasha to speak of him as a reincarnation, so separate and withdrawn he seemed at the end of the evening, yet with an uncanny mastery in his dark-brown eyes. One of the Ulema, or holy men, present had said in reply to Diaz, "It is the look of one who hath walked with Death and bought and sold with Sheitan the accursed." To Nahoum Pasha, Diaz had said, as the former left the Palace, a cigarette between his fingers: "Sleep not nor slumber, Nahoum. The world was never lost by one earthquake." And Nahoum had replied with a smooth friendliness, "The world is not reaped in one harvest."

"The day is at hand—the East against the West," murmured old Diaz, as he passed on.

"The day is far spent," answered Nahoum, in a voice unheard by Diaz; and, with a word to his coachman, who drove off quickly, he disappeared in the shrubbery.

A few minutes later he was tapping at the door of Mizraim, the Chief Eunuch. Three times he tapped in the same way. Presently the door opened, and he stepped inside. The lean, dark figure of Mizraim bowed low; the long, slow fingers touched the forehead, the breast, and the lips.

"May God preserve thy head from harm, excellency, and the night give thee sleep," said Mizraim. He looked inquiringly at Nahoum.

"May thy head know neither heat nor cold, and thy joys increase," responded Nahoum mechanically, and sat down.

To a European it would have seemed a shameless mockery to have wished joy to this lean, hateful dweller in the between-worlds; to Nahoum it was part of a life which was all ritual and intrigue, gabbling superstition and innate fatalism, decorated falsehood and a brave philosophy.

"I have work for thee at last, Mizraim," said Nahoum.

"At last?"

"Thou hast but played before. To-night I must see the sweat of thy brow."

Mizraim's cold fingers again threw themselves against his breast, forehead, and lips, and he said:

"As a woman swims in a fountain, so shall I bathe in

sweat for thee, who hath given with one hand and hath never taken with the other."

"I did thee service once, Mizraim—eh?"

"I was as a bird buffeted by the wind; upon thy masts my feet found rest. Behold, I build my nest in thy sails, excellency."

"There are no birds in last year's nest, Mizraim, thou dove," said Nahoum, with a cynical smile.

"When I build, I build. Where I swear by the stone of the corner, there am I from dark to dark and from dawn to dawn, pasha." Suddenly he swept his hand low to the ground and a ghastly sort of smile crossed over his face. "Speak—I am thy servant. Shall I not hear? I will put my hand in the entrails of Egypt, and wrench them forth for thee."

He made a gesture so cruelly, so darkly suggestive that Nahoum turned his head away. There flashed before his mind the scene of death in which his own father had lain, butchered like a beast in the shambles, a victim to the rage of Ibrahim Pasha, the son of Mehemet Ali.

"Then listen, and learn why I have need of thee to-night."

First, Nahoum told the story of David's coming, and Kaïd's treatment of himself, the foreshadowing of his own doom. Then of David and the girl, and the dead body he had seen; of the escape of the girl, of David's return with Kaïd—all exactly as it had happened, save that he did not mention the name of the dead man.

It did not astonish Mizraim that Nahoum had kept all this secret. That crime should be followed by secrecy and further crime, if need be, seems natural to the Oriental mind. Mizraim had seen removal follow upon removal, and the dark Nile flowed on gloomily, silently, faithful to the helpless ones tossed into its bosom. It would much have astonished him if Nahoum had not shown a gaping darkness somewhere in his tale, and he felt for the key to the mystery.

"And he who lies dead, excellency?"

"My brother."

"Foorgat Bey!"

"Even he, Mizraim. He lured the girl here—a madman ever. The other madman was in the next room. He struck—come, and thou shalt see."

Together they felt their way through the passages and rooms, and presently entered the room where Foorgat Bey was lying. Nahoum struck a light, and, as he held the candle, Mizraim knelt and examined the body closely. He found the slight wound on the temple, then took the candle from Nahoum and held it close to the corner of the marble pedestal. A faint stain of blood was there. Again he examined the body, and ran his fingers over the face and neck. Suddenly he stopped, and held the light close to the skin beneath the right jaw. He motioned, and Nahoum laid his fingers also on the spot. There was a slight swelling.

"A blow with the fist, excellency—skilful, and English." He looked inquiringly at Nahoum. "As a weasel hath a rabbit by the throat, so is the Inglesi in thy hands."

Nahoum shook his head. "And if I went to Kaïd, and said, 'This is the work of the Inglesi,' would he believe? Kaïd would hang me for the lie—would it be truth to him? What proof have I, save the testimony of mine own eyes? Egypt would laugh at that. Is it the time, while yet the singers are beneath the windows, to assail the bride? All bridegrooms are mad. It is all sunshine and morning with the favorite, the Inglesi. Only when the shadows lengthen may he be stricken. Not now."

"Why dost thou hide this from Kaïd, O thou brother of the eagle?"

"For my gain and thine, keeper of the gate. To-night I am weak, because I am poor. To-morrow I shall be rich—and, it may be, strong. If Kaïd knew of this to-night, I should be a prisoner before cockcrow. What claims has a prisoner? Kaïd would be in my brother's house at dawn seizing all that is there and elsewhere, and I on my way to Fazougli, to be strangled or drowned."

"O wise and far-seeing! Thine eye pierces the earth. What is there to do? What is my gain—what thine?"

"Thy gain? The payment of thy debt to me."

Mizraim's face lengthened. His was a loathsome sort of gratitude. He was willing to pay in kind; but what Oriental ever paid a debt without a gift in return, even as a bartering Irishman demands his lucky penny.

"So be it, Excellency, and my life is thine to spill upon the ground, a scarlet cloth for thy feet. And backsheesh?"

Nahoum smiled grimly. "For backsheesh, thy turban full of gold."

Mizraim's eyes glittered—the dull black shine of a mongrel terrier's. He caught the sleeve of Nahoum's coat and kissed it, then kissed his hand.

Thus was their bargain made over the dead body; and Mizraim had an almost superstitious reverence for the fulfilment of a bond, the one virtue rarely found in the Oriental. Nothing else had he, but of all men in Egypt he was the best instrument Nahoum could have chosen; and of all men in Egypt he was the one man who could surely help him.

"What is there now to do, excellency?"

"My coachman is with the carriage at the gate by which the English girl left. It is open still. The key is in Foorgat's pocket, no doubt; stolen by him, no doubt also. . . . This is my design. Thou wilt drive him"—he pointed to the body—"to his palace, seated in the carriage as though he were alive. There is a secret entrance. The *bowáb* at the gate will show the way; I know it not. But who will deny thee? Thou comest from high places—from Kaïd. Who will speak of this? Will the bowáb? In the morning Foorgat will be found dead in his bed! The slight bruise thou canst heal—thou canst?"

Mizraim nodded. "I can smooth it from the sharpest eye."

"At dawn he will be found dead; but at dawn I shall be knocking at his gates. Before the world knows I shall be in possession. All that is his shall be mine, for at once the men of law shall be summoned, and my inheritance secured before Kaïd shall even know of his death. I shall take my chances for my life."

"And the coachman, and the bowáb, and others it may be?"

"Shall not these be with thee—thou, Kaïd's keeper of the harem, the lion at the door of his garden of women? Would it be strange that Foorgat, who ever flew at fruit above his head, perilous to get or keep, should be found on forbidden ground, or in design upon it? Would it be strange to the bowáb or the slave that he should return with thee stark and still? They would not but count it mercy of Kaïd that he was not given to the serpents of the Nile? A word from thee—would one open his mouth? Would not the shadow of thy hand, of the swift doom, be over them? Would not a handful of gold bind them to me? Is not the man dead? Are they not mine—mine to bind or break as I will?"

"So be it! Wisdom is of thee as the breath of man is his life. I will drive Foorgat Bey to his home."

A few moments later all that was left of Foorgat Bey was sitting in his carriage beside Mizraim, the Chief Eunuch—sitting upright, stony, and still, and in such wise was driven swiftly to his palace.

VIII

FOR HIS SOUL'S SAKE AND THE LAND'S SAKE

DAVID came to know a startling piece of news the next morning—that Foorgat Bey had died of heart-disease in his bed, and was so found by his servants. He at once surmised that Foorgat's body had been carried out of the Palace; no doubt, that it might not be thought he had come to his death by command of Kaïd. His mind became easier. Death, murder, crime, in Egypt was not a nine days' wonder; it scarce outlived one day. When a man was gone, none troubled. The dead man was in the bosom of Allah; then why should the living be beset or troubled? If there was foul play, why make things worse by sending another life after the life gone, even in the way of justice?

The girl David saved had told him her own name, and had given him the name of the hotel at which she was staying. He had an early breakfast, and prepared to go to her hotel, wishing to see her once more. There were things to be said for the first and last time and then be buried forever. She must leave the country at once. In this sick, mad land, in this whirlpool of secret murder and conspiracy, no one could tell what plot was hatching, what deeds were forward; and he could not yet be sure that no one save himself and herself knew who had killed Foorgat Bey. Her perfect safety lay in instant flight. It was his duty to see that she went—this very day. He would go and see her.

He went to the hotel. There he learned that, with her aunt, she had left that morning for Alexandria *en route* to England.

He approved her wisdom, he applauded her decision. Yet—yet, somehow, as he bent his footsteps towards his lodgings again he had a sense of disappointment, of revelation. What might happen to him—evidently that had not occurred to her. How could she know but that his life might be in danger; that, after all, they might have been seen leaving the fatal room? Well, she had gone, and with all his heart he was glad that she was safe.

His judgment upon last night's event was not colored by a single direct criticism upon the girl. But he could not prevent the suggestion suddenly flashing into his mind, that she had thought of herself first and last. Well, she had gone; and he was here to face the future, unencumbered by aught save the weight of his own conscience.

Yet, the weight of his conscience! His feet were still free—free for one short hour before he went to Kaïd; but his soul was in chains. As he turned his course to the Nile, and crossed over the great bridge, there went clanking by in chains a hundred conscripts, torn from their homes in the Fayoum, bidding farewell forever to their friends, receiving their last offerings; for they had no hope of return. He looked at their haggard and dusty faces, at their excoriated ankles, and his eyes closed in pain. All they felt he felt. What their homes were to them, these fellaheen, dragged forth to defend their country, to go into the desert and waste their lives under leaders tyrannous, cruel, and incompetent, his old open life, his innocence, his integrity, his truthfulness and character, were to him. By an impulsive act, by a rash blow, he had asserted his humanity; but he had killed his fellow-man in anger. He knew that as that fatal blow had been delivered, there was no thought of punishment—it was blind anger and hatred: it was the ancient virus working which had filled the world with war, and armed it at the expense, the bitter and oppressive expense, of the toilers and the poor. The taxes for wars were wrung out of the sons of labor and sorrow. These poor fellaheen had paid taxes on everything they possessed. Taxes, taxes, nothing but taxes from the cradle! Their lands, houses, and palm-trees would be taxed still, when they would reap no more. And having given all save their lives, these lives they must now give under the whip and the chain and the sword.

As David looked at them in their single blue calico coverings, in which they had lived and slept — shivering in the cold night air upon the bare ground—these thoughts came to him; and he had a sudden longing to follow them and put the chains upon his own arms and legs, and go forth and suffer with them, and fight and die? To die were easy. To fight? . . . Was it then come to that? He was no longer a man of peace, but a man of the sword; no longer a man of the palm and the evangel, but a man of blood and of crime! He shrank back out of the glare of the sun; for it suddenly seemed to him that there was written upon his forehead, "*This is a brother of Cain.*" For the first time in his life he had a shrinking from the light, and from the sun which he had loved like a Persian—had, in a sense, unconsciously worshipped.

He was scarcely aware where he was. He had wandered on until he had come to the end of the bridge and into the great groups of traffickers who, at this place, made a market of their wares. Here sat a seller of sugar-cane, there wandered, clanking his brasses, a merchant of sweet waters, there shouted a cheap-jack of the Nile the virtues of a knife from Sheffield. Yonder a camel-driver squatted and counted his earnings; and a sheep-dealer haggled with the owner of a ghiassa bound for the sands of the North. The curious came about him and looked at him, but he did not see or hear. He sat upon a stone, his gaze upon the river, following with his eyes, yet without consciously observing, the dark riverine population whose ways are hidden, who know only the law of the river and spend their lives in eluding it—pirates and brigands now, and yet again the peaceful porters of commerce.

To his mind never a criminal in this land but less a criminal than he! For their standard was a standard of might the only right; but he—his whole life had been nurtured in an atmosphere of right and justice, had been a spiritual demonstration against force. He was without fear, as he was without an undue love of life. The laying down of his life had never been presented to him; and yet, now that his conscience was his only judge, and it condemned him, he would gladly have given his life to pay the price of blood.

That was impossible. His life was not his own to give, save by suicide; and that would be the unpardonable insult to God and humanity. He had given his word to the woman, and he would keep it. In those brief moments she must have suffered more than most men suffer in a long life. Not her hand, however, but his, had committed the deed. And yet—a sudden wave of pity for her rushed over him, because the conviction seized him that she would also in her heart take upon herself the burden of his guilt, as though it were her own. He had seen it in the look of her face last night. For the sake of her future it was her duty to shield herself from any imputation which might as unjustly as scandalously arise, if the facts of that black hour ever became known— Ever became known? The thought that there might be some human eye which had seen, which knew, sent a shiver through him.

"I would give my life a thousand times rather than

"FOR THIS LAND—HIS LIFE, AND HIS LOVE, AND HIS FAITH"

that," he said aloud to the swift-flowing river. His head sank on his breast. His lips murmured in prayer:

"But be merciful to me, Thou just judge of Israel, for Thou hast made me, and Thou knowest whereof I am made. Here will I dedicate my life to Thee for the land's sake. Not for my soul's sake, O my God! If it be Thy will, let my soul be cast away; but for the soul of him whose body I slew, and for his land, let my life be the long sacrifice."

Dreams he had had the night before—terrible dreams, which he could never forget; dreams of a fugitive being hunted through the world, escaping and eluding, only to be hemmed in once more; on and on, till he grew gray and gaunt, and the hunt suddenly ended in a great morass, into which he plunged with the howling world behind him. The gray, dank mists came down on him, his footsteps sank deeper and deeper, and ever the cries, as of damned spirits, grew in his ears. Mocking shapes flitted past him, the wings of obscene birds buffeted him, the morass grew up about him; and now it was all a red moving mass like a dead sea heaving about him. With a moan of agony he felt the dolorous flood above his shoulders, and then a cry pierced the gloom and the loathsome misery, and a voice he knew called to him, "David, David, I am coming!" and he had awaked with the old hallucination of his uncle's voice calling to him in the dawn.

It came to him now as he sat by the waterside, and he raised his face to the sun and to the world. The idlers had left him alone; none were staring at him now. They were all intent on their own business, each man laboring after his kind. He heard the voice of a river-man as he toiled at a rope standing on the corn that filled his ghiassa from end to end, from keel to gunwale. The man was singing a wild chant of cheerful labor, the soul of the hard-smitten of the earth rising above the rack and burden of the body:

> "O, the garden where to-day we sow and to-morrow we reap!
> O, the sakkia turning by the garden walls;
> O, the onion-field and the date-tree growing,
> And my hand on the plough—by the blessing of God;
> Strength of my soul, O my brother, all's well!"

The meaning of the song got into his heart. He pressed his hand to his breast with a sudden gesture. It touched something hard. It was his flute. Mechanically he had put it in his pocket when he dressed in the morning. He took it out and looked at it lovingly. Into it he had poured his soul in the old days—days, centuries away, it seemed now. It should still be the link with the old life.

He rose and walked towards his home again. The future spread clearly before him. Rapine, murder, tyranny, oppression, were round him on every side, and the ruler of the land called him to his counsels. Here a great duty lay—his life for this land, his life, and his love, and his faith. He would expiate his crime and his sin, the crime of homicide for which he alone was responsible, the sin of secrecy for which he and another were responsible. And that other? If only there had been but one word of understanding between them before she left!

At the door of his house stood the American whom he had met at the citadel yesterday—it seemed a hundred years ago.

"I've got a letter for you," Lacey said. "The lady's aunt and herself are cousins of mine more or less removed, and originally at home in the U. S. A. a generation ago. Her mother was an American. She didn't know your name—Miss Hylda Maryon, I mean. I told her, but there wasn't time to put it on." He handed over the unaddressed envelope.

David opened the letter, and read:

"I have seen the papers. I do not understand what has happened, but I know that all is well. If it were not so, I would not go. That is the truth. Grateful I am, oh, believe me! So grateful that I do not yet know what is the return which I must make. But the return will be made. I hear of what has come to you—how easily I might have destroyed all! My thoughts blind me. You are great and good; you will know at least that I go because it is the only thing to do. I fly from the storm with a broken wing. Take now my promise to pay what I owe in the hour Fate wills—or in the hour of your need. You can trust him who brings this to you; he is a distant cousin of my own. Do not judge him by his odd and foolish words. They hide a good character, and he has a strong nature. He wants work to do. Can you give it? Farewell."

David put the letter in his pocket, a strange quietness about his heart.

He scarcely realized what Lacey was saying. "Great girl that. Troubled about something in England, I guess. Going straight back."

David thanked him for the letter. Lacey became red in the face. He tried to say something, but failed.

"Thee wishes to say something to me, friend?" asked David.

"I'm full up; I can't speak. But, say—"

"I am going to the Palace now. Come back at noon if you will."

He wrung David's hand in gratitude. "You're going to do it. You're going to do it. I see it. It's a great game—like Abe Lincoln's. Say, let me black your boots while you're doing it, will you?"

David pressed his hand.

IX

THE LETTER, THE NIGHT, AND THE WOMAN

"To-day has come the fulfilment of my dream, Faith. I am given to my appointed task; I am set on a road of life in which there is no looking back. My dreams of the past are here begun in very truth and fact. When, in the night, I heard Uncle Benn calling, when in the Meeting-house voices said, 'Come away, come away, and labor; thou art idle,' I could hear my heart beat in the ardor to be off. Yet I knew not whither. Now I know.

"Last night the Prince Pasha called me to his Council, made me adviser, confidant, as one who has the ear of his captain—after he had come to terms with me upon that which Uncle Benn left of land and gold. Think not that he tempted me.

"Last night I saw favorites look upon me with hate because of Kaïd's favor, though the great hall was filled with show of cheerful splendor, and men smiled and feasted. To-day I know that in the Palace where I was summoned to my first duty with the Prince, every step I took was shadowed, every motion recorded, every look or word noted and set down. I have no fear of them. They are not subtle enough for the unexpected acts of honesty in the life of a true man. Yet I do not wonder men fail to keep honest in the midst of this splendor, where all is strife as to who shall have the Prince's favor; who shall enjoy the fruits of bribery, backsheesh, and monopoly; who shall wring from the slave and the toil-ridden fellah the coin his poor body mints at the *corvée*, in his own taxed fields of dourha and cucumbers.

"Is this like anything we ever dreamed at Hamley, Faith? Yet here am I set, and here shall I stay till the skein be ravelled out. Soon I shall go into the desert upon a mission to the cities of the South, to Dongola, Khartoum, and Darfûr and beyond; for there is trouble yonder, and war is near, unless it is given to me to bring peace. So I must bend to my study of Arabic, which I am thankful I learned long ago. And I must not forget to say that I shall take with me on my journey that faithful Muslim Ebn Ezra. Others I shall take also, but of them I shall write hereafter.

"I shall henceforth be moving in the midst of things which I was taught to hate. I pray that I may not hate them less as time goes on. To-morrow I shall breathe the air of intrigue, shall hear footsteps of spies behind me wherever I go; shall know that even the roses in the garden have ears; that the ground under my feet will telegraph my thoughts. Shall I be true? Shall I at last whisper, and follow, and evade, believe in no one, much less in myself, steal in and out of men's confidences to use them for my own purposes? Does any human being know what he can bear of temptation or of the daily pressure of the life around him? what powers of resistance are in his soul? how long the vital energy will continue to throw off the never-ending seduction, the freshening force of evil? Therein lies the power of evil, that it is ever new, ever fortified by continuous conquest and achievements. It has the rare fire of aggression; is ever more upon the offence than upon the defence; has, withal, the false lure of freedom from restraint, the throbbing force of sympathy.

"Such things I dreamed not of in Soolsby's hut upon the hill, Faith, though, indeed, that seemed a time of trial and sore-heartedness. How large do small issues seem till we have faced the momentous things! It is true that the larger life has pleasures and expanding capacities; but it is truer still that it has perils, events which try the soul as it is never tried in the smaller life—unless, indeed, the soul be that of the Epicurean. The Epicurean I well understand, and in his way I might have walked with a wicked grace. I have in me some hidden depths of luxury, a secret heart of pleasure, an understanding for the forbidden thing. I could have walked the broad way with a laughing heart, though, in truth, habit of mind and desire have kept me in the better path. But offences must come, and woe to him from whom the offence cometh! I have begun now, and only now, to feel the storms that shake us to our farthest cells of life. I begin to see how near good is to evil: how near faith is to unfaith; and how difficult it is to judge from actions only; how little we can know to-day what we shall feel to-morrow. Yet one must learn to see deeper, to find motive, not in acts that shake the faith, but in character which needs no explanation, which—" He paused, disturbed.

Then he raised his head, as though not conscious of what was breaking the course of his thoughts. Presently he realized a low, hurried knocking at his door. He drew a hand over his eyes, and sprang up. An instant later the figure of a woman, deeply veiled, stood within the room, beside the table where he had been writing. There was silence as they faced each other, his back against the door.

"Oh, do you not know me?" she said at last, and sank into the chair where he had been sitting.

The question was unnecessary, and she knew it was so; but she could not bear the strain of the silence. She seemed to have risen out of the letter he had been writing; and had he not been writing of her—of what concerned them both? How mean and small-hearted he had been, to have thought for an instant that she had not the highest courage, though in going she had done the discreeter, safer thing! But she had come—she had come!

All this was in his eyes, though his face was pale and still. He was almost rigid with emotion, for the ancient habit of repose and self-command of the Quaker people was upon him.

"Can you not see—do you not know?" she repeated, her back upon him now, her face still veiled, her hands making a swift motion of distress.

"Has thee found in the past that thee is so soon forgotten?"

"Oh, do not blame me!" She raised her veil suddenly and showed a face as pale as his own, and in the eyes a fiery brightness. "I did not know. It was so hard to come—do not blame me. I went to Alexandria—I felt that I must fly, the air around me seemed full of voices crying out. Did you not understand why I went?"

"I understand," he said, coming forward slowly. "Thee should not have returned. In the way I go now the watchers go also."

"If I had not come, you would never have understood," she answered quickly. "I am not sorry I went. I was so frightened, so shaken. My only thought was to get away from the terrible Thing. But I should have been sorry all my life long, had I not come back to tell you what I feel, and that I shall never forget. All my life I shall be grateful. You have saved me from a thousand deaths! Ah, if I could give you but one life! Yet—yet—oh, do not think but that I would tell you the whole truth, though I am not wholly truthful. See, I love my place in the world more than I love my life: and but for you I should have lost all."

He made a protesting motion. "The debt is mine,

in truth. But for you I should never have known what, perhaps—" He paused.

His eyes were on hers, gravely speaking what his tongue faltered to say. She looked and looked, but did not understand. She only saw troubled depths lighted by a soul of kindling purpose. "Tell me," she said, awed.

"Through you I have come to know—" He paused again. What he was going to say, truthful though it was, must hurt her, and she had been sorely hurt already. He put his thoughts more gently, more vaguely.

"By what happened I have come to see what matters in life. I was behind the hedge. I have broken through upon the road. I know my goal now. The highway is before me."

She felt the tragedy in his words, and her voice shook as she spoke. "I wish I knew life better. Then I could make a better answer. You are on the road, you say. But I feel that it is a hard and cruel road—oh, I understand that at least! Tell me, please, tell me the whole truth. You are hiding from me what you feel. I have upset your life, have I not? You are a Quaker, and Quakers are better than all other Christian people, are they not? Their faith is peace, and for me, you—" She covered her face with her hands for an instant, but turned quickly and looked him in the eyes. "For me you put your hand upon the clock of a man's life, and stopped it."

She got to her feet with a passionate gesture, but he put a hand gently upon her arm, and she sank back again. "Oh, it was not you; it was I who did it!" she said. "You did what any man of honor would have done, what a brother would have done."

"What I did is a matter for myself only," he responded quickly. "Had I never seen your face again it would have been the same. You were the occasion; the thing I did had only one source, my own heart and mind. There might have been another way; but for that way, or for the way I did take, you could not be responsible."

"How generous you are!" Her eyes swam with tears; she leaned over the table where he had been writing, and the tears dropped upon his letter. Presently she realized this, and drew back, then made as though to dry the tears from the paper with her handkerchief. As she did so the words that he had written met her eye: "*But offences must come, and woe to him from whom the offence cometh!* I have begun now, and only now, to feel the storms that shake us to our farthest cells of life."

She became very still. He touched her arm and said heavily, "Come away, come away."

She pointed to the words she had read. "I could not help but see, and now I know what this must mean to you."

"Thee must go at once," he urged. "Thee should not have come. Thee was safe—none knew. A few hours and it would all have been far behind. We might never have met again."

Suddenly she gave a low hysterical laugh. "You think you hide the real thing from me. I know I'm ignorant and selfish and feeble-minded, but I can see farther than you think. You want to tell the truth about—about *it*, because you are honest and hate hiding things, because you want to be punished, and so pay the price. Oh, I can understand! If it were not for me you would not. . . ." With a sudden wild impulse she got to her feet. "And you shall not," she cried. "I will not have it." Color came rushing to her cheeks. "I will not have it. I will not put myself so much in your debt. I will not demand so much of you. I will face it all. I will stand alone."

There was a touch of indignation in her voice. Somehow she seemed moved to anger against him. Her hands were clasped at her side rigidly, her pulses throbbing. He stood looking at her fixedly, as though trying to realize her. His silence agitated her still further, and she spoke excitedly.

"I could have, would have, killed him myself without a moment's regret. He had planned, planned—ah, God, can you not see it all! I would have taken his life without a thought. I was mad to go upon such an adventure, but I meant no ill. I had not one thought that I could not have cried out from the house-tops, and he had in his heart—he had what you saw. But you repent that you killed him—by accident, it was by accident. Do you realize how many times others have been trapped by him as was I! Do you not see what he was—as I see now? Did he not say as much to me before you came, when I was dumb with terror? Did he not make me understand what his whole life had been? Did I not see in a flash the women whose lives he had spoiled and killed? Would I have had pity? Would I have had remorse? No, no, no! I was frightened when it was done, I was horrified, but I was not sorry; and I am not sorry. It was to be. It was the true end to his vileness. Ah!"

She shuddered, and buried her face in her hands for a moment, then went on: "I can never forgive myself for going to the Palace with him. I was mad for experience, for mystery; I wanted more than the ordinary share of knowledge. I wanted to probe things. Yet I meant no wrong. I thought then nothing of which I shall ever be ashamed. But I shall always be ashamed because I knew him, because he thought that I—oh, if I were a man, I should be glad that I had killed him, for the sake of all honest women!"

He remained silent. His look was not upon her, he seemed lost in a dream; but his face was fixed in trouble.

She misunderstood his silence. "You had the courage, the impulse to—to do it," she said keenly; "you have not the courage to justify it. I will not have it so. I will tell the truth to all the world. I will not shrink. I shrank yesterday because I was afraid of the world; to-day I will face it, I will—"

She stopped suddenly, and another look flashed into her face. Presently she spoke in a different tone; a new light had come upon her mind. "But I see," she added. "To tell all is to make you the victim, too, of what he did. It is in your hands; it is all in your hands; and I cannot speak unless—unless you are ready also."

There was an unintended touch of scorn in her voice. She had been troubled and tried beyond bearing, and her impulsive nature revolted at his silence. She misunderstood him, or, if she did not wholly misunderstand him, she was angry at what she thought was a needless remorse or sensitiveness. Did not the man deserve his end?

"There is only one course to pursue," he rejoined quietly, "and that is the course we entered upon last night. I neither doubted yourself nor your courage. Thee must not turn back now. Thee must not alter the course which was your own making, and the only course which thee could, or I should, take. I have planned my life according to the word I gave you. I could not turn back now. We are strangers, and we must remain so. Thee will go from here now, and we must not meet again. I am—"

"I know who you are," she broke in. "I know what your religion is; that fighting and war and bloodshed is a sin to you."

"I am of no family or place in England," he went on calmly. "I come of yeoman and trading stock; I have nothing in common with people of rank and riches. Our lines of life will not cross. It is well that it should be so. As to what happened—that which I may feel has nothing to do with whether I was justified or no. But if thee has thought that I have repented doing what I did, let that pass forever from your mind. I know that I should do the same, yes, even a hundred times. I did according to my nature. Thee must not now be punished cruelly for a thing thee did not do. Silence is the only way of safety or of justice. We must not speak of this again. We must each go our own way."

Her eyes were moist. She reached out a hand to him timidly. "Oh, forgive me," she added brokenly. "I am so vain, so selfish, and that makes one blind to the truth. It is all clearer now. You have shown me that I was right in my first impulse, and that is all I can say for myself. I shall pray all my life that it will do you no harm in the end."

She remained silent, for a moment adjusting her veil, preparing to go. Presently she spoke again: "I shall always want to know about you—what is happening to you. How could it be otherwise?"

She was half realizing one of the deepest things in existence, that the closest bond between two human beings is a bond of secrecy upon a thing which vitally, fatally concerns both or either. It is a power at once malevolent and beautiful. A secret like that of David and Hylda will do in a day what a score of years could not accomplish, will insinuate confidences which might never be given to the nearest or dearest. In neither was any feeling of the heart begotten by their experiences; and yet they had gone deeper in each other's lives than any one either had known in a lifetime. They had struck a deeper note than love or friendship. They had touched the chord of a secret and mutual experience which had gone so far that their lives would be influenced by it forever after. Each understood this in a different way.

Hylda looked towards the letter lying on the table.

It had raised in her mind, not a doubt, but an undefined, undefinable anxiety. He saw the glance, and said: "I was writing to one who has been as a sister to me. She was my mother's sister though she is almost, as young as I. Her name is Faith. There is nothing there of what concerns thee and me, though it would make no difference if she knew." Suddenly a thought seemed to strike him. "The secret is of thee and me. There is safety. If it became another's, there might be peril. The thing shall be between us only, forever?"

"Do you think that I—"

"My instinct tells me a woman of sensitive mind might one day, out of an unmerciful honesty, tell her husband—"

"I am not married—"

"But one day—"

She interrupted him. "Sentimental egotism will not rule me. Tell me," she added—"tell me one thing before I go. You said that your course was set. What is it?"

"I remain here," he answered quietly. "I remain in the service of Prince Kaïd."

"It is a dreadful government, an awful service—"

"That is why I stay."

"You are going to try and change things here—you alone?"

"I hope not alone, in time."

"You are going to leave England, your friends, your family, your place—in Hamley, was it not? My aunt has read of you—my cousin—" She paused.

"I had no place in Hamley. Here is my place. Distance has little to do with understanding or affection. I had an uncle here in the East for twenty-five years, yet I knew him better than all others in the world. Space is nothing if minds are in sympathy. My uncle talked to me over seas and lands. I felt him, heard him speak."

"You think that minds can speak to minds, no matter what the distance—real and definite things?"

"If I were parted from one very dear to me, I would try to say to him or her what was in my mind, not by written word only, but by the flying thought."

She sat down suddenly, as though overwhelmed. "Oh, if that were possible!" she said. "If only one could send a thought like that!" Then with an impulse, and the flicker of a sad smile, she reached out a hand. "If ever in the years to come you want to speak to me, will you try to make me understand, as your uncle did with you?"

"I cannot tell," he answered. "That which is deepest within us obeys only the laws of its need. By instinct it turns to where help lies, as a wild deer, fleeing from captivity, makes for the veldt and the watercourse."

She got to her feet again. "I want to pay my debt," she said solemnly. "It is a debt that one day must be paid — so awful — so awful!" A swift change passed over her. She shuddered, and grew white. "I said brave words just now," she added in a hoarse whisper, "but now I see him lying there cold and still, and you stooping over him. I see you touch his breast, his pulse. I see you close his eyes. One instant full of the pulse of life, the next struck out into infinite space. Oh, I shall never—how can I ever—forget!" She turned her head away from him, then composed herself again, and said quietly, with anxious eyes: "Why was nothing said or done? Perhaps they are only waiting. Perhaps they know. Why was it announced that he died in his bed at home?"

"I cannot tell. When a man in high places dies in Egypt, it may be one death or another. No one inquires too closely. He died in Kaïd Pasha's Palace, where other men have died, and none has inquired too closely. To-day they told me at the Palace that his carriage was seen to leave with himself and Mizraim the Chief Eunuch. Whatever the object, he was secretly taken to his house from the Palace, and his brother Nahoum seized upon his estate in the early morning. I think that no one knows the truth. But it is all in the hands of God. We can do nothing more. Thee must go. Thee should not have come. In England thee will forget, as thee should forget. In Egypt I shall remember, as I should remember."

"*Thee*," she repeated softly. "I love the Quaker *thee*. My grandmother was an American Quaker. She always spoke like that. Will you not use *thee* and *thou* in speaking to me, always?"

"We are not likely to speak together in any language in the future," he answered. "But now thee must go, and I will—"

"My cousin, Mr. Lacey, is waiting for me in the garden," she answered. "I shall be safe with him."

She moved towards the door. He caught the handle to turn it, when there came the noise of loud talking, and the sound of footsteps in the courtyard. He opened the door slightly and looked out, then closed it quickly.

"It is Nahoum Pasha," he said. "Please, the other room," he added, and pointed to a curtain. "There is a window leading on a garden. The garden-gate opens on a street leading to the Ezbekiah Square and your hotel."

"But, no, I shall stay here," she said. She drew down her veil, then taking from her pocket another, arranged it also, so that her face was hidden.

"Thee must go," he said—"go quickly." Again he pointed.

"I will remain," she rejoined, with determination, and seated herself in a chair.

X

THE FOUR WHO KNEW

THERE was a knocking at the door. David opened it. Nahoum Pasha stepped inside, and stood still a moment looking at Hylda. Then he made low salutation to her, touched his hand to his lips and breast saluting David, and waited.

"What is thy business, pasha?" asked David quietly, and motioned towards a chair.

"May thy path be on the high hills, Saadat-el-básha. I come for a favor at thy hands." Nahoum sat down.

"What favor is mine to give to Nahoum Pasha?"

"The Prince has given thee supreme place—it was mine but yesterday. It is well. To the deserving be the fruits of deserving."

"Is merit, then, so truly rewarded here?" asked David quietly.

"The Prince saw merit at last when he chose your excellency for councillor."

"How shall I show merit, then, in the eyes of Nahoum Pasha?"

"Even by urging the Prince to give me place under him again. Not as heretofore,—that is thy place—yet where it may be. I have capacity. I can aid thee in the great task. Thou wouldst remake our Egypt—and my heart is with you. I would rescue, not destroy. In years gone by I tried to do good to this land, and I failed. I was alone. I had not the strength to fight the forces around me. I was overcome. I had too little faith. But my heart was with the right—I am an Armenian and a Christian of the ancient faith. I am in sorrow. Death has humbled me. My brother Foorgat Bey—may flowers bloom forever on his grave!—he is dead,"—his eyes were fixed on those of David, as with a perfectly assured candor—"and my heart is like an empty house. But man must not be idle and live—if Kaïd lets me live. I have riches. Are not Foorgat's riches mine, his palace, his gardens, his cattle, and his plantations, are they not mine? I may sit in the courtyard and hear the singers, may listen to the tale-tellers by the light of the moon; I may hear the tales of Al-Raschid chanted by one whose tongue never falters, and whose voice is like music; after the manner of the East I may give bread and meat to the poor at sunset; I may call the dancers to the feast. But what comfort shall it give? I am no longer a youth. I would work. I would labor for the land of Egypt, for by work shall we fulfil ourselves, redeem ourselves. Saadat, I would labor, but my master has taken away from me the anvil, the fire, and the hammer, and I sit without the door like an armless beggar. What work to do in Egypt save to help the land, and how shall one help, save in the Prince's service? There can be no reform from outside. If I labored for better things outside Kaïd's Palace, how long dost thou think I should escape the Nile, or the diamond-dust in my coffee? The work which I did, is it not so that it, with much more, falls now to thy hands, Saadat, with a confidence from Kaïd that never was mine?"

"I sought not the office."

"Have I a word of blame? I come to ask for work to do with thee. Do I not know Prince Kaïd? He had come to distrust us all. As stale water were we in his taste. He had no pleasure in us, and in our deeds he found only stones of stumbling. He knew not whom to trust. One by one we all had yielded to ceaseless intrigue and common distrust of each other, until no honest man was left; till all were intent to save their lives by holding power; for in this land to lose power is to lose life. No man who has been in high place, has had the secrets of the Palace and the ear of the Prince, lives after he has lost favor. The Prince, for his safety, must ensure silence, and the only silence in Egypt is the grave. In thee, Saadat, Kaïd has found an honest man. Men will call thee mad, if thou remainest honest, but that is within thine own bosom and with fate. For me, thou hast taken my place, and more. Malaish, it is the decree of fate, and I have no anger! I come to ask thee to save my life, and then to give me work."

"How shall I save thy life?"

"By reconciling the Effendina to my living, and then by giving me service, where I shall be near to thee, where I can share with thee, though it be as the ant beside the beaver, the work of salvation in Egypt. I am rich since my brother was"— He paused; no covert look was in his eyes, no sign of knowledge, nothing but meditation and sorrowful frankness—"since Foorgat passed away in peace, praise be to God! He lay on his bed in the morning, when one came to wake him, like a sleeping child, no sign of the struggle of death upon him.

A gasping sound came from the chair where Hylda sat; but he took no notice. He appeared to be unconscious of David's pain-drawn face, as he sat with his hands upon his knees, his head bent forward listening, as though lost to the world.

"So did Foorgat, my brother, die while yet in the fulness of his manhood, life beating high in his veins, with years before him to waste. He was a pleasure-lover, alas! he laid up no treasure of work accomplished; and so it was meet that he should die as he lived, in a moment of ease. And already he is forgotten. It is the custom here. He might have died by diamond-dust, and men would have set down their coffee-cups in surprise, and then would have forgotten; or he might have been struck down by the hand of an assassin, and, unless it was in the Palace, none would have paused to note it! And so the sands sweep over his steps upon the shore of time."

After the first exclamation of horror, Hylda had sat rigid, listening as though under a spell. Through her veil she gazed at Nahoum with a cramping pain at her heart, for he seemed ever on the verge of the truth she dreaded; and when he spoke the truth, as though unconsciously, she felt she must cry out and rush from the room. He recalled to her the scene in the little tapestried room as vividly as though it was there before her eyes, and it had for the moment all the effect of a hideous nightmare. At last, however, she met David's eyes, and they guided her, for in them was a steady strength and force which gave her confidence. At first he also had been overcome inwardly, but his nerves were cool, his head was clear, and he listened to Nahoum, thinking out his course meanwhile.

He owed this man much. He had taken his place, and by so doing had placed his life in danger. He had killed the brother upon the same day that he had dispossessed the favorite of office; and the debt was heavy. In office Nahoum had done after his kind, after the custom of the place and the people; and yet, as it would seem, the man had had stirrings within him towards a higher path. He, at any rate, had not amassed riches out of his position, and so much could not be said of any other servant of the Prince Pasha. Much he had heard of Nahoum's powerful will, hidden under a genial exterior, and behind his friendly, smiling blue eyes. He had heard also of cruelty—of banishment, and of enemies removed from his path suddenly, never to be seen again; but, on the whole, men spoke with more admiration of him than of any other public servant, Armenian Christian in a Mahommedan country though he was. That very day Kaïd had said that if Nahoum had been less eager to control the state, he might still have held his place. Besides, the man was a Christian—of a mystic, half-legendary, obscured Christianity; yet having in his mind the old faith, its essence and its meaning, perhaps. Might not this Oriental mind, with that faith, be a power to redeem the land? It was a wonderful dream, in which he found the way, as he thought, to atone somewhat to this man for a dark injury done.

When Nahoum stopped speaking, David said: "But if I would have it, if it were well that it should be, I doubt I have the power to make it so."

"Saadat-el-básha, Kaïd believes in thee to-day; he will not believe to-morrow if thou dost remain without initiative. Action, however startling, will be proof of fitness. His Highness shakes a long spear. Those who ride with him must do battle with the same valor. Excellency, I have now great riches — since Death smote Foorgat Bey in the forehead"—still his eyes conveyed no meaning, though Hylda shrank back—"and I would use them for the good thou wouldst do here. Money will be needed, and sufficient will not be at thy hand—not till new ledgers be opened, new balances struck."

He turned to Hylda quietly and with a continued air of innocence said: "Shall it not be so—madame? Thou, I doubt not, are of his kin. It would seem so, though I ask pardon if it be not so—wilt thou not urge his excellency to restore me to Kaïd's favor? I know little of the English, though I know them humane and honest; but my brother Foorgat Bey, he was much among them, lived much in England, was a friend to many great English. Indeed, on the evening that he died I saw him in the gallery of the banquet-room with an English lady—can one be mistaken in an English face?

Perhaps he cared for her; perhaps that was why he smiled as he lay upon his bed, never to move again. Madame, perhaps in England thou mayst have known my brother. If that is so, I ask thee to speak for me to his excellency. My life is in danger, and I am too young to go as my brother went. I do not wish to die in middle age, as my brother died."

He had gone too far. In David's mind there was no suspicion that Nahoum knew the truth. The suggestion in his words had seemed natural; but, from the first, a sharp suspicion was in the mind of Hylda, and his last words had convinced her that if Nahoum did not surely know the truth, he suspected it all too well. Her instinct had pierced far; and as she realized his suspicions, perhaps his certainty, and heard his words of covert insult, which, as she saw, David did not appreciate, anger and determination grew in her. Yet she felt that caution must mark her words, and that nothing but danger lay in resentment. She felt the everlasting indignity behind the quiet, youthful eyes, the determined power of the man; but she saw also that, for the present, the course Nahoum suggested was the only course to take. And David must not even feel the suspicion in her own mind, that Nahoum knew or suspected the truth. If David thought that Nahoum knew, the end of all would come at once. It was clear, however, that Nahoum meant to be silent, or he would have taken another course of action. Danger lay in every direction, but, to her mind, the least danger lay in following Nahoum's wish.

She slowly raised her veil, showing a face very still now, with eyes as steady as David's. David started at her action, he thought it rash; but the courage of it pleased him, too.

"You are not mistaken," she said slowly, in French; "your brother was known to me. I had met him in England. It will be a relief to all his friends to know that he passed away peacefully!" She looked him in the eyes determinedly. "Monsieur Claridge is not my kinsman, but he is my fellow-countryman. If you mean well by monsieur, your knowledge and your riches should help him on his way. But your past is no guarantee of good faith, as you will acknowledge."

He looked her in the eyes with a far meaning. "*But I am giving guarantees of good faith now*," he said softly. "Will you—not?"

She understood. It was clear that he meant peace, for the moment at least.

"If I had influence I would advise him to reconcile you to Prince Kaïd," she said quietly, then turned to David with an appeal in her eyes.

David stood up. "I will do what I can," he said. "If thee means as well by Egypt as I mean by thee, all may be well for all!"

"Saadat! Saadat!" said Nahoum, with show of assumed feeling, and made salutation. Then to Hylda, making lower salutation still, he said: "Thou hast lifted from my neck the yoke. Thou hast saved me from the shadow and the dust. I am thy slave." His eyes were like a child's, wide and confiding.

He turned towards the door, and was about to open it, when there came a knocking, and he stepped back. Hylda drew down her veil. David opened the door cautiously and admitted Mizraim the Chief Eunuch. Mizraim's eyes searched the room, and found Nahoum.

"Pasha," he said to Nahoum, "may thy bones never return to dust, nor the light of thine eyes darken! There is danger."

Nahoum nodded, but did not speak.

"Shall I speak, then?" He paused and made low salutation to David, saying, "Excellency, I am thine ox to be slain."

"Speak, son of the flowering oak," said Nahoum, with a sneer in his voice. "What blessing dost thou bring?"

"The Effendina has sent for thee."

Nahoum's eyes flashed. "By thee, lion of Abdin?"

The lean, ghastly being smiled. "He has sent a company of soldiers and Achmet Pasha."

"Achmet! Is it so?" "They are here, Mizraim, watcher of the morning?"

"They are at thy palace—I am here, light of Egypt."

"How knewest thou I was here?"

Mizraim salaamed. "A watch was set upon thee this morning early. The watcher was of my slaves. He brought the word to me that thou wast here now. A watcher also was set upon thee, excellency," he turned to David. "He also was of my slaves. Word was delivered to his Highness that thou"—he turned to Nahoum again—"wast in thy palace, and Achmet Pasha went thither. He found thee not. Now the city is full of watchers, and Achmet goes from bazaar to bazaar, from house to house which thou wast wont to frequent —and thou art here!"

"What wouldst thou have me do, Mizraim?"

"Thou art here; is it the house of a friend or a foe?"

Nahoum did not answer. His eyes were fixed in thought upon the floor, but he was smiling. He seemed without fear.

"But if this be the house of a friend, is he safe here?" asked David.

"For this night, it may be," answered Mizraim, "till other watchers be set, who are no slaves of mine. To-night, here, of all places in Cairo, he is safe; for who could look to find him, where thou art who hast taken from him his place and office, excellency—on whom the stars shine forever! But in another day, if my lord Nahoum be not forgiven by the Effendina, a hundred watchers will pierce the darkest corner of the Bazaar, the smallest room in Cairo."

David turned to Nahoum. "Peace be to thee, friend. Abide here till to-morrow, when I will speak for thee to his Highness, and, I trust, bring thee pardon. It shall be so—but I shall prevail," he added, with slow decision; "I shall prevail with him. My reasons shall convince his Highness."

"I can help you with great reasons, Saadat," said Nahoum. "Thou shalt prevail. I can tell thee that which will convince Kaïd."

While they were speaking, Hylda had sat motionless, watching. At first it seemed to her that a trap had been set, and that David was to be the victim of Oriental duplicity; but revolt, as she did, from the miserable creature before them, she saw at last that he spoke the truth.

"Thee will remain under this roof to-night, pasha?" asked David.

"I will stay if thy goodness will have it so," answered Nahoum slowly. "It is not my way to hide, but when the storm comes it is well to shelter."

Salaaming low, Mizraim withdrew, his last glance being thrown towards Hylda, who met his look with a repugnance which made her face rigid. She rose and put on her gloves. Nahoum rose also, and stood watching her respectfully.

"Thee will go?" asked David with a movement towards her.

She inclined her head. "We have finished our business, and it is late," she answered.

David looked at Nahoum. "Thee will rest here, pasha, in peace. In a moment I will return." He took up his hat.

There was a sudden flash of Nahoum's eyes, as though he saw an outcome of the intention which pleased him, but Hylda saw the flash, and her senses were at once alarmed.

"There is no need to accompany me," she said. "My cousin waits for me."

David opened the door leading into the courtyard. It was dark, save for the light of a brazier of coals. A short distance away, near the outer gate, glowed a star of red light, and the fragrance of a strong cigar came over.

"Say, looking for me?" said a voice, and a figure moved towards David. "Yours to command, pasha, yours to command." Lacey from Chicago held out his hand.

"Thee is welcome, friend," said David.

"She's ready, I suppose. Wonderful person, that. Stands on her own feet every time. She don't seem as though she came of the same stock as me, does she?"

"I will bring her if thee will wait, friend."

"I'm waiting." Lacey drew back to the gateway again and leaned against the wall, his cigar blazing in the dusk.

A moment later David appeared in the garden again, with the slim, graceful figure of the girl who stood "upon her own feet." David drew her aside for a moment.

"Thee is going at once to England?" he asked.

"To-morrow to Alexandria. There is a steamer next day for Marseilles. In a fortnight I shall be in England."

"Thee must forget Egypt," he said.

"Remembrance is not a thing of the will," she answered.

"It is thy duty to forget. Thee is young, and it is spring with thee. Spring should be in thy heart. Thee has seen a shadow; but let it not fright thee."

"My only fear is that I may forget," she answered.

"Yet thee will forget."

With a motion towards Lacey he moved to the gate. Suddenly she turned to him and touched his arm. "You will be a great man here in Egypt," she said. "You will have enemies without number. The worst of your enemies always will be your guest to-night."

He did not, for a moment, understand. "Nahoum?" he asked. "I take his place. It would not be strange; but I will win him to me."

"You will never win him," she answered. "Oh, trust my instinct in this! Watch him. Beware of him."

David smiled slightly. "I shall have need to beware of many. I am sure thee does well to caution me. Farewell," he added.

"If it should be that I can ever help you—" she said, and paused.

"Thee has helped me," he replied. "The world is a desert. Caravans from all quarters of the sun meet at the cross-roads. One gives the other food or drink or medicine, and they all move on again. And all grows dim with time. And the camel-drivers are forgotten; but the cross-roads remain, and the food and the drink and the medicine and the cattle helped each caravan upon the way. Is it not enough?"

She placed her hand in his. It lay there for a moment. "God be with thee, friend," he said.

The next instant Thomas Tilman Lacey's drawling voice broke the silence.

"There's something catching about these nights in Egypt. I suppose it's the air. No wind—just the stars, and the ultramarine, and the nothing to do but lay me down and sleep. It doesn't give you the jim-jumps like Mexico. It makes you forget the world, doesn't it? You'd do things here that you wouldn't do anywhere else."

The gate was opened by the bowáb and the two passed through. David was standing by the brazier, his hand held unconsciously over the coals, his eyes turned towards them. The reddish flame from the fire lit up his face under the broad-brimmed hat. His head slightly bowed, was thrust forward to the dusk. Hylda looked at him steadily for a moment. Their eyes met, though hers were in the shade. Again Lacey spoke.

"Don't be anxious. I'll see her safe back. Good-bye. Give my love to the girls."

David stood looking at the closed gate with eyes full of thought and wonder and trouble. He was not thinking of the girl. There was no sentimental reverie in his look. Already his mind was engaged in scrutiny of the circumstances in which he was set. He realized fully his situation. The idealism which had been born with him had met its reward in a labor herculean at the least, and the infinite drudgery of the practical issues came in a terrible pressure of conviction to his mind. The mind did not shrink from any thought of the dangers in which he would be placed, from any vision of the struggle he must have with intrigue and treachery and vileness. In a dim, half-realized way he felt that honesty and truth would be invincible weapons with a people who did not know them. They would be embarrassed, if not baffled, by a formula of life and conduct which they could not understand.

It was not these matters that vexed him now, but the underlying forces of life set in motion by the blow which killed a fellow-man. This fact had driven him to an act of redemption unparalleled in its intensity and scope; but he could not tell—and this was the thought that shook his being—how far this act itself, inspiring him to a dangerous and immense work in life, would sap the best that was in him, since it must remain a secret crime, for which he could not openly atone. He asked himself as he stood by the brazier, the bowáb apathetically rolling cigarettes at his feet, whether, in the flow of circumstance, the fact that he could not make open restitution, or take punishment for his unlawful act, would undermine the structure of his character. He was on the threshold of his career; action had not yet begun; he was standing like a swimmer on a high shore, looking into depths beneath, which have never been plumbed by mortal man, wondering what currents, what rocks, lay beneath the surface of the blue. Would his strength, his knowledge, his skill, be equal to the enterprise? Would he emerge safe and successful, or be carried away by some strong undercurrent, be battered on unseen rocks?

He turned with a calm face to the door behind which sat the displaced favorite of the Prince, his mind at rest, the trouble gone out of his eyes.

"Uncle Benn! Uncle Benn!" he said to himself, with a warmth at his heart as he opened the door and stepped inside.

Nahoum sat sipping coffee. A cigarette was between his fingers. He touched his hand to his forehead and his breast as David closed the door and hung his hat upon a nail. David's servant, Mahommed Hassan, whom he had had since first he came to Egypt, was gliding from the room—a large, square-shouldered fellow of near six feet, dressed in a plain blue yelek, but on his head the green turban of one who had done a pilgrimage to Mecca. Nahoum waved a hand after Mahommed and said:

"Whence came thy servant, Saadat?"

"He was my guide to Cairo. I picked him from the street."

Nahoum smiled. There was no malice in the smile, only, as it might seem, a frank humor. "Ah, your excellency used independent judgment. Thou art a judge of men. But does it make any difference that the man is a thief and a murderer—a murderer?"

David's eyes darkened, as they were wont to do when he was moved or shocked.

"Shall one only deal, then, with those who have

neither stolen nor slain—is that the rule of the just in Egypt?"

Nahoum raised his eyes to the ceiling as though in amiable inquiry, and began to finger a string of beads as a nun might tell her paternosters. "If that were the rule," he answered, after a moment, "how should any man be served in Egypt? Hereabouts is a man's life held cheap, else I had not been thy guest to-night; and Kaïd's Palace itself would be empty, if every man in it must be honest. But it is the custom of the place for political errors to be punished by a hidden hand; we do not call it murder."

"What is murder, friend?"

"It is such a crime as that of Mahommed yonder, who killed—"

David interposed. "I do not wish to know his crime. That is no affair between thee and me."

Nahoum fingered his beads meditatively. "It was an affair of the housetops in his town of Manfaloot. I have only mentioned it because I know what view the English take of killing, and how set thou art to have thy household above reproach, as is meet in a Christian land. So, I took it, would be thy mind—which Heaven fill with light for Egypt's sake!—that thou wouldst have none about thee who were not above reproach, neither liars, nor thieves, nor murderers."

"But thee would serve with me, friend," rejoined David quietly. "Thee has men's lives against thy account."

"Else had mine been against their account."

"Was it not so with Mahommed? If so, according to the custom of the land, then Mahommed is as immune as thou art."

"Excellency, like thee I am a Christian, yet am I also Oriental, and what is crime with one race is none with another. At the Palace two days past thou saidst thou hadst never killed a man; and I know that thy religion condemns killing even in war. Yet in Egypt thou wilt kill, or thou shalt thyself be killed, and thy aims will come to naught. When, as thou wouldst say, thou hast sinned, hast taken a man's life, then thou wilt understand! Thou wilt keep this fellow Mahommed, then?"

"I understand; and I will keep him."

"Surely thy heart is large and thy mind great. It moveth above small things. Thou dost not seek riches here?"

"I have enough; my wants are few."

"There is no precedent for one in office to withhold his hand from profit and backsheesh."

"Shall we not try to make a precedent?"

"Truthfulness will be desolate—like a bird blown to sea, beating 'gainst its doom."

"Truth will find an island in the sea."

"If Egypt is that sea, Saadat, there is no island."

David came over close to Nahoum, and looked him in the eyes.

"Surely I can speak to thee, friend, as to one understanding. Thou art a Christian—of the ancient fold. Out of the East came the light. Thy Church has preserved the faith. It is still like a lamp in the mist and the cloud in the East. Thou saidst but now that thy heart was with my purpose. Shall the truth that I would practise here not find an island in this sea—and shall it not be the soul of Nahoum Pasha?"

"Have I not given my word? Nay, then, I swear it by the tomb of my brother, whom Death met in the highway, and because he loved the sun, and the talk of men, and the ways of women, rashly smote him out of the garden of life into the void. Even by his tomb I swear it."

"Hast thou, then, such malice against Death? These things cannot happen save by the will of God."

"And by the hand of man. But I have no cause for revenge. Foorgat died in his sleep like a child. Yet if it had been the hand of man, Prince Kaïd or any other, I would not have held my hand until I had a life for his."

"Thou art a Christian, yet thou wouldst meet one wrong by another?"

"I am an Oriental." Then, with a sudden change of manner, he added: "But thou hast a Christianity the like of which I have never seen. I will learn of thee, Saadat, and thou shalt learn of me also many things which I know. They will help thee to understand Egypt and the place where thou wilt be set—if so be my life is saved, and by thy hand."

Mahommed entered, and came to David.

"Where wilt thou sleep, Saadat?" he asked.

"The pasha will sleep yonder," David replied, pointing to another room. "I will sleep here." He laid a hand upon the couch where he sat.

Nahoum rose, and, salaaming, followed Mahommed to the other room.

In a few moments the house was still, and remained so for hours. Just before dawn the curtain of Nahoum's room was drawn aside, the Armenian entered stealthily, and moved a step towards the couch where David lay. Suddenly he was stopped by a sound. He glanced towards a corner near David's feet. There sat Mahommed watching, a neboot of dom-wood across his knees.

Their eyes remained fixed upon each other for a moment. Then Nahoum passed back into his bedroom as stealthily as he had come.

Mahommed looked closely at David. He lay with an arm thrown over his head, resting softly, a moisture on his forehead as on that of a sleeping child.

"Saadat! Saadat!" said Mahommed softly to the

sleeping figure, scarcely above his breath, and then, with his eyes upon the curtained room opposite, began to whisper words from the Koran:

"*In the name of Allah, the Compassionate, the Merciful—*"

XI

AGAINST THE HOUR OF MIDNIGHT

Achmet the Rope-maker was ill at ease. He had been set a task in which he had failed. The bright Cairene sun starkly glittering on the French chandeliers and Viennese mirrors, and beating on the brass trays and braziers by the window, irritated him. He watched the flies on the wall abstractedly; he listened to the early peripatetic salesmen crying their wares in the streets leading to the Palace; he stroked his cadaverous cheek with yellow fingers; he listened anxiously for a footstep. Presently he straightened himself up, and his fingers ran down the front of his coat to make sure that it was buttoned from top to bottom. He grew a little paler. He was less stoical and apathetic than most Egyptians. Also he was absurdly vain, and he knew that his vanity would receive rough usage.

Now the door swung open, and a portly figure entered quickly. For so large a man Prince Kaïd was light and subtle in his movements. His face was mobile, his eye keen and human.

Achmet salaamed low. "The gardens of the First Heaven be thine, and the uttermost joy, Effendina," he said elaborately.

"A thousand colors to the rainbow of thy happiness," answered Kaïd mechanically, and seated himself cross-legged on a divan, taking a narghileh from the black slave who had glided ghostlike behind him.

"What hour didst thou find him? Where hast thou placed him?" he added, after a moment.

Achmet salaamed once more. "I have burrowed without ceasing, but the holes are empty, Effendina," he returned, abjectly and nervously.

He had need to be concerned. The reply was full of amazement and anger. "Thou hast not found him? Thou hast not brought Nahoum to me!" Kaïd's eyes were growing reddish; no good sign for those around him, for any that crossed him or his purpose.

"A hundred eyes failed to search him out. Ten thousand piastres did not find him; the kourbash did not reveal him."

Kaïd's frown grew heavier. "Thou shalt bring Nahoum to me by midnight to-morrow!"

"But if he has escaped, Effendina?" Achmet asked desperately. He had a peasant's blood; fear of power was ingrained.

"What was thy business but to prevent escape? Son of a Nile crocodile, if he has escaped, thou too shalt escape from Egypt—into Fazougli. Fool, Nahoum is no coward! He would remain. He is in Egypt."

"If he be in Egypt, I will find him, Effendina. Have I ever failed? When thou hast pointed, have I not brought? Have there not been many, Effendina? Should I not bring Nahoum, who has held over our heads the rod?"

Kaïd looked at him meditatively, and gave no answer to the question. "He reached too far," he muttered. "Egypt has one master only."

The door opened softly and the black slave stole in. His lips moved, but scarce a sound travelled across the room. Kaïd understood, and made a gesture. An instant afterwards the vast figure of Higli Pasha bulked into the room. Again there were elaborate salutations and salaams, and Kaïd presently said:

"Foorgat?"

"Effendina," answered Higli, "it is not known how he died. He was in this Palace alive at night. In the morning he was found dead in bed at his own home."

"There was no wound?"

"None, Effendina."

"The thong?"

"There was no mark, Effendina."

"Poison?"

"There was no sign, Effendina."

"Diamond-dust?"

"Impossible, Effendina. There was not time. He was alive and well here at the Palace at eleven, and—"

Kaïd made an impatient gesture. "By the stone in the Kaabah, but it is not reasonable that Foorgat should die in his bed like a babe and sleep himself into heaven! Fate meant him for a violent end; but ere that came there was work to do for me. He had a gift for scenting treason—and he had treasure!" His eyes shut and opened again with a look not pleasant to see. "But since it was that he must die so soon, then the loan he promised must now be a gift from the dead, if he be dead, if he be not shamming! Foorgat was a dire jester."

"But now it is no jest, Effendina. He is in his grave."

"In his grave! *Bismillah!* In his grave, dost thou say?"

Higli's voice quavered. "Yesterday before sunset, Effendina. By Nahoum's orders."

"I ordered the burial for to-day. By the gates of Hell, but who shall disobey me!"

"He was already buried when the Effendina's orders came," Higli pleaded anxiously.

"Nahoum should have been taken yesterday," he rejoined, with malice in his eyes.

"If I had received the orders of the Effendina on the night when the Effendina dismissed Nahoum—" Achmet said softly, and broke off.

"A curse upon thine eyes that did not see thy duty!" Kaïd replied gloomily. Then he turned to Higli. "My seal has been put upon Foorgat's doors? His treasure-places have been found? The courts have been commanded as to his estate—the banks—?"

"It was too late, Effendina," replied Higli hopelessly.

Kaïd got to his feet slowly, rage possessing him. "Too late! Who makes it too late when I command?"

"When Foorgat was found dead, Nahoum at once seized the Palace and the treasures. Then he went to the courts and to the holy men and claimed succession. That was while it was yet early morning. Then he instructed the banks. The banks hold Foorgat's fortune against us, Effendina."

"Foorgat was a Mohammedan. Nahoum is a Christian. My will is law. Shall a Christian dog inherit from a true believer? The courts, the Wakfs shall obey me. And thou, son of a burnt father, shalt find Nahoum! Kaïd shall not be cheated. Foorgat pledged the loan. It is mine. Allah scorch thine eyes!" he added fiercely to Achmet, "but thou shalt find this Christian gentleman, Nahoum."

Suddenly, with a motion of disgust, he sat down, and taking the stem of the narghileh, puffed vigorously in silence. Presently in a red fury he cried: "Go—go—go, and bring me back by midnight Nahoum and Foorgat's treasures—to the last piastre. Let every soldier be a spy, if thine own spies fail."

As they turned to go, the door opened again, the black slave appeared, and ushered David into the room.

David salaamed, but not low, and stood still.

On the instant Kaïd changed. The rage left his face.

He leaned forward eagerly; the cruel and ugly look faded slowly from his eyes.

"May thy days of life be as a river with sands of gold, effendi," he said gently. He had a voice like music.

"May the sun shine in thy heart and fruits of wisdom flourish there, Effendina," answered David quietly. He saluted the others gravely, and his eyes rested upon Achmet in a way which Higli Pasha noted for subsequent gossip.

Kaïd pulled at his narghileh for a moment, mumbling good-humoredly to himself and watching the smoke reel away; then, with half-shut eyes, he said to David:

"Am I master in Egypt or no, effendi?"

"In ruling this people the Prince of Egypt stands alone," answered David. "There is no one between him and the people. There is no Parliament."

"It is in my hand, then, to give or to withhold, to make or to break?" Kaïd chuckled to have this tribute, as he thought, from a Christian, who did not blink at Oriental facts, and was honest.

David bowed his head to Kaïd's words.

"Then if it be my hand that lifts up or casts down, that rewards or that punishes, shall my arm not stretch into the darkest corner of Egypt to bring forth a traitor? Shall it not be so?"

"It belongs to thy power," answered David. "It is the ancient custom of princes here. Custom is law, while it is yet the custom."

Kaïd looked at him enigmatically for a moment, then smiled grimly—he saw the course of the lance which David had thrown. He bent his look fiercely on Achmet and Higli. "Ye have heard. Truth is on his lips. I have stretched out my arm. Ye are my arm, to reach for and gather in Nahoum and all that is his." He turned quickly to David again. "I have given this hawk,

Achmet, till to-morrow night to bring Nahoum to me," he explained.

"And if he fails—a penalty? He will lose his place?" asked David, with cold humor.

"More than his place," Kaïd rejoined, with a cruel smile.

"Then is his place mine, Effendina," rejoined David, with a look which could give Achmet no comfort.

"Thou wilt bring Nahoum—thou?" asked Kaïd, in amazement.

"I have brought him," answered David. "Is it not my duty to know the will of the Effendina and to do it, when it is just and right?"

"Where is he—where does he wait?" questioned Kaïd eagerly.

"Within the Palace—here," replied David. "He awaits his fate in thine own dwelling, Effendina."

Kaïd glowered upon Achmet. "In the years which Time, the Scytheman, will cut from thy life, think, as thou fastest at Ramadan or feastest at Beiram, how Kaïd filled thy plate when thou wast a beggar, and made thee from a dog of a fellah into a pasha. Go to thy dwelling, and come here no more," he added sharply. "I am sick of thy yellow, sinful face."

Achmet made no reply, but as he passed beyond the door with Higli, he said in a whisper: "Come—to Harrik and the army! He shall be deposed. The hour is at hand!" Higli answered him faintly, however. He had not the courage of the true conspirator, traitor though he was.

As they disappeared, Kaïd made a wide gesture of friendliness to David, and motioned to a seat, then to a narghileh. David seated himself, took the stem of a narghileh in his mouth for an instant, then laid it down again and waited.

"Nahoum—I do not understand," Kaïd said presently, his eyes gloating.

"He comes of his own will, Effendina."

"Wherefore?" Kaïd could not realize the truth. This truth was not Oriental on the face of it.

"Effendina, he comes to place his life in thy hands. He would speak with thee."

"How is it thou dost bring him?"

"He sought me to plead for him with your Highness, and because I knew his peril, I kept him with me and brought him hither but now."

"Nahoum went to thee!" Kaïd's eyes peered abstractedly into the distance between the almost shut lids. That Nahoum should seek David, who had displaced him from his high office, was scarcely Oriental, when his every cue was to have revenge on his rival. This was a natural sequence to his downfall. It was understandable. But here was David safe and sound. Was it, then, some deeper scheme of future vengeance? The Oriental instinctively pierced the mind of the Oriental. He could have realized fully the fierce, blinding passion for revenge which had almost overcome Nahoum's calculating mind in the dark night, with his foe in the next room, which had driven him suddenly from his bed to fall upon David, only to find Mahommed Hassan watching—also with the instinct of the Oriental.

Some future scheme of revenge? Kaïd's eyes gleamed red. *There would be no future for Nahoum!*

"Why did Nahoum go to thee?" he asked again presently.

"That I might beg his life of thee, Highness, as I said," David replied.

"I have not ordered his death."

David looked meditatively at him. "It was agreed between us yesterday that I should speak plainly—is it not so?"

Kaïd nodded, and leaned back among the cushions.

"If what the Effendina intends is fulfilled, there is no other way but death for Nahoum," added David.

"What is my intention, effendi?"

"To confiscate the fortune left by Foorgat Bey. Is it not so?"

"I had a pledge from Foorgat—a loan."

"That is the merit of the case, Effendina. I am otherwise concerned. There is the law. Nahoum inherits. Shouldst thou send him to Fazougli, he would still inherit."

"He is a traitor."

"Highness, where is the proof?"

"I know. My friends have disappeared one by one—Nahoum. Lands have been alienated from me—Nahoum. My income has declined—Nahoum. I have given orders and they have not been fulfilled—Nahoum. Always, always some rumor of assassination, or of conspiracy, or the influence and secret agents of the Sultan—all Nahoum. He is a traitor. He has grown rich while I borrow from Europe to pay my army and to meet the demands of the Sultan."

"What man can offer evidence in this save the Effendina who would profit by his death?"

"I speak of what I know. I satisfy myself. It is enough."

"Highness, there is a better way: to satisfy the people, for whom thee lives. None should stand between. Is not the Effendina a father to them?"

"The people! Would they not say Nahoum had got his due if he were blotted from their sight?"

"None has been so generous to the poor, so it is said by all. His hand has been upon the rich only. Now, Effendina, he has brought hither the full amount of all he has received and acquired in thy service. He would offer it in tribute."

Kaïd smiled sardonically. "It is a thin jest. When a traitor dies the state confiscates his goods!"

"Thee calls him traitor. Does thee believe he has ever conspired against thy life?"

Kaïd shrugged his shoulders.

"Let me answer for thee, Effendina. Again and again he has defeated conspiracy. He has blotted it out—by the sword and other means. He has been a faithful servant to his prince at least. If he has done after the manner of all others in power here, the fault is in the system, not in the man alone. He has been a friend to thee, Kaïd."

"I hope to find in thee a better."

"Why should he not live?"

"Thou hast taken his place."

"Is it, then, the custom to destroy those who have served thee, when they cease to serve?" David rose to his feet quickly. His face was shining with a strange excitement. It gave him a look of exaltation, his lips quivered with indignation. "Does thee kill because there is silence in the grave?"

Kaïd blew a cloud of smoke slowly. "Silence in the grave is a fact beyond dispute," he said cynically.

"Highness, thee changes servants not seldom," rejoined David meaningly. "It may be that my service will be short. When I go, will the long arm reach out for me in the burrows where I shall hide!"

Kaïd looked at him with ill-concealed admiration. "Thou art an Englishman, not an Egyptian; a guest, not a subject, and under no law save my friendship." Then he added scornfully: "When an Englishman in England leaves office, no matter how unfaithful, though he be a friend of any country save his own, they send him to the House of Lords—or so I was told in France when I was there. What does it matter to thee what chances to Nahoum? Thou hast his place with me. My secrets are thine. They shall be all thine—for years I have sought an honest man. Thou art safe whether to go or to stay."

"It may be so. I heed it not. My life is as that of a

gull—if the wind carry it out to sea, it is lost! As my uncle went I shall go one day. Thee will never do me ill, but do I not know that I shall have foes at every corner, behind every mooshrabieh screen, on every mastaba, in the pasha's courtyard, by every mosque? Do I not know in what peril I serve Egypt?"

"Yet thou wouldst keep alive Nahoum! He will dig thy grave deep, and wait long."

"He will work with me for Egypt, Effendina."

Kaïd's face darkened. "What is thy meaning?"

"I ask Nahoum's life that he may serve under me, to do those things thou and I planned yesterday—the land, taxation, the army, agriculture, the Soudan! Together we will make Egypt better and greater and richer—the poor richer, even though the rich be poorer."

"And Kaïd—poorer?"

"When Egypt is richer, the Prince is richer, too. Is not the Prince Egypt? Highness, yesterday—yesterday thee gave me my commission. If thee will not take Nahoum again into service to aid me, I must not remain. I cannot work alone."

"Thou must have this Christian Oriental to work with thee?" He looked at David closely, then smiled sardonically, but with friendliness to David in his eyes. "Nahoum has prayed to work with thee, to be a slave where he was master? He says to thee that he would lay his heart upon the altar of Egypt?" Mordant, questioning humor was in his voice.

David inclined his head.

"He would give up all that is his?"

"It is so, Effendina."

"All save Foorgat's heritage?"

"It belonged to their father. It is a due inheritance."

Kaïd laughed sarcastically. "It was got in Mehemet Ali's service."

"Nathless, it is a heritage, Effendina. He would give

that fortune back again to Egypt in work with me, as I shall give of what is mine, and of what I am, in the name of God, the all-merciful!"

The smile faded out of Kaïd's face, and wonder settled on it. What manner of man was this! His life, his fortune for Egypt, a country alien to him, which he had never seen till six months ago! What kind of being was behind the dark, fiery eyes and the pale, impassioned face? Was he some new prophet? If so, why should he not have cast a spell upon Nahoum? Had he not bewitched himself, Kaïd, one of the ablest princes since Alexander or Amenhotep? Had Nahoum, then, been mastered and won? Was ever such power? In how many ways had it not been shown! He had fought for his uncle's fortune, and had got it at last yesterday without a penny of backsheesh. Having got his will, he was now ready to give that same fortune to the good of Egypt—but not to beys and pashas and eunuchs (and that he should have escaped Mizraim was the marvel beyond all others!), or even to the Prince Pasha; but to that which would make "Egypt better and greater and richer—the poor richer, even if the rich be poorer!" Kaïd chuckled to himself at that. To make the rich poorer would suit him well, so long as he remained rich. And, if riches could be got, as this pale Frank proposed, by less extortion from the fellah and less kourbash, so much the happier for all.

He was capable of patriotism, and this Quaker dreamer had stirred it in him a little. Egypt, industrial in a real sense; Egypt, paying her own way without tyranny and loans; Egypt, without *corvée*, and with an army hired from a full public purse; Egypt, grown strong and able to resist the suzerainty and cruel tribute—that touched his native goodness of heart, so long in disguise; it appealed to the sense of leadership in him; to the love of the soil deep in his bones; to regard for the common people—for was not his mother a slave? Some distant nobleness trembled in him, while yet the arid humor of the situation flashed into his eyes, and, getting to his feet, he said to David: "Where is Nahoum?"

David told him, and he clapped his hands. The black slave entered, received an order, and disappeared. Neither spoke, but Kaïd's face was full of cheerfulness.

Presently Nahoum entered and salaamed low, then put his hand upon his turban. There was submission, but no cringing or servility in his manner. His blue eyes looked fearlessly before him. His face was not paler than its wont. He waited for Kaïd to speak.

"Peace be to thee," Kaïd murmured mechanically.

"And to thee, peace, O Prince," answered Nahoum. "May the feet of Time linger by thee, and Death pass thy house forgetful!"

There was silence for a moment, and then Kaïd spoke again. "What are thy properties and treasure?" he asked sternly.

Nahoum drew forth a paper from his sleeve and handed it to Kaïd without a word. Kaïd glanced at it hurriedly, then said: "This is but nothing. What hast thou hidden from me?"

"It is all I have got in thy service, Highness," he answered boldly. "All else I have given to the poor; also to spies—and to the army."

"To spies—and to the army?" asked Kaïd slowly, incredulously.

"Wilt thou come with me to the window, Effendina?"

Kaïd, wondering, went to the great windows which looked on to the Palace square. There, drawn up, were a thousand mounted men as black as ebony, wearing shining white metal helmets and fine chain-armor and swords and lances, like medieval crusaders. The horses, too, were black, and the mass made a barbaric display belonging more to another period in the world's history.

This regiment of Nubians Kaïd had recruited from the far south, and had maintained at his own expense. When they saw him at the window now, their swords clashed on their thighs and across their breasts, and they raised a great shout of greeting.

"Well?" asked Kaïd, with a ring to the voice.

"They are loyal, Effendina, every man. But the army otherwise is honeycombed with treason. Effendina, my money has been busy in the army paying and bribing officers, and my spies were costly. There has been sedition—conspiracy; but until I could get the full proofs I waited; I could but bribe and wait. Were it not for the money I had spent, there might have been another Prince of Egypt."

Kaïd's face darkened. He was startled, too. He had been taken unaware. "My brother Harrik—!"

"And I should have lost my place, lost all for which I cared. I had no love for money; it was but a means. I spent it for the state—for the Effendina, and to keep my place. I lost my place, however, in another way."

"Proofs! Proofs!" Kaïd's voice was hoarse with feeling.

"I have no proofs against Prince Harrik, no word upon paper. But there are proofs that the army is seditious, that at any moment it may revolt."

"Thou hast kept this secret?" questioned Kaïd darkly and suspiciously.

"The time had not come. Read, Effendina," he added, handing some papers over.

"But it is the whole army!" said Kaïd aghast, as he read. He was convinced.

"*There is only one guilty!*" returned Nahoum. Their eyes met. Oriental fatalism met inveterate Oriental distrust, and then instinctively Kaïd's eyes turned to David. In the eyes of the Inglesi was a different thing.

The test of the new relationship had come.

Ferocity was in his heart, a vitriolic note was in his voice as he said to David: "If this be true—the army rotten, the officers disloyal, treachery under every tunic—bismillah, speak!"

"Shall it not be one thing at a time, Effendina?" asked David. He made a gesture towards Nahoum.

Kaïd motioned to a door. "Wait yonder," he said darkly to Nahoum. As the door opened, and Nahoum disappeared leisurely and composedly, David caught a glimpse of a guard of armed Nubians in leopard-skins filed against the white wall of the other room.

"What is thy intention towards Nahoum, Effendina?" David asked presently.

Kaïd's voice was impatient. "Thou hast asked his life—take it; it is thine; but if I find him within these walls again until I give him leave, he shall go as Foorgat went."

"What was the manner of Foorgat's going?" asked David quietly.

"As a wind blows through a courtyard and the lamp goes out, so he went, in the night. Who can say? Wherefore speculate! He is gone. It is enough. Were it not for thee, Egypt should see Nahoum no more."

David sighed, and his eyes closed for an instant. "Effendina, Nahoum has proved his faith—is it not so?" He pointed to the documents in Kaïd's hands.

A grim smile passed over Kaïd's face. Distrust of humanity, incredulity, cold cynicism, were in it. "Wheels within wheels, proofs within proofs," he said. "Thou hast yet to learn the Eastern heart. When thou seest white in the East, call it black, for in an instant it will be black. Malaish, it is the East! Have I not trusted—did I not mean well by all? Did I not deal justly? Yet my justice was but darkness of purpose, the hidden terror to them all. So did I become what thou findest me and dost believe me—a tyrant, in whose name a thousand do evil things of which I neither hear nor know. Proof! When a woman lies in your arms it is not the moment to prove her fidelity. Nahoum has crawled back to my feet with these things, and by the beard of the Prophet they are true!" He looked at the papers with loathing. "But what his purpose was when he spied upon and bribed my army I know not. Yet, it shall be said, he has held Harrik back—Harrik, my brother. Son of Sheitan and slime of the Nile, have I not spared Harrik all these years!"

"Hast thou proof, Effendina?"

"I have proof enough; I shall have more soon. To save their lives, these, these will tell—I have their names here!" He tapped the papers. "There are ways to make them tell. Now, speak, effendi, and tell me what I shall do to Harrik."

"Wouldst thou proclaim to Egypt, to the Sultan, to the world that the army is disloyal? If these guilty men are seized, can the army be trusted? Will it not break away in fear? Yonder Nubians are not enough—a handful lost in the *mêlée*. Prove the guilt of him who perverted the army and sought to destroy thee. Punish him."

"How shall there be proof save through those whom he has perverted? There is no writing."

"There is proof," answered David calmly.

"Where shall I find it?" Kaïd laughed contemptuously.

"I have the proof," answered David gravely.

"Against Harrik?"

"Against Prince Harrik Pasha."

"Thou—what dost thou know?"

"A woman of the Prince heard him give instructions for thy disposal, Effendina, when the Citadel should turn its guns upon Cairo and the Palace. She was once of thy harem. Thou didst give her in marriage, and she came to the harem of Prince Harrik at last. A woman from without who sang to her—a singing girl, an *al'mah*—she trusted with the paper to warn thee, Effendina, in her name. Her heart had remembrance of thee. Her foster-brother Mahommed Hassan is my servant. Him she told, and Mahommed laid the matter before me this morning. Here is a sign by which thee will remember her, so she said. Zaida she was called here." He handed over an amulet which had one red gem in the centre.

Kaïd's face had set into fierce resolution, but as he took the amulet his eyes softened.

"Zaida. Inshallah! Zaida she was called. She has the truth almost of the English. She could not lie ever. My heart smote me concerning her, and I gave her in marriage." Then his face darkened again, and his teeth showed in malice. A demon was roused in him. He might long ago have banished the handsome and insinuating Harrik, but he had allowed him wealth and safety—and now . . . !

His intention was unmistakable.

"He shall die the death," he said. "Is it not so?" he added fiercely to David, and gazed at him fixedly. Would this man of peace plead for the traitor, the would-be fratricide?

"He is a traitor; he must die," answered David slowly.

Kaïd's eyes showed burning satisfaction. "If he were thy brother, thou wouldst kill him?"

"I would give a traitor to death for the country's sake. There is no other way."

"To-night he shall die."

"But with due trial, Effendina?"

"Trial—is not the proof sufficient?"

"But if he confess, and give evidence himself, and so offer himself to die?"

"Is Harrik a fool?" answered Kaïd, with scorn.

"If there be a trial and sentence is given, the truth

concerning the army must appear. Is that well? Egypt will shake to its foundations—to the joy of its enemies."

"Then he shall die secretly."

"The Prince Pasha of Egypt will be called a murderer."

Kaïd shrugged his shoulders.

"The Sultan—Europe—is it well?"

"I will tell the truth," Kaïd rejoined angrily.

"If the Effendina will trust me, Prince Harrik shall confess his crime and pay the penalty also."

"What is thy purpose?"

"I will go to his palace and speak with him."

"Seize him?"

"I have no power to seize him, Effendina."

"I will give it. My Nubians shall go also."

"Effendina, I will go alone. It is the only way. There is great danger to the throne. Who can tell what a night will bring forth?"

"If Harrik should escape—"

"If I were an Egyptian and permitted Harrik to escape, my life would pay for my failure. If I failed, thou wouldst not succeed. If I am to serve Egypt, there must be trust in me from thee, or it were better to pause now. If I go, as I shall go, alone, I put my life in danger—is it not so?"

Suddenly Kaïd sat down again among his cushions.

"Inshallah! In the name of God, be it so. Thou art not as other men. There is something in thee above my thinking. But I will not sleep till I see thee again."

"I shall see thee at midnight, Effendina. Give me the ring from thy finger."

Kaïd passed it over, and David put it in his pocket. Then he turned to go.

"Nahoum?" he asked.

"Take him hence. Let him serve thee if it be thy will. Yet I cannot understand it. The play is dark. Is he not an Oriental?"

"He is a Christian."

Kaïd laughed sourly, and clapped his hands for the slave.

In a moment David and Nahoum were gone.

"Nahoum, a Christian! Bismillah!" murmured Kaïd scornfully, then fell to pondering darkly over the evil things he had heard.

Meanwhile the Nubians in their glittering armor waited without in the blistering square.

XII

THE JEHAD AND THE LIONS

"*Allah hu Achbar! Allah hu Achbar! Ashhadu an la illaha illalla!*" The sweetly piercing, resonant voice of the Muezzin rang far and commandingly on the clear evening air, and from bazaar and crowded street the faithful silently hurried to the mosques, leaving their slippers at the door, while others knelt where the call found them, and touched their foreheads to the ground.

In his palace by the Nile, Harrik, the half-brother of the Prince Pasha, heard it, and breaking off from conversation with two urgent visitors, passed to an alcove near, dropping a curtain behind him. Kneeling reverently on the solitary furniture of the room—a prayer-rug from Medina—he lost himself as completely in his devotions as though his life were an even current of unforbidden acts and motives.

Cross-legged on the great divan of the room he had left, his less pious visitors, unable to turn their thoughts from the dark business on which they had come, smoked their cigarettes, talking to each other in tones so low as would not have been heard by a European, and with apparent listlessness.

Their manner would not have indicated that they were weighing matters of life and death, of treason and infamy, of massacre and national shame. Only the sombre, smouldering fire of their eyes was evidence of the lighted fuse of conspiracy burning towards the magazine. One look of surprise had been exchanged when Harrik Pasha left them suddenly—time was short for what they meant to do; but they were Muslims, and they resigned themselves.

"The Inglesi must be the first to go; shall a Christian dog rule over us?"

It was Achmet the Rope-maker who spoke, his yellow face wrinkling with malice, though his voice but murmured hoarsely.

"Nahoum will kill him." Higli Pasha laughed low—it was like the gurgle of water in the narghileh—a voice of good nature and persuasiveness from a heart that knew no virtue. "Bismillah! Who shall read the meaning of it? Why has he not already killed?"

"Nahoum would choose his own time—after he has saved his life by the white carrion. Kaïd will give him his life if the Inglesi asks. The Inglesi, he is mad. If he were not mad, he would see to it that Nahoum was now drying his bones in the sands."

"What each has failed to do for the other shall be done for them," answered Achmet, a hateful leer on his immobile features. "To-night many things shall be made right. To-morrow there will be places empty and places filled. Egypt shall begin again to-morrow."

"Kaïd?"

Achmet stopped smoking for a moment. "When the khamsin comes, when the camels stampede, and the children of the storm fall upon the caravan, can it be foretold in what way Fate shall do her work? So but the end be the same—malaish! We shall be content to-morrow."

Now he turned and looked at his companion as though his mind had chanced on a discovery. "To him who first brings word to a prince who inherits, that the reigning prince is dead, belong honor and place!" he said.

"Then shall it be between us twain," said Higli, and

laid his hot palm against the cold, snaky palm of the other. "And he to whom the honor falls shall help the other."

"*Aiwa*, but it shall be so," answered Achmet, and then they spoke in lower tones still, their eyes on the curtain behind which Harrik prayed.

Presently Harrik entered, impassive, yet alert, his slight, handsome figure in sharp contrast to the men lounging in the cushions before him, who salaamed as he came forward. The features were finely chiselled, the forehead white and high, the lips sensuous, the eyes fanatical, the look concentrated yet abstracted. He took a seat among the cushions, and—after a moment—said to Achmet in a voice abnormally deep and powerful, "Diaz—there is no doubt of Diaz?"

"He awaits the signal. The hawk flies not swifter than Diaz will act."

"The people—the bazaars—the markets?"

"As the air stirs a moment before the hurricane comes, so the whisper has stirred them. From one lip to another, from one street to another, from one quarter to another, the word has been passed—'Nahoum was a Christian, but Nahoum was an Egyptian whose heart was Muslim. The stranger is a Christian and an Inglesi. Reason has fled from the Prince Pasha, the Inglesi has bewitched him. But the hour of deliverance draweth nigh. Be ready! To-night!' So has the whisper gone."

Harrik's eyes burned. "God is great," he said. "The time has come. The Christians spoil us. From France, from England, from Austria—it is enough. Kaïd has handed us over to the Greek usurers, the Inglesi and the Frank are everywhere. And now this new-comer who would rule Kaïd, and lay his hand upon Egypt like Joseph of old, and bring back Nahoum, to the shame of every Muslim—behold, the spark is to the tinder, it shall burn."

"And the hour, Effendina?"

"At midnight. The guns to be trained on the Citadel, the Palace surrounded. Kaïd's Nubians?"

"A hundred will be there, Effendina, the rest a mile away at their barracks." Achmet rubbed his cold palms together in satisfaction.

"And Prince Kaïd, Effendina?" asked Higli cautiously.

The fanatical eyes turned away. "The question is foolish—have ye no brains?" he said impatiently.

A look of malignant triumph flashed from Achmet to Higli, and he said, scarce above a whisper: "May thy footsteps be as the wings of the eagle, Effendina. The heart of the pomegranate is not redder than our hearts are red for thee. Cut deep into our hearts, and thou shalt find the last beat is for thee—and for the *Jehad!*"

"The Jehad—ay, the Jehad! The time is at hand," answered Harrik, glowering at the two. "The sword shall not be sheathed till we have redeemed Egypt. Go your ways, effendis, and peace be on you and on all the righteous worshippers of God!"

As Higli and Achmet left the palace, the voice of a holy man—admitted everywhere and treated with reverence—chanting the Koran, came somnolently through the courtyard: "*Bismillah hirrahmah, nirraheem. El-hamdu lillahi sabbila!*"

Rocking his body backwards and forwards and dwelling sonorously on each vowel, the holy man seemed the incarnation of Muslim piety; but as the two conspirators passed him with scarce a glance, and made their way to a small gate leading into the great garden bordering on the Nile, his eyes watched them sharply. When they had passed through, he turned towards the windows of the harem, still chanting. For a long time he chanted. An occasional servant came and went, but his voice ceased not, and he kept his eyes fixed ever on the harem windows.

At last his watching had its reward. Something fluttered from a window to the ground. Still chanting, he rose and began walking round the great courtyard. Twice he went round, still chanting, but the third time he stooped to pick up a little strip of linen which had fallen from the window, and concealed it in his sleeve. Presently he seated himself again, and, still chanting, spread out the linen in his palm and read the characters upon it. For an instant there was a jerkiness to the voice, and then it droned on resonantly again. Now the eyes of the holy man were fixed on the great gates through which strangers entered, and he was seated in the way which any one must take who came to the palace doors.

It was almost dark when he saw the bowáb, after repeated knocking, sleepily and grudgingly open the gates to admit a visitor. There seemed to be a moment's hesitation on the bowáb's part, but he was presently assured by something the visitor showed him, and the latter made his way deliberately to the Palace doors. As the visitor neared the holy man, who chanted on monotonously, he was suddenly startled to hear between the long-drawn syllables the quick words in Arabic:

"Beware, Saadat! See, I am Mahommed Hassan, thy servant! At midnight they surround Kaïd's Palace—Achmet and Higli—and kill the Prince Pasha. Return, Saadat. Harrik will kill thee."

David made no sign, but with a swift word to the faithful Mahommed Hassan, passed on, and was presently admitted to the Palace. As the doors closed behind him, he could hear the voice of the holy man still chanting—"*Waladalleen—Ameen—Ameen! Waladalleen—Ameen!*"

The voice followed him, fainter and fainter, as he passed through the great bare corridors with the thick carpets on which the footsteps made no sound, until it came, soft and undefined, as it were from a great distance. Then suddenly there fell upon him a sense of the peril of his enterprise. He had been left alone in the vast dim hall while a slave, made obsequious by the sight of the ring of the Prince Pasha, sought his master. As he waited he was conscious that people were moving about behind the great screens of mooshrabieh which separated this room from others, and that eyes were following his every motion. He had gained easy ingress to this place; but egress was a matter of some speculation. The doors which had closed behind him might swing one way only! He had voluntarily put himself in the power of a man whose fatal secret he knew. He only felt a moment's apprehension, however. He had been moved to come from a whisper in his soul; and he had the sure conviction of the predestinarian that he was not to be the victim of "The Scytheman" before his appointed time. His mind resumed its composure, and he watchfully waited the return of the slave.

Suddenly he was conscious of some one behind him, though he had heard no one approach. He swung round and was met by the passive face of the black slave in personal attendance on Harrik. The slave did not speak, but motioned towards a screen at the end of the room, and moved towards it. David followed. As they reached it, a broad panel opened, and they passed through, between a line of black slaves. Then there was a sudden darkness, and a moment later David was ushered into a room blazing with light. Every inch of the walls was hung with red curtains. No door was visible. He was conscious of this as the panel clicked behind him, and the folds of the red velvet caught his shoulder in falling. Now he saw sitting on a divan on the opposite side of the room Prince Harrik.

David had never before seen him, and his imagination

had fashioned a different personality. Here was a combination of intellect, refinement, and savagery. The red, sullen lips stamped the delicate, fanatical face with cruelty and barbaric indulgence, while yet there was an intensity in the eyes that showed the man was possessed of an idea which mastered him—a root-thought. David was at once conscious of a complex personality, of a man in whom two natures fought. He understood it. By instinct the man was a Mahdi, by heredity he was a voluptuary, that strange commingling of the religious and the evil found in so many criminals. In some far corner of his nature David felt something akin. The rebellion in his own blood against the fine instinct of his Quaker faith and upbringing made him grasp the personality before him. Had he himself been born in these surroundings, under these influences—! The thought flashed through his mind like lightning, even as he salaamed before Harrik, who salaamed and said, "Peace be unto thee!" and motioned him to a seat on a divan near and facing him.

"What is thy business with me, effendi?" asked Harrik.

"I come on the business of the Prince Pasha," answered David.

Harrik touched his fez mechanically, then his breast and lips, and a cruel smile lurked at the corners of his mouth as he rejoined,—

"The feet of them who wear the ring of his Prince wait at no man's door. The carpet is spread for them. They go and they come as the feet of the doe in the desert. Who shall say, They shall not come; who shall say, They shall not return!"

Though the words were spoken with an air of ingenuous welcome, David felt the malignity in the last phrase, and knew that now was come the most fateful moment of his life. In his inner being he heard the dreadful challenge of fate. If he failed in his purpose with his man, he would never begin his work in Egypt. Of his life he did not think—his life was his purpose, and the one was nothing without the other. No other man would have undertaken so Quixotic an enterprise, none would have exposed himself so recklessly to the dreadful accidents of circumstance. There had been other ways to overcome this crisis, but he had rejected them for a course fantastic and fatal when looked at in the light of ordinary reason. A struggle between the East and the West was here to be fought out between two wills; between an intellectual libertine steeped in Oriental guilt and cruelty and self-indulgence, and a being selfless, human, and in an agony of remorse for a life lost by his hand.

Involuntarily David's eyes ran round the room before he replied. How many slaves and retainers waited behind those velvet curtains?

Harrik saw the glance and interpreted it correctly. With a look of dark triumph he clapped his hands. As if by magic fifty black slaves appeared, armed with daggers. They folded their arms and waited like statues.

David made no sign of discomposure, but said slowly: "Dost thou think I did not know my danger, eminence? Do I seem to thee such a fool? I came alone as one would come to the tent of a Bedouin chief whose son one had slain, and ask for food and safety. A thousand men were mine to command, but I came alone. Is thy guest imbecile? Let them go. I have that to say which is for Prince Harrik's ear alone."

An instant's hesitation, and Harrik motioned the slaves away. "What is the private word for my ear?" he asked presently, fingering the stem of the narghileh.

"To do right by Egypt, the land of thy fathers and thy land; to do right by the Prince Pasha, thy brother."

"What is Egypt to thee? Why shouldst thou bring

"'DOST THOU THINK I DID NOT KNOW MY DANGER, EMINENCE?'"

thine insolence here? Couldst thou not preach in thine own bazaars beyond the sea?"

David showed no resentment. His reply was composed and quiet. "I am come to save Egypt from the work of thy hands."

"Dog of an unbeliever, what hast thou to do with me, or the work of my hands?"

David held up Kaïd's ring which had lain in his hand. "I come from the master of Egypt—master of thee, and of thy life, and of all that is thine."

"What is Kaïd's message to me?" Harrik asked, with an effort at unconcern, for David's boldness had in it something chilling to his fierce passion and pride.

"The word of the Effendina is to do right by Egypt, to give thyself to justice and to peace."

"Have done with parables. To do right by Egypt—wherein, wherefore?" The eyes glinted at David like bits of fiery steel.

"I will interpret to thee, eminence."

"Interpret." Harrik muttered to himself in rage. His heart was dark, he thirsted for the life of this arrogant Inglesi. Did the fool not see his end? Midnight was at hand! He smiled grimly.

"This is the interpretation, O Prince! Prince Harrik has conspired against his brother the Prince Pasha, has treacherously seduced officers of the army, has planned to seize Cairo, to surround the Palace and take the life of the Prince of Egypt. For months, Prince, thee has done this: and the end of it is that thee shall do right ere it be too late. Thee is a traitor to thy country and thy lawful lord."

Harrik's face turned pale; the stem of the narghileh shook in his fingers. All had been discovered, then! But there was a thing of dark magic here. It was not a half-hour since he had given the word to strike at midnight, to surround the Palace, and to seize the Prince

Pasha. Achmet—Higli, had betrayed him, then! Who other? No one else knew save Zaida, and Zaida was in the harem. Perhaps even now his own palace was surrounded. If it was so, then, come what might, this masterful Inglesi should pay the price. He thought of the den of lions hard by, of the cage of tigers—the menagerie not a thousand feet away. He could hear the distant roaring now, and his eyes glittered. The Christian to the wild beasts! That at least before the end. A Muslim would win heaven by sending a Christian to hell.

Achmet—Higli! No others knew. The light of a fateful fanaticism was in his eyes. David read him as an open book, and saw the madness come upon him.

"Neither Higli, nor Achmet, nor any of thy fellow-conspirators has betrayed thee," David said. "God has other voices to whisper the truth than those who share thy crimes. I have ears, and the air is full of voices."

Harrik stared at him. Was this Inglesi, then, with the gray coat, buttoned to the chin, and the broad black hat which remained on his head unlike the custom of the English—was he one of those who saw visions and dreamed dreams, even as himself? Had he not heard last night a voice whisper through the dark: "*Harrik, Harrik, flee to the desert! The lions are loosed upon thee!*" Had he not risen with the voice still in his ears and fled to the harem, seeking Zaida, she who had never cringed before him, whose beauty he had conquered, but whose face turned from him when he would lay his lips on hers? And, as he fled, had he not heard, as it were, footsteps lightly following him—or were they going before him? Finding Zaida, had he not told her of the voice, and had she not said, "*In the desert all men are safe—safe from themselves and safe from others; from their own acts and from the acts of others*"? Were the lions, then, loosed upon him? Had he been betrayed?

Suddenly the thought flashed into his mind that his

challenger would not have thrust himself into danger, given himself to the mouth of the Pit, if violence were intended. There was that inside his robe, than which lightning would not be more quick to slay. Had he not been a hunter of repute? Had he not been in deadly peril with wild beasts, and was he not quicker than they? This man before him was like no other he had ever met. Did voices speak to him? Were there, then, among the Christians such holy men as among the Muslims, who saw things before they happened, and read the human mind? Were there sorcerers among them, as among the Arabs?

In any case his treason was known. What were to be the consequences? Diamond-dust in his coffee? To be dropped into the Nile like a dog? To be smothered in his sleep?—For who could be trusted among all his slaves and retainers when it was known he was disgraced, and that the Prince Pasha would be happier if Harrik were quiet forever?

Mechanically he drew out his watch and looked at it. It was nine o'clock. In three hours more would have fallen the *coup*. But from this man's words he knew that the stroke was now with the Prince Pasha. Yet, if this pale Inglesi, this Christian sorcerer, knew the truth in a vision only, and had not declared it to Kaïd, there might still be a chance of escape. The lions were near—it would be a joy to give a Christian to the lions to celebrate the capture of Cairo and the throne. He listened intently to the distant rumble of the lions. There was one cage dedicated to vengeance. Five human beings on whom his terrible anger fell in times past had been thrust into it alive. Two were slaves, one was an enemy, one an invader of his harem, and one was a woman, his wife, his favorite, the darling of his heart. When his chief eunuch accused her of a guilty love, he had given her paramour and herself to that awful death. A stroke of the vast paw, a smothered roar as the teeth gave into the neck of the beautiful Fatima, and then—no more. Fanaticism had caught a note of savage music that tuned it to its height.

"Why art thou here? For what hast thou come? Do the spirit voices give thee that counsel?" he snarled.

"I am come to ask Prince Harrik to repair the wrong he has done. When the Prince Pasha came to know of thy treason—"

Harrik started. "Kaïd believes thy tale of treason?" he burst out.

"Prince Kaïd knows the truth," answered David quietly. "He might have surrounded this Palace with his Nubians, and had thee shot against the Palace walls. That would have meant a scandal in Egypt and in Europe. I besought him otherwise. It may be the scandal must come, but in another way, and—"

"That I, Harrik, must die?" Harrik's voice seemed far away. In his own ears it sounded strange and unusual. All at once the world seemed to be a vast vacuum in which his brain strove for air, and all his senses were numbed and overpowered. Distempered and vague, his soul seemed spinning in an aching chaos. It was being overpowered by vast elements, and life and being were atrophied in a deadly smother. The awful forces behind visible being hung him in the middle space between consciousness and dissolution. He heard David's voice, at first dimly, then understandingly.

"There is no other way. Thou art a traitor. Thou wouldst have been a fratricide. Thou wouldst have put back the clock in Egypt by a hundred years, even to the days of the Mamelukes—a race of slaves and murderers. God ordained that thy guilt should be known in time. Prince, thou art guilty. It is now but a question how thou shalt pay the debt of treason."

In David's calm voice was the ring of destiny. It

was dispassionate, judicial; it had neither hatred nor pity. It fell on Harrik's ear as though from some far height. Destiny, the controller—who could escape it? Had he not heard the voices in the night—"*The lions are loosed upon thee*"? He did not answer David now, but murmured to himself like one in a dream.

David saw his mood, and pursued the startled mind into the pit of confusion. "If it become known to Europe that the army is disloyal, that its officers are traitors like thee, what shall we find? England, France, Turkey will land an army of occupation. Who shall gainsay Turkey if she chooses to bring an army here and recover control, remove thy family from Egypt, and seize upon its lands and goods? Dost thou not see that the hand of God has been against thee? He has spoken, and thy evil is discovered."

He paused. Still Harrik did not reply, but looked at him with dilated, fascinated eyes. Death had hypnotized him, and against death and destiny who could struggle? Had not a past Prince Pasha of Egypt safeguarded himself from assassination all his life, and, in the end, had he not been smothered in his sleep by slaves?

"There are two ways only," David continued—"to be tried and die publicly for thy crimes, to the shame of Egypt, its present peril, and lasting injury; or to send a message to those who conspired with thee, commanding them to return to their allegiance, and another to the Prince Pasha, acknowledging thy fault, and exonerating all others. Else, how many of thy dupes shall die! Thy choice is not life or death, but how thou shalt die, and what thou shalt do for Egypt as thou diest. Thou didst love Egypt, eminence?"

David's voice dropped low, and his last words had a suggestion which went like an arrow to the source of all Harrik's crimes, and that also which redeemed him in a little. It got into his inner being. He roused himself and spoke, but at first his speech was broken and smothered.

"Day by day I saw Egypt given over to the Christians," he said. "The Greek, the Italian, the Frenchman, the Englishman, everywhere they reached out their hands and took from us our own. They defiled our mosques; they corrupted our life; they ravaged our trade, they stole our customers, they crowded us from the streets where once the faithful lived alone. Such as thou had the ear of the Prince, and such as Nahoum, also an infidel, who favored the infidels of Europe. And now thou hast come, the most dangerous of them all! Day by day the Muslim has loosed his hold on Cairo, and Alexandria, and the cities of Egypt. Street upon street knows him no more. My heart burned within me. I conspired for Egypt's sake. I would have made her Muslim once again. I would have fought the Turk and the Frank, as did Mehemet Ali; and if the infidels came, I would have turned them back; or if they would not go, I would have destroyed them here. Such as thou should have been stayed at the door. In my own house I would have been master. We seek not to take up our abode in other nations and in the cities of the infidel. Shall we give place to them on our own mastaba, in our own courtyard, hand to them the keys of our harems? I would have raised the Jehad if they vexed me with their envoys and their armies!" He paused, panting.

"It would not have availed," was David's quiet answer. "This land may not be as Tibet—a prison for its own people. If the door opens outward, then must it open inward also. Egypt is the bridge between the East and the West. Upon it the peoples of all nations pass and repass. Thy plan was folly, thy hope madness, thy means to achieve horrible. Thy dream is done.

The army will not revolt, the Prince will not be slain. Now only remains what thou shalt do for Egypt."

"And thou—thou wilt be left here to lay thy will upon Egypt. Kaïd's ear will be in thy hand—thou hast the sorcerer's eye. I know thy meaning. Thou wouldst have me absolve all, even Achmet, and Higli, and Diaz, and the rest, and at thy bidding go out into the desert" —he paused—"or into the grave."

"*Not into the desert*," rejoined David firmly. "Thou wouldst not rest. There, in the desert, thou wouldst be a Mahdi. Since thou must die, wilt thou not order it after thine own choice? It is to die for Egypt."

"Is this the will of Kaïd?" asked Harrik, his voice thick with wonder, his brain still dulled by the blow of Fate.

"It was not the Effendina's will, but it hath his assent. Wilt thou write the word to the army and also to the Prince?"

He had conquered. There was a moment's hesitation, then Harrik picked up paper and ink that lay near and said: "I will write to Kaïd. I will have naught to do with the army."

"It shall be the whole, not the part," answered David determinedly. "The truth is known. It can serve no end to withhold the writing to the army. Remember what I have said to thee. The disloyalty of the army must not be known. Canst thou not act after the will of Allah, the all-powerful, the all-just, the all-merciful?"

There was an instant's pause, and then suddenly Harrik placed the paper in his palm and wrote swiftly and at some length to Kaïd. Laying it down, he took another and wrote but a few words—to Achmet and Diaz. This message said in brief, "Do not strike. It is the will of Allah. The army shall keep faithful until the day of the Mahdi be come. I spoke before the time. I go to the bosom of my Lord Mahomet."

He threw the papers on the floor before David, who picked them up, read them, and put them into his pocket.

"It is well," he said. "Egypt shall have peace. And thou, eminence?"

"Who shall escape Fate? What I have written I have written."

David rose and salaamed. Harrik rose also.

"Thou wouldst go, having accomplished thy will?" Harrik asked, a thought flashing to his mind again, in keeping with his earlier purpose. Why should this man be left to trouble Egypt?

David touched his breast. "I must bear thy words to the Palace and the Citadel."

"Are there not slaves for messengers?" Involuntarily Harrik turned his eyes to the velvet curtains. No fear possessed David, but he felt the keenness of the struggle, and prepared for the last critical moment of fanaticism.

"It were a foolish thing to attempt my death," he said calmly. "I have been thy friend to urge thee to do that which saves thee from public shame, and Egypt from peril. I came alone, because I had no fear that thou wouldst go to thy death shaming hospitality."

"Thou wast sure I would give myself to death?"

"Even as that I breathe. Thou wert mistaken; a madness possessed thee; but thou, I knew, wouldst choose the way of honor. I too have had dreams—and of Egypt. If it were for her good, I would die for her."

"Thou art mad. But the mad are in the hands of God, and—"

Suddenly Harrik stopped. There came to his ears two distant sounds—the faint click of horses' hoofs and that dull rumble they had heard as they talked, a sound he loved, the roar of his lions.

He clapped his hands twice, the curtains parted opposite, and a slave slid silently forward.

"Quick! The horses! What are they? Bring me word," he said.

The slave vanished. For a moment there was silence. The eyes of the two men met. In the minds of both was the same thing.

"Kaïd! The Nubians!" Harrik said, at last. David made no response.

The slave returned, and his voice murmured softly, as though the matter were of no concern, "The Nubians—from the Palace!" In an instant he was gone again.

"Kaïd had not faith in thee!" Harrik said grimly. "But see, infidel though thou art, thou trustest me, and thou shalt go thy way. Take them with thee, yonder jackals of the desert. I will not go with them. I did not choose to live; others chose for me; but I will die after my own choice. Thou hast heard a voice, even as I. It is too late to flee to the desert. Fate tricks me. '*The lions are loosed on thee*'—so the voice said to me in the night. Hark! dost thou not hear them—the lions, Harrik's lions, got out of the uttermost desert?"

David could hear the distant roar, for the menagerie was even part of the Palace itself.

"Go in peace," continued Harrik soberly and with dignity, "and when Egypt is given to the infidel and Muslims are their slaves, remember that Harrik would have saved it for his Lord Mahomet, the prophet of God."

He clapped his hands, and fifty slaves slid from behind the velvet curtains.

"I have thy word by the tomb of thy mother that thou wilt take the Nubians hence, and leave me in peace?" he asked.

David raised a hand above his head. "As I have trusted thee, trust thou me, Harrik, son of Mahomet." Harrik made a gesture of dismissal, and David salaamed and turned to go. As the curtains parted for his exit, he faced Harrik again. "Peace be to thee," he said.

But, seated in his cushions, the haggard, fanatical face of Harrik was turned from him, the black, flaring eyes fixed on vacancy. The curtain dropped behind David, and through the dim rooms and corridors he passed, the slaves gliding beside him, before him, and behind him, until they reached the great doors. As they swung open and the cool night breeze blew in his face, a great suspiration of relief passed from him. What he had set out to do would be accomplished in all. Harrik would keep his word. It was the only way.

As he emerged from the doorway some one fell at his feet, caught his sleeve and kissed it. It was Mahommed Hassan. Behind Mahommed was a little group of officers and a hundred stalwart Nubians. David motioned them towards the great gates, and, without speaking, passed swiftly down the pathway and emerged upon the road without. A moment later he was riding towards the Citadel with Harrik's message to Achmet.

In the red-curtained room Harrik sat alone, listening until he heard the far clatter of hoofs, and knew that the Nubians were gone. Then the other distant sound which had captured his ear came to him again. In his fancy it grew louder and louder. With it came the voice that called him in the night, the voice of a woman—of the wife he had given to the lions for a crime against him which she did not commit, which had haunted him all the years. He had seen her thrown to the king of them all, killed in one swift instant, and dragged about the den by her warm white neck—this slave wife from Albania, his adored Fatima. And when, afterwards, he came to know the truth, and of her innocence, from the chief eunuch who with his last breath cleared her name, a terrible anger and despair had come upon him. Time and intrigue and conspiracy had distracted his mind, and the Jehad became the fixed aim and end of his life. Now this was gone. Destiny had tripped him up. Kaïd and the infidel Inglesi had won.

As the one great passion went out like smoke, the woman he loved, whom he had given to the lions, the memory of her, some haunting part of her possessed him, overcame him. In truth, he had heard a voice in the night, but not the voice of a spirit. It was the voice of Zaida, who, preying upon his superstitious mind—she knew the hallucination which possessed him concerning her he had cast to the lions—and having given the terrible secret to Kaïd, whom she had ever loved, would still save Harrik from the sure vengeance which must fall upon him. Her design had worked, but not as she intended. She had put a spell of superstition on him, and the end would be accomplished, but not by flight to the desert.

Harrik chose the other way. He had been a hunter. He was without fear. The voice of the woman he loved called him. It came to him through the distant roar of the lions as clear as when, with one cry of "*Harrik!*" she had fallen beneath the lion's paw. He knew now why he had kept the great beast until this hour, though tempted again and again to slay him.

Like one in a dream, he drew a dagger from the cushions where he sat, and rose to his feet. Leaving the room and passing dark groups of waiting slaves, he travelled empty chambers and long corridors, the voices of the lions growing nearer and nearer. He sped faster now, and presently came to two great doors, on which he knocked thrice. The doors opened, and two slaves held up lights for him to enter. Taking a torch from one of them, he bade them retire, and the doors clanged behind them.

Harrik held up the torch and came nearer. In the

centre of the room was a cage in which one great lion paced to and fro in fury. It roared at him savagely. It was his roar which had come to Harrik through the distance and the night. He it was who had carried Fatima, the beloved, about his cage by that neck in which Harrik had laid his face so often.

The hot flush of conflict and the long anger of the years were on him. Since he must die, since Destiny had befooled him, left him the victim of the avengers, he would end it here. Here, against the thing of savage hate which had drunk of the veins and crushed the bones of his fair wife, he would strike one blow deep and strong, and shed the blood of sacrifice before his own was shed.

He thrust the torch into the ground, and, with the dagger grasped tightly, carefully opened the cage and stepped inside. The door clicked behind him. The lion was silent now, and in a far corner prepared to spring, crouching low.

"Fatima!" Harrik cried, and sprang forward as the wild beast rose at him. He struck deep, drew forth the dagger—and was still.

XIII

ACHMET THE ROPE-MAKER STRIKES

War! War! The chains of the conscripts clanked in the river villages; the wailing of the women affrighted the pigeons in a thousand dove-cotes on the Nile; the dust of despair was heaped upon the heads of the old, who knew that their young would no more return, and that the fields of dourha would go ungathered, the water-channels go unattended, and the onion-fields be bare. *War! War! War!* The strong, the broad-shouldered—Aka, Mahmoud, Raschid, Selim, they with the bodies of Seti and the faces of Rameses, in their blue yeleks and unsandalled feet, would go into the desert as their forefathers did for the Shepherd Kings. But there would be no spoil for them—no slaves with swelling breasts and lips of honey, no straight-limbed servants of their pleasure to wait on them with caressing fingers; no rich spoils carried back from the fields of war to the mud hut, the earth oven, and the thatched roof; no rings of soft gold and necklaces of amber snatched from the fingers and bosoms of the captive and the dead. Those days were no more. No vision of loot or luxury allured these. They saw only the yellow sand, the ever-receding oasis, the brackish, undrinkable water, the withered and fruitless date-tree, handfuls of dourha for their food by day, and the keen sharp night to chill their half-dead bodies in a half-waking sleep. And then the savage struggle for life—with all the gain to the pashas and the beys, and those who ruled over them; while their own wounds grew foul, and, in the torturing noonday heat of the white waste, Death reached out and dragged them from the drooping lines to die. Fighting because they must fight — not patriot love, nor understanding, nor sacrifice in their hearts. *War! War! War! War!*

David had been too late to stop it. It had grown to a head with revolution and conspiracy. For months before he came conscripts had been gathered in the Nile country from Rosetta to Assouan, and here and there, far south, tribes had revolted. He had come to power too late to devise another course. One day, when this war was over, he would go alone, save for a faithful few, to deal with these tribes and peoples upon another plane than war; but here and now the only course was that which had been planned by Kaïd and those who counselled him. Troubled by a deep danger drawing near, Kaïd had drawn him into his tough service, half-blindly catching at his help, with a strange, almost superstitious belief that luck and good would come from the alliance; seeing in him a protection against wholesale robbery and debt—were not the English masters of finance, and was not this Englishman honest, and with a brain of fire and an eye that pierced things?

David had accepted the inevitable. The war had its value. It would draw off to the south—he would see that it was so—Achmet and Higli and Diaz and the rest, who were ever a danger. Not to himself: he did not think of that; but to Kaïd and to Egypt. They had been outmanœuvred, beaten, foiled, knew who had foiled them and what they had escaped; congratulated themselves, but had no gratitude to him, and still plotted his destruction. More than once his death had been planned, but the dark design had come to light—now from the workers of the bazaars, whose wires of intelligence pierced everywhere; now from some hungry fellah, whose yelek he had filled with cakes of dourha beside a bread-shop; now from Mahommed Hassan, who was for him a thousand eyes and feet and hands, who cooked his food, and gathered round him fellaheen or Copts or Soudanese or Nubians whom he himself had tested and found true, and ruled them with a hand of plenty and a rod of iron. Also, from Nahoum's spies he learned of plots and counterplots, chiefly on Achmet's part; and these he hid from Kaïd, while he trusted Nahoum—and not without reason, as yet.

The day of Nahoum's wrath and revenge was not yet come; it was his deep design to lay the foundation for his own dark actions strong on a rock of apparent confidence and devotion. A long torture and a great overwhelming was his design. He knew himself to be in the scheme of a master workman, and by and by he would blunt the chisel and bend the saw; but not yet. Meanwhile, he hated, admired, schemed, and got a sweet taste on his tongue from aiding David to foil Achmet—Higli and Diaz were of little account; only the injury they felt in seeing the sluices being closed on the stream of bribery and corruption kept them in the toils of Achmet's conspiracy. They had saved their heads, but they had not learned their lesson yet; and Achmet, blinded by rage, not at all. Achmet did not understand clemency. One by one his plots had failed, until the day came when David advised Kaïd to send him and his friends into the Soudan, with the punitive expedition under loyal generals. It was David's dream that in the field of war a better spirit might enter into Achmet and his friends; that patriotism might stir in them.

The day was approaching when the army must leave. Achmet threw dice once more.

Evening was drawing down. Over the plaintive pink and golden glow of sunset was slowly being drawn a pervasive silver veil of moonlight. A caravan of camels hunched alone in the middle distance, making for the western desert. Near by, village life manifested itself in heavily laden donkeys; in wolfish curs stealing away with refuse into the waste; in women, upright and modest, bearing jars of water on their heads; in evening fires, where the cover of the pot clattered over the boiling mass within; in the voice of the muezzin calling to prayer.

Returning from Alexandria to Cairo in the special train which Kaïd had sent for him, David watched the scene with grave and friendly interest. There was far to go before those mud huts of the thousand years would give place to rational modern homes; and as he saw a solitary horseman spread his sheepskin on the ground and kneel to say his evening prayer, as Mahomet had done in his flight between Mecca and Medina, the distance between the Egypt of his desire and the ancient Egypt that moved round him sharply impressed his mind, and the magnitude of his task settled heavily on his spirit.

"But it is the beginning — the beginning," he said aloud to himself, looking out upon the green expanses of dourha and lucerne, and eying lovingly the cotton-fields here and there,—the beginning of the industrial movement he foresaw—"and some one had to begin. The rest is as it must be—"

There was a touch of Oriental philosophy in his mind—was it not Galilee and the Nazarene, that Oriental source from which Mahomet also drew? But he added to the "as it must be" the words, "and as God wills!"

He was alone in the compartment with Lacey, whose natural garrulity had had a severe discipline in the months that had passed since he had asked to be allowed to black David's boots! He could now sit for an hour silent, talking to himself, carrying on unheard conversations. Seeing David's mood, he had not spoken twice on this journey, but had made notes in a little "Book of Experience,"—as once he had done in Mexico. At last, however, he raised his head, and looked eagerly out of the window as David did, and sniffed.

"The Nile again," he said, and smiled. The attraction of the Nile was upon him, as it grows on every one who lives in Egypt. The Nile and Egypt—Egypt and the Nile—its mystery, its greatness, its benevolence, its life-giving power, without which Egypt is as Sahara, it conquers the mind of every man at last.

"The Nile, yes," rejoined David, and smiled also. "We shall cross it presently."

Again they relapsed into silence, broken only by the *clang, clang* of the metal on the rails, and then presently another, more hollow sound—the engine was upon the bridge. Lacey got up and put his head out of the window. Suddenly there was a cry of fear and horror over his head, a warning voice shrieking:

"The bridge is open—we are lost. Effendi—master—Allah!" It was the voice of Mahommed Hassan, who had been perched on the roof of the car.

Like lightning, Lacey realized the danger and saw the only way of escape. He swung open the door, even as the engine touched the edge of the abyss and shrieked its complaint under the hand of the terror-stricken driver, caught David's shoulder, and cried: "Jump—jump into the river—quick!"

As the engine toppled, David jumped—there was no time to think, obedience was the only way. After him sprang, far down into the gray-blue water, Lacey and Mahommed. When they came again to the surface, the little train with its handful of human freight had disappeared.

Two people had seen the train plunge to destruction—the solitary horseman whom David had watched kneel upon his sheepskin, and who now from a far hill had seen the disaster, but had not seen the three jump for their lives, and a fisherman on the bank, who ran shouting towards a village standing back from the river.

As the fisherman sped shrieking and beckoning to the villagers, David, Lacey, and Mahommed, fought for their lives in the swift current, swimming at an angle upstream towards the shore; for, as Mahommed warned them, there were rocks below. Lacey was a good swimmer, but he was heavy, and David was a better, but Mahommed had proved his merit in the past on many an occasion when the laws of the river were reaching out strong hands for him. Now, as Mahommed swam, he kept moaning to himself, cursing his father and his father's son, as though he himself were to blame for the crime which had been committed. Here was a plot, and he had discovered more plots than one against his master. The bridge-opener—when he found him he would take him into the desert and flay him alive; and find him he would. His watchful eyes were on the hut by the bridge where this man should be. No one was visible. He cursed the man and all his ancestry and all his posterity, sleeping and waking, until the day when he, Mahommed, would pinch his flesh with red-hot irons. But now he had other and nearer things to occupy him, for in the fierce struggle towards the shore Lacey found himself failing, and falling down the stream. Presently both Mahommed and David were beside him, Lacey angrily protesting to David that he must save himself.

"Say, think of Egypt and all the rest. You've got to save yourself—let me splash along!" he spluttered, breathing hard, his shoulders low in the water, his mouth almost submerged.

But David and Mahommed fought along beside him, each determined that it must be all or none; and presently the terror-stricken fisherman who had roused the village, still shrieking deliriously, came upon them in a flat-bottomed boat manned by four stalwart fellaheen, and the tragedy of the bridge was over— But not the tragedy of Achmet the Rope-maker.

XIV

BEYOND THE PALE

MAHOMMED HASSAN had vowed a vow in the river, and he kept it in so far as was seemly. His soul hungered for the face of the bridge-opener, and the hunger grew. He was scarce passed from the shivering Nile into a dry yelek, had hardly taken a juicy piece from the cooking-pot at the house of the village sheikh, before he began to cultivate friends who could help him, including the sheikh himself; for what money Mahommed lacked was supplied by Lacey, who had a reasoned confidence in him, and by the fiercely indignant Kaïd himself, to whom Lacey and Mahommed went secretly, hiding their purpose from David. So, there were a score of villages where every sheikh, eager for gold, listened for the whisper of the doorways, and every slave and villager listened at the sheikh's door. But neither to sheikh nor to villager was it given to find the man.

But one evening there came a-knocking at the door of the house which Mahommed still kept in the lowest Muslim quarter of the town, a woman who hid her face and was of more graceful figure than was familiar in those dark purlieus. The door was at once opened, and Mahommed, with a cry, drew her inside.

"Zaida—the peace of God be upon thee," he said, and gazed lovingly yet sadly upon her, for she had greatly changed.

"And upon thee peace, Mahommed," she answered, and sat upon the floor, her head upon her breast.

"Thou hast trouble—eat," he said, and put some cakes of dourha and a meated cucumber beside her.

She touched the food with her fingers, but did not eat.

"Is thy grief, then, for thy prince who gave himself to the lions?" he asked.

"Inshallah! Harrik is in the bosom of Allah. He is with Fatima in the fields of heaven—was I as Fatima to him? Nay, the dead have done with hurting."

"Since that night thou hast been lost, even since Harrik went. I searched for thee, but thou wert hid. Surely, thou knewest mine eyes were aching and my heart was cast down—did not thou and I feed at the same breast?"

"I was dead, and am come forth from the grave; but I shall go again into the dark where all shall forget, even I myself; but there is that which I would do, which thou must do for me, even as I shall do good to thee, that which is the desire of my heart."

"Speak, light of the morning and blessing of thy mother's soul," he said, and crowded into his mouth a roll of meated cucumber. "Against thy feddan shall be set my date-tree; it hath been so ever."

"Listen, then, and by the stone of the Kaabah, keep the faith which has been thine and mine since my mother, dying, gave me to thy mother, whose milk gave me health and, in my youth, beauty—and, in my youth, beauty!" Suddenly she buried her face in her veil, and her body shook with sobs which had no voice.

Presently she continued: "Listen, and by Abraham and Christ and all the Prophets, and by Mahomet the true revealer, give me thine aid. When Harrik gave his life to the lions, I fled to her whom I had loved in the house of Kaïd—Laka the Syrian, afterwards the wife of Achmet Pasha. By Harrik's death I was free—no more a slave. Once Laka had been the joy of Achmet's heart, but because she had no child she was despised and forgotten. Was it not meet I should fly to her whose sorrow would hide my loneliness? And so it was—I was hidden in the harem of Achmet. But miserable tongues—may God wither them!—told Achmet of my presence. And though I was free and not a bondswoman, he broke upon my sleep. . . ."

Mahommed's eyes blazed, his dark skin blackened like a coal, and he muttered maledictions between his teeth.

". . . In the morning there was a horror upon me for which there is no name. But I laughed also when I took a dagger and stole from the harem to find him in the quarters beyond the women's gate. I found him, but I held my hand, for one was with him who spake with a tone of anger and of death, and I listened. Then, indeed, I rejoiced for thee, for I have found thee a road to honor and fortune. The man was a bridge-opener—"

"Ah!—O light of a thousand eyes, fruit of the tree of Eden!" cried Mahommed, and fell on his knees at her feet, and would have kissed them but that, with a cry, she said, "Nay, nay, touch me not. But listen. . . . Ay, it was Achmet who sought to drown thy Pasha in the Nile. Thou shalt find the man in the little street called Singat in the Moosky, at the house of Haleel the date-seller."

Mahommed rocked backwards and forwards in his delight. "Oh, now art thou like a lamp of Paradise, even as a star which leadeth an army of stars, beloved," he said. He rubbed his hands together. "Thy witness and his shall send Achmet to a hell of scorpions, and I shall slay the bridge-opener with my own hand—hath not the Effendina secretly said so to me, knowing that my Pasha, the Inglesi, upon whom be peace forever and forever, would forgive him. Ah, thou blossom of the tree of trees—"

She rose hastily, and when he would have kissed her hand she drew back to the wall. "Touch me not—nay, then, Mahommed, touch me not—"

"Why should I not pay thee honor, thou princess among women? Hast thou not the brain of a man, and thy beauty, like thy heart, is it not—"

She put out both her hands and spoke sharply. "Enough, my brother," she said. "Thou hast thy way to great honor. Thou shalt yet have a thousand feddans of well-watered land and slaves to wait upon thee. Get thee to the house of Haleel. There shall the blow fall on the head of Achmet, the blow which was mine to strike, but that Allah stayed my hand that I might do thee and thy Pasha good, and to give the soul-slayer and the body-slayer into the hands of Kaïd, upon whom be everlasting peace!" Her voice dropped low. "Thou saidst but now that I had beauty. Is there yet any beauty in my face?" She lowered her yashmak and looked at him with burning eyes.

"Thou art altogether beautiful," he answered, "but there is a strangeness to thy beauty like none I have seen; as if upon the face of an angel there fell a mist—nay, I have not words to make it plain to thee."

With a great sigh, and yet with the tenseness gone from her eyes, she slowly drew the veil up again till only her eyes were visible. "It is well," she answered. "Now, I have heard that to-morrow night Prince Kaïd will sit in the small courtyard of the blue tiles by the harem to feast with his friends, ere the army goes into the desert at the next sunrise. Achmet is bidden to the feast."

"It is so, O beloved!"

"There will be dancers and singers to make the feast worthy?"

"At such a time it will be so."

"Then this thou shalt do. See to it that I shall be among the singers, and when all have danced and sung, that I shall sing, and be brought before Kaïd."

"Inshallah! It shall be so. Thou dost desire to see Kaïd—in truth, thou hast memory, beloved!"

She made a gesture of despair. "Go upon thy business. Dost thou not desire the blood of Achmet and the bridge-opener?"

Mahommed laughed, and joyfully beat his breast, with whispered exclamations, and made ready to go. "And thou?" he asked.

"Am I not welcome here?" she replied wearily.

"O my sister, thou art the master of my life and all that I have," he exclaimed, and a moment afterwards he was speeding towards Kaïd's Palace.

For the first time since the day of his banishment, Achmet the Rope-maker was invited to Kaïd's palace. Coming, he was received with careless consideraton by the Prince. Behind his long, harsh face and sullen eyes a devil was raging, because of all his plans that had gone awry, and because the man he had sought to kill still served the Effendina, putting a blight upon Egypt. To-morrow he, Achmet, must go into the desert with the army, and this hated Inglesi would remain behind to have his will with Kaïd. The one drop of comfort in his cup was the fact that the displeasure of the Effendina against himself was removed, and that he had, therefore, his foot once more inside the Palace. When he came back from the war he would win his way to power again. Meanwhile, he cursed the man who had eluded the death he had prepared for him. With his own eyes had he not seen, from a hilltop, the train plunge to destruction, and had he not once more got off his horse and knelt upon his sheepskin and given thanks to Allah—a devout Arab obeying the sunset call to prayer, as David had observed from the train?

One by one, two by two, group by group, the unveiled dancers came and went; the singers sang behind the screen provided for them, so that none might see their faces, after the custom. At last, however, Kaïd and his guests grew listless, and smoked and talked idly. Yet there was in the eyes of Kaïd a watchfulness unseen by any save a fellah who squatted in a corner eating sweetmeats, and a hidden singer waiting until she should be called before the Prince Pasha. The singer's glances continually flashed between Kaïd and Achmet. At last, with gleaming eyes, she saw six Nubian slaves steal silently behind Achmet. One, also, of great strength, came suddenly and stood before him. In his hands was a leathern thong.

Achmet saw, felt the presence of the slaves behind him, and shrank back numbed and appalled. A mist came before his eyes; the voice he heard summoning him to stand up seemed to come from infinite distances. The hand of doom had fallen like a thunderbolt. The leathern thong in the hands of the slave was the token of instant death. There was no chance of escape. The Nubians had him at their mercy. As his brain struggled to regain its understanding, he saw, as in a dream, David enter the courtyard and come towards Kaïd.

Suddenly David stopped in amazement, seeing Achmet. Inquiringly he looked at Kaïd, who spoke earnestly to him in a low tone. Whereupon David turned his head away, but after a moment fixed his eyes on Achmet.

Kaïd motioned all his startled guests to come nearer. Then in strong, unmerciful voice he laid Achmet's crime before them, and told the story of the bridge-opener, who had that day expiated his crime in the desert by the hands of Mahommed—but not with torture, as Mahommed had hoped might be.

"What shall be his punishment—so foul, so wolfish?" Kaïd asked of them all. A dozen voices answered, some one terrible thing, some another.

"Mercy!" moaned Achmet aghast. "Mercy, Saadat!" he cried to David.

David looked at him calmly. There was little mercy in his eyes as he answered: "Thy crimes sent to their death in the Nile those who never injured thee. Dost thou quarrel with justice? Compose thy soul, and I pray only the Effendina to give thee that seemly death thou didst deny thy victims." He bowed respectfully to Kaïd.

Kaïd frowned. "The ways of Egypt are the ways of Egypt, and not of the land once thine," he answered shortly. Then, under the spell of that influence which he had never yet been able to resist, he added to the slaves: "Take him aside. I will think upon it. . . . But he shall die at sunrise ere the army goes. Shall not justice be the gift of Kaïd for an example and a warning? Take him away a little. I will decide."

As Achmet and the slaves disappeared into a dark corner of the courtyard, Kaïd rose to his feet, and, upon the hint, his guests, murmuring praises of his justice and his mercy and his wisdom, slowly melted from the courtyard; but once outside they hastened to proclaim in the four quarters of Cairo how yet again the English Pasha had picked from the Tree of Life an apple of fortune.

The courtyard was now empty, save for the servants of the Prince, David and Mahommed, and two officers in whom David had advised Kaïd to put trust. Presently one of these officers said: "There is another singer, and the last. Is it the Effendina's pleasure?"

Kaïd made a gesture of assent, sat down, and took the stem of a narghileh between his lips. For a moment there was silence, and then, out upon the sweet, perfumed night, over which the stars hung brilliant and soft and near, a voice, at first quietly, then fully, and palpitating with feeling, poured forth an Eastern love-song:

"Take thou thy flight, O soul! Thou hast no more
The gladness of the morning! Ah, the perfumed roses
My love laid on my bosom as I slept!
How did he wake me with his lips upon mine eyes,

How did the singers carol—the singers of my soul
That nest among the thoughts of my beloved! . . .
All silent now, the choruses are gone,
The windows of my soul are closed; no more
Mine eyes look gladly out to see my lover come.
There is no more to do, no more to say:
Take flight, my soul, my love returns no more!"

At the first note Kaïd started, and his eyes fastened upon the screen behind which sat the singer. Then, as the voice, in sweet anguish, filled the courtyard, entrancing them all, rose higher and higher, fell and died away, he got to his feet, and called out hoarsely, "Come—come forth!"

Slowly a graceful veiled figure came from behind the great screen. He took a step forward.

"Zaida! Zaida!" he said gently, amazedly.

She salaamed low. "Forgive me, O my lord," she said in a whispering voice, drawing her veil about her head. "It was my soul's desire to look upon thy face once more."

"Whither didst thou go at Harrik's death? I sent to find thee, and give thee safety; but thou wert gone, none knew where."

"O my lord, what was I but a mote in thy sun, that thou shouldst seek me?"

Kaïd's eyes fell, and he murmured to himself a moment, then he said slowly: "Thou didst save Egypt, thou and my friend"—he gestured towards David—"and my life also, and all else that is worth. Therefore bounty, and safety, and all thy desires were thy due. Kaïd is no ingrate—no, by the hand of Moses that smote at Siniai!"

She made a pathetic motion of her hands. "By Harrik's death I am free, a slave no longer. O my lord, where I go bounty and famine are the same."

Kaïd took a step forward. "Let me see thy face," he

said, something strange in her tone moving him with awe.

She lowered her veil and looked him in the eyes. Her wan beauty smote him, conquered him, the exquisite pain in her face filled Kaïd's eyes with foreboding, and pierced his heart.

"O cursed day that saw thee leave these walls! I did it for thy good—thou wert so young; thy life was all before thee! But now — come, Zaida, here in Kaïd's Palace thou shalt have a home, and be at peace, for I see that thou hast suffered. Surely it shall be said that Kaïd honors thee." He reached out to take her hand.

She had listened like one in a dream, but, as he was about to touch her, she suddenly drew back, veiled her face, save for the eyes, and said in a voice of agony: "*Unclean, unclean! My lord, I am a leper!*"

An awed and awful silence fell upon them all. Kaïd drew back as though smitten by a blow.

Presently, upon the silence, her voice sharp with agony said,—"I am a leper, and I go to that desert place which my lord has set apart for lepers, where, dead to the world, I shall watch the dreadful years come and go. Behold, I would die, but that I have a sister there these many years, and her sick soul lives in loneliness. O my lord, forgive me. Here was I happy; here of old I did sing to thee, and I came to sing to thee once more a death-song. Also, I came to see thee do justice, ere I went from thy face forever."

Kaïd's head was lowered on his breast. He shuddered. "Thou art so beautiful—thy voice, all! Thou wouldst see justice—speak! Justice shall be made plain before thee."

Twice she essayed to speak, and could not; but from his sweetmeats and the shadows Mahommed crept forward, kissed the ground before Kaïd, and said, "Effendina, thou knowest me as the servant of thy high servant, Claridge Pasha."

"I know thee—proceed."

"Behold, she whom God has smitten man smote first. I am her foster-brother—from the same breast we drew the food of life. Thou wouldst do justice, O Effendina; but canst thou do double justice—ay, a thousandfold? Then"—his voice raised almost shrilly—"then do it upon Achmet Pasha. She — Zaida — told me where I should find the bridge-opener."

"Zaida once more!" Kaïd murmured.

"She had learned all in Achmet's harem — hearing speech between Achmet and the man whom thou didst deliver to my hands yesterday."

"Zaida—in Achmet's harem?" Kaïd turned upon her.

Swiftly she told her dreadful tale, how, after Achmet had murdered all of her except her body, she rose up to kill herself; but fainting, fell upon a burning brazier, and her hand thrust accidentally in the live coals felt no pain. "And behold, O my lord, I knew I was a leper; and I remembered my sister and lived on." So she ended, in a voice numbed and tuneless.

Kaïd trembled with rage, and he cried in a loud voice, "Bring Achmet forth."

As a slave sped upon the errand, David laid a hand on Kaïd's arm, and whispered to him earnestly. Kaïd's savage frown cleared away, and his rage calmed down; but an inflexible look came into his face, a look which petrified the ruined Achmet as he salaamed before him.

"Know thy punishment, son of a dog with a dog's heart, and prepare for a daily death," said Kaïd. "This woman thou didst so foully wrong, even when thou didst wrong her, she was a leper."

A low cry broke from Achmet, for now when death came he must go unclean to the after-world, forbidden Allah's presence. Broken and abject, he listened.

"She knew not, till thou wert gone," continued Kaïd. "She is innocent before the law. But thou—beast of the slime—hear thy sentence. There is in the far desert a place where lepers live. There, once a year, one caravan comes, and, at the outskirts of the place unclean, leaves food and needful things for another year, and returns again to Egypt after many days. From that place there is no escape—the desert is as the sea, and upon that sea there is no ghiassa to sail to a farther shore. It is the leper land. Thither thou shalt go to wait upon this woman thou hast savagely wronged, and upon her kind, till thou diest. It shall be so."

"Mercy! mercy!" Achmet cried, horror-stricken, and turned to David. "Thou art merciful. Speak for me, Saadat."

"When didst thou have mercy?" asked David. "Thy crimes are against humanity."

Kaïd made a motion, and, with dragging feet, Achmet passed from the haunts of familiar faces.

For a moment Kaïd stood and looked at Zaida, rigid and stricken in that awful isolation which is the leper's doom. Her eyes were closed, but her head was high.

"Wilt thou not die?" Kaïd asked her gently.

She shook her head slowly, and her hands folded on her breast. "My sister is there," she said at last.

There was an instant's stillness, then Kaïd added with a voice of grief: "Peace be upon thee, Zaida. Life is but a spark. If death comes not to-day, it will to-morrow, for thee—for me. Inshallah, peace be upon thee!"

She opened her eyes and looked at him. Seeing what was in his face, they lighted with a great light for a moment.

"And upon thee peace, O my lord, forever and forever!" she said softly, and, turning, left the courtyard, followed at a distance by Mahommed Hassan.

Kaïd remained motionless, looking after her.

David broke in on his abstraction. "The army at sunrise—thou wilt speak to it, Effendina?"

Kaïd roused himself. "What shall I say?" he asked anxiously.

"Tell them they shall be clothed and fed, and to every man or his family three hundred piastres at the end."

"Who will do this?" asked Kaïd incredulously.

"Thou, Effendina—Egypt and thou and I."

"So be it," answered Kaïd.

As they left the courtyard, he said suddenly to an officer behind him:

"The caravan to the Place of Lepers—add to the stores fifty camel-loads this year, and each year hereafter. Have heed to it. Ere it starts, come to me. I would see all with mine own eyes."

BOOK III

XV

SOOLSBY'S HAND UPON THE CURTAIN

FAITH raised her eyes from the paper before her and poised her head meditatively.

"How long is it, friend, since—"

"Since *he* went to Egypt?"

"Nay, since thee—"

"Since I went to Mass?" he grumbled humorously.

She laughed whimsically. "Nay, then, since thee made the promise—"

"That I would drink no more till his return—ay, that was my bargain; till then and no longer! I am not to be held back then, unless I change my mind when I see him. Well, 'tis three years since—"

"Three years! Time hasn't flown. Is it not like an old memory, his living here in this house, Soolsby, and all that happened then?"

Soolsby looked at her over his glasses, resting his chin on the back of the chair he was caning, and his lips worked in and out with a suppressed smile.

"Time's got naught to do with you. He's afeard of you," he continued. "He lets you be."

"Friend, thee knows I am almost an old woman now." She made marks abstractedly upon the corner of a piece of paper. "Unless my hair turns gray presently I must bleach it, for 'twill seem improper it should remain so brown."

She smoothed it back with her hand. Try as she

would to keep it trim after the manner of her people, it still waved loosely on her forehead and over her ears. And the gray bonnet she wore but added piquancy to its luxuriance, gave a sweet gravity to the demure beauty of the face it sheltered.

"I am thirty now," she murmured with a sigh, and went on writing.

The old man's fingers moved quickly among the strips of cane, and, after a silence, without raising his head, he said: "Thirty, it means naught."

"To those without understanding," she rejoined dryly.

"'Tis tough understanding why there's no wedding-ring on yonder finger. There's been many a man that's wanted it, that's true—the Squire's son from Bridgley, the lord of Axwood Manor, the long soldier from Shipley Wood, and doctors and such folk a-plenty. There's where understanding fails."

Faith's face flushed, then it became pale, and her eyes, suffused, dropped upon the paper before her. At first it seemed as though she must resent his boldness; but she had made a friend of him these years past, and she knew he meant no rudeness. In the past they had talked of things deeper and more intimate still. Yet there was that in his words which touched a sensitive corner of her nature.

"Why should I be marrying?" she asked presently. "There was my sister's son all those years—I had to care for him."

"Ay, older than him by a thimbleful!" he rejoined.

"Nay, till he came to live in this hut alone, older by many a year. Since then he is older than me by fifty. I had not thought of marriage before he went away. Squire's son, soldier, or pillman, what were they to me! He needed me. They came, did they? Well, and if they came?"

"And since the Egyptian went?"

A sort of sob came into her throat. "He does not need me now, but he may—he will one day; and then I shall be ready. But now—"

Old Soolsby's face turned away. His house overlooked every house in the valley beneath; he could see nearly every garden; he could even recognize many in the far streets. Besides, there hung along two nails on the wall a telescope, relic of days when he sailed the main. The grounds of the Cloistered House and the fruit-decked garden wall of the Red Mansion were ever within his vision. Once, twice, thrice, he had seen what he had seen, and dark feelings, harsh emotions, had been roused in him.

"He will need us both — the Egyptian will need us both one day," he answered now; "you more than any, me because I can help him, too—ay, I can help him. But married or single you could help him; so why waste your days here?"

"Is it wasting my days to stay with my father? He is lonely; most lonely since our Davy went away; and troubled, too, for the dangers of that life yonder. His voice used to shake when he prayed, in those days when Davy was away in the desert, down at Darfûr and elsewhere among the rebel tribes. He frightened me then, he was so stern and still. Ah, but that day when we knew he was safe, I was eighteen, and no more!" she added, smiling. "But, think you, I could marry while my life is so tied to him and to our Egyptian?"

No one looking at her limpid, shining, blue eyes but would have set her down for twenty-three or twenty-four, for not a line showed on her smooth face; she was exquisite of limb and feature, and had the lissomeness of a girl of fifteen. There was in her eyes, however, an unquiet sadness; she had abstracted moments when her mind seemed fixed on some vexing problem. Such a mood suddenly came upon her now. The pen lay by the paper untouched, her hands folded in her lap, and a long silence fell upon them, broken only by the twanging of the strips of cane in Soolsby's hands. At last, however, even this sound ceased; and the two scarce moved as the sun drew towards the middle afternoon. At last they were roused by the sound of a horn, and, looking down, they saw a four-in-hand drawing smartly down the road to the village over the gorse-spread common, till it stopped at the Cloistered House. As Faith looked, her face slightly flushed. She bent forward till she saw one figure get down and, waving a hand to the party on the coach as it moved on, disappear into the gateway of the Cloistered House.

"What is the office they have given him?" asked Soolsby, disapproval in his tone, his eyes fixed on the disappearing figure.

"They have made Lord Eglington Under-Secretary for Foreign Affairs," she answered.

"And what means that to a common mind?"

"That what his Government does in Egypt will mean good or bad to our Egyptian," she returned.

"That he can do our man good or ill?" Soolsby asked sharply—"that he, yonder, can do that?"

She inclined her head.

"When I see him doing ill—well, when I see him doing that"—he snatched up a piece of wood from the floor—"then I will break him so!"

He snapped the stick across his knee, and threw the pieces on the ground. He was excited. He got to his feet and walked up and down the little room, his lips shut tight, his round eyes flaring.

Faith watched him in astonishment. In the past she had seen his face cloud over, his eyes grow sulky, at the mention of Lord Eglington's name; she knew that Soolsby hated him; but his aversion now was more definite and violent than he had before shown, save on that night long ago when David went first to Egypt, and she had heard hard words between them in this same hut. She supposed it one of those antipathies which often grow in inverse ratio to the social position of those concerned. She replied in a soothing voice:

"Then we shall hope that he will do our Davy only good."

"You would not wish me to break his lordship? *You* would not wish it?" He came over to her, and looked sharply at her. "You would not wish it?" he repeated meaningly.

She evaded his question. "Lord Eglington will be a great man one day perhaps," she answered. "He has made his way quickly. How high he has climbed in three years—how high!"

Soolsby's anger was not lessened. "Pooh! Pooh! He is an Earl. An Earl has all with him at the start—name, place, and all. But look at our Egyptian! Look at Egyptian David—what had he but his head and an honest mind? What is he? He is the great man of Egypt. Tell me, who helped Egyptian David? That second-best lordship yonder, he crept about coaxing this one and wheedling that. I know him—I know him. He wheedles and wheedles. No matter whether 'tis a babe or an old woman, he'll talk, and talk, and talk, till they believe in him, poor folks! No one's too small for his net. There's Martha Higham yonder. She's forty-five. If he sees her, as sure as eggs he'll make love to her, and fill her ears with words she'd never heard before, and 'd never hear at all if not from him. Ay, there's no man too sour and no woman too old that he'll not blandish, if he gets the chance."

As he spoke Faith shut her eyes, and her fingers clasped tightly together—beautiful, long, tapering fingers, like those in Romney's pictures. When he stopped, her eyes opened slowly, and she gazed before her down towards that garden by the Red Mansion where her lifetime had been spent.

"Thee says hard words, Soolsby," she rejoined gently. "But maybe thee is right." Then a flash of humor passed over her face. "Suppose we ask Martha Higham if the Earl has 'blandished' her. If the Earl has blandished Martha, he is the very captain of deceit. Why, he has himself but twenty-eight years. Will a man speak so to one older than himself, save in mockery? So, if thee is right in this, then—then if he speak well to deceive and to serve his turn, he will also speak ill; and he will do ill when it may serve his turn; and so he may do our Davy ill, as thee says, Soolsby."

She rose to her feet and made as if to go, but she kept her face from him. Presently, however, she turned and looked at him. "If he does ill to Davy—there will be those like thee, Soolsby, who will not spare him."

His fingers opened and shut maliciously, he nodded dour assent. After an instant, while he watched her, she added: "Thee has not heard my lord is to marry?"

"Marry—who is the blind lass?"

"Her name is Maryon, Miss Hylda Maryon; and she has a great fortune. But within a month it is to be. You remember the woman of the cross-roads, her that our Davy—"

"Her the Egyptian kissed, and put his watch in her belt—ay, Kate Heaver!"

"She is now maid to her Lord Eglington will wed. She is to spend to-night with us."

"Where is her lad that was, that the Egyptian rolled like dough in a trough?"

"Jasper Kimber? He is at Sheffield. He has been up and down, now sober for a year, now drunken for a month, now in now out of a place, until this past year. But for this whole year he has been sober, and he may keep his pledge. He is working in the trades-unions,

Among his fellow-workers he is called a politician — if loud speaking and boasting can make one. Yet if these doings give him stimulant instead of drink, who shall complain?"

Soolsby's head was down. He was looking out over the far hills, while the strips of cane were idle in his hands. "Ay, 'tis true—'tis true," he nodded. "Give a man an idee which keeps him cogitating, makes him think he's greater than he is, and sets his pulses beating, why, that's the cure to drink. Drink is friendship and good company and big thoughts while it lasts; and it's lonely without it, if you've been used to it. Ay, but Kimber's way is best. Get an idee in your noddle, to do a thing that's more to you than work or food or bed, and 'twill be more than drink, too."

He nodded to himself, then began weaving the strips of cane furiously. Presently he stopped again, and threw his head back with a chuckle. "Now, wouldn't it be a joke, a reg'lar first-class joke, if Kimber and me both had the same idee; if we was both workin' for the same thing—an' didn't know it? I reckon it might be so."

"What end is thee working for, friend? If the public prints speak true, Kimber is working to stand for Parliament against Lord Eglington."

Soolsby grunted and laughed in his throat. "Now, is that the game of Mister Kimber? Against my Lord Eglington! Hey, but that's a joke, my lord!"

"And what is thee working for, Soolsby?"

"What do I be working for? To get the Egyptian back to England—what else?"

"That is no joke."

"Ay, but 'tis a joke." The old man chuckled. "'Tis the best joke in the boilin'." He shook his head and moved his body backwards and forwards with glee. "Me and Kimber! Me and Kimber!" he roared, "and neither of us drunk for a year—not drunk for a whole year. Me and Kimber—and *him!*"

Faith put her hand on his shoulder. "Indeed, I see no joke, but only that which makes my heart thankful, Soolsby."

"Ay, you will be thankful, you will be thankful, by and by," he said, still chuckling, and stood up respectfully to show her out.

XVI

THE DEBT AND THE ACCOUNTING

HIS forehead frowning, but his eyes full of friendliness, Soolsby watched Faith go down the hillside and until she reached the main road. Here, instead of going to the Red Mansion, she hesitated a moment, and then passed along a wooded path leading to the Meeting-house and the graveyard. It was a perfect day of early summer, the gorse was in full bloom, and the may and the hawthorn were alive with color. The path she had taken led through a narrow lane, overhung with blossoms and greenery. By bearing away to the left into another path, and making a *détour*, she could reach the Meeting-house through a narrow lane leading past a now disused mill and a small, strong stream flowing from the hill above.

As she came down the hill, other eyes than Soolsby's watched her. From his laboratory—the laboratory in which his father had worked, in which he had lost his life—Eglington had seen the trim, graceful figure. He watched it till it moved into the wooded path. Then he left his garden, and, moving across a field, came into the path ahead of her. Walking swiftly, he reached the old mill, and waited.

She came slowly, now and again stooping to pick a flower and place it in her belt. Her bonnet was slung on her arm, her hair had broken a little loose and made a sort of hood round the face, so still, so composed, into which the light of steady, soft, apprehending eyes threw a gentle radiance. It was a face to haunt a man when the storm of life was round him. It had, too, a courage which might easily become a delicate stubbornness, a sense of duty which might become sternness, if roused by a sense of wrong to herself or others.

She reached the mill and stood and listened towards the stream and the waterfall. She came here often. The scene quieted her in moods of restlessness which came from a feeling that her mission was interrupted, that half her life's work had been suddenly taken from her. When David went, her life had seemed to shrivel; for with him she had developed as he had developed; and when her busy care of him was withdrawn, she had felt a sort of paralysis which, in a sense, had never left her. Then suitors had come—the soldier from Shipley Wood, the lord of Axwood Manor, and others, and, in a way, a new sense was born in her, though she was alive to the fact that the fifteen thousand pounds inherited from her Uncle Benn had served to warm the air about her into a wider circle. Yet it was neither to soldier, nor squire, nor civil engineer, nor surgeon that the new sense stirring in her was due. The spring was too far beneath to be found by them.

When, at last, she raised her head, Lord Eglington was in the path, looking at her with a half-smile. She did not start, but her face turned white, and a mist came before her eyes.

Quickly, however, as though fearful lest he should think he could trouble her composure, she laid a hand upon herself.

He came near to her and held out his hand. "It has been a long six months since we met here," he said.

She made no motion to take his hand. "I find days grow shorter as I grow older," she rejoined steadily, and smoothed her hair with her hand, making ready to put on her bonnet.

"Ah, do not put it on," he urged quickly, with a gesture. "It becomes you so—on your arm."

She had regained her self-possession. Pride, the best weapon of a woman, the best tonic, came to her resource. "Thee loves to please thee at any cost," she replied. She fastened the gray strings beneath her chin.

"Would it be costly to keep the bonnet on your arm?"

"It is my pleasure to have it on my head, and my pleasure has some value to myself."

"A moment ago," he rejoined laughing, "it was your pleasure to have it on your arm."

"Are all to be monotonous except Lord Eglington? Is he to have the only patent of change?"

"Do I change?" He smiled at her with a sense of inquisition, with an air that seemed to say, "I have lifted the veil of this woman's heart; I am the master of the situation."

She did not answer to the obvious meaning of his words, but said:

"Thee has done little else but change, so far as eye can see. Thee and thy family were once of Quaker faith, but thee is a High Churchman now. Yet they said a year ago thee was a sceptic or an infidel."

"There is force in what you say," he replied. "I have an inquiring mind; I am ever open to reason. Confucius said, 'It is only the supremely wise or the deeply ignorant who never alter.'"

"Thee has changed politics. Thee made a sensation, but that was not enough. Thee that was a rebel became a deserter."

He laughed. "Ah, I was open to conviction! I took my life in my hands, defied consequences." He laughed again.

"It brought office."

"I am Under-Secretary for Foreign Affairs," he murmured complacently.

"Change is a policy with thee, I think. It has paid thee well, so it would seem."

"Only a fair rate of interest for the capital invested and the risks I've taken," he answered with an amused look.

"I do not think that interest will increase. Thee has climbed quickly, but fast climbing is not always safe climbing."

His mood changed. His voice quickened, his face lowered. "You think I will fail? You wish me to fail?"

"In so far as thee acts uprightly, I wish thee well. But if, out of office, thee disregards justice and conscience and the rights of others, can thee be just and faithful in office? Subtilty will not always avail. The strong man takes the straight course. Subtilty is not intellect."

He flushed. She had gone to the weakest point in his defences. His vanity was being hurt. She had an advantage now.

"You are wrong," he protested. "You do not understand public life, here in a silly Quaker village."

"Does thee think that all that happens in 'public life' is of consequence? That is not sensible. Thee is in the midst of a thousand immaterial things, though they have importance for the moment. But the chief things that matter to all, does thee not know that a 'silly Quaker village' may realize them to the full—more fully because we see them apart from the thousand little things that do not matter? I remember a thing in political life that mattered. It was at Heddington after the massacre at Damascus. Does thee think that we did not know thee spoke without principle then, and only to draw notice?"

"You would make me into a demagogue," he said irritably.

"Thee is a demagogue," she answered candidly.

"Why did you never say all this to me long ago? Years have passed since then, and since then you and I have—have been friends. You have—"

He paused, for she made a protesting motion, and a fire sprang into her eyes. Her voice got colder.

"Thee made me believe—ah, how many times did we speak together? Six times it was, not more. Thee made me believe that what I thought or said helped thee to see things better. Thee said I saw things truly like a child, with the wisdom of a woman. Thee remembers that?"

"It was so," he put in hastily.

"Oh, not for a moment so, though I was blinded to think for an instant that it was. Thee subtly took the one way which could have made me listen to thee. Thee wanted help, thee said; and if a word of mine could help thee now and then, should I withhold it, so long as I thought thee honest?"

"Do you think I was not honest in wanting your friendship?"

"Nay, it was not friendship thee wanted, for friendship means a giving and a getting. Thee was bent on getting what was, indeed, of but little value save to the giver; but thee gave nothing; thee remembered nothing of what was given thee."

"It is not so, it is not so," he urged eagerly, nervously. "I gave, and I still give."

"In those old days, I did not understand," she went on, "what it was thee wanted. I know now. It was to know the heart and mind of a woman—of a woman older than thee! So that thee should have such sort of experience, though I was but a foolish choice of the experiment They say thee has a gift for chemistry like thy father; but if thee experiments no more wisely in the laboratory than with me, thee will not reach distinction."

"Your father hated my father and did not believe in him, I know not why, and you are now hating and disbelieving me."

"I do not know why my father held the late Earl in abhorrence; I know he has no faith in thee; and I did ill in listening to thee, in believing for one moment there was truth in thee. But no, no, I think I never believed it. I think that even when thee said most, at heart I believed least."

"You doubt that? You doubt all I said to you?" he urged softly, coming close to her.

She drew aside slightly. She had steeled herself for this inevitable interview, and there was no weakening of her defences; but a great sadness came into her eyes, and spread over her face, and to this was added, after a moment, a pity which showed the distance she was from him, the safety in which she stood.

"I remember that the garden was beautiful, and that thee spoke as though thee was part of the garden. Thee remembers that, at our meeting in the Cloistered House, when the woman was ill, I had no faith in thee; but thee spoke with grace, and turned common things round about, so that they seemed different to the ear from any past hearing; and I listened. I did not know, and I do not know now, why it is my duty to shun any of thy name, and above all thyself; but it has been so commanded by my father all my life; and though what he says may be in a little wrong, in much it must ever be right."

"And so, from a hatred handed down, your mind has been tuned to shun even when your heart was learning to give me a home—Faith?"

She straightened herself. "Friend, thee will do me the courtesy to forget to use my Christian name. I am not a child—indeed, I am well on in years"—he smiled —"and thee has no friendship or kinship for warrant.

If my mind was tuned to shun thee, I gave proof that it was willing to take thee at thine own worth, even against the will of my father, against the desire of David, who knew thee better than I—he gauged thee at first glance."

"You have become a philosopher and a statesman," he said ironically. "Has your nephew, the new Joseph in Egypt, been giving you instructions in high politics? Has he been writing the Epistles of David to the Quakers?"

"Thee will leave his name apart," she answered with dignity. "I have studied neither high politics nor statesmanship, though in the days when thee did flatter me thee said I had a gift for such things. Thee did not speak the truth. And now I will say that I do not respect thee. No matter how high thee may climb, still I shall not respect thee; for thee will ever gain ends by flattery, by subtilty, and by using every man and every woman for selfish ends. Thee cannot be true—not even to that which by nature is greatest in thee."

He withered under her words.

"And what is greatest in me?" he asked abruptly, his coolness and self-possession striving to hold their own.

"That which will ruin thee in the end." Her eyes looked beyond his into the distance, rapt and shining; she seemed scarcely aware of his presence. "That which will bring thee down—thy hungry spirit of discovery. It will serve thee no better than it served the late Earl. But thee it will lead into paths ending in a gulf of darkness."

"Deborah!" he answered, with a rasping laugh. "*Continuez!* Forewarned is forearmed."

"Oh, do not think I shall be glad," she answered, still like one in a dream. "I shall lament it as I lament—as I lament now. All else fades away into the end which I see for thee. Thee will live alone without a near and true friend, and thee will die alone, never having had a true friend. Thee will never be a true friend, thee will never love truly man or woman, and thee will never find man or woman who will love thee truly, or will be with thee to aid thee in the dark and falling days."

"Then," he broke in sharply, querulously, "then, I will stand alone. I shall never come whining that I have been ill used, to fate or fortune, to men or to the Almighty."

"That I believe. Pride will build up in thee a strength which will be like water in the end. Oh, my lord," she added, with a sudden change in her voice and manner, "if thee could only be true—thee who never has been true to any one!"

"Why does a woman always judge a man after her own personal experience with him, or what she thinks is her own personal experience?"

A robin hopped upon the path before her. She watched it for a moment intently, then lifted her head as the sound of a bell came through the wood to her. She looked up at the sun, which was slanting towards evening. She seemed about to speak, but with second thought, moved on slowly past the mill and towards the Meeting-house. He stepped on beside her. She kept her eyes fixed in front of her, as though oblivious of his presence.

"You shall hear me speak. You shall listen to what I have to say, though it is for the last time," he urged stubbornly. "You think ill of me. Are you sure you are not pharisaical?"

"I am honest enough to say that which hurts me in the saying. I do not forget that to believe thee what I think is to take all truth from what thee said to me last year, and again this spring when the tulips first came and there was good news from Egypt."

"I said," he rejoined boldly, "that I was happier with you than with any one else alive. I said that what you thought of me meant more to me than what any one else in the world thought; and that I say now, and will always say it."

The old look of pity came into her face. "I am older than thee by two years," she answered quaintly, "and I know more of real life, though I have lived always here. I have made the most of the little I have seen; thee has made little of the much that thee has seen. Thee does not know the truth concerning thee. Is it not, in truth, vanity which would have me believe in thee? If thee was happier with me than with any one alive, why then did thee make choice of a wife even in the days thee was speaking to me as no man shall ever speak again? Nothing can explain so base a fact. No, no, no, thee said to me what thee said to others, and will say again without shame. But—but see, I will forgive; yes, I will follow thee with good wishes, if thee will promise to help David, whom thee has ever disliked, as, in the place held by thee, thee can do now. Will thee offer this one proof, in spite of all else that disproves, that thee spoke any words of truth to me in the Cloistered House, in the garden by my father's house, by yonder mill, and hard by the Meeting-house yonder—near to my sister's grave by the willow-tree? Will thee do that for me?"

He was about to reply, when there appeared in the path before them Luke Claridge. His back was upon them, but he heard their footsteps and swung round. As though turned to stone, he waited for them. As they approached, his lips, dry and pale, essayed to speak, but no sound came. A fire was in his eyes which boded no good. Amazement, horror, deadly anger, were all there; but, after a moment, the will behind the tumult commanded it, the wild light died away, and he stood calm and still awaiting them. Faith was as pale as when she had met Eglington. As she came nearer, Luke Claridge said, in a low voice:

"How do I find thee in this company, Faith?"

There was reproach unutterable in his voice, in his face. He seemed humiliated and shamed, though all the while a violent spirit in him was struggling for the mastery.

"As I came this way to visit my sister's grave, I met my lord by the mill. He spoke to me, and, as I wished a favor of him, I walked with him thither—but a little way. I was going to visit my sister's grave."

"Thy sister's grave!" The fire flamed up again, but the masterful will chilled it down, and he answered, "What secret business can thee have with any of that name which I have cast out of knowledge or notice?"

Ignorant as he was of the old man's cause for quarrel or dislike, Eglington felt himself aggrieved, and, therefore, with an advantage.

"You had differences with my father, sir," he said. "I do not know what they were, but they lasted his lifetime, and all my life you have treated me with aversion. I am not a pestilence. I have never wronged you. I have lived your peaceful neighbor under great provocation, for your treatment would have done me harm if my place were less secure. I think I have cause for complaint."

"I have never acted in haste concerning thee, or those who went before thee. What business had thee with him, Faith?" he asked again. His voice was dry and hard.

Her impulse was to tell the truth, and so forever have her conscience clear, for there would never be any more need for secrecy. The wheel of understanding between Eglington and herself had come full circle, and there was an end. But to tell the truth would be to wound her father, to vex him against Eglington even as he had never yet been vexed. Besides, it was hard, while Eglington was there, to tell what, after all, was the sole affair of her own life. In one literal sense, Eglington was not guilty of deceit. Never in so many words had he said to her, "I love you"; never had he made any promise to her or exacted one; he had done no more than lure her to feel one thing, and then to call it another thing. Also there was no direct and vital injury, for she had never loved him; though how far she had travelled towards that land of light and trial she could never now declare. These thoughts flashed through her mind as she stood looking at her father. Her tongue seemed imprisoned, yet her soft and candid eyes conquered the austerity in the old man's gaze.

Eglington spoke for her.

"Permit me to answer, neighbor," he said. "I wished to speak with your daughter, because I am to be married soon, and my wife will, at intervals, come here to live. I wished that she should not be shunned by you and yours as I have been. She would not understand, as I do not. Yours is a constant call to war, while all your religion is an appeal for peace. I wished to ask your daughter to influence you to make it possible for me and mine to live in friendship among you. My wife will have some claims upon you. Her mother was an American, of a Quaker family from Derbyshire. She has done nothing to merit your aversion."

Faith listened, astonished and baffled. Nothing of this had he said to her. Had he meant to say it to her? Had it been in his mind? Or was it only a swift adaptation to circumstances, an adroit means of working upon the sympathies of her father, who, she could see, was in a quandary. Eglington had indeed touched the old man as he had not been touched in thirty years and more by one of his name. For a moment the insinuating quality of the appeal submerged the fixed idea in a mind to which the name of Eglington was anathema.

Eglington saw his advantage. He had felt his way

carefully, and he pursued it quickly. "For the rest, your daughter asked what I was ready to offer—such help as in my new official position I can give to Claridge Pasha in Egypt. As a neighbor, as Minister in the Government, I will do what I can to aid him."

Silent and embarrassed, the old man tried to find his way. Presently he said tentatively, "David Claridge has a title to the esteem of all civilized people."

Eglington was quick with his reply. "If he succeeds, his *title* will become a concrete fact. There is no honor the Crown would not confer for such remarkable service."

The other's face darkened. "I did not speak, I did not think of handles to his name. I find no good in them, but only means for deceiving and deluding the world. Such honors as might make him baronet, or duke, would add not a cubit to his stature. If he had such a thing by right"—his voice hardened, his eyes grew angry once again—"I would wish it sunk into the sea."

"You are hard on us, sir, who did not give ourselves our titles, but took them with our birth as a matter of course. There was nothing inspiring in them. We became at once distinguished and respectable by patent."

He laughed good-humoredly. Then suddenly he changed, and his eyes took on a far-off look which Faith had seen so often in the eyes of David, but in David's more intense and meaning, and so different. With what deftness and diplomacy had he worked upon her father! He had crossed a stream which seemed impassable by adroit, insincere diplomacy.

She saw that it was time to go, while yet Eglington's disparagement of rank and aristocracy was ringing in the old man's ears; though she knew there was nothing in Eglington's equipment he valued more than his title and the place it gave him. Grateful, however, for his successful intervention, Faith now held out her hand.

"I must take my father away, or it will be sunset

before we reach the Meeting-house," she said. "Good-bye—friend," she added gently.

For an instant Luke Claridge stared at her, scarce comprehending that his movements were being directed by any one save himself. Truth was, Faith had come to her cross-roads in life. For the first time in her memory she had seen her father speak to an Eglington without harshness; and, as he weakened for a moment, she moved to take command of that weakness, though she meant it to seem like leading. While loving her and David profoundly, her father had ever been quietly imperious. If she could but gain ascendency even in a little, it might lead to a more open book of life for them both.

Eglington held out his hand to the old man. "I have kept you too long, sir. Good-bye—if you will."

The offered hand was not taken, but Faith slid hers into the old man's palm, and pressed it, and he said quietly to Eglington:

"Good-evening, friend."

"And when I bring my wife, sir?" Eglington added, with a smile.

"When thee brings the lady, there will be occasion to consider—there will be occasion then."

Eglington raised his hat, and turned back upon the path he and Faith had travelled.

The old man stood watching him until he was out of view. Then he seemed more himself. Still holding Faith's hand, he walked with her on the gorse-covered hill towards the graveyard.

"Was it his heart spoke or his tongue—is there any truth in him?" he asked at last.

Faith pressed his hand. "If he help Davy, father—"

"If he help Davy; ay, if he help Davy! . . . Nay, I cannot go to the graveyard, Faith. Take me home," he said with emotion.

His hand remained in hers. She had conquered. She

was set upon a new path of influence. Her hand was upon the door of his heart.

"Thee is good to me, Faith," he said, as they entered the door of the Red Mansion.

She glanced over towards the Cloistered House. Smoke was coming from the little chimney of the laboratory.

XVII

THE WOMAN OF THE CROSS-ROADS

THE night came down slowly. There was no moon, the stars were few, but a mellow warmth was in the air. At the window of her little sitting-room up-stairs Faith sat looking out into the stillness. Beneath was the garden, with its profusion of flowers and fruit; away to the left was the common; and beyond — far beyond — was a glow in the sky, a suffused light, of a delicate orange, merging away into a gray-blueness, deepening into a darker blue; and then a purple depth, palpable and heavy with a comforting silence.

There was something alluring and suggestive in the soft, smothered radiance. It had all the glamour of some distant place of pleasure and quiet joy, of happiness, and ethereal being. It was, in fact, the far-off mirror of the flaming furnace of the great Heddington factories. The light of the sky above was a soft radiance, as of a happy Arcadian land; the fire of the toil beneath was the output of human striving, an intricate interweaving of vital forces which, like some Titanic machine, wrought out in pain a vast destiny.

As Faith looked, she thought of the thousands beneath struggling and striving, none with all desires satisfied, some in an agony of want and penury, all straining for the elusive Enough; like Sisyphus ever rolling the rock of labor up a hill too steep for them.

Her mind flew to the man Kimber and his task of

organizing labor for its own advance. What a life-work for a man! Here might David have spent his days, here among his own countrymen, instead of in that far-off land where all the forces of centuries were fighting against him. Here the forces would have been fighting for him; the trend was towards the elevation of the standards of living and the wider rights of labor, to the amelioration of hard conditions of life among the poor. David's mind, with its equity, its balance, and its fire—what might it not have accomplished in shepherding such a cause, guiding its activity?

The gate of the garden clicked. Kate Heaver had arrived. Faith got to her feet and left the room.

A few minutes later the woman of the cross-roads was seated opposite Faith at the window. She had changed greatly since the day David had sent her on her way to London and into the unknown. Then there had been recklessness, something of coarseness in the fine face. Now it was strong and quiet, marked by purpose and self-reliance. Ignorance had been her only peril in the past, as it had been the cause of her unhappy connection with Jasper Kimber. The atmosphere in which she was raised had been unmoral; it had not been consciously immoral. Her temper and her indignation against her man for drinking had been the means of driving them apart. He would have married her in those days, if she had given the word, for her will was stronger than his own; but she had broken from him in an agony of rage and regret and despised love.

She was now, again, as she had been in those first days before she went with Jasper Kimber; when she was the rose-red angel of the quarters; when children were lured by the touch of her large, shapely hands; when she had been counted a great nurse among her neighbors. The old simple untutored sympathy was in her face.

They sat for a long time in silence, and at length Faith said, "Thee is happy now—with her who is to marry Lord Eglington?"

Kate nodded, smiling. "Who could help but be happy with her! Yet a temper, too—so quick, and then all over in a second. Ah, she is one that 'd break her heart if she was treated bad; but I'd be sorry for him that did it. For the like of her goes mad with hurting, and the mad cut with a big scythe."

"Has thee seen Lord Eglington?"

"Once before I left these parts and often in London." Her voice was constrained; she seemed not to wish to speak of him.

"Is it true that Jasper Kimber is to stand against him for Parliament?"

"I do not know. They say my lord has to do with foreign lands now. If he helps Mr. Claridge there, then it would be a foolish thing for Jasper to fight him; and so I've told him. You've got to stand by those that stand by you. Lord Eglington has his own way of doing things. There's not a servant in my lady's house that he hasn't made his friend. He's one that's bound to have his will. I heard my lady say he talks better than any one in England, and there's none she doesn't know, from duchesses down."

"She is beautiful?" asked Faith, with hesitation.

"Taller than you, but not so beautiful."

Faith sighed, and was silent for a moment, then she laid a hand upon the other's shoulder. "Thee has never said what happened when thee first got to London. Does thee care to say?"

"It seems so long ago," was the reply. . . . "No need to tell of the journey to London. When I got there it frightened me at first. My head went round. But somehow it came to me what I should do. I asked my way to a hospital. I'd helped a many that was hurt at

Heddington and thereabouts, and doctors said I was as good as them that was trained. I found a hospital at last, and asked for work, but they laughed at me—it was the porter at the door. I was not to be put down, and asked to see some one that had rights to say yes or no. So he opened the door and told me to go. I said he was no man to treat a woman so, and I would not go. Then a fine white-haired gentleman came forward. He had heard all we had said, standing in a little room at one side. He spoke a kind word or two, and asked me to go into the little room. Before I had time to think, he came to me with the matron, and left me with her. I told her the whole truth, and she looked at first as if she'd turn me out. But the end of it was I stayed there for the night, and in the morning the old gentleman came again, and with him his lady, as kind and sharp of tongue as himself, and as big as three. Some things she said made my tongue ache to speak back to her; but I choked it down. I went to her to be a sort of nurse and maid. She taught me how to do a hundred things, and by-and-by I couldn't be too thankful she had taken me in. I was with her till she died. Then, six months ago I went to Miss Maryon, who knew about me long before from her that died. With her I've been ever since—and so that's all!"

"Surely God has been kind to thee."

"I'd have gone down—down—down, if it hadn't been for Mr. Claridge at the cross-roads."

"Does thee think I shall like her that will live yonder?" She nodded towards the Cloistered House.

"There's none but likes her. She will want a friend, I'm thinking. She'll be lonely by-and-by. Surely, she will be lonely."

Faith looked at her closely, and at last leaned over, and again laid a soft hand on her shoulder. "Thee thinks that—why?"

"He cares only what matters to himself. She will be naught to him but one that belongs. He'll never try to do her good. Doing good to any but himself never comes to his mind."

"How does thee know him, to speak so surely?"

"When, at the first, he gave me a letter for her one day, and slipped a sovereign into my hand, and nodded, and smiled at me, I knew him right enough. He never could be true to aught."

"Did thee keep the sovereign?" Faith asked anxiously.

"Ay, that I did. If he was for giving his money away, I'd take it fast enough. The gold gave father boots for a year. Why should I mind?"

Faith's face suffused. How low was Eglington's estimate of humanity!

In the silence that followed the door of her room opened, and her father entered. He held in one hand a paper, in the other a candle. His face was passive, but his eyes were burning.

"David—David is coming," he cried, in a voice that rang. "Does thee hear, Faith? Davy is coming home!"

A woman laughed exultantly. It was not Faith.

But still two years passed before David came.

XVIII

TIME, THE IDOL-BREAKER

LORD WINDLEHURST looked meditatively round the crowded and brilliant salon. His host, the Foreign Minister, had gathered in the vast golden chamber the most notable people of a most notable season, and in as critical a period of the world's politics as had been known for a quarter of a century. After a moment's survey, the ex-Prime-Minister turned to answer the frank and caustic words addressed to him by the Duchess of Snowdon concerning the Under-Secretary for Foreign Affairs. Presently he said:

"But there is method in his haste, dear lady. He is good at his dangerous gam He plays high, he plunges; but, somehow, he makes it do. I've been in Parliament a generation or so, and I've never known an amateur more daring and skilful. I should have given him office had I remained in power. Look at him, and tell me if he wouldn't have been worth the backing."

As Lord Windlehurst uttered the last word with an arid smile, he looked quizzically at the central figure of a group of people gayly talking.

The Duchess impatiently tapped her knee with a fan. "Be thankful you haven't got him on your conscience," she rejoined. "I call Eglington unscrupulous and unreliable. He has but one god — getting on; and he has got on, with a vengeance. Whenever I look at that dear thing he's married, I feel there's no trusting

Providence, who seems to make the deserving a footstool for the undeserving. I've known Hylda since she was ten, and I've known him since the minute he came into the world, and I've got the measure of both. She is the finest essence the middle class can distil, and he, oh, he's paraffin—*vin ordinaire*, if you like it better, a selfish, calculating adventurer!"

Lord Windlehurst chuckled mordantly. "Adventurer! That's what they called me—with more reason. I spotted him as soon as he spoke in the House. There was devilry in him, and unscrupulousness, as you say; but, I confess, I thought it would give way to the more profitable habit of integrity, and that some cause would seize him, make him sincere and mistaken, and give him a few falls. But in that he was more original than I thought. He is superior to convictions. You don't think he married yonder Queen of Hearts from conviction, do you?"

He nodded towards a corner where Hylda, under a great palm, and backed by a bank of flowers, stood surrounded by a group of people palpably amused and interested; for she had a reputation for wit—a wit that never hurt, and irony that was only whimsical.

"Oh, there you are wrong," the Duchess answered. "He married from conviction, if ever a man did. Look at her beauty, look at her fortune, listen to her tongue! Don't you think conviction was easy?"

Lord Windlehurst looked at Hylda approvingly. "She has the real gift—little information, but much knowledge, the primary gift of public life. Information is full of traps; knowledge avoids them; it reads men; and politics is men—and foreign affairs perhaps! She is remarkable. I've made some hay in the political world, not so much as the babblers think, but I hadn't her ability at twenty-five."

"Why didn't she see through Eglington?"

"My dear Betty, he didn't give her time. He carried her off her feet. You know how he can talk."

"That's the trouble. She was clever, and liked a clever man—and he—!"

"Quite so. He'd disprove his own honest parentage, if it would help him on—as you say."

"I didn't say it. Now don't repeat that as from me. I'm not clever enough to think of such things. But that Eglington lot—I knew his father and his grandfather! Old Broadbrim they called his grandfather after he turned Quaker, and he didn't do that till he had had his fling, so my father used to say. And Old Broadbrim's father was called I-want-to-know. He was always poking his nose into things, and playing at being a chemist—like this one and the one before. They all fly off. This one's father used to disappear for two or three years at a time. This one will fly off, too! You'll see!"

"He is too keen on Number One for that, I fancy. He calculates like a mathematician. As cool as a cracksman of fame and fancy."

The Duchess dropped the fan in her lap. "My dear, I've said nothing as bad as that about him. And there he is at the Foreign Office!"

"Yet, what has he done, Betty, after all? He has never cheated at cards, or forged a check, or run away with his neighbor's wife."

"There's no credit in not doing what you don't want to do. There's no virtue in not falling, when you're not tempted. Neighbor's wife! He hasn't enough feeling to face it. Oh no, he'll not break the heart of his neighbor's wife. That's melodrama, and he's a cold-blooded artist. He will torture that sweet child over there until she poisons him, or runs away."

"Isn't he too clever for that? She has a million!"

"He'll not realize it till it's all over. He's too selfish to see—how I hate him!"

Lord Windlehurst smiled indulgently at her. "Ah, you never hated any one—not even the Duke."

"I will not have you take away my character. Of course I've hated, or I wouldn't be worth a button. I'm not the silly thing you've always thought me."

His face became gentler. "I've always thought you one of the wisest women of this world—adventurous, but wise. If it weren't too late, if my day weren't over, I'd ask the one great favor, Betty, and—"

She tapped his arm sharply with her fan. "What a humbug you are—the Great Pretender! But tell me, am I not right about Eglington?"

Windlehurst became grave. "Yes, you are right—but I admire him, too. He is determined to test himself to the full. His ambition is boundless and ruthless, but his mind has a scientific turn—the obligation of energy to apply itself, of intelligence to engage itself to the farthest limit. But service to humanity—"

"Service to humanity!" she sniffed.

"Of course he would think it 'flap-doodle'—except in a speech; but I repeat, I admire him. Think of it all. He was a poor Irish peer, with no wide circle of acquaintance, come of a family none too popular. He strikes out a course for himself—a course which had its dangers, because it was original. He determines to become celebrated—by becoming notorious first. He uses his title as a weapon for advancement as though he were a butter-merchant. He plans carefully and adroitly. He writes a book of travel. It is impudent, and it traverses the observations of authorities, and the scientific geographers prance with rage. That was what he wished. He writes a novel. It sets London laughing at me, his political chief. He knew me well enough to be sure I would not resent it. He would have lampooned his grandmother, if he was sure she would not, or could not, hurt him. Then he becomes more audacious. He publishes a monograph on the painters of Spain, artificial, confident, rhetorical, acute—as fascinating as a hide-and-seek drawing-room play — he is so cleverly escaping from his ignorance and indiscretions all the while. Connoisseurs laugh, students of art shriek a little, and Ruskin writes a scathing letter, which was what he had played for. He had got something for nothing cheaply. The few who knew and despised him did not matter, for they were able and learned and obscure, and, in the world where he moves, most people are superficial, mediocre, and 'tuppence-colored.' It was all very brilliant. He pursued his notoriety, and got it."

"Industrious Eglington!"

"But, yes, he is industrious. It is all business. It was an enormous risk, rebelling against his party, and leaving me, and going over; but his temerity justified itself, and it didn't matter to him that people said he went over to get office as we were going out. He got the office—and people forget so soon! Then, what does he do—"

"He brings out another book, and marries a wife, and abuses his old friends—and you."

"Abuse? With his tongue in his cheek, hoping that I should reply. Dev'lishly ingenious! But on that book of 'Electricity and Disease,' he scored. In most other things he's a barber-shop philosopher, but in science he has got a flare, a real talent. So he moves modestly in this thing, for which he had a fine natural gift and more knowledge than he ever had before in any department, whose boundaries his impertinent and ignorant mind had invaded. That book gave him a place. It wasn't full of new things, but it crystallized the discoveries, suggestions, and expectations of others; and, meanwhile, he had got a name at no cost. He is so various. Look at it dispassionately, and you will see much to admire in his skill. He pleases, he amuses, he startles, he baffles, he mystifies."

The Duchess made an impatient exclamation. "The silly newspapers call him 'a remarkable man, a personality.' Now, believe me, Windlehurst, he will overreach himself one of these days, and he'll come down like a stick."

"There you are on solid ground. He thinks that Fate is with him, and that, in taking risks, he is infallible. But the best system breaks at political roulette sooner or later. You have got to work for something outside yourself, something that is bigger than the game, or the end is sickening."

"Eglington hasn't far to go, if that's the truth."

"Well, well, when it comes, we must help him—we must help him up again."

The Duchess nervously adjusted her wig, with ludicrously tiny fingers for one so ample, and said petulantly: "You are incomprehensible. He has been a traitor to you and to your party, he has thrown mud at you, he has played with principles as my terrier plays with his rubber ball, and yet you'll run and pick him up when he falls, and—"

"'And kiss the spot to make it well,'" he laughed softly, then added with a sigh: "Able men in public life are few; 'far too few, for half our tasks; we can spare not one.' Besides, my dear Betty, there is his pretty lass o' London."

The Duchess was mollified at once. "I wish she had been my girl," she said, in a voice a little tremulous. "She never needed looking after. Look at the position she has made for herself. Her father wouldn't go into society, her mother knew a mere handful of people, and—"

"She knew you, Betty."

"Well, suppose I did help her a little— I was only a kind of reference. She did the rest. She's set a half-dozen fashions herself—pure genius. She was born to lead. Her turnouts were always a little smarter, her horses travelled a little faster, than other people's. She took risks, too, but she didn't play a game; she only wanted to do things well. We all gasped when she brought Adelaide to recite from 'Romeo and Juliet' at an evening party, but all London did the same the week after."

"She discovered, and the Duchess of Snowdon applied the science. Ah, Betty, don't think I don't agree. She has the gift. She has temperament. No woman should have temperament. She hasn't scope enough to wear it out in some passion for a cause. Men are saved in spite of themselves by the law of work. Forty comes to a man of temperament, and then a passion for a cause seizes him, and he is safe. A woman of temperament at forty is apt to cut across the bows of iron-clad convention and go down. She has temperament, has my lady yonder, and I don't like the look of her eyes sometimes. There's dark fire smouldering in them. She should have a cause; but a cause to a woman nowadays means 'too little of pleasure, too much of pain,' for others."

"What was your real cause, Windlehurst? You had one, I suppose, for you've never had a fall!"

"My cause? You ask that? Behold the barren fig-tree! A lifetime in my country's service, and you who have driven me home from the House in your own brougham, and told me that you understood—oh, Betty!"

She laughed. "You'll say something funny as you're dying, Windlehurst."

"Perhaps. But it will be funny to know that presently I'll have a secret that none of you know, who watch me 'launch my pinnace into the dark.' But causes? There are hundreds, and all worth while. I've come here to-night for a cause—no, don't start, it's not you, Betty, though you are worth any sacrifice. I've come here to-night to see a modern Paladin, a real crusader:

> "Then felt I like some watcher of the skies,
> When a new planet swims into his ken."

"Yes, that's poetry, Windlehurst, and you know I love it—I've always kept yours. But who's the man—the planet?"

"Egyptian Claridge."

"Ah, he is in England?"

"He will be here to-night; you shall see him."

"Really! What is his origin?"

He told her briefly, adding: "I've watched the rise of Claridge Pasha. I've watched his cause grow, and now I shall see the man—ah, but here comes our lass o' London!"

The eyes of both brightened, and a whimsical pleasure came to the mask-like face of Lord Windlehurst. There was an eager and delighted look in Hylda's face also, as she quickly came to them, her cavaliers following.

The five years that had passed since that tragic night in Cairo had been more than kind to her. She was lissome, radiant, and dignified, her face was alive with expression, and a delicate grace was in every movement. The dark lashes seemed to have grown longer, the brown hair fuller, the smile softer and more alluring.

"She is an invaluable asset to the Government," Lord Windlehurst murmured as she came. "No wonder the party helped the marriage on. London conspired for it, her feet got tangled in the web—and he gave her no time to think. Thinking had saved her till he came."

By instinct Lord Windlehurst knew. During the first year after the catastrophe at Kaïd's Palace, Hylda could scarcely endure the advances made by her many admirers, the greatly eligible and the eager ineligible, all with as real an appreciation of her wealth as of her personal attributes. But she took her place in London life with more than the old will to make for herself, with the help of her aunt Conyngham, an individual position.

The second year after her visit to Egypt, she was less haunted by the dark episode of the Palace, memory tortured her less; she came to think of David and the part he had played with less agitation. At first the thought of him had moved her alternately to sympathy and to revolt. His chivalry had filled her with admiration, with a sense of confidence, of dependence, of touching and vital obligation; but there was, too, another overmastering feeling. He had seen her life naked, as it were, stripped of all independence, with the knowledge of a dangerous indiscretion which, to say the least, was a deformity; and she inwardly resented it, as one would resent the exposure of a long-hidden physical deformity, even by the surgeon who saved one's life. It was not a very lofty attitude of mind, but it was human—and feminine.

These moods had been always dissipated, however, when she recalled, as she did so often, David as he stood before Nahoum Pasha, his soul fighting in him to make of his enemy—of the man whose brother he had killed—a fellow-worker in the path of altruism he had mapped out for himself. David's name had been continually mentioned in telegraphic reports and journalistic correspondence from Egypt; and from this source she had learned that Nahoum Pasha was again high in the service of Prince Kaïd. When the news of David's southern expedition to the revolting slave-dealing tribes began to appear, she was deeply roused. Her agitation was the more intense because she never permitted herself to talk of him to others, even when his name was discussed at dinner-tables, accompanied by strange legends of his origin and stranger romances regarding his call to power by Kaïd.

She had surrounded him with romance; he seemed more a hero of history than of her own real and living world, a being apart. Even when there came rumblings of disaster, dark dangers to be conquered by the Quaker crusader, it all was still as of another life. True it was, that when his safe return to Cairo was announced she had cried with joy and relief; but there was nothing emotional or passionate in her feeling; it was the love of the lower for the higher, the hero-worship of an idealist in passionate gratitude.

And, amid it all, her mind scarcely realized that they would surely meet again. At the end of the second year the thought had receded into an almost indefinite past. She was beginning to feel that she had lived two lives, and that this life had no direct or vital bearing upon her previous existence, in which David had moved. Yet now and then the perfume of the Egyptian garden, through which she had fled to escape from tragedy, swept over her senses, clouded her eyes in the daytime, made them burn at night.

At last she had come to meet and know Eglington. From the first moment they met he had directed his course towards marriage. He was the man of the moment. His ambition seemed but patriotism, his ardent and overwhelming courtship the impulse of a powerful nature. As Lord Windlehurst had said, he carried her off her feet, and, on a wave of devotion and popular encouragement, he had swept her to the altar.

The Duchess held both her hands for a moment, admiring her, and, presently, with a playful remark upon her unselfishness, left her alone with Lord Windlehurst.

As they talked, his mask-like face became lighted from the brilliant fire in the inquisitorial eyes, his lips played with topics of the moment in a mordant fashion, which drew from her flashing replies. Looking at her, he was conscious of the mingled qualities of three races in her—English, Welsh, and American-Dutch of the Knickerbocker strain; and he contrasted her keen perception and her exquisite sensitiveness with the pure-bred Englishwomen round him, stately, kindly, handsome, and monotonously intelligent.

"Now I often wonder," he said, conscious of, but indifferent to, the knowledge that he and the brilliant person beside him were objects of general attention—"I often wonder, when I look at a gathering like this, how many undiscovered crimes there are playing about among us. They never do tell—or, shall I say, *we* never do tell?"

All day, she knew not why, Hylda had been nervous and excited. Without reason his words startled her. Now there flashed before her eyes a room in a palace at Cairo, and a man lying dead before her. The light slowly faded out of her eyes, leaving them almost lustreless, but her face was calm, and the smile on her lips stayed. She fanned herself slowly, and answered nonchalantly: "Crime is a word of many meanings. I read in the papers of political crimes—it is a common phrase; yet the criminals appear to go unpunished."

"There you are wrong," he answered cynically. "The punishment is, that political virtue goes unrewarded, and in due course crime is the only refuge to most. Yet in politics the temptation to be virtuous is great."

She laughed now with a sense of relief. The intellectual stimulant had brought back the light to her face. "How is it, then, with you—inveterate habit or the strain of the ages? For they say you have not had your due reward?"

He smiled grimly. "Ah, no, with me virtue is the act of an inquiring mind—to discover where it will lead me. I began with political crime—I was understood! I practise political virtue: it embarrasses the world, it fogs them, it seems original, because so unnecessary. Mine is the scientific life. Experiment in old substance gives new—well, say, new precipitations. But you are scientific, too. You have a laboratory, and have much to do—with retorts."

"No, you are thinking of my husband. The laboratory is his."

"But the retorts are yours."

"The precipitations are his."

"Ah, well, at least you help him to fuse the constituents! . . . But, now, be quite confidential to an old man who has experimented too. Is your husband really an amateur scientist, or is he a scientific amateur? Is it a pose or a taste? I fiddled once—and wrote sonnets; one was a pose, the other a taste."

It was mere persiflage, but it was a jest which made an unintended wound. Hylda became conscious of a sudden sharp inquiry going on in her mind. There flashed into it the question, Does Eglington's heart ever really throb for love of any object or any cause? Even in moments of greatest intimacy, soon after marriage, when he was most demonstrative towards her, he had seemed preoccupied, except when speaking about himself and what he meant to do. Then he made her heart throb in response to his confident, ardent words—concerning himself. But his own heart, did it throb? Or was it only his brain that throbbed?

Suddenly, with an exclamation, she involuntarily laid a hand upon Windlehurst's arm. She was looking down the room straight before her to a group of people towards which other groups were now converging, attracted by one who seemed to be a centre of interest.

Presently the eager onlookers drew aside, and Lord Windlehurst observed moving up the room a figure he had never seen before. The new-comer was dressed in a gray and blue official dress, unrelieved save by silver braid at the collar and at the wrists. There was no decoration, but on the head was a red fez, which gave prominence to the white, broad forehead, with the dark hair waving away behind the ears. Lord Windlehurst held his eye-glass to his eye in interested scrutiny.

"H'm," he said, with lips pursed out, "a most notable figure, a most remarkable face! My dear, there's a fortune in that face. It's a national asset."

He saw the flush, the dumb amazement, the poignant look in Lady Eglington's face, and registered it in his mind. "Poor thing," he said to himself, "I wonder what it is all about—I wonder. I thought she had no unregulated moments. She gave promise of better things."

The Foreign Minister was bringing his guest towards them. The new-comer did not look at them till within a few steps of where they stood. Then his eyes met those of Lady Eglington. For an instant his steps were arrested. A swift light came into his face, softening its quiet austerity and strength.

It was David.

XIX

SHARPER THAN A SWORD

A GLANCE of the eye was the only sign of recognition between David and Hylda; nothing that others saw could have suggested that they had ever met before. Lord Windlehurst at once engaged David in conversation.

At first when Hylda had come back from Egypt, those five years ago, she had often wondered what she would think or do if she ever were to see this man again; whether, indeed, she could bear it. Well, the moment and the man had come. Her eyes had gone blind for an instant; it had seemed for one sharp, crucial moment as though she could not bear it; then the gulf of agitation was passed, and she had herself in hand.

While her mind was engaged subconsciously with what Lord Windlehurst and David said, comprehending it all, and, when Lord Windlehurst appealed to her, offering by a word contribution to the *pourparler*, she was studying David as steadily as her heated senses would permit her.

He seemed to her to have put on twenty years in the steady force of his personality—in the composure of his bearing, in the self-reliance of his look, though his face and form were singularly youthful. The face was handsome and alight, the look was that of one who weighed things; yet she was conscious of a great change. The old delicate quality of the features was not so marked, though there was nothing material in the look, and the head had not a sordid line, while the hand that he now and again raised, brushing his forehead meditatively, had gained much in strength and force. Yet there was something—something different, that brought a slight cloud into her eyes. It came to her now, a certain melancholy in the bearing of the figure, erect and well-balanced as it was. Once the feeling came, the certainty grew. And presently she found a strange sadness in the eyes, something that lurked behind all that he did and all that he was, some shadow over the spirit. It was even more apparent when he smiled.

As she was conscious of this new reading of him, a motion arrested her glance, a quick lifting of the head to one side, as though the mind had suddenly been struck by an idea, the glance flying upward in abstracted questioning. This she had seen in her husband, too, the same brisk lifting of the head, the same quick smiling. But this face, unlike Eglington's, expressed a perfect single-mindedness; it wore the look of a self-effacing man of luminous force, a concentrated battery of energy. Since she had last seen him every sign of the provincial had vanished. He was now the well-modulated man of affairs, elegant in his simplicity of dress, with the dignified air of the intellectual, yet with the decision of a man who knew his mind.

Lord Windlehurst was leaving. Now David and she were alone. Without a word they moved on together through the throng, the eyes of all following them, until they reached a quiet room at one end of the salon, where were only a few people watching the crowd pass the doorway.

"You will be glad to sit," he said, motioning her to a chair beside some palms. Then, with a change of tone, he added, "Thee is not sorry I am come?"

Thee—the old-fashioned simple Quaker word! She

put her fingers to her eyes. Her senses were swimming with a distant memory. The East was in her brain, the glow of the skies, the gleam of the desert, the swish of the Nile, the cry of the sweet-seller, the song of the dance-girl, the strain of the *darabukheh*, the call of the *sáis*. She saw again the ghiassas drifting down the great river, laden with dourha; she saw the mosque of the blue tiles with its placid fountain, and its handful of worshippers praying by the olive-tree. She watched the moon rise above the immobile Sphinx, she looked down on the banqueters in the Palace, David among them, and Foorgat Bey beside her. She saw Foorgat Bey again lying dead at her feet. She heard the stir of the leaves; she caught the smell of the lime-trees in the Palace garden as she fled. She recalled her reckless return to Cairo from Alexandria. She remembered the little room where she and David, Nahoum and Mizraim, crossed a bridge over a chasm, and stood upon ground which had held good till now—till this hour, when the man who had played a most vital part in her life had come again out of a land which, by some forced obliquity of mind and stubbornness of will, she had assured herself she would never see again.

She withdrew her hand from her eyes, and saw him looking at her calmly, though his face was alight.

"Thee is fatigued," he said. "This is labor which wears away the strength." He made a motion towards the crowd.

She smiled a very little, and said: "You do not care for such things as this, I know. Your life has its share of it, however, I suppose."

He looked out over the throng before he answered. "It seems an eddy of purposeless waters. Yet there is great depth beneath, or there were no eddy; and where there is depth and the eddy there is danger—always."

As he spoke she became almost herself again. "You think that deep natures have most perils?"

"Thee knows it is so. Human nature is like the earth: the deeper the plough goes into the soil unploughed before, the more evil substance is turned up —evil that becomes alive as soon as the sun and the air fall upon it."

"Then, women like me who pursue a flippant life, who ride in this merry-go-round"—she made a gesture towards the crowd beyond—"who have no depth, we are safest, we live upon the surface." Her gaiety was forced; her words were feigned.

"Thee has passed the point of danger, thee is safe," he answered meaningly.

"Is that because I am not deep, or because the plough has been at work?" she asked. "In either case I am not sure you are right."

"Thee is happily married," he said reflectively; "and the prospect is fair."

"I think you know my husband," she said in answer, and yet not in answer.

"I was born in Hamley where he has a place—thee has been there?" he asked eagerly.

"Not yet. We are to go next Sunday—for the first time—to the Cloistered House. I had not heard that my husband knew you, until I saw in the paper a few days ago that your home was in Hamley. Then I asked Eglington, and he told me that your family and his had been neighbors for generations."

"His father was a Quaker," David rejoined, "but he forsook the faith."

"I did not know," she answered, with some hesitation. There was no reason why, when she and Eglington had talked of Hamley, he should not have said his own father had once been a Quaker; yet she had dwelt so upon the fact that she herself had Quaker blood, and he had laughed so much over it, with the amusement of the superior person, that his silence on this one point struck her now with a sense of confusion.

"You are going to Hamley—we shall meet there?" she continued.

"To-day I should have gone, but I have business at the Foreign Office to-morrow. One needs time to learn that all 'private interests and partial affections' must be sacrificed to public duty."

"But you are going soon? You will be there on Sunday?"

"I shall be there to-morrow night, and Sunday, and for one long week at least. Hamley is the centre of the world, the axle of the universe—you shall see. You doubt it?" he added, with a whimsical smile.

"I shall dispute most of what you say, and all that you think, if you do not continue to use the Quaker 'thee' and 'thou'—ungrammatical as you are so often."

"Thee is now the only person in London, or in England, with whom I use 'thee' and 'thou.' I am no longer my own master, I am a public servant, and so I must follow custom."

"It is destructive of personality. The 'thee' and 'thou' belonged to you. I wonder if the people of Hamley will say 'thee' and 'thou' to me. I hope, I do hope they will."

"Thee may be sure they will. They are no respecters of persons there. They called your husband's father, Robert—his name was Robert. Friend Robert they called him, and afterwards they called him Robert Denton till he died."

"Will they call me Hylda?" she asked, with a smile.

"More like they will call thee Friend Hylda; it sounds simple and strong," he replied.

"As they call Claridge Pasha, Friend David," she answered, with a smile. "David is a good name for a strong man."

"That David threw a stone from a sling and smote a giant in the forehead. The stone from this David's sling falls into the ocean and is lost beneath the surface."

His voice had taken on a somewhat sombre tone, his eyes looked away into the distance; yet he smiled too, and a hand upon his knee suddenly closed in sympathy with an inward determination.

A light of understanding came into her face. They had been keeping things upon the surface, and, while it lasted, he seemed a lesser man than she had thought him these past years. But now—now there was the old unschooled simplicity, the unique and lonely personality, the homely soul and body bending to one root-idea, losing themselves in a wave of duty. Again he was to her, once more, the dreamer, the worker, the conqueror—the conqueror of her own imagination. She had in herself the soul of altruism, the heart of the crusader. Touched by the fire of a great idea, she was of those who could have gone out into the world without wallet or scrip, to work passionately for some great end. . . . And she had married the Earl of Eglington!

She leaned towards David, and said eagerly, "But you are satisfied—you *are* satisfied with your work for poor Egypt?"

"Thee says 'poor Egypt,'" he answered, "and thee says well. Even now she is not far from the day of Rameses and Joseph. Thee thinks perhaps thee knows Egypt—none knows her."

"You know her—now?"

He shook his head slowly. "It is like putting one's ear to the mouth of the Sphinx. Yet sometimes, almost in despair, when I have lain down in the desert beside my camel, set about with enemies, I have got a message from the barren desert, the wide silence, and the stars." He paused.

"What is the message that comes?" she asked softly.

"It is always the same: *Work on!* Seek not to know too much, nor think that what you do is of vast value. Work, because it is yours to be adjusting the machinery in your own little workshop of life to the wide mechanism of the universe and time. One wheel set right, one flying belt adjusted, and there is a step forward to the final harmony—ah, but how I preach!" he added hastily.

His eyes were fixed on hers with a great sincerity, and they were clear and shining, yet his lips were smiling—what a trick they had of smiling! He looked as though he should apologize for such words in such a place.

She rose to her feet with a great suspiration, with a light in her eyes and a trembling smile.

"Ah, no, no, no, you inspire one. *Thee* inspires me," she said with a little laugh, in which there was a note of sadness. "I may use 'thee,' may I not, when I will? I am a little a Quaker also, am I not? My people came from Derbyshire, my American people, that is—and only forty years ago. Almost thee persuades me to be a Quaker now," she added. "And perhaps I shall be, too," she went on, her eyes fixed on the crowd passing by, Eglington among them.

David saw Eglington also, and moved forward with her.

"We shall meet in Hamley," she said composedly, as she saw her husband leave the crush and come towards her. As Eglington noticed David a curious enigmatical glance flashed from his eyes. He came forward, however, with outstretched hand.

"I am sorry I was not at the Foreign Office when you called to-day. Welcome back to England, home—and beauty." He laughed in a rather mirthless way, but with a certain *empressement*, conscious, as he always was, of the onlookers. "You have had a busy time in Egypt?" he continued cheerfully, and laughed again.

David laughed slightly, also, and Hylda noticed that it had a certain resemblance in its quick naturalness to that of her husband; but the one was different.

"I am not sure that we are so busy there as we ought to be," David answered. "I have no real standards. I am but an amateur, and have known nothing of public life. But you should come and see."

"It has been in my mind. An ounce of eyesight is worth a ton of print. My lady was there once, I believe"—he turned towards her—"but before your time, I think. Or did you meet there, perhaps?" He glanced at both curiously. He scarcely knew why a thought flashed into his mind—as though by some telepathic sense; for it had never been there before, and there was no reason for its being there now.

Hylda saw what David was about to answer, and she knew instinctively that he would say they had never met. It shamed her. She intervened as she saw he was about to speak.

"We were introduced for the first time to-night," she said; "but Claridge Pasha is part of my education in the world. It is a miracle that Hamley should produce two such men," she added gayly, and laid her fan upon her husband's arm lightly. "You should have been a Quaker, Harry, and then you two would have been—"

"Two Quaker Don Quixotes," interrupted Eglington ironically.

"I should not have called you a Don Quixote," his wife lightly rejoined, relieved at the turn things had taken. "I cannot imagine you tilting at windmills—"

"Or saving maidens in distress? Well, perhaps not; but you do not suggest that Claridge Pasha tilts at windmills either—or saves maidens in distress. Though, now I come to think, there was an episode!" He laughed maliciously. "Some time ago it was — a lass of the cross-roads! I think I heard of such an adventure, which did credit to Claridge Pasha's heart, though it shocked Hamley at the time. But I wonder, was the maiden really saved?"

Lady Eglington's face became rigid. "Ah, yes," she said slowly, "the maiden was saved. She is now my maid. Hamley may have been shocked, but Claridge Pasha has every reason to be glad that he helped a fellow-being in trouble."

"Your maid—Heaver?" asked Eglington in surprise, a swift shadow crossing his face.

"Yes; she only told me this morning. Perhaps she had seen that Claridge Pasha was coming to England. I had not, however. At any rate, Quixotism saved her."

David smiled. "It is better than I dared to hope," he remarked quietly.

"But that is not all," continued Hylda. "There is more. She had been used badly by a man who now wants to marry her—has tried to do so for years. Now, be prepared for a surprise, for it concerns you rather closely, Eglington. Fate is a whimsical jade. Whom do you think it is? Well, since you could never guess —Jasper Kimber."

Eglington's eyes opened wide. "This is nothing but a coarse and impossible stage coincidence," he laughed. "It is one of those tricks played by Fact to discredit the imagination. Life is laughing at us again. The longer I live, the more I am conscious of being an object of derision by the scene-shifters in the wings of the stage. What a cynical comedy life is at the best!"

"It all seems natural enough," rejoined David.

"It is all paradox."

"Isn't it all inevitable law? I have no belief in 'antic Fate!'"

Hylda realized, with a new and poignant understanding, the difference of outlook on life between the two men. She suddenly remembered the words of Confucius, which she had set down in her little book of daily life: "By nature we approximate, it is only experience that drives us apart."

David would have been content to live in the desert all his life for the sake of a cause, making no calculations as to reward. Eglington must ever have the counters for the game.

"Well, if you do not believe in 'antic Fate,' you must be greatly puzzled as you go on," he rejoined, laughing; "especially in Egypt, where the East and the West collide, race against race, religion against religion, Oriental mind against Occidental intellect. You have an unusual quantity of Quaker composure, to see in it all 'inevitable law.' And it must be dull. But you always were, so they say in Hamley, a monument of seriousness."

"I believe they made one or two exceptions," answered David dryly. "I had assurances."

Eglington laughed boyishly. "You are right. You achieved a name for humor in a day—'a glass, a kick, and a kiss,' it was. Do you have such days in Egypt?"

"You must come and see," David answered lightly, declining to notice the insolence. "These are critical days there. The problems are worthy of your care. Will you not come?"

Eglington was conscious of a peculiar persuasive influence over himself that he had never felt before. In proportion, however, as he felt its compelling quality, there came a jealousy of the man who was its cause. The old antagonism, which had had its sharpest expression the last time they had met on the platform at Heddington came back. It was one strong will resenting another—as though there was not room enough in the wide world of being for these two atoms of life, sparks from the ceaseless wheel, one making a little brighter flash than the other for the moment, and then presently darkness, and the whirring wheel which threw them off, throwing off millions of others again.

On the moment Eglington had a temptation to say something with an edge, which would show David that his success in Egypt hung upon the course that he himself and the weak Foreign Minister, under whom he served, would take. And this course would be his own course largely, since he had been appointed to be a force and strength in the Foreign Office which his chief did not supply. He refrained, however, and, on the moment, remembered the promise he had given to Faith to help David.

A wave of feeling passed over him. His wife was beautiful, a creature of various charms, a centre of attraction. Yet he had never really loved her—so many sordid elements had entered into the thought of marriage with her, lowering the character of his affection. With a perversity which only such men know, such heart as he had turned to the unknown Quaker girl who had rebuked him, scathed him, laid bare his soul before himself, as no one ever had done. To Eglington it was a relief that there was one human being—he thought there was only one—who read him through and through; and that knowledge was in itself as powerful an influence as was the secret between David and Hylda. It was a kind of confessional, comforting to a nature not self-contained. Now he restrained his cynical intention to deal David a side-thrust, and said quietly:

"We shall meet at Hamley, shall we not? Let us talk there, and not at the Foreign Office. You would care to go to Egypt, Hylda?"

She forced a smile. "Let us talk it over at Hamley."

With a smile to David she turned away to some friends.

Eglington offered to introduce David to some notable people, but he said that he must go—he was fatigued after his journey. He had no wish to be lionized.

As he left the salon, the band was playing a tune that made him close his eyes, as though against something he would not see. The band in Kaïd's Palace had played it that night when he had killed Foorgat Bey.

XX

EACH AFTER HIS OWN ORDER

WITH the passing years new feelings had grown up in the heart of Luke Claridge. Once David's destiny and career were his own peculiar and self-assumed responsibility. "Inwardly convicted," he had wrenched the lad away from the natural circumstances of his life, and created a scheme of existence for him out of his own conscience—a pious egoist.

After David went to Egypt, however, his mind involuntarily formed the resolution that "Davy and God should work it out together."

He had grown very old in appearance, and his quiet face was almost painfully white; but the eyes burned with more fire than in the past. As the day approached when David should arrive in England, he walked by himself continuously, oblivious of the world round him. He spoke to no one, save the wizened Elder Meacham, and to Elder Fairley, who rightly felt that he had a share in the making of Claridge Pasha.

With head perched in the air and face half hidden in his great white collar, the wizened Elder, stopping Luke Claridge in the street one day, said:

"Does thee think the lad will ride in Pharaoh's chariot here?"

There were sly lines of humor about the mouth of the wizened Elder as he spoke, but Luke Claridge did not see.

"Pride is far from his heart," he answered portentously. "He will ride in no chariot. He has written that he will walk here from Hedding on, and none is to meet him."

"He will come by the cross-roads, perhaps," rejoined the other piously. "Well, well, memory is a flower or a rod, as John Fox said, and the cross-roads have memories for him."

Again flashes of humor crossed his face, for he had a wide humanity, of insufficient exercise.

"He has made full atonement, and thee does ill to recall the past, Reuben," rejoined the other sternly.

"If he has done no more that needs atonement than he did that day at the cross-roads, then has his history been worthy of Hamley," rejoined the wizened Elder, eyes shut and head buried in his collar. "Hamley made him—Hamley made him. We did not spare advice, or example, or any correction that came to our minds—indeed, it was almost a luxury. Think you, does he still play the flute—an instrument none too grave, Luke?"

But, to this, Luke Claridge exclaimed impatiently and hastened on; and the little wizened Elder chuckled to himself all the way to the house of John Fairley. None in Hamley took such pride in David as did these two old men, who had loved him from a child, but had discreetly hidden their favor, save to each other. Many times they had met and prayed together in the weeks when his life was in notorious danger in the Soudan.

As David walked through the streets of Heddington making for the open country, he was conscious of a new feeling regarding the place. It was familiar, but in a new sense. Its grimy, narrow streets, unlovely houses, with shut windows, summer though it was, and no softening influences anywhere, save here and there a box of sickly geraniums in the windows, all struck his mind in a way they had never done before. A mile away were the green fields, the woods, the roadsides gay with flowers and shrubs—loveliness was but over the wall, as it were; yet here the barrack-like houses, the gray, harsh streets, seemed like prison walls, and the people in them prisoners who, with every legal right to call themselves free, were as much captives as the criminal on some small island in a dangerous sea. Escape—where? Into the gulf of no work and degradation?

They never lifted their eyes above the day's labor. They were scarce conscious of anything beyond. What were their pleasures? They had imitations of pleasures. To them a funeral or a wedding, a riot or a vociferous band, a dog-fight or a strike, were alike in this, that they quickened feelings which carried them out of themselves, gave them a sense of intoxication.

Intoxication? David remembered the far-off day of his own wild rebellion in Hamley. From that day forward he had better realized that in the hearts of so many of the human race there was a passion to forget themselves; to blot out, if for a moment only, the troubles of life and time; or, by creating a false air of exaltation, to rise above them. Once in the desert, when men were dying round him of fever and dysentery, he had been obliged, exhausted and ill, scarce able to drag himself from his bed, to resort to an opiate to allay his own sufferings, that he might minister to others. He remembered how, in the atmosphere it had created,—an intoxication, a soothing exhilaration and pervasive thrill—he had saved so many of his followers. Since then the temptation had come upon him often when trouble weighed or difficulties surrounded him—accompanied always by recurrence of fever—to resort to the insidious medicine. Though he had fought the temptation with every inch of his strength, he could too well understand those who sought for "surcease of pain"—

"Seeking for surcease of pain,
Pilgrim to Lethe I came;
Drank not, for pride was too keen
Stung by the sound of a name!"

As the plough of action had gone deep into his life and laid bare his nature to the light, there had been exposed things which struggled for life and power in him, with the fiery strength which only evil has.

The western heavens were aglow. On every hand the gorse and the may were in bloom, the lilacs were coming to their end, but wild rhododendrons were glowing in the bracken, as he stepped along the road towards the place where he was born. Though every tree and road-mark was familiar, yet he was conscious of a new outlook. He had left these quiet scenes inexperienced and untravelled, to be thrust suddenly into the thick of a struggle of nations over a sick land. He had worked in a vortex of debilitating local intrigue. All who had to do with Egypt gained except herself, and if she moved in revolt or agony, they threatened her. Once when resisting the pressure and the threats of war of a foreign diplomatist, he had, after a trying hour, written to Faith in a burst of passionate complaint, and his letter had ended with these words:

"In your onward march, O men,
White of face, in promise whiter,
You unsheath the sword, and then
Blame the wrongèd as the fighter!

"Time, ah, Time, rolls onward o'er
All these fœtid fields of evil,
While hard at the nation's core
Eats the burning rust and weevil!

"Nathless, out beyond the stars
Reigns the Wiser and the Stronger,
Seeing in all strifes and wars
Who the wrongèd, who the wronger."

Privately he had spoken thus, but before the world he had given way to no impulse, in silence finding safety from the temptation to diplomatic evasion. Looking back over five years, he felt now that the sum of his accomplishment had been small.

He did not realize the truth. When his hand was almost upon the object for which he had toiled and striven—whether pacifying a tribe, meeting a loan by honest means, building a barrage, irrigating the land, financing a new industry, or experimenting in cotton —it suddenly eluded him. Nahoum had snatched it away by subterranean wires. On such occasions Nahoum would shrug his shoulders, and say with a sigh, "Ah, my friend, let us begin again. We are both young; time is with us; and we will flourish palms in the face of Europe yet. We have our course set by a bright star. We will continue."

Yet, withal, David was the true altruist. Even now as he walked this road which led to his old home, dear to him beyond all else, his thoughts kept flying to the Nile and to the desert.

Suddenly he stopped. He was at the cross-roads. Here he had met Kate Heaver, here he had shamed his neighbors—and begun his work in life. He stood for a moment, smiling, as he looked at the stone where he had sat those years ago, his hand feeling instinctively for his flute. Presently he turned to the dusty road again.

Walking quickly away, he swung into the path of the wood which would bring him by a short cut to Hamley, past Soolsby's cottage. Here was the old peace, the old joy of solitude among the healing trees. Experience had broadened his life, had given him a vast theatre of work; but the smell of the woods, the touch of the turf, the whispering of the trees, the song of the birds, had the ancient entry to his heart.

At last he emerged on the hill where Soolsby lived. He had not meant, if he could help it, to speak to any one until he had entered the garden of the Red Mansion, but he had inadvertently come upon this place where he had spent the most momentous days of his life, and a feeling stronger than he cared to resist drew him to the open doorway. The afternoon sun was beating in over the threshold as he reached it, and, at his footstep, a figure started forward from the shadow of a corner.

It was Kate Heaver.

Surprise, then pain, showed in her face; she flushed, was agitated.

"I am sorry. It's too bad—it's hard on him you should see," she said in a breath, and turned her head away for an instant; but presently looked him in the face again, all trembling and eager. "He'll be sorry enough to-morrow," she added solicitously, and drew away from something she had been trying to hide.

Then David saw. On a bench against the wall lay old Soolsby—drunk. A cloud passed across his face and left it pale.

"Of course," he said simply, and went over and touched the heaving shoulders reflectively. "Poor Soolsby!"

"He's been sober four years—over four," she said eagerly. "When he knew you'd come again, he got wild, and he would have the drink in spite of all. Walking from Heddington, I saw him at the tavern, and brought him home."

"At the tavern—" David said reflectively.

"The Fox and Goose, sir." She turned her face away again, and David's head came up with a quick motion. There it was, five years ago, that he had drunk at the bar, and had fought Jasper Kimber.

"Poor fellow!" he said again, and listened to Soolsby's stertorous breathing, as a physician looks at a patient whose case he cannot control, does not wholly understand.

The hand of the sleeping man was suddenly raised, his head gave a jerk, and he said mumblingly, "Claridge forever!"

Kate nervously intervened. "It fair beat him, your coming back, sir. It's awful temptation, the drink. I lived in it for years, and it's cruel hard to fight it when you're worked up either way, sorrow or joy. There's a real pleasure in being drunk, I'm sure. While it lasts you're rich, and you're young, and you don't care what happens. It's kind of you to take it like this, sir, seeing you've never been tempted and mightn't understand."

David shook his head sadly, and looked at Soolsby in silence.

"I don't suppose he took a quarter what he used to take, but it made him drunk. 'Twas but a minute of madness. You've saved him right enough."

"I was not blaming him. I understand—I understand."

He looked at her clearly. She was healthy and fine-looking, with large, eloquent eyes. Her dress was severe and quiet, as became her occupation—a plain dark gray, but the shapely fulness of the figure gave softness to the outlines. It was no wonder Jasper Kimber wished to marry her; and, if he did, the future of the man was sure. She had a temperament which might have made her an adventuress—or an opera-singer. She had been touched in time, and she had never looked back.

"You are with Lady Eglington now, I have heard?" he asked.

She nodded.

"It was hard for you in London at first?"

She met his look steadily. "It was easy in a way. I could see round me what was the right thing to do. Oh, that was what was so awful in the old life over there at Heddington." She pointed beyond the hill. "We didn't know what was good and what was bad. The poor people in big working-places like Heddington ain't much better than heathens, leastways as to most things that matter. They haven't got a sensible religion, not one that gets down into what they do. The parson doesn't reach them — he talks about church and the sacraments, and they don't get at what good it's going to do them. And the chapel preachers ain't much better. They talk and sing and pray, when what the people want is light and hot water and soap, and being showed how to live, and how to bring up children healthy and strong, and decent-cooked food. I'd have food-hospitals if I could, and I'd give the children in the schools one good meal a day. I'm sure the children of the poor go wrong and bad more through the way they live than anything. If only they was taught right—not as though they was paupers! Give me enough nurses of the right sort, and enough good plain cooks, and meat three times a week, and milk and bread and rice and porridge every day, and I'd make a new place of any town in England in a year. I'd—"

She stopped all at once, however, and flushing, said, "I didn't stop to think I was talking to you, sir."

"I am glad you speak to me so," he answered gently. "You and I are both reformers at heart."

"Me? I've done nothing, sir, not any good to anybody or anything."

"Not to Jasper Kimber?"

"You did that, sir; he says so; he says you made him."

A quick laugh passed David's lips. "Men are not made so easily. I think I know the trowel and the mortar that built that wall! Thee will marry him, friend?"

Her eyes burned as she looked at him. She had been eternally dispossessed of what every woman has the right to have—one memory possessing the elements of beauty. Even if it remain but for the moment, yet that moment is hers by right of her sex, which is denied the wider rights of those they love and serve. She had tasted the cup of bitterness and drunk of the waters of sacrifice. Married life had no lure for her. She wanted none of it. The seed of service had, however, taken root in a nature full of fire and light and power, undisciplined and undeveloped as it was. She wished to do something—the spirit of toil, the first habit of the life of the poor, the natural medium for the good that may be in them, had possession of her.

This man was to her the symbol of work. To have cared for his home, to have looked after his daily needs, to have sheltered him humbly from little things, would have been her one true happiness. And this was denied her. Had she been a man, it had been so easy. She could have offered to be his servant; could have done those things which she could do better than any, since hers would be a heart-service.

But even as she looked at him now, she had a flash of insight and prescience. She had, from little things said or done, from newspapers marked and a hundred small indications, made up her mind that her mistress's mind dwelt much upon "the Egyptian." The thought flashed now that she might serve this man, after all; that a day might come when she could say that she had played a part in his happiness, in return for all he had done for her. Life had its chances—and strange things had happened. In her own mind she had decided that her mistress was not happy, and who could tell what might happen? Men did not live forever! The thought came and went, but it left behind a determination to answer David as she fel .

"I will not marry Jasper," she answered, slowly. "I want work, not marriage."

"There would be both," he urged.

"With women there is the one or the other, not both."

"Thee could help him. He has done credit to himself, and he can do good work for England. Thee can help him."

"I want work alone, not marriage, sir."

"He would pay thee his debt."

"He owes me nothing. What happened was no fault of his, but of the life we were born in. He tired of me, and left me. Husbands tire of their wives, but stay on and beat them."

"He drove thee mad almost, I remember!"

"Wives go mad and are never cured, so many of them. I've seen them die, poor things, and leave the little ones behind. I had the luck wi' me. I took the right turning at the cross-roads yonder."

"Thee must be Jasper's wife if he asks thee again," he urged.

"He will come when I call, but I will not call," she answered.

"But still thee will marry him when the heart is ready," he persisted. "It shall be ready soon. He needs thee. Good-bye, friend. Leave Soolsby alone. He will be safe. And do not tell him that I have seen him so." He stooped over and touched the old man's shoulder gently.

He held out his hand to her. She took it, then suddenly leaned over and kissed it. She could not speak.

He stepped to the door and looked out. Behind the Red Mansion the sun was setting, and the far garden looked cool and sweet. He gave a happy sigh, and stepped out and down.

As he disappeared, the woman dropped into a chair, her arms upon a table. Her body shook with sobs.

She sat there for an hour, and then, when the sun was

setting, she left the drunken man sleeping, and made her way down the hill to the Cloistered House.

Entering, she was summoned to her mistress's room.

"I did not expect my lady so soon," she said, surprised.

"No; we came sooner than we expected. Where have you been?"

"At Soolsby's hut on the hill, my lady."

"Who is Soolsby?"

Kate told her all she knew, and of what had happened that afternoon—but not all.

XXI

"THERE IS NOTHING HIDDEN WHICH SHALL NOT BE REVEALED"

A FORTNIGHT had passed since they had come to Hamley—David, Eglington, and Hylda—and they had all travelled a long distance in mutual understanding during that time, too far, thought Luke Claridge, who remained neutral and silent. He would not let Faith go to the Cloistered House, though he made no protest against David going; because he recognized in these visits the duty of diplomacy and the business of the nation—more particularly David's business, which, in his eyes, swallowed all. Three times David had gone to the Cloistered House; once Hylda and he had met in the road leading to the old mill, and once at Soolsby's hut. Twice, also, in the garden of his old home he had seen her, when she came to visit Faith, who had captured her heart at once. Eglington and Faith had not met, however. He was either busy in his laboratory, or with his books, or riding over the common and through the woods, and their courses lay apart.

But there came an afternoon when Hylda and David were a long hour together at the Cloistered House. They talked freely of his work in Egypt. At last she said, "And Nahoum Pasha?"

"He has kept faith."

"He is in high place again?"

"He is a good administrator."

"You put him there!"

"Thee remembers what I said to him, that night in Cairo?"

Hylda closed her eyes and drew in a long breath. Had there been a word spoken that night when she and David and Nahoum met which had not bitten into her soul! That David had done so much in Egypt without ruin or death was a tribute to his power. Nevertheless, though Nahoum had not struck yet, she was certain he would one day. All that David now told her of the vicissitudes of his plans, and Nahoum's sympathy and help, only deepened this conviction. She could well believe that Nahoum gave David money from his own pocket, which he replaced by extortion from other sources, while gaining credit with David for co-operation. Armenian Christian, Nahoum might be, but he was ranged with the East against the West, with the reactionary and corrupt against advance, against civilization and freedom and equality. Nahoum's Christianity was permeated with Orientalism, the Christian belief obscured by the theism of the Muslim. David was in a deadlier struggle than he knew. Yet it could serve no good end to attempt to warn him now. He had outlived peril so far, might it not be that, after all, he would win?

So far she had avoided Nahoum's name in talks with David. She could scarcely tell why she did, save that it opened a door better closed, as it were; but the restraint had given way at last.

"Thee remembers what I said that night?" David repeated slowly.

"I remember—I understand. You devise your course and you never change. It is like building on a rock. That is why nothing happens to you as bad as might happen."

"Nothing bad ever happens to me."

"The philosophy of the desert," she commented, smiling. "You are living in the desert even when you are here. This is a dream, the desert and Egypt only are real."

"That is true, I think. I seem sometimes like a sojourner here, like a spirit 'revisiting the scenes of life and time!'" He laughed boyishly.

"Yet you are happy here. I understand now why and how you are what you are. Even I that have been here so short a time feel the influence upon me. I breathe an air that, somehow, seems a native air. The spirit of my Quaker grandmother revives in me. Sometimes I sit hours thinking, scarcely stirring; and I believe I know now how people might speak to each other without words. Your Uncle Benn and you—it was so with you, was it not? You heard his voice speaking to you sometimes, you understood what he meant to say to you? You told me so, long ago."

David inclined his head. "I heard him speak as one might speak through a closed door. Sometimes, too, in the desert I have heard Faith speak to me."

"And your grandfather?"

"Never my grandfather—never. It would seem as though, in my thoughts, I could never reach him; as though masses of opaque things lay between. Yet he and I—there is love between us. I don't know why I never hear him."

"Tell me of your childhood, of your mother. I have seen her grave under the ash by the Meeting-house, but I want to know of her from you."

"Has not Faith told you?"

"We have only talked of the present. I could not ask her; but I can ask you. I want to know of your mother and you together."

"We were never together. When I opened my eyes she closed hers. It was so little to get for the life she gave. See, was it not a good face?" He drew from his pocket a little locket which Faith had given him years ago, and opened it before her.

Hylda looked long. "She was exquisite," she said, "exquisite."

"My father I never knew either. He was a captain of a merchant ship. He married her secretly while she was staying with an aunt at Portsmouth. He sailed away, my mother told my grandfather all, and he brought her home here. The marriage was regular, of course, but my grandfather, after announcing it, and bringing it before the Elders, declared that she should never see her husband again. She never did, for she died a few months after, when I came, and my father died very soon also. I never saw him, and I do not know if he ever tried to see me. I never had any feeling about it. My grandfather was the only father I ever knew, and Faith, who was born a year before me, became like a sister to me, though she soon made other pretensions!" He laughed again, almost happily. "To gain an end she exercised authority as my aunt!"

"What was your father's name?"

"Fetherdon—James Fetherdon."

"Fetherdon—James Fetherdon!" Involuntarily Hylda repeated the name after him. Where had she heard the name before—or where had she seen it? It kept flashing before her eyes. Where had she seen it? For days she had been rummaging among old papers in the library of the Cloistered House, and in an old box full of correspondence and papers of the late countess, who had died suddenly. Was it among them that she had seen the name? She could not tell. It was all vague, but that she had seen it or heard it she was sure.

"Your father's people, you never knew them?"

He shook his head. "Nor of them. Here was my

home—I had no desire to discover them. We draw in upon ourselves here."

"There is great force in such a life and such a people," she answered. "If the same concentration of mind could be carried into the wide life of the world, we might revolutionize civilization, or vitalize and advance it, I mean—as you are doing in Egypt."

"I have done nothing in Egypt. I have sounded the bugle—I have not had my fight."

"That is true in a sense," she replied. "Your real struggle is before you. I do not know why I say it, but I do say it; I feel it. Something here"—she pressed her hand to her heart—"something here tells me that your day of battle is yet to come." Her eyes were brimming and full of excitement. "We must all help you." She gained courage with each word. "You must not fight alone. You work for civilization; you must have civilization behind you." Her hands clasped nervously; there was a catch in her throat. "You remember—*then*, that I said I would call to you one day, as your Uncle Benn did, and you should hear and answer me. It shall not be that I will call. You—you will call, and I will help you if I can! I will help, no matter what may seem to prevent, if there is anything I can do. I, surely I, of all the world owe it to you to do what I can, always. I owe so much—you did so much. Oh, how it haunts me! Sometimes in the night I wake with a start and see it all—all!"

The flood which had been dyked back these years past had broken loose in her heart.

Out of the stir and sweep of social life and duty, of official and political ambition—heart-hungry, for she had no child; heart-lonely, though she had scarce recognized it in the duties and excitements round her—she had floated suddenly into this backwater of a motionless life in Hamley. Its quiet had settled upon her, the shackles of her spirit had been loosed, and dropped from her; she had suddenly bathed her heart and soul in a freer atmosphere than they had ever known before. And David and Hamley had come together. The old impulses, dominated by a divine altruism, were swinging her out upon a course leading she knew not, recked not, whither—for the moment recked not. This man's career, the work he was set to do, the ideal before him, the vision of a land redeemed, captured her, carried her panting into a resolve, which, however she might modify her speech or action, must be an influence in her life hereafter. Must the penance and the redemption be his only? This life he lived had come from what had happened to her and to him in Egypt. In a deep sense her life was linked with his.

In a flash David now felt the deep significance of their relations. A curtain seemed suddenly to have been drawn aside. He was blinded for a moment. Her sympathy, her desire to help, gave him a new sense of hope and confidence, but—but there was no room in his crusade for any woman; the dear egotism of a life-dream was masterful in him, possessed him.

Yet, if ever his heart might have dwelt upon a woman with thought of the future, this being before him —he drew himself up with a start! . . . He was going to Egypt again in a few days; they might probably never meet again — would not, no doubt — should not. He had pressed her husband to go to Egypt, but now he would not encourage it; he must "finish his journey alone."

He looked again in her eyes, and their light and beauty held him. His own eyes swam. The exaltation of a great idea was upon them, was a bond of fate between them. It was a moment of peril not fully realized by either. David did realize, however, that she was beautiful beyond all women he had ever seen—or was he now for the first time really aware of the beauty of woman? She had an expression, a light of eye and face, finely alluring beyond mere outline of feature. Yet the features were there, too, regular and fine; and her brown hair, waving away from her broad, white forehead over eyes a grayish violet in color, gave her a classic distinction. In the quietness of the face there was that strain of the Quaker, descending to her through three generations, yet enlivened by a mind of impulse and genius.

They stood looking at each other for a moment, in which both had taken a long step forward in life's experience. But presently his eyes looked beyond her, as though at something that fascinated them.

"Of what are you thinking? What do you see?" she asked.

"You, leaving the garden of my house in Cairo, I standing by the fire," he answered, closing his eyes for an instant.

"It is what I saw also," she said breathlessly. "It is what I saw and was thinking of that instant." When, as though she must break away from the cords of feeling drawing her nearer and nearer to him, she said with a little laugh, "Tell me again of my Chicago cousin? I have not had a letter for a year."

"Lacey, he is with me always. I should have done little had it not been for him. He has remarkable resource; he is never cast down. He had but one fault."

"What is that?"

"He is no respecter of persons. His humor cuts deep. He has a wide heart for your sex. When leaving the court of the King of Abyssinia he said to his Majesty, 'Well, good-bye, King. Give my love to the girls.'"

She laughed again. "How absurd and childish he is! But he is true. And how glad you should be that you are able to make true friends, without an effort. Yesterday I met neighbor Fairley, and another little old Elder who keeps his chin in his collar and his eyes on the sky. They did little else but sing your praises. One might have thought that you had invented the world — or Hamley."

"Yet they would chafe if I were to appear among them without these." He glanced down at the Quaker clothes he wore, and made a gesture towards the broad-brimmed hat reposing on a footstool near by.

"It is good to see that you are not changed, not spoiled at all," she remarked smiling. "Though, indeed, how could you be, who always work for others and never for yourself? All I envy you is your friends. You make them—and keep them so!"

She sighed, and a shadow came into her eyes suddenly. She was thinking of Eglington. Did he make friends—true friends? In London—was there one she knew who would cleave to him for love of him? In England—had she ever seen one? In Hamley, where his people had been for so many generations, had she found one?

Herself? Yes, she was his true friend. She would do—what would she not do to help him, to serve his interests? What had she not done since she married! Her fortune, it was his; her every waking hour had been filled with something devised to help him on his way. Had he ever said to her, "Hylda, you are a help to me"? He had admired her—but was he singular in that? Before she married there were many—since, there had been many—who had shown, some with tact and carefulness, others with a crudeness making her shudder, that they admired her; and, if they might, would have given their admiration another name with other manifestations. Had she repelled it all? She had been too sure of herself to draw her skirts about her; she was too proud to let any man put her at any disadvantage. She had been safe, because her heart had been untouched. The Duchess of Snowdon, once beautiful, but now with a face like a mask, enamelled and rouged and lifeless, had said to her once, "My dear, I ought to have died at thirty. When I was twenty-three I wanted to squeeze the orange dry in a handful of years, and then go out suddenly, and let the dust of forgetfulness cover my bones. I had one child, a boy, and would have no more; and I squeezed the orange! But I didn't go at thirty, and yet the orange was dry. My boy died; and you see what I am—a fright, I know it; and I dress like a child of twenty; and I can't help it!"

There had been moments, once, when Hylda too had wished to squeeze the orange dry, but something behind, calling to her, had held her back. She had dropped her anchor in perilous seas, but it had never dragged.

"Tell me how to make friends—and keep them," she added gayly.

"If it be true I make friends, thee taught me how," he answered, "for thee made me a friend, and I forget not the lesson."

She smiled. "Thee has learnt another lesson too well!" she answered brightly. "Thee must not flatter. It is not that which makes thee keep friends. Thee sees I also am speaking as they do in Hamley—am I not bold? I love grammarless speech."

"Then use it freely to-day, for this is farewell," he answered, not looking at her.

"This—is—farewell," she said slowly, vaguely. Why should it startle her so? "You are going so soon—where?"

"To-morrow to London, next week to Egypt."

She laid a hand upon herself, for her heart was beating violently. "Thee is not fair to give no warning—there is so much to say," she said in so low a tone that he could scarcely hear her. "There is the future, your work, what we are to do here to help. What am I to do?"

"SHE WATCHED HIM PASS THROUGH THE GARDEN"

"Thee will always be a friend to Egypt, I know," he answered. "She needs friends. Thee has a place where thee indeed can help."

"Will not right be done without my voice?" she asked, her eyes half closing. "There is the Foreign Office, and English policy, and the ministers, and—and Eglington. What need of me?"

He saw the thought had flashed into her mind that he did not trust her husband. "Thee knows and cares for Egypt, and knowing and caring make policy easier to frame," he rejoined.

Suddenly a wave of feeling went over her. He whose life had been flung into this field of labor by an act of her own, who should help him but herself?

But it all baffled her, hurt her, shook her. She was not free to help as she wished. Her life belonged to another; and he exacted the payment of tribute to the uttermost farthing. She was blinded by the thought. Yet she must speak. "I will come to Egypt—we will come to Egypt," she said quickly. "Eglington shall know, too; he shall understand. You shall have his help. You shall not work alone."

"Thee can work here," he said. "It may not be easy for Lord Eglington to come."

"You pressed it on him."

Their eyes met. She suddenly saw what was in his mind.

"You know best what will help you most," she added gently.

"You will not come?" he asked.

"I will not say I will not come—not ever," she answered firmly. "It may be I should have to come." Resolution was in her eyes. She was thinking of Nahoum. "I may have to come," she added after a pause, "to do right by you."

He read her meaning. "Thee will never come," he continued confidently. He held out his hand.

"Perhaps I shall see you in town," she rejoined, as her hand rested in his, and she looked away. "When do you start for Egypt?"

"To-morrow week, I think," he answered. "There is much to do."

"Perhaps we shall meet in town," she repeated. But they both knew they would not.

"Farewell," he said, and picked up his hat.

As he turned again, the look in her eyes brought the blood to his face, then it became pale. A new force had come into his life.

"God be good to thee," he said, and turned away.

She watched him leave the room and pass through the garden.

"David! David!" she said softly after him.

At the other end of the room her husband, who had just entered, watched her. He heard her voice, but did not hear what she said.

"Come, Hylda, and have some music," he said brusquely.

She scrutinized him calmly. His face showed nothing. His look was enigmatical.

"Chopin is the thing for me," he said, and opened the piano.

XXII

AS IN A GLASS DARKLY

It was very quiet and cool in the Quaker Meeting-house, though outside there was the rustle of leaves, the low din of the bees, the whistle of a bird, or the even tread of horses' hoofs as they journeyed on the London road. The place was full. For a half-hour the worshippers had sat voiceless. They were waiting for the spirit to move some one to speak. As they waited, a lady entered and glided into a seat. Few saw, and these gave no indication of surprise, though they were little used to strangers, and none of the name borne by this lady had entered the building for many years. It was Hylda.

At last the silence was broken. The wizened Elder, with eyes upon the ceiling and his long white chin like ivory on his great collar, began to pray, sitting where he was, his hands upon his knees. He prayed for all who wandered "into by and forbidden paths." He prayed for one whose work was as that of Joseph, son of Jacob; whose footsteps were now upon the sea, and now upon the desert; whose way was set among strange gods and divers heresies—"'*For there must also be heresies, that they which are approved may be made manifest among the weak.*'" A moment more, and then he added: "He hath been tried beyond his years; do Thou uphold his hands. Once with a goad did we urge him on, when in ease and sloth he was among us, but now he spurreth on his spirit and body in too great haste. O put Thy hand upon the bridle, Lord, that he ride soberly upon Thy business."

There was a longer silence now, but at last came the voice of Luke Claridge.

"Father of the fatherless," he said, "my days are as the sands in the hour-glass hastening to their rest; and my place will soon be empty. He goeth far, and I may not go with him. He fighteth alone, like him that strove with wild beasts at Ephesus; do Thou uphold him that he may bring a nation captive. And if a viper fasten on his hand, as chanced to Paul of old, give him grace to strike it off without hurt. O Lord, he is to me, Thy servant, as the one ewe lamb, let him be Thine when Thou gatherest for Thy vineyard!"

"*And if a viper fasten on his hand—!*" David passed his hand across his forehead and closed his eyes. The beasts at Ephesus he had fought, and he would fight them again — there was fighting enough to do in the land of Egypt. And the viper would fasten on his hand —it had fastened on his hand, and he had struck it off; but it would come again, the dark thing against which he had fought in the desert.

Their prayers had unnerved him, had got into that corner of his nature where youth and its irresponsibility loitered yet. For a moment he was shaken, and then looking into the faces of the Elders, said, "Friends, I go again upon paths that lead into the wilderness. I know not if I ever shall return. Howsoe'er that may be, I shall walk with firmer step because of all ye do for me."

He closed his eyes and prayed: "O God, I go into the land of ancient plagues and present pestilence. If it be Thy will, bring me home to this good land, when my task is done. If not, by Thy goodness let me be as a stone set by the wayside for others who come after;

and save me from the beast and from the viper. '*Thou art faithful, who wilt not suffer us to be tempted above that we are able; but wilt with the temptation also make a way of escape, that we may be able to bear it!*' "

He sat down, and all grew silent again; but suddenly some one sobbed aloud—sobbed, and strove to stay the sobbing, and could not, and, getting up, hastened towards the door.

It was Faith. David heard, and came quickly after her. As he took her arm gently, his eyes met those of Hylda. She rose and came out also.

"Will thee take her home?" he said huskily. "I can bear no more."

Hylda placed her arm round Faith, and led her out under the trees and into the wood. As they went, Faith looked back.

"Oh, forgive me, forgive me, Davy," she said softly.

Three lights burned in Hamley: one in the Red Mansion, one in the Cloistered House, and one in Soolsby's hut upon the hill. In the Red Mansion old Luke Claridge, his face pale with feeling, his white hair tumbling about, his head thrust forward, his eyes shining, sat listening, as Faith read aloud letters which Benn Claridge had written from the East many years before. One letter, written from Bagdad, he made her read twice. The faded sheet had in it the glow and glamour of the East; it was like a heart beating with life; emotion rose and fell in it like the waves of the sea. Once the old man interrupted Faith.

"Davy—it is as though Davy spoke. It is like Davy—both Claridge, both Claridge," he said. "But is it not like Davy? Davy is doing what it was in Benn's heart to do. Benn showed the way; Benn called, and Davy came."

He laid both hands upon his knees and raised his

eyes. "O Lord, I have sought to do according to Thy will," he whispered. He was thinking of a thing he had long hidden. Through many years he had had no doubt, no qualm; but, since David had gone to Egypt, some spirit of unquiet had worked in him. He had acted against the prayer of his own wife, lying in her grave—a quiet-faced woman, who had never crossed him, who had never shown a note of passion in all her life, save in one thing concerning David. Upon it, like some prophetess, she had flamed out. With the insight which only women have where children are concerned, she had told him that he would live to repent of what he had done. She had died soon after, and was laid beside the deserted young mother, whose days had budded and blossomed, and fallen like petals to the ground, while yet it was the spring.

Luke Claridge had understood neither, not his wife when she had said, "Thee should let the Lord do His own work, Luke," nor his dying daughter Mercy, whose last words had been, "With love and sorrow I have sowed; he shall reap rejoicing — my babe. Thee will set him in the garden in the sun, where God may find him—God will not pass him by. He will take him by the hand and lead him home." The old man had thought her touched by delirium then, though her words were but the parable of a mind fed by the poetry of life, by a shy spirit, to which meditation gave fancy and far-seeing. David had come by his idealism honestly. The half-mystical spirit of his Uncle Benn had flowed on to another generation through the filter of a woman's sad soul. It had come to David a pure force, a constructive and practical idealism.

Now, as Faith read, there were ringing in the old man's ears the words which David's mother had said before she closed her eyes and passed away: "*Set him in the garden in the sun, where God may find him—God will not pass him by.*" They seemed to weave themselves into the symbolism of Benn Claridge's letter, written from the hills of Bagdad.

"But," the letter continued, "the Governor passed by with his suite, the buckles of the harness of his horses all silver, his carriage shining with inlay of gold, his turban full of precious stones. When he had passed, I said to a shepherd standing by, 'If thou hadst all his wealth, shepherd, what wouldst thou do?' and he answered, 'If I had his wealth, I would sit on the south side of my house in the sun all day and every day.' To a messenger of the Palace, who must ever be ready night and day to run at his master's order, I asked the same. He replied, 'If I had all the Effendina's wealth, I would sleep till I died.' To a blind beggar, shaking the copper in his cup in the highways, pleading dumbly to those who passed, I made similar inquisition, and he replied, 'If the wealth of the exalted one were mine, I would sit on the mastaba by the bakehouse, and eat three times a day, save at Ramadan, when I would bless Allah the compassionate and merciful, and breakfast at sunset, with the flesh of a kid and a bowl of wine.' To a woman at the door of a tomb hung with relics of hundreds of poor souls in misery, who besought the buried saint to intercede for her with Allah, I made the same catechism, and she answered, 'Oh, effendi, if his wealth were mine, I would give my son what he has lost.' 'What has he lost, woman?' said I; and she answered, 'A little house with a garden, and a flock of ten goats, a cow and a dovecote, his inheritance of which he has been despoiled by one who carried a false debt 'gainst his dead father. And I said to her, 'But if thy wealth were as that of the ruler of the city, thy son would have no need of the little house and garden and the flock of goats, and a cow and a dovecote.' Whereupon she turned upon me in bitterness, and said: 'Were they not his own as the seed of his father? Shall not one cherish that which is his own, which cometh from seed to seed? Is it not the law?' 'But,' said I, 'if his wealth were thine, there would be herds of cattle, and flocks of sheep, and carpets spread, and the banquet-tables, and great orchards.' But she stubbornly shook her head. 'Where the eagle built shall not the young eagle nest? How should God meet me in the way and bless him who stood not by his birthright? The plot of ground was the lad's, and all that is thereon. I pray thee, mock me not!' God knows I did not mock her, for her words were wisdom. So did it work upon me that, after many days, I got for the lad his own again, and there he is happier, and his mother happier, than the Governor in his palace. Later I did learn some truths from the shepherd, the messenger, and the beggar, and the woman with the child; but chiefly from the woman and the child. The material value has no relation to the value each sets upon that which is his own. Behind this feeling lies the strength of the world. Here on this hill of Bagdad I am thinking these things. And, Luke, I would have thee also think on my story of the woman and the child. There is in it a lesson for thee."

When Luke Claridge first read this letter years before, he had put it from him sternly. Now he heard it with a soft emotion. He took the letter from Faith at last, and put it in his pocket. With no apparent relevancy, and laying his hand on Faith's shoulder, he said:

"We have done according to our conscience by Davy —God is our witness, so!"

She leaned her cheek against his hand, but did not speak.

In Soolsby's hut upon the hill David sat talking to the old chairmaker. Since his return he had visited the place several times, only to find Soolsby absent. The old man, on awaking from his drunken sleep, had been visited by a terrible remorse, and, whenever he had seen David coming, had fled into the woods. This evening, however, David came in the dark, and Soolsby was caught.

When David entered first, the old man broke down. He could not speak, but leaned upon the back of a chair, and though his lips moved, no sound came forth. But David took him by the shoulders and set him down, and laughed gently in his face, and at last Soolsby got voice and said:

"Egyptian! O Egyptian!"

Then his tongue was loosened and his eye glistened, and he poured out question after question, many pertinent, some whimsical, all frankly answered by David. But suddenly he stopped short, and his eyes sank before the other, who had laid a hand upon his knee.

"Oh, don't, Egyptian, don't! Don't have aught to do with me. I'm only a drunken swine. I kept sober four years, as she knows—as the Angel down yonder in the Red Mansion knows; but the day you came, going out to meet you, I got drunk — blind drunk. I had only been pretending al the time. I was being coaxed along—made believe I was a real man, I suppose. But I wasn't. I was a pillar of sand. When pressure came I just broke down—broke down, Egyptian. Don't be surprised if you hear me grunt. It's my natural speech. I'm a hog, a drink-swilling hog. I wasn't decent enough to stay sober till you had said 'Good day,' and 'How goes it, Soolsby?' I tried it on; it was no good. I began to live like a man, but I've slipped back into the ditch. You didn't know that, did you?"

David let him have his say, and then in a low voice said, "Yes, I knew thee had been drinking, Soolsby."

He started. "She told you—Kate Heaver—"

"She did not tell me. I came and found you here with her. You were asleep."

"A drunken sweep!" He spat upon the ground in disgust at himself.

"I ought never have come back here," he added. "It was no place for me. But it drew me. I didn't belong; but it drew me."

"Thee belongs to Hamley. Thee is an honor to Hamley, Soolsby."

Soolsby's eyes widened; the blurred look of rage and self-reproach in them began to fade away.

"Thee has made a fight, Soolsby, to conquer a thing that has had thee by the throat. There's no fighting like it. It means a watching every hour, every minute—thee can never take the eye off it. Some days it's easy, some days it's hard, but it's never so easy that you can say, 'There is no need to watch.' In sleep it whispers and wakes you; in the morning, when there are no shadows, it casts a shadow on the path. It comes between you and your work; you see it looking out of the eyes of a friend. And one day, when you think it has been conquered, that you have worn it down into oblivion and the dust, and you close your eyes and say, 'I am master,' up it springs with fury from nowhere you can see, and catches you by the throat; and the fight begins again. But you sit stronger, and the fight becomes shorter; and after many battles, and you have learned never to be off guard, to know by instinct where every ambush is, then at last the victory is yours. But it is hard, it is bitter, and sometimes it seems hardly worth the struggle! But it is—it is worth the struggle, dear old man."

Soolsby dropped on his knees and caught David by the arms. "How did you know—how did you know?" he asked hoarsely. "It's been just as you say. You've watched some one fighting?"

"I have watched some one fighting—fighting," answered David clearly, but his eyes were moist.

"With drink, the same as me?"

"No, with opium—laudanum."

"Oh, I've heard that's worse, that it makes you mad, the wanting it."

"I have seen it so."

"Did the man break down like me?"

"Only once, but the fight is not yet over with him."

"Was he—an Englishman?"

David inclined his head. "It's a great thing to have a temptation to fight, Soolsby. Then we can understand others."

"It's not always true, Egyptian, for you have never had temptation to fight. Yet you know it all."

"God has been good to me," David answered, putting a hand on the old man's shoulder. "And thee is a credit to Hamley, friend. Thee will never fall again."

"You know that—you say that to me! Then, by Mary the mother of God, I never will be a swine again," he said, getting to his feet.

"Well, good-bye, Soolsby. I go to-morrow," David said presently.

Soolsby frowned; his lips worked. "When will you come back?" he asked eagerly.

David smiled. "There is so much to do, they may not let me come—not soon. I am going into the desert again."

Soolsby was shaking. He spoke huskily. "Here is your place," he said. "You shall come back— Oh, but you shall come back, here, where you belong."

David shook his head and smiled, and clasped the strong hand again. A moment later he was gone.

From the door of the hut Soolsby muttered to himself:

"I will bring you back. If Luke Claridge doesn't, then

I will bring you back. If he dies, I will bring you—no, by the love of God, I will bring you back while he lives!"

Two thousand miles away, in a Nile village, women sat wailing in dark doorways, dust on their heads, black mantles covering their faces. By the pond where all the people drank, performed their ablutions, bathed their bodies and rinsed their mouths, sat the sheikh-el-beled, the village chief, taking counsel in sorrow with the barber, the holy man, and others. Now speaking, now rocking their bodies to and fro, in the evening sunlight, they sat and watched the Nile in flood covering the wide wastes of the Fayoum, spreading over the land rich deposits of earth from the mountains of Abyssinia. When that flood subsided there would be fields to be planted with dourha and onions and sugar-cane; but they whose strong arms should plough and sow and wield the sickle, the youth, the upstanding ones, had been carried off in chains to serve in the army of Egypt, destined for the far Soudan, for hardship, misery, and death, never to see their kindred any more. Twice during three months had the dread servant of the Palace come and driven off their best like sheep to the slaughter. The brave, the stalwart, the bread-winners were gone; and yet the tax-gatherer would come and press for every impost—on the onion-field, the date-palm, the dourha-field, and the clump of sugar-cane, as though the young men, the toilers, were still there. The old and infirm, the children, the women, must now double and treble their labor. The old men must go to the *corvée*, and mend the banks of the Nile for the Prince and his pashas, providing their own food, their own tools, their own housing, if housing there would be—if it was more than sleeping under a bush by the riverside, or crawling into a hole in the ground, their yeleks their clothes by day, their only covering at night.

They sat like men without hope, yet with the proud, bitter mien of those who had known good and had lost it, had seen content and now were desolate.

Presently one—a lad — the youngest of them, lifted up his voice and began to chant a recitative, while another took a small drum and beat it in unison. He was but just recovered from an illness, or he had gone also in chains to die for he knew not what, leaving behind without hope all that he loved—

"How has the cloud fallen, and the leaf withered on the tree,
The lemon-tree, that standeth by the door.
The melon and the date have gone bitter to the taste,
The weevil, it has eaten at the core—
The core of my heart, the mildew findeth it.
My music, it is but the drip of tears,
The garner empty standeth, the oven hath no fire,
Night filleth me with fears.
O Nile that floweth deeply, hast thou not heard his voice?
His footsteps hast thou covered with thy flood?
He was as one who lifteth up the yoke,
He was as one who taketh off the chain,
As one who sheltereth from the rain,
As one who scattereth bread to the pigeons flying.
His purse was at his side, his mantle was for me,
For any who passeth were his mantle and his purse,
And now like a gourd is he withered from our eyes.
His friendship, it was like a shady wood—
Whither has he gone?—Who shall speak for us?
Who shall save us from the kourbash and the stripes?
Who shall proclaim us in the palace?
Who shall contend for us in the gate?
The sakkia turneth no more; the oxen they are gone;
The young go forth in chains, the old waken in the night,
They waken and weep, for the wheel turns backward,
And the dark days are come again upon us—
Will he return no more?
His friendship was like a shady wood,
O Nile that floweth deeply, hast thou not heard his voice?
Hast thou covered up his footsteps with thy flood?
The core of my heart, the mildew findeth it!"

Another—an old man—took up the strain, as the drum kept time to the beat of the voice with its undulating call and refrain—

"When his footsteps were among us there was peace;
War entered not the village, nor the call of war.
Now our homes are as those that have no roofs.
As a nest decayed, as a cave forsaken,
As a ship that lieth broken on the beach,
Is the house where we were born.
Out in the desert did we bury our gold,
We buried it where no man robbed us, for his arm was strong.
Now, are the jars empty, gold did not avail
To save our young men, to keep them from the chains.
God hath swallowed his voice, or the sea hath drowned it,
Or the Nile hath covered him with its flood;
Else would he come when our voices call.
His word was honey in the prince's ear—
Will he return no more?"

And now the sheikh-el-beled spoke. "It hath been so since Nahoum Pasha passed this way four months agone. He hath changed all. War will not avail. David Pasha, he will come again. His word is as the centre of the world. Ye have no hope, because ye see the hawks among the starving sheep. But the shepherd will return from behind the hill, and the hawks will flee away. . . . Behold, once was I in the desert. Listen, for mine are the words of one who hath travelled far—was I not at Damascus and Palmyra and Bagdad, and at Mecca by the tomb of Mahomet?"

Reverently he touched the green turban on his head, evidence of his journey to Mahomet's tomb. "Once in the desert I saw afar off an oasis of wood and water, and flying things, and houses where a man might rest. And I got me down from my camel, and knelt upon my sheepskin, and gave thanks in the name of Allah. Thereupon I mounted again and rode on towards that goodly place. But as I rode it vanished from my sight. Then did I mourn. Yet once again I saw the trees, and flocks of pigeons and waving fields, and I was hungry and thirsty, and longed exceedingly. Yet got I down, and, upon my sheepskin, once more gave thanks to Allah. And I mounted thereafter in haste and rode on; but once again was I mocked. Then I cried aloud in my despair. It was in my heart to die upon the sheepskin where I had prayed; for I was burned up within, and there seemed naught to do but say malaish, and go hence. But that goodly sight came again. My heart rebelled that I should be so mocked. I bent down my head upon my camel that I might not see, yet once more I loosed the sheepskin. Lifting up my heart, I looked again, and again I took hope and rode on. Farther and farther I rode, and lo! I was no longer mocked; for I came to a goodly place of water and trees, and was saved. So shall it be with us. We have looked for his coming again, and our hearts have fallen and been as ashes, for that he has not come. Yet there be mirages, and one day soon David Pasha will come hither, and our pains shall be eased."

"*Aiwa*, *aiwa*—yes, yes," cried the lad who had sung to them.

"*Aiwa*, *aiwa*," rang softly over the pond, where naked children stooped to drink.

The smell of the cooking-pots floated out from the mud-houses near by.

"Malaish " said one after another, "I am hungry. He will come again—perhaps to-morrow." So they moved towards the houses over the way.

One cursed his woman for wailing in the doorway; one snatched the lid from a cooking-pot; one drew from an oven cakes of dourha and gave them to those who had none; one knelt and bowed his forehead to the ground in prayer; one shouted the name of him whose coming they desired.

So was David missed in Egypt.

XXIII

THE TENTS OF CUSHAN

"*I saw the tents of Cushan in affliction, and the curtains of the Land of Midian did tremble.*"

A HURDY-GURDY was standing at the corner, playing with shrill insistence a medley of Scottish airs. Now "Loch Lomond" pleaded for pennies from the upper windows:

"For you'll tak' the high road, and I'll tak' the low road,
And I'll be in Scotland before ye:
But I and my true love will never meet again,
On the bonnie, bonnie banks of Loch Lomond!"

The hurdy-gurdy was strident and insistent, but for a long time no response came. At last, however, as the strains of "Loch Lomond" ceased, a lady appeared on the balcony of a drawing-room, and, leaning over a little forest of flowers and plants, threw a half-crown to the sorry street musician. She watched the grotesque thing trundle away, then entering the house again, took a 'cello from the corner of the room and tuned the instrument tenderly. It was Hylda.

Something of the peace of Hamley had followed her to London, but the poignant pain of it had come also. Like Melisande, she had looked into the quiet pool of life, and had seen her own face, its story and its foreshadowings. Since then she had been "apart." She had watched life move on rather than shared in its movement. Things stood still for her. That apathy of soul was upon her which follows the inward struggle that exhausts the throb and fret of inward emotions, leaving the mind dominant, the will in abeyance.

She had become conscious that her fate and future were suspended over a chasm, as on the trapeze of a balloon, an adventurous aeronaut hangs uncertain over the hungry sea, waiting for the coming wind which will either blow the hazardous vessel to its doom or to safe refuge on the land.

She had not seen David after he left Hamley. Their last words had been spoken at the Meeting-house when he gave Faith to her care. That scene came back to her now, and a flush crept slowly over her face and faded away again. She was recalling, too, the afternoon of that day when she and David had parted in the drawing-room of the Cloistered House, and Eglington had asked her to sing. She thought of the hours with Eglington that followed, first at the piano, and afterwards in the laboratory, where in his long blue smock he made experiments. Had she not been conscious of something enigmatical in his gaiety that afternoon, in his cheerful yet cheerless words, she would have been deeply impressed by his appreciation of her playing, and his keen reflections on the merits of the composers; by his still keener attention to his subsequent experiments, and his amusing comments upon them. But, somehow, that very cheerless cheerfulness seemed to proclaim him superficial. Though she had no knowledge of science, she instinctively doubted his earnestness even in this work, which certainly was not pursued for effect. She had put the feeling from her, but it kept returning. She felt that in nothing did he touch the depths. Nothing could possess him wholly; nothing inherent could make him self-effacing.

Yet she wondered, too, if she was right, when she saw his fox-terrier watching him, ever watching him with his big brown eyes as he buoyantly worked, and saw him stoop to pat its head. Or was this, after all, mere animalism, mere superficial vitality, love of health and being? She shuddered, and shut her eyes, for it came home to her that to him she was just such a being of health, vitality, and comeliness, on a little higher plane. She put the thought from her, but it had had its birth, and it would not down. He had immense vitality, he was tireless, and abundant in work and industry; he went from one thing to another with ease and swiftly changing eagerness. Was it all mere force—mere man and mind? Was there no soul behind it? There in the laboratory she had laid her hand on the terrier, and prayed in her heart that she might understand him—for her own good, her own happiness, and his. Above all else she wanted to love him truly, and to be loved truly, and duty was to her a daily sacrifice, a constant memorial. She realized to the full that there lay before her a long race unilluminated by the sacred lamp which, lighted at the altar, should still be burning beside the grave.

Now, as she thought of him, she kept saying to herself, "We should have worked out his life together. Work together would have brought peace. He shuts me out. He shuts me out."

At last she drew the bow across the instrument, once, twice, and then she began to play, forgetful of the world. She had a contralto voice, and she sang with a depth of feeling and a delicate form worthy of a professional; on the piano she was effective and charming, but into the 'cello she poured her soul.

For quite an hour she played with scarce an interruption. At last, with a sigh, she laid the instrument against her knee and gazed out of the window. As she sat lost in her dream—a dream of the desert—a servant entered with letters. One caught her eye. It was from Egypt—from her cousin Lacey! Her heart throbbed violently, yet she opened the official-looking envelope with steady fingers. She would not admit even to herself that news from the desert could move her so. She began to read slowly, but presently, with a little cry, she hastened through the pages. It ran:

"THE SOUDAN.

"DEAR LADY COUSIN,—I'm still not certain how I ought to style you, but I thought I'd compromise as per above. Anyway, it's a sure thing that I haven't bothered you much with country-cousin letters. I figure, however, that you've put some money in Egypt, so to speak, and what happens to this sandy-eyed foundling of the Nile you would like to know. So I've studied the only 'complete letter-writer' I could find between the tropic of Capricorn and Khartoum, and this is the contemptible result, as the dagos in Mexico say. This is a hot place by reason of the sun that shines above us, and likewise it is hot because of the niggers that swarm around us. I figure, if we get out of this portion of the African continent inside our skins, that we will have put up a pretty good bluff, and pulled off a ticklish proposition.

"It's a sort of early Christian business. You see, David the Saadat is great on moral suasion—he's a master of it; and he's never failed yet—not altogether; though there have been minutes by a stop-watch when I've thought it wouldn't stand the strain—like the Mississippi steamboat which was so weak that when the whistle blew the engines stopped! When those frozen minutes have come to us, I've tried to remember the correct religious etiquette, but I've not had much practice since I stayed with Aunt Melissa, and lived on skim-milk and early piety. When things were looking as bad as they did for Dives, 'Now I lay me down to sleep,' and 'For what we are about to receive,' was all that I could think of. But the Saadat, he's a wonder from Wondertown. With a little stick, or maybe his flute under his arm, he'll smile and string these heathen along, when you'd think they weren't waiting for anybody. A spear took off his fez yesterday. He never blinked—he's a jim-dandy at keeping cool; and when a hundred mounted heathens made a rush down on him the other day, spears sticking out like quills on a porcupine—2.5 on the shell-road the chargers were going—did he stir? Say, he watched 'em as if they were playing for his benefit. And sure enough, he was right. They parted either side of him when they were ten feet away, and there he was quite safe, a blessing in the storm, a little rock island in the rapids—but I couldn't remember a proper hymn of praise to say.

"There's no getting away from the fact that he's got a will or something, a sort of force different from most of us, or perhaps any of us. These heathen feel it, and keep their hands off him. They say he's mad, but they've got great respect for mad people, for they think that God has got their souls above with Him, and that what's left behind on earth is sacred. He talks to 'em, too, like a father in Israel; tells 'em they must stop buying and selling slaves, and that if they don't he will have to punish them! And I sit holding my sides, for we're only two white men and forty 'friendlies' altogether, and two revolvers among us; and I've got the two! And they listen to his blarneying, and say, '*Aiwa, Saadat! aiwa, Saadat!*' as if he had an army of fifty thousand behind him. Sometimes I've sort of hinted that his canoe was carrying a lot of sail; but my! he believes in it all as if there wasn't a spear or a battle-axe or a rifle within a hundred miles of him. We've been at this for two months now, and a lot of ground we covered till we got here. I've ridden the gentle camel at the rate of sixty and seventy miles a day—sort of sweeping through the land, making treaties, giving presents, freeing slaves, appointing governors and sheikhs-el-beled, doing it as if we owned the continent. He mesmerized 'em, simply mesmerized 'em—till we got here. I don't know what happened then. Now we're distinctly rating low, the laugh is on us somehow. But he—mind it? He goes about talking to the sheikhs as though we were all eating off the same corn-cob, and it seems to stupefy them; they don't grasp it. He goes on arranging for a post here and a station there, and it never occurs to him that it ain't really actual. He doesn't tell me, and I don't ask him, for I came along to wipe his stirrups, so to speak. I put my money on him, and I'm not going to worry him. He's so dead certain in what he does, and what he is, that I don't lose any sleep guessing about him. It will be funny if we do win out on this proposition—funnier than anything.

"Now, there's one curious thing about it all which ought to be whispered, for I'm only guessing, and I'm not a good guesser; I guessed too much in Mexico about three railways and two silver-mines. The first two days after we came here, everything was all right. Then there came an Egyptian, Halim Bey, with a handful of niggers from Cairo, and letters for Claridge Pasha. From that minute there was trouble. I figure it out this way: Halim was sent by Nahoum Pasha to bring letters that said one thing to the Saadat, and, when quite convenient, to say other things to Mustafa, the boss sheikh of this settlement. Halim Bey has gone again, but he has left his tale behind him. I'd stake all I lost, and more than I ever expect to get out of Mexico on that, and maybe I'll get a hatful out of Mexico yet! I had some good mining propositions down there. The Saadat believes in Nahoum, and has made Nahoum what he is; and on the surface Nahoum pretends to help him; but he is running underground all the time. I'd like to help give him a villa at Fazougli. When the Saadat was in England there was a bad time in Egypt. I was in Cairo; I know. It was the same bad old game—the *corvée*, the kourbash, conscription, a war manufactured to fill the pockets of a few, while the poor starved and died. It didn't come off, because the Saadat wasn't gone long enough, and he stopped it when he came back. But Nahoum—he laid the blame on others, and the Saadat took his word for it, and, instead of a war, there came this expedition of his own.

"*Ten days later.*—Things have happened. First, there's been awful sickness among the natives, and the Saadat has had his chance. His medicine-chest was loaded,—he had a special camel for it—and he has fired it off. Night and day he has worked, never resting, never sleeping, curing most, burying a few. He looks like a ghost now, but it's no use saying or doing anything. He says, 'Sink your own will; let it be subject to a higher, and you need take no thought.' It's eating away his life and strength, but it has given us our return tickets, I guess. They hang about him as if he was Moses in the wilderness smiting the rock. It's his luck. Just when I get scared to death, and run down, and want a tonic, and it looks as if there'd be no need to put out next week's washing, then his luck steps in, and we get another run. But it takes a heap out of a man, getting scared. Whenever I look on a lot of green trees and cattle and horses, and the sun, to say nothing of women and children, and listen to music, or feel a horse eating up the ground under me, 2.10 in the sand, I hate to think of leaving it, and I try to prevent it. Besides, I don't like the proposition of going, I don't know where. That's why I get scared. But he says that it's no more than turning down the light and turning it up again.

"They used to call me a dreamer in Mexico, because

I kept seeing things that no one else had thought of, and laid out railways and tapped mines for the future; but I was nothing to him. I'm a high-and-dry hedge-clipper alongside. I'm betting on him all the time; but no one seems to be working to make his dreams come true, except himself. I don't count; I'm no good, no real good. I'm only fit to run the commissariat, and see that he gets enough to eat, and has a safe camel, and so on. Why doesn't some one else help him? He's working for humanity. Give him half a chance, and Haroun-al-Raschid won't be in it. Kaïd trusts him, depends on him, stands by him, but doesn't seem to know how to help him when help would do most good. The Saadat does it all himself; and if it wasn't that the poor devil of a fellah sees what he's doing, and cottons to him, and the dervishes and Arabs *feel* he's right, he might as well leave. But it's just there he counts. There's something about him, something that's Quaker in him, primitive, silent, and perceptive—if that's a real word—which makes them feel that he's honest, and isn't after anything for himself. Arabs don't talk much; they make each other understand without many words. They think with all their might on one thing at a time, and they think things into happening—and so does he. He's a thousand years old, which is about as old-fashioned as I mean, and as wise, and as plain to read as though you'd write the letters of words as big as a date-palm. That's where he makes the running with them, and they can read their title clear to mansions in the skies!

"You should hear him talk with Ebn Ezra Bey—perhaps you don't know of Ezra? He was a friend of his Uncle Benn, and brought the news of his massacre to England, and came back with the Saadat. Well, three days ago Ebn Ezra came, and there came with him, too, Halim Bey, the Egyptian, who had brought the letters to us from Cairo. Ebn Ezra found him down the river deserted by his niggers, and sick with this new sort of fever, which the Saadat is knocking out of time. And there he lies, the Saadat caring for him as though he was his brother. But that's his way; though, now I come to think of it, the Saadat doesn't suspect what I suspect, that Halim Bey brought word from Nahoum to our sheikhs here to keep us here, or lose us, or do away with us. Old Ebn Ezra doesn't say much himself, doesn't say anything about *that;* but he's guessing the same as me. And the Saadat looks as though he was ready for his grave, but keeps going, going, going. He never seems to sleep. What keeps him alive I don't know. Sometimes I feel clean knocked out myself with the little I do, but he's a travelling hospital all by his lonesome.

"*Later.*—I had to stop writing, for things have been going on—several. I can see that Ebn Ezra has told the Saadat things that make him want to get away to Cairo as soon as possible. That it's Nahoum Pasha and others—oh, plenty of others, of course—I'm certain; but what the particular game is I don't know. Perhaps you know over in England, for you're nearer Cairo than we are by a few miles, and you've got the telegraph. Perhaps there's a revolution, perhaps there's been a massacre of Europeans, perhaps Turkey is kicking up a dust, perhaps Europe is interfering—all of it, all at once.

"*Later still.*—I've found out it's a little of all, and the Saadat is ready to go. I guess he can go now pretty soon, for the worst of the fever is over. But something has happened that's upset him—knocked him stony for a minute. Halim Bey was killed last night—by order of the sheikhs, I'm told; but the sheikhs won't give it away. When the Saadat went to them, his eyes blazing, his face pale as a sheet, and as good as swore at them, and treated them as though he'd string them up the next minute, they only put their hands on their heads, and said they were 'the fallen leaves for his foot to scatter,' the 'snow on the hill for his breath to melt'; but they wouldn't give him any satisfaction. So he came back and shut himself up in his tent, and he sits there like a ghost all shrivelled up for want of sleep, and his eyes like a lime-kiln burning; for now he knows this at least, that Halim Bey had brought some word from Kaïd's Palace that set these Arabs against him, and nearly stopped my correspondence. You see, there's a widow in Cairo—she's a sister of the American consul, and I've promised to take her with a party camping in the Fayoum—cute as she can be, and plays the guitar! But it's all right now, except that the Saadat is running too close and fine. If he has any real friends in England among the Government people, or among those who can make the Government people sit up, and think what's coming to Egypt and to him, they'll help him now when he needs it. He'll need help real bad when he gets back to Cairo—if we get that far. It isn't yet a sure thing, for we've got to fight in the next day or two—I forgot to tell you that sooner. There's a bull-Arab on the rampage with five thousand men, and he's got a cla m out on our sheikh, Mustafa, for ivory he has here, and there's going to be a scrimmage. We've got to make for a better position to-morrow, and meet Abdullah, the bull-Arab, further down the river. That's one reason why Mustafa and all our friends here are so sweet on us now. They look on the Saadat as a kind of mascot, and they think that he can wipe out the enemy with his flute, which they believe is a witch-stick to work wonders.

"He's just sent for me to come, and I must stop soon. Say, he hasn't had sleep for a fortnight. It's too much; he can't stand it. I tried it, and couldn't. He wore me down. He's killing himself for others. I can't manage him; but I guess you could. I apologize, dear Lady

Cousin. I'm only a hayseed, and a failure, but I guess you'll understand that I haven't thought only of myself as I wrote this letter. The higher *you* go in life the more *you'll* understand; that's your nature. I'll get this letter off by a nigger to-morrow, with those the Saadat is sending through to Cairo by some friendlies. It's only a chance; but everything's chance here now. Anyhow, it's safer than leaving it till the scrimmage. If you get this, won't you try and make the British Government stand by the Saadat? Your husband, the lord, could pull it off, if he tried; and if you ask him, I guess he'd try. I must be off now. David Pasha will be waiting. Well, give my love to the girls!

"Your affectionate cousin,

"TOM LACEY.

"P. S.—I've got a first-class camel for our scrimmage day after to-morrow. Mustafa sent it to me this morning. I had a fight on mules once, down at Oaxaca, but that was child's play. This will be 'slaughter in the pan,' if the Saadat doesn't stop it somehow. Perhaps he will. If I wasn't so scared I'd wish he couldn't stop it, for it will be a way-up Barbarian scrap, the tongs and the kettle, a bully panjandrum. It gets mighty dull in the desert when you're not moving. But 'it makes to think,' as the French say. Since I came out here I've had several real centre thoughts, sort of main principles—key-thoughts, that's it. What I want now is a sort of safety-ring to string 'em on and keep 'em safe; for I haven't a good memory, and I get mighty rattled sometimes. Thoughts like these are like the secret of a combination-lock; they let you into the place where the gold and securities and title-deeds of life are. Trouble is, I haven't got a safety-ring, and I'm certain to lose them. I haven't got what you'd call an intellectual memory. Things come in flashes to me out of experiences, and pull me up short, and I say, 'Yes, that's it—*that's* it; I understand!' I see why it's so, and what it means, and where it leads, and how far it spreads. It's five thousand years old. Adam thought it after Cain killed Abel, or Abel thought it just before he died, or Eve learned it from Lilith, or it struck Abraham when he went to sacrifice Isaac. Sometimes things hit me deep like that here in the desert. Then I feel I can see just over on the horizon the tents of Moab in the wilderness; that yesterday and to-day are the same; that I've crossed the prairies of the everlasting years, and am playing about with Ishmael in the wild hills, or fighting with Ahab. Then the world and time seem pretty small potatoes.

"You see how it is. I never was trained to think, and I get stunned by thoughts that strike me as being dug right out of the centre. Sometimes I'd like to write them down; but I can't write; I can only talk as I'm talking to you. If you weren't so high up, and so much cleverer than I am, and such a thinker, I'd like you to be my safety-ring, if you would. I could tell the key-thoughts to you when they came to me, before I forgot them with all their bearings; and by and by they'd do me a lot of good when I got away from this influence, and back into the machinery of the Western world again. If you could come out here, if you could feel what I feel here—and you would feel a thousand times as much—I don't know what you wouldn't do! It's pretty wonderful. The nights with the stars so white and glittering, and so near that you'd think you could reach up and hand them down; the dark, deep blue beyond; such a width of life all round you, a sort of never-ending space, that everything you ever saw or did seems little, and God so great in a kind of hovering sense like a pair of wings; and all the secrets of time coming out of it all, and sort of touching your face like a velvet wind. I expect you'll think me sentimental, a first-class squash out of the pumpkin-garden; but it's in the desert, and it gets into you and saturates you, till you feel that this is a kind of middle space between the world of cities, and factories, and railways, and tenement-houses, and the quiet world to come — a place where they think out things for the benefit of future generations, and convey them through incarnations, or through the desert. Say, your ladyship, I'm a chatterer, I'm a two-cent philosopher, I'm a baby; but you are too much like your grandmother, who was the daughter of a Quaker like David Pasha, to laugh at me.

"I've got a suit of fine chain-armor which I bought of an Arab down by Darfûr. I'm wondering if it would be too cowardly to wear it in the scrap that's coming. I don't know, though, but what I'll wear it, I get so scared. But it will be a frightful hot thing under my clothes, and it's hot enough without that, so I'm not sure. It depends how much my teeth chatter when I see 'the dawn of battle.'

"I've got one more thing before I stop. I'm going to send you a piece of poetry which the Saadat wrote, and tore in two, and threw away. He was working off his imagination, I guess, as you have to do out here. I collected it and copied it, and put in the punctuation—he didn't bother about that. Perhaps he can't punctuate. I don't understand quite what the poetry means, but maybe you will. Anyway, you'll see that it's a real desert piece. Here it is:

THE DESERT ROAD

"In the sands I lived in a hut of palm,
There was never a garden to see;
There was never a path through the desert calm,
Nor a way through its storms for me.

"Tenant was I of a lone domain;
The far pale caravans wound
To the rim of the sky, and vanished again;
My call in the waste was drowned.

"The vultures came and hovered and fled;
And once there stole to my door
A white gazelle, but its eyes were dread
With the hurt of the wounds it bore.

"It passed in the dusk with a foot of fear,
And the white cold mists rolled in;
And my heart was the heart of a stricken deer,
Of a soul in the snare of sin.

"My days they withered like rootless things,
And the sands rolled on, rolled wide;
Like a pelican I, with broken wings,
Like a drifting barque on the tide.

"But at last, in the light of a rose-red day,
In the windless glow of the morn,
From over the hills and from far away,
You came—ah, the joy of the morn!

"And wherever your footsteps fell, there crept
A path—it was fair and wide:
A desert-road which no sands have swept,
Where never a hope has died.

"I followed you forth, and your beauty held
My heart like an ancient song;
By that desert road to the blossoming plains
I came—and the way was long!

"So I set my course by the light of your eyes;
I care not what fate may send;
On the road I tread shine the love-starred skies—
The road with never an end.

"Not many men can do things like that, and the other things, too, that he does. Perhaps he will win through, by himself, but is it fair to have him run the risk? If he ever did you a good turn, as you once said to me he did, won't you help him now? You are on the inside of political things, and if you make up your mind to help, nothing will stop you—that was your grandmother's way. He ought to get his backing pretty soon, or it won't be any good. . . . I hear him at his flute. I expect he's tired waiting for me. Well, give my love to the girls!

"T. L."

As Hylda read, she passed through phases of feeling begotten of new understanding which shook her composure. She had seen David and all that David was doing; Egypt, and all that was threatening the land through the eyes of another who told the whole truth—except about his own cowardice, which was untrue. She felt the issues at stake. While the mention of David's personal danger left her sick for a moment, she saw the wider peril also to the work he had set out to do.

What was the thing without the man? It could not exist—it had no meaning. Where was he now? What had been the end of the battle? He had saved others, had he saved himself? The most charmed life must be pierced by the shaft of doom sooner or later; but he was little more than a youth yet, he had only just begun!

"*And the Saadat looks as if he was ready for his grave—and he keeps going, going, going!*" The words kept ringing in her ears. Again: "*And he sits there like a ghost all shrivelled up for want of sleep, and his eyes like a lime-kiln burning. . . . He hasn't had sleep for a fortnight. . . . He's killing himself for others.*"

Her own eyes were shining with a dry, hot light, her lips were quivering, but her hands upon the letter were steady and firm. What could she do?

She went to a table, picked up the papers, and scanned

them hurriedly. Not a word about Egypt. She thought for a moment, then left the drawing-room. Passing up a flight of stairs to her husband's study, she knocked and entered. It was empty; but Eglington was in the house, for a red despatch-box lay open on his table. Instinctively she glanced at the papers exposed in the box, and at the letters beside it. The document on the top of the pile in the box related to Cyprus—the name caught her eye. Another document was half-exposed beneath it. Her hand went to her heart. She saw the words "Soudan" and "Claridge Pasha." She reached for it, then drew back her hand, and her eyes closed as though to shut it out from her sight. Why should she not see it? They were her husband's papers, husband and wife were one. Husband and wife one! She shrank back. Were they one? An overmastering desire was on her. It seemed terrible to wait, when here before her was news of David, of life or death. Suddenly she put out her hand and drew the Cyprus paper over the Egyptian document, so that she might not see it.

As she did so, the door opened on her, and Eglington entered. He had seen the swift motion of her hand, and again a look peculiar to him crossed his face, enigmatical, cynical, not pleasant to see.

She turned on him slowly, and he was aware of her inward distress to some degree, though her face was ruled to quietness.

He nodded at her and smiled. She shrank, for she saw in his nod and his smile that suggestion of knowing all about everything and everybody, and thinking the worst, which had chilled her so often. Even in their short married life it had chilled those confidences which she would gladly have poured out before him, if he had been a man with an open soul. Had there been joined to his intellect and temperament a heart capable of true convictions and abiding love, what a man he might have been! But his intellect was superficial, and his temperament was dangerous, because there were not the experiences of a soul of truth to give the deeper hold upon the meaning of life. She shrank now, as with a little laugh and glancing suggestively at the despatch-box, he said:

"And what do you think of it all?"

She felt as though something was crushing her heart within its grasp, and her eyes took on a new look of pain. "I did not read the papers," she answered quietly.

"I saw them in your fingers. What creatures women are—so dishonorable in little things," he said ironically.

She laid a hand on his. "I did not read them, Harry," she urged.

He smiled and patted her arm. "There, there, it doesn't matter," he laughed. He watched her narrowly.

"It matters greatly," she answered gently, though his words had cut her like a knife. "I did not read the papers. I only saw the word 'Cyprus' on the first paper, and I pushed it over the paper which had the word 'Egypt' on it—'Egypt' and 'Claridge,' lest I should read it. I did not wish to read it. I am not dishonorable, Harry."

He had hurt her more than he had ever done; and only the great matter at stake had prevented the lesser part of her from bursting forth in indignation, from saying things which she did not wish to say. She had given him devotion—such devotion, such self-effacement in his career as few women ever gave. Her wealth—that was so little in comparison with the richness of her nature—had been his; and yet his vast egotism took it all as his right, and she was repaid in a kind of tyranny, the more galling and cruel because it was wielded by a man of intellect and culture, and ancient name and tradition. If he had been warned that he was losing his wife's love, he would have scouted the idea, his self-assurance was so strong, his vanity complete. If, however, he had been told that another man was thinking of his wife, he would have believed it, as he believed now that David had done; and he cherished that belief, and let resentment grow. He was the Earl of Eglington, and no matter what reputation David had reached, he was still a member of a Quaker trader's family, with an origin slightly touched with scandal. Another resentment, however, was steadily rising in him. It galled him that Hylda should take so powerful an interest in David's work in Egypt; and he knew now that she had always done so. It did not ease his vexed spirit to know that thousands of others of his fellow-countrymen did the same. They might do so, but she was hi wife, and his own work was the sun round which her mind and interest should revolve.

"Why should you be so keen about Egypt and Claridge Pasha?" he said to her now.

Her face hardened a little. Had he the right to torture her so? To suspect her? She could read it in his eyes. Her conscience was clear. She was no man's slave. She would not be any man's slave. She was master of her own soul. What right had he to catechize her—as though she were a servant or a criminal? But she checked the answer on her tongue, because she was hurt deeper than words could express, and she said, composedly:

"I have here a letter from my cousin, Lacey, who is with Claridge Pasha. It has news of him, of events in the Soudan. He had fever, there was to be a fight, and I wished to know if you have any later news. I thought that document there might contain news, but I did not read it. I realized that it was not yours, that it belonged to the Government, that I had no right. Perhaps you will tell me if you have news. Will you?" She leaned against the table wearily, holding her letter.

"Let me read your letter first," he said wilfully.

A mist seemed to come before her eyes; but she was schooled to self-command, and he did not see he had given her a shock. Her first impulse was to hand the letter over at once; then there came the remembrance of all it contained, all it suggested. Would he see all it suggested? She recalled the words Lacey had used regarding a service which David had once done her. If Eglington asked, what could she say? It was not her secret alone, it was another's. Would she have the right, even if she wished it, to tell the truth, or part of the truth? Or, would she be entitled to relate some immaterial incident which would evade the real truth? What good could it do to tell the dark story? What could it serve? Eglington would horribly misunderstand it—that she knew. There were the verses also. They were more suggestive than anything else, though, indeed, they might have referred to another woman, or were merely impersonal; but she felt that was not so. And there was Eglington's innate unbelief in man and woman! Her first impulse held, however. She would act honestly. She would face whatever there was to face. She would not shelter herself; she would not give him the right in the future to say she had not dealt fairly by him, had evaded any inquest of her life or mind which he might make.

She gave him the letter, her heart standing still, but she was filled with a regnant determination to defend herself, to defend David against any attack, or from any consequences.

All her life and hopes seemed hanging in the balance, as he began to read the letter. With fear she saw his face cloud over, heard an impatient exclamation pass his lips. She closed her eyes to gather strength for the conflict which was upon her. He spoke, and she vaguely wondered what passage in the letter had fixed his attention. His voice seemed very far away. She scarcely understood. But presently it pierced the clouds of numbness between them, and she realized what he was saying:

"Vulgar fellow—I can't congratulate you upon your American cousin. So, 'the Saadat is great on moral suasion, master of it—never failed yet—not altogether—and Aunt Melissa and skim-milk and early piety!' And 'the Saadat is a wonder from Wondertown'—like a side-show to a circus, a marvel on the flying trapeze! Perhaps you can give me the sense of the letter, if there is any sense in it. I can't read his writing, and it seems interminable. Would you mind?"

A sigh of relief broke from her. A weight slipped away from her heart and brain. It was as though one in armor awaited the impact of a heavy, cruel, overwhelming foe, who suddenly disappeared, and the armor fell from the shoulders, and breath came easily once again.

"Would you mind?" he repeated dryly, as he folded up the letter slowly.

He handed it back to her, the note of sarcasm in his voice pricking her like the point of a dagger. She felt angered with herself that he could rouse her temper by such small mean irony. She had a sense of bitter disappointment in him—or was it a deep hurt?—that she had not made him love her, truly love her. If he had only meant the love that he swore before they had married! Why had he deceived her? It had all been in his hands, her fate and future; but almost before the bridal flowers had faded, she had come to know two bitter things: that he had married with a sordid mind; that he was incapable of the love which transmutes the half-comprehending, half-developed affection of the maid into the absorbing, understanding, beautiful passion of the woman. She had married not knowing what love and passion were; uncomprehending; and innocent because uncomprehending; with a fine affection, but capable of loving wholly. One thing had purified her motives and her life—the desire to share with Eglington his public duty and private hopes, to be his *confidante*, his friend, his coadjutor, proud of him, eager for him, determined to help him. But he had blocked the path to all inner companionship. He did no more than let her share the obvious and outer responsibilities of his life. From the vital things, if there were vital things, she was shut out. What would she not give for one day of simple tenderness and quiet affection, a true day with a true love!

She was now perfectly composed. She told him the substance of the letter, of David's plight, of the fever, of the intended fight, of Nahoum Pasha, of the peril to David's work. He continued to interrogate her, while she could have shrieked out the question, "What is in yonder document? What do you know? Have you news of his safety?" Would he never stop his questioning? It was trying her strength and patience beyond endurance. At last he drew the document slowly from the despatch-box, and glanced up and down it musingly.

"I fancy he won the battle," he said slowly, "for they have news of him much farther down the river. But from this letter I take it he is not yet within the zone of safety—so Nahoum Pasha says." He flicked the document upwards with his thumb.

"What is our Government doing to help him?" she asked, checking her eagerness.

His heart had gradually hardened towards Egypt. Power had emphasized a certain smallness in him. Personal considerations informed the policy of the moment. He was not going to be dragged at the chariot wheels of the Quaker. To be passive, when David in

Egypt had asked for active interest; to delay, when urgency was important to Claridge Pasha; to speak coldly on Egyptian affairs to his chief, the weak Foreign Secretary—this was the policy he had begun.

So he answered now: "It is the duty of the Egyptian government to help him—of Prince Kaïd, of Nahoum Pasha, who is acting for him in his absence, who governs finance and therefore the army. Egypt does not belong to England."

"Nahoum Pasha is his enemy. He will do nothing to help, unless you force him."

"Why do you say that?"

"Because I know Nahoum Pasha."

"When did you know Nahoum?"

"In Egypt, years ago."

"Your acquaintance is more varied than I thought," he said sarcastically.

"Oh, do not speak to me like that," she returned in a low, indignant voice. "Do not patronize me; do not be sarcastic."

"Do not be so sensitive," he answered unemotionally.

"You surely do not mean that you—that the Government will not help him? He is doing the work of Europe, of civilization, of Christianity there. He is sacrificing himself for the world. Do you not see it? Oh, but you do! You would realize his work if you knew Egypt as I have seen it."

"Expediency must govern the policy of nations," he answered critically.

"But, if through your expediency he is killed like a rat in a trap, and his work goes to pieces—all undone! Is there no right in the matter?"

"In affairs of state other circumstances than absolute 'right' enter. Here and there the individual is sacrificed who otherwise would be saved—if it were expedient."

"Oh, Eglington! He is of your own county, of your

own village, is your neighbor, a man of whom all England should be proud. You can intervene if you will—be just, and say you will. I know that intervention has been discussed in the Cabinet."

"You say he is of my county. So are many people, and yet they are not county people. A neighbor he was, but more in a Scriptural than social sense." He was hurting her purposely.

She made a protesting motion of her hand. "No, no, no, do not be so small. This is a great matter. Do a great thing now; help it to be done for your own honor, for England's honor—for a good man's sake, for your country's sake."

There came a knock at the door. An instant afterwards a secretary entered. "A message from the Prime Minister, sir." He handed over a paper.

"Will you excuse me?" he asked Hylda suavely, in his eyes the enigmatical look that had chilled her so often before. She felt that her appeal had been useless. She prepared to leave the room. He took her hand, kissed it gallantly, and showed her out. It was his way—too civil to be real.

Blindly she made her way to her room. Inside, she suddenly swayed and sank fainting to the ground, as Kate Heaver ran forward to her. Kate saw the letter in the clenched hand. Loosening it, she read two or three sentences with a gasp. They contained Tom Lacey's appeal for David. She lifted Hylda's head to her shoulder with endearing words, and chafed the cold hands, murmuring to herself the while.

XXIV

THE QUESTIONER

"WHAT has thee come to say?"

Sitting in his high-backed chair, Luke Claridge seemed a part of its dignified severity. In the sparsely furnished room with its uncarpeted floor, its plain teak table, its high wainscoting and undecorated walls, the old man had the look of one who belonged to some ancient consistory, a judge whose piety would march with an austerity that would save a human soul by destroying the body, if need be.

A crisis had come, vaguely foreseen, sombrely eluded. A questioner was before him who, poor, unheeded, an ancient victim of vice, could yet wield a weapon whose sweep of wounds would be wide. Stern and masterful as he looked in his arid isolation, beneath all was a shaking anxiety.

He knew well what the old chairmaker had come to say, but, in the prologue of the struggle before him, he was unwittingly manœuvring for position.

"Speak," he added presently, as Soolsby fumbled in his great loose pockets, and drew forth a paper. "What has thee to say?"

Without a word, Soolsby handed over the paper, but the other would not take it.

"What is it?" he asked, his lips growing pale. "Read —if thee can read."

The gibe in the last words made the color leap into

Soolsby's face, and a fighting look came. He too had staved off this inevitable hour, had dreaded it, but now his courage shot up high.

"Doost think I have forgotten how to read since the day I put my hand to a writing you've hid so long from them it most concerns? Ay, I can read, and I can write, and I will prove that I can speak too before I've done."

"Read — read," rejoined the old man hoarsely, his hands tightly gripping the chair-arm.

"The fever caught him at Shendy—that is the place—"

"He is not dead—David is not dead?" came the sharp, pained interruption. The old man's head strained forward, his eyes were misty and dazed.

Soolsby's face showed no pity for the other's anxiety; it had a kind of triumph in it. "Nay, he is living," he answered. "He got well of the fever, and came to Cairo, but he's off again into the desert. It's the third time. You can't be tempting Providence forever. This paper here says it's too big a job for one man—like throwing a good life away. Here in England is his place, it says. And so say I; and so I have come to say, and to hear you say so, too. What is he there? One man against a million. What put it in his head that he thinks he can do it?"

His voice became lower; he fixed his eyes meaningly on the other. "When a man's life got a twist at the start, no wonder it flies off madlike to do the thing that isn't to be done, and leave undone the thing that's here for it to do. Doost think a straight line could come from the crooked line you drew for him?"

"He is safe—he is well and strong again?" asked the old man painfully. Suddenly he reached out a hand for the paper. "Let me read," he said, in a voice scarce above a whisper.

He essayed to take the paper calmly, but it trembled in his hands. He spread it out and fumbled for his glasses, but could not find them, and he gazed helplessly at the page before him. Soolsby took the paper from him and read slowly:

". . . Claridge Pasha has done good work in Egypt, but he is a generation too soon, it may be two or three too soon. We can but regard this fresh enterprise as a temptation to Fate to take from our race one of the most promising spirits and vital personalities which this generation has produced. It is a forlorn hope. Most Englishman familiar with Claridge Pasha's life and aims will ask—"

An exclamation broke from the old man. In the pause which followed he said: "It was none of my doing. He went to Egypt against my will."

"Ay, so many a man's said that's not wanted to look his own acts straight in the face. If Our Man had been started different, if he'd started in the path where God A'mighty dropped him, and not in the path Luke Claridge chose, would he have been in Egypt to-day wearing out his life? He's not making carpets there, he's only beating them."

The homely illustration drawn from the business in which he had been interested so many years went home to Claridge's mind. He shrank back, and sat rigid, his brows drawing over the eyes, till they seemed sunk in caverns of the head. Suddenly Soolsby's voice rose angrily. Luke Claridge seemed so remorseless and unyielding, so set in his vanity and self-will! Soolsby misread the rigid look in the face, the pale sternness. He did not know that there had suddenly come upon Luke Claridge the full consciousness of an agonizing truth—that all he had done where David was concerned had been a mistake. The hard look, the sternness, were the signals of a soul challenging itself.

"Ay, you've had your own will," cried Soolsby mercilessly. "You've said to God A'mighty that He wasn't able to work out to a good end what He'd let happen; and so you'd do His work for Him. You kept the lad hid away from the people that belonged to him, you kept him out of his own, and let others take his birthright. You put a shame upon him, hiding who his father and his father's people were, and you put a shame upon her that lies in the graveyard—as sweet a lass, as good, as ever lived on earth. Ay, a shame and a scandal! For your eyes were shut always to the sidelong looks, your ears never heard the things people said—'*A good-for-nothing ship-captain, a scamp and a ne'er-do-weel, one that had a lass at every port, and, maybe, wives too; one that none knew or ever had seen—a pirate maybe, or a slave-dealer, or a jail-bird, for all they knew! Married—oh yes, married right enough, but nothing else—not even a home. Just a ring on the finger, and then, beyond and away!*' Around her life that brought into the world our lad yonder you let a cloud draw down; and you let it draw round his, too, for he didn't even bear his father's name, much less knew who his father was—or live in his father's home, or come by his own in the end. You gave the lad shame and scandal. Do you think he didn't feel it, was it much or little? He wasn't walking in the sun, but—"

"Mercy! Mercy!" broke in the old man, his hand before his eyes. He was thinking of Mercy his daughter, of the words she had said to him when she died, "*Set him in the sun, father, where God can find him,*" and her name now broke from his lips.

Soolsby misunderstood. "Ay, there'll be mercy when right's been done Our Man, and not till then. I've held my tongue for half a lifetime, but I'll speak now and bring him back. Ay, he shall come back and take the place that is his, and all that belongs to him. That lordship yonder—let him go out into the world and make his place as the Egyptian did. He's had his chance to help Our Man, and he has only hurt, not helped him. We've had enough of his second-best lordship and his ways."

The old man's face was painful in its stricken stillness now. He had regained control of himself, his brain had recovered greatly from its first suffusion of excitement.

"How does thee know my lord yonder has hurt and not helped him?" he asked in an even voice, his lips tightening, however. "How does thee know it surely?"

"From Kate Heaver, my lady's maid. My lady's illness—what was it? Because she would help Our Man, and, out of his hatred, yonder second son said that to her which no woman can bear that's a true woman; and then, what with a chill and fever, she's been yonder ailing these weeks past. She did what she could for him, and her husband did what he could against him."

The old man settled back in his chair again. "Thee has kept silent all these years? Thee has never told any that lives?"

"I gave my word to her that died—to our Egyptian's mother—that I would never speak unless you gave me leave to speak, or if you should die before me. It was but a day before the lad was born. So have I kept my word. But now you shall speak. Ay, then, but you shall speak, or I'll break my word to her, to do right by her son. She herself would speak if she was here, and I'll answer her, if ever I see her after Purgatory, for speaking now."

The old man drew himself up in his chair as though in pain, and said very slowly, almost thickly: "I shall answer also for all I did. The spirit moved me. He is of my blood—his mother was dead—in his veins is the blood that runs in mine. His father—aristocrat, spendthrift, adventurer, renegade, who married her in secret, and left her, bidding her return to me, until he came again, and she to bear him a child—was he fit to bring up the boy?"

He breathed heavily, his face became wan and haggard, as he continued: "Restless on land or sea, forever seeking some new thing, and when he found it, and saw what was therein, he turned away forgetful. God put it into my heart to abjure him and the life around him. The Voice made me rescue the child from a life empty and bare and heartless and proud. When he returned, and my child was in her grave, he came to me in secret; he claimed the child of that honest lass whom he had married under a false name. I held my hand lest I should kill him, man of peace as I am. Even his father—Quaker though he once became—did we not know ere the end that he had no part or lot with us, that he but experimented with his soul, as with all else? Experiment—experiment—experiment, until at last an Eglington went exploring in my child's heart, and sent her to her grave—the God of Israel be her rest and refuge! What should such high-placed folk do stooping out of their sphere to us who walk in plain paths? What have we in common with them? My soul would have none of them—masks of men, the slaves of riches and titles, and tyrants over the poor!"

His voice grew hoarse and high, and his head bent forward. He spoke as though forgetful of Soolsby's presence. "As the East is from the West, so were we separate from these lovers of this world, the self-indulgent, the hard-hearted, the proud. I chose for the child that he should stay with me and not go to him, to remain among his own people and his own class. He was a sinister, an evil man. Was the child to be trusted with him?"

"The child was his own child," broke in Soolsby. "Your daughter was his lady—the Countess of Eglington! Not all the Quakers in heaven or earth could alter that. His first-born son is Earl of Eglington, and has been so these years past; and you, nor his second-best lordship there, nor all the courts in England can alter that. . . . Ay, I've kept my peace, but I will speak out now. I was with the Earl—James Fetherdon he called himself—when he married her that's gone to heaven, if any ever went to heaven; and I can prove all. There's proof aplenty, and 'tis a pity, ay, God's pity! that 'twas not used long ago. Well I knew, as the years passed, that the Earl's heart was with David, but he had not the courage to face it all, so worn away was the man in him. Ah, if the lad had always been with him—who can tell? —he might have been different! Whether so or not, it was the lad's right to take his place his mother gave him, let be whatever his father was. 'Twas a cruel thing done to him. His own was his own, to run his race as God A'mighty had laid the hurdles, not as Luke Claridge willed. I'm sick of seeing yonder fellow in Our Man's place, he that will not give him help, when he may; he that would see him die like a dog in the desert, brother or no brother—"

"He does not know—Lord Eglington does not know the truth?" interposed the old man in a heavy whisper.

"He does not know but, if he knew, would it matter to him? So much the more would he see Our Man die yonder in the sands. I know the breed. I know him yonder, the skim-milk lord. There is no blood of justice, no milk of kindness in him. Do you think his father that I friended in this thing—did he ever give me a penny, or aught save that hut on the hill that was not worth a pound a year? Did he ever do aught to show that he remembered?—Like father like son? I wanted naught. I held my peace, not for him, but for her—for the promise I made her when she smiled at me and said, '*If I shouldn't be seeing thee again, Soolsby, remember; and if thee can ever prove a friend to the child that is to be, prove it!'* And I will prove it now. He must come back to his own. Right's right, and I will have it so. More brains you may have, and wealth you have, but not more common sense than any common man like me. If the spirit moved you to hold your peace, it moves me to make you speak. With all your meek face you've been a hard, stiff-necked man, a tyrant too, and as much an aristocrat to such as me as any lord in the land. But I've drunk the mug of silence to the bottom. I've—"

He stopped short, seeing a strange look come over the other's face, and stepped forward quickly as the old man half rose from his chair, murmuring thickly.

"Mercy—David, my lord, come—!" he muttered, and staggered, and fell into Soolsby's arms.

His head dropped forward on his breast, and with a great sigh he sank into unconsciousness. Soolsby laid him on a couch, and ran to the door and called aloud for help.

The man of silence was silent indeed now. In the room where paralysis had fallen on him a bed was brought, and he lay nerveless on the verge of a still deeper silence. The hours went by. His eyes opened, he saw and recognized them all, but his look rested only on Faith and Soolsby; and, as time went on, these were the only faces to which he gave an answering look of understanding. Days wore away, but he neither spoke nor moved.

People came and went softly, and he gave no heed. There was ever a trouble in his eyes when they were open. Only when Soolsby came did it seem to lessen. Faith saw this, and urged Soolsby to sit by him. She had questioned much concerning what had happened before the stroke fell, but Soolsby said only that the old man had been greatly troubled about David. Once Lady Eglington, frail and gentle and sympathetic, came, but the trouble deepened in his eyes, and the lids closed over them, so that he might not see her face.

When she had gone, Soolsby, who had been present and had interpreted the old man's look according to a knowledge all his own, came over to the bed, leaned down, and whispered, "I will speak now."

Then the eyes opened, and a smile faintly flickered at the mouth.

"I will speak now," Soolsby said again into the old man's ear.

XXV

THE VOICE THROUGH THE DOOR

THAT night Soolsby tapped at the door of the lighted laboratory of the Cloistered House where Lord Eglington was at work, opened it, peered in, and stepped inside.

With a glass retort in his hand, Eglington faced him. "What's this—what do you want?" he demanded.

"I want to try an experiment," answered Soolsby grimly.

"Ah, a scientific turn!" rejoined Eglington coolly—looking at him narrowly, however. He was conscious of danger of some kind.

Then for a minute neither spoke. Now that Soolsby had come to the moment for which he had waited for so many years, the situation was not what he had so often prefigured. The words he had chosen long ago were gone from his memory; in his ignorance of what had been a commonplace to Soolsby's dark reflection so long, the man he had meant to bring low stood up before him on his own ground, powerful and unabashed.

Eglington wore a blue smock, and over his eyes was a green shade to protect them from the light, but they peered sharply out at the chairmaker, and were boldly alive to the unexpected. He was no physical coward—and, in any case, what reason had he for physical fear in the presence of this man weakened by vice and age? Yet ever since he was a boy there had existed between them an antagonism which had shown itself in many ways. There had ever been something sinister in Soolsby's attitude to his father and himself.

Eglington vaguely knew that now he was to face some trial of mind and nerve, but with great deliberation he continued dropping liquid from a bottle into the glass retort he carried, his eyes, however, watchful of his visitor, who involuntarily stared around the laboratory.

It was fifteen years since Soolsby had been in this room; and then he had faced this man's father with a challenge on his tongue such as he meant to speak now. The smell of the chemicals, the carboys filled with acids, the queer tapering glasses with engraved measurements showing against the colored liquids, the great blue bottles, the mortars and pestles, the microscopic instruments—all brought back the far-off, acrid scene between the late Earl and himself. Nothing had changed, except that now there were wires which gave out hissing sparks, electrical instruments invented since the earlier day; except that this man, gently dropping acids into the round white bottle upon a crystal which gave off musty fumes, was bolder, stronger, had more at stake than the other.

Slowly Eglington moved back to put the retort on a long table against the wall, and Soolsby stepped forward till he stood where the electri sparks were gently hissing about him. Now Eglington leaned against the table, poured some alcohol on his fingers to cleanse the acid from them, and wiped them with a piece of linen, while he looked inquiringly at Soolsby. Still, Soolsby did not speak. Eglington lit a cigarette, and took away the shade from his eyes.

"Well, now, what is your experiment?" he asked, "and why bring it here? Didn't you know the way to the stables or the scullery?"

"I knew my way better here," answered Soolsby, steadying himself.

"Ah, you've been here often?" asked Eglington nonchalantly, yet feeling for the cause of this midnight visit.

"It is fifteen years since I was here, my lord. Then I came to see the Earl of Eglington."

"And so history repeats itself every fifteen years! You came to see the Earl of Eglington then; you come to see the Earl of Eglington again—after fifteen years!"

"I come to speak with him that's called the Earl of Eglington."

Eglington's eyes half closed, as though the light hurt them. "That sounds communistic, or is it pure Quakerism? I believe they used to call my father *Friend Robert* till he backslided. But you are not a Quaker, Soolsby, so why be too familiar? Or is it merely the way of the old family friend?"

"I knew your father before you were born, my lord—he troosted me then."

"So long? And fifteen years ago—here?" He felt a menace, vague and penetrating. His eyes were hard and cruel.

"It wasn't a question of troost then; 'twas one of right or wrong—naught else."

"Ah—and who was right, and what was wrong?"

At that moment there came a tap at the door leading into the living part of the house, and the butler entered.

"The doctor—he has used up all his oxygen, my lord. He begs to know if you can give him some for Mr. Claridge. Mr. Claridge is bad to-night."

A sinister smile passed over Eglington's face. "Who brings the message, Garry?"

"A servant—Miss Claridge's, my lord."

An ironical look came into Eglington's eyes; then they softened a little. In a moment he placed a jar of oxygen in the butler's hands.

"My compliments to Miss Claridge, and I am happy

to find my laboratory of use at last to my neighbors," he said, and the door closed upon the man.

Then he came back thoughtfully. Soolsby had not moved.

"Do you know what oxygen's for, Soolsby?" he asked quizzically.

"No, my lord, I've never heerd tell of it."

"Well, if you brought the top of Ben Lomond to the bottom of a coal-mine—breath to the breathless—that's it."

"You've been doing that to Mr. Claridge, my lord?"

"A little oxygen more or less makes all the difference to a man—it probably will to neighbor Claridge, Soolsby; and so I've done him a good turn."

A grim look passed over Soolsby's face. "It's the first, I'm thinking, my lord, and none too soon; and it 'll be the last, I'm thinking, too. It's many a year since this house was neighborly to that."

Eglington's eyes almost closed, as he studied the other's face; then he said: "I asked you a little while ago who was right and what was wrong when you came to see my father here fifteen years ago. Well?"

Suddenly a thought flashed into his eyes, and it seemed to course through his veins like some anæsthetic, for he grew very still, and a minute passed before he added quietly: "Was it a thing between my father and Luke Claridge? There was trouble—well, what was it?" All at once he seemed to rise above the vague anxiety that possessed him, and he fingered inquiringly a long tapering glass of acids on the bench beside him. "There's been so much mystery, and I suppose it was nothing, after all. What was it all about? Or do you know—eh? Fifteen years ago you came to see my father, and now you have come to see me—all in the light o' the moon, as it were; like a villain in a play. Ah, yes, you said it was to make an experiment—yet you didn't know what oxygen was! It's foolish making experiments, unless you know what you are playing with, Soolsby. See, here are two glasses." He held them up. "If I poured one into the other, we'd have an experiment—and you and I would be picked up in fragments and carried away in a basket. And that wouldn't be a successful experiment, Soolsby."

"I'm not so sure of that, my lord. Some things would be put right then."

"H'm, there would be a new Under-Secretary for Foreign Affairs, and—"

"And Claridge Pasha would come back from Egypt, my lord," was the sharp interjection. Suddenly Soolsby's anger flared up, his hands twitched. "You had your chance to be a friend to him, my lord. You promised her yonder at the Red Mansion that you would help him —him that never wronged you, him you always wronged, and you haven't lifted hand to help him in his danger. A moment since you asked me who was right and what was wrong. You shall know. If you had treated him right, I'd have held my peace, and kept my word to her that's gone these thirty-odd years. I'll hold it no more, and so I told Luke Claridge. I've been silent, but not for your father's sake or yours, for he was as cruel as you, with no heart, and a conscience like a pin's head, not big enough for use. . . . Ay, you shall know! You are no more the Earl of Eglington than me. The Earl of Eglington is your elder brother, called David Claridge."

As Soolsby's words poured forth passionately, weighty, Eglington listened like one in a dream. Since this man entered the laboratory fifty reasons for his coming had flashed across his mind; he had prepared himself at many corners for defence, he had rallied every mental resource, he had imagined a dozen dangerous events which his father and Luke Claridge shared—with the balance against his father; but this thing was beyond all speculation. Yet on the instant the words were said he had a conviction of their inevitable truth. Even as they were uttered, kaleidoscopic memories rushed in, and David's face, figure, personal characteristics, flashed before him. He saw, he felt, the likeness to his father and himself; a thousand things were explained that could only be explained by this fatal fact launched at him without warning. It was as though, fully armed for his battle of life, he had suddenly been stripped of armor and every weapon, and left naked on the field. But he had the mind of the gamester, and the true gamester's self-control. He had taken chances so often that the tornado of ill-luck left him standing.

"What proof have you?" he asked quietly.

Soolsby's explicit answer left no ground for doubt. He had not asked the question with any idea of finding gaps in the evidence, but rather to find if there were a chance for resistance, of escape, anywhere. The marriage certificate existed; identification of James Fetherdon with his father could be established by Soolsby and Luke Claridge.

Soolsby and Luke Claridge! Luke Claridge—he could not help but smile cynically, for he was composed and calculating now. But a few minutes ago he had sent a jar of oxygen to keep Luke Claridge alive! But for it one enemy to his career, to his future, would be gone. He did not shrink from the thought. Born a gentleman, there were in him some degenerate characteristics which heart could not drown or temperament refine. Selfishness was inwoven with every fibre of his nature.

Now, as he stood with eyes fixed on Soolsby, the world seemed to narrow down to this laboratory. It was a vacuum where sensation was suspended and the million facts of ordinary existence disappeared into inactivity. There was a fine sense of proportion in it all. Only the bare essential things that concerned him remained: David Claridge was the Earl of Eglington, this man before him knew, Luke Claridge knew; and there was one thing yet to know! When he spoke his voice showed no excitement—the tones were even, colorless.

"*Does he know?*" In these words he acknowledged that he believed the tale told him.

Soolsby had expected a different attitude; he was not easier in mind because his story had not been challenged. He blindly felt working in the man before him a powerful mind, more powerful because it faced the truth unflinchingly; but he knew that this did not mean calm acceptance of the consequences. He, not Eglington, was dazed and embarrassed, was not equal to the situation. He moved uneasily, changed his position.

"*Does he know?*" Eglington questioned again quietly. There was no need for Eglington to explain who *he* was.

"Of course he does not know—I said so. If he knew, do you think he'd be in Egypt and you here, my lord?"

Eglington was very quiet. His intellect more than his passions were now at work.

"I am not sure. You never can tell. This might not mean much to him. He has got his work cut out; he wasn't brought up to this. What he has done is in line with the life he has lived as a pious Quaker. What good would it do to bring him back? I have been brought up to it; I am used to it; I have worked things out 'according to the state of life to which I was called.' Take what I've always had away from me, and I am crippled; give him what he never had, and it doesn't work into his scheme. It would do him no good and me harm— Where's the use? Besides, I am still my father's son. Don't you see how unreasonable you are? Luke Claridge was right. He knew that he and his belonged to a different sphere. He didn't speak. Why do you speak now after all these years when we are all set in our grooves? It's silly to disturb us, Soolsby."

The voice was low, persuasive, and searching; the mind was working as it had never worked before, to achieve an end by peaceful means, when war seemed against him. And all the time he was fascinated by the fact that Soolsby's hand was within a few inches of a live electric wire, which, if he touched, would probably complete "the experiment" he had come to make; and what had been the silence of a generation would continue indefinitely. It was as though Fate had deliberately tempted him and arranged these necessary conditions, for Soolsby's feet were in a little pool of liquid which had been spilled on the floor—the experiment was exact and real.

For minutes he had watched Soolsby's hand near the wire—had watched as he talked, and his talk was his argument for non-interference against warning the man who had come to destroy him and his career. Why had Fate placed that hand so near the wire there, and provided the other perfect conditions for tragedy? Why should he intervene? It would never have crossed his mind to do Soolsby harm, yet here, as the man's arm was stretched out to strike him, Fate offered an escape. Luke Claridge was stricken with paralysis, no doubt would die; Soolsby alone stood in his way.

"You see, Soolsby, it has gone on too long," he added, in a low, penetrating tone. "It would be a crime to alter things now. Give him the earldom and the estates, and his work in Egypt goes to pieces; he will be spoiled for all he wants to do. I've got my faults, but, on the whole, I'm useful, and I play my part here, as I was born to it, as well as most. Anyhow, it's no robbery for me to have what has been mine by every right except the accident of being born after him. I think you'll see that you will do a good thing to let it all be. Luke Claridge, if he was up and well, wouldn't thank you for it—have you got any right to give him trouble, too? Besides, I've saved his life to-night, and . . . and perhaps I might save yours, Soolsby, if it was in danger."

Soolsby's hand had moved slightly. It was only an inch from the wire. For an instant the room was terribly still.

An instant, and it might be too late. An instant, and Soolsby would be gone. Eglington watched the hand which had been resting on the table turn slowly over to the wire. Why should he intervene? Was it his business? This thing was not his doing. Destiny had laid the train of circumstance and accident, and who was stronger than Destiny? In spite of himself his eyes fixed themselves on Soolsby's hand. It was but a hair's breadth from the wire. The end would come now.

Suddenly a voice was heard outside the door. "Eglington!" it called.

Soolsby started, his hand drew spasmodically away from the wire, and he stepped back quickly.

The door opened—and Hylda entered.

"Mr. Claridge is dead, Eglington," she said.

Destiny had decided.

XXVI

"I OWE YOU NOTHING"

BESIDE the grave under the willow-tree another grave had been made. It was sprinkled with the fallen leaves of autumn. In the Red Mansion Faith's delicate figure moved forlornly among relics of an austere, beloved figure vanished from the apricot-garden and the primitive simplicity of wealth combined with narrow thought.

Since her father's death, the bereaved girl had been occupied by matters of law and business, by affairs of the estate; but the first pressure was over, long letters had been written to David which might never reach him; and now, when the strain was withdrawn, the gentle mind was lost in a gray mist of quiet suffering. In Hamley there were but two in whom she had any real comfort and help — Lady Eglington and the old chair-maker. Of an afternoon or evening one or the other was to be seen in the long, high-wainscoted room, where a great fire burned, or in the fruitless garden where the breeze stirred the bare branches.

Almost as deep a quiet brooded in the Cloistered House as in the home where mourning enjoined movement in a minor key. Hylda had not recovered wholly from the illness which had stricken her down on that day in London when she had sought news of David from Eglington, at such cost to her peace and health and happiness. Then had come her slow convalescence in Hamley, and long days of loneliness, in which Eglington seemed to retreat farther and farther from her inner life. Inquiries had poured in from friends in town, many had asked to come and see her; flowers came from one or two who loved her benignly, like Lord Windlehurst; and now and then she had some cheerful friend with her who cared for music or could sing; and then the old home rang; but she was mostly alone, and Eglington was kept in town by official business the greater part of each week. She did not gain strength as quickly as she ought to have done, and this was what brought the Duchess of Snowdon down on a special mission one day of early November.

Ever since the night she had announced Luke Claridge's death to Eglington, had discovered Soolsby with him, had seen the look in her husband's face and caught the tension of the moment on which she had broken, she had been haunted by a hovering sense of trouble. What had Soolsby been doing in the laboratory at that time of night? What was the cause of this secret meeting? All Hamley knew—she had long known—how Luke Claridge had held the Cloistered House in abhorrence, and she knew also that Soolsby worshipped David and Faith, and, whatever the cause of the family antipathy, championed it. She was conscious of a shadow somewhere, and behind it all was the name of David's father, James Fetherdon. That last afternoon when she had talked with him, and he had told her of his life, she had recalled the name as one she had seen or heard, and it had floated into her mind at last that she had seen it among the papers and letters of the late Countess of Eglington.

As the look in Eglington's face the night she came upon him and Soolsby in the laboratory haunted her, so the look in her own face had haunted Soolsby. Her voice announcing Luke Claridge's death had suddenly opened up a new situation to him. It stunned him; and afterwards, as he saw Hylda with Faith in the apricot-garden, or walking in the grounds of the Cloistered House hour after hour alone or with her maid, he became vexed by a problem greater than had yet perplexed him. It was one thing to turn Eglington out of his lands and home and title; it was another thing to strike this beautiful being, whose smile had won him from the first, whose voice, had he but known, had saved his life. Perhaps the truth in some dim way was conveyed to him, for he came to think of her a little as he thought of Faith.

Since the moment when he had left the laboratory and made his way to the Red Mansion, he and Eglington had never met face to face; and he avoided a meeting. He was not a blackmailer, he had no personal wrongs to avenge, he had not sprung the bolt of secrecy for evil ends; and when he saw the possible results of his disclosure, he was unnerved. His mind had seen one thing only, the rights of "Our Man," the wrong that had been done him and his mother; but now he saw how the sword of justice which he had kept by his hand these many years would cut both ways. His mind was troubled, too, that he had spoken while yet Luke Claridge lived, and so broken his word to Mercy Claridge. If he had but waited till the old man died—but one brief half-hour—his pledge would have been kept. Nothing had worked out wholly as he expected. The heavens had not fallen. The "second-best lordship" still came and went, the wheels went round as usual. There was no change; yet, as he sat in his hut and looked down into the grounds of the Cloistered House, he kept saying to himself:

"It had to be told. It's for my lord now. He knows the truth. I'll wait and see. It's for him to do right by Our Man that's beyond and away."

The logic and fairness of this position, reached after

much thinking, comforted him. He had done his duty so far. If, in the end, the "second-best lordship" failed to do his part, hid the truth from the world, refused to do right by his half-brother, the true Earl, then would be time to act again. Also he waited for word out of Egypt; and he had a superstitious belief that David would return, that any day might see him entering the door of the Red Mansion.

Eglington himself was haunted by a spectre which touched his elbow by day and said, "You are not the Earl of Eglington," and at night laid a clammy finger on his forehead, waking him, and whispering in his ear, "If Soolsby had touched the wire, all would now be well!" And as deep as thought and feeling in him lay, he felt that Fate had tricked him—Fate and Hylda. If Hylda had not come at that crucial instant, the chair-maker's hut on the hill would be empty. Why had not Soolsby told the world the truth since? Was the man waiting to see what course he himself would take? Had the old chairmaker perhaps written the truth to the Egyptian—to his brother David!

His brother! The thought irritated every nerve in him. No note of kindness or kinship or blood stirred in him. If, before, he had had innate antagonism and a dark, hovering jealousy, he had a black repugnance now—the antipathy of the lesser to the greater nature, of the man in the wrong to the man in the right.

And behind it all was the belief that his wife had set David above him—by how much or in what fashion he did not stop to consider; but it made him desire that death and the desert would swallow up his father's son and leave no trace behind.

Policy? His work in the Foreign Office now had but one policy so far as Egypt was concerned. The active sophistry in him made him advocate non-intervention in Egyptian affairs as diplomatic wisdom, though it was but personal purpose; and he almost convinced himself that he was acting from a national standpoint. Kaïd and Claridge Pasha pursued their course of civilization in the Soudan, and who could tell what danger might not bring forth? If only Soolsby held his peace yet a while!

Did Faith know? Luke Claridge was gone without speaking, but had Soolsby told Faith? How closely had he watched the faces round him at Luke Claridge's funeral, to see if they betrayed any knowledge!

Anxious days had followed that night in the laboratory. His boundless egotism had widened the chasm between Hylda and himself, which had been made on the day when she fell ill in London, with Lacey's letter in her hand. It had not grown less in the weeks that followed. He nursed a grievance which had, so far as he knew, no foundation in fact; he was vaguely jealous of a man—his brother—thousands of miles away; he was not certain how far Hylda had pierced the disguise of sincerity which he himself had always worn, or how far she understood him. He thought that she shrank from what she had seen of his real self, much or little, and he was conscious of so many gifts and abilities and attractive personal qualities that he felt a sense of injury. Yet what would his position be without her? Suppose David should return and take the estates and titles, and suppose that she should close her hand upon her fortune and leave him, where would he be?

He thought of all this as he sat in his room at the Foreign Office and looked over St. James's Park, his day's work done. He was suddenly seized by a newborn anxiety, for he had been so long used to the open purse and the unchecked stream of gold, had taken it so much as a matter of course, as not to realize the possibility of its being withdrawn. He was conscious of a kind of meanness and ugly sordidness in the suggestion; but the stake—his future, his career, his position in the world—was too high to allow him to be too chivalrous. His sense of the real facts was perverted. He said to himself that he must be practical.

Moved by the new thought, he seized a time-table and looked up the trains. He had been ten days in town, receiving every morning a little note from Hylda telling of what she had done each day; a calm, dutiful note, written without pretence, and out of a womanly affection with which she surrounded the man who, it seemed once—such a little while ago—must be all in all to her. She had no element of pretence in her. What she could give she gave freely, and it was just what it appeared to be. He had taken it all as his due, with an underlying belief that, if he chose to make love to her again, he could blind her to all else in the world. Hurt vanity and egotism and jealousy had prevented him from luring her back to that fine atmosphere in which he had hypnotized her so few years ago. But suddenly, as he watched the swans swimming in the pond below, a new sense of approaching loss, all that Hylda had meant in his march and progress, came upon him; and he hastened to return to Hamley.

Getting out of the train at Heddington, he made up his mind to walk home by the road that David had taken on his return from Egypt, and he left word at the station that he would send for his luggage.

His first objective was Soolsby's hut, and, long before he reached it, darkness had fallen. From a light shining through the crack of the blind he knew that Soolsby was at home. He opened the door and entered without knocking. Soolsby was seated at a table, a map and a newspaper spread out before him. Egypt and David, always David and Egypt!

Soolsby got to his feet slowly, his eyes fixed inquiringly on his visitor.

"I didn't knock," said Eglington, taking off his great-coat and reaching for a chair; then added, as he seated himself, "Better sit down, Soolsby."

After a moment he continued, "Do you mind my smoking?"

Soolsby did not reply, but sat down again. He watched Eglington light a cigar and stretch out his hands to the wood fire with an air of comfort.

A silence followed. Eglington appeared to forget the other's presence, and to occupy himself with thoughts that glimmered in the fire.

At last Soolsby said moodily, "What have you come for, my lord?"

"Oh, I am *my lord* still, am I?" Eglington returned lazily. "Is it a genealogical tree you are studying there?" He pointed to the map.

"I've studied your family tree with care, as you should know, my lord; and a map of Egypt"—he tapped the parchment before him—"goes well with it. And see, my lord, Egypt concerns you too. Lord Eglington is there, and 'tis time he was returning—ay, 'tis time."

There was a baleful look in Soolsby's eyes. Whatever he might think, whatever considerations might arise at other times, a sinister feeling came upon him when Eglington was with him.

"And, my lord," he went on, "I'd be glad to know that you've sent for him, and told him the truth."

"Have *you?*" Eglington flicked the ash from his cigar, speaking coolly.

Soolsby looked at him with his honest blue eyes aflame, and answered deliberately: "I was not for taking your place, my lord. 'Twas my duty to tell you, but the rest was between you and the Earl of Eglington."

"That was thoughtful of you, Soolsby. And Miss Claridge?"

"I told you that night, my lord, that only her father and myself knew; and what was then is now."

A look of relief stole across Eglington's face. "Of course—of course. These things need a lot of thought, Soolsby. One must act with care—no haste, no flurry, no mistakes."

"I would not wait too long, my lord, or be too careful." There was menace in the tone.

"But if you go at things blind, you're likely to hurt where you don't mean to hurt. When you're mowing in a field by a school-house, you must look out for the children asleep in the grass. Sometimes the longest way round is the shortest way home."

"Do you mean to do it or not, my lord? I've left it to you as a gentleman."

"It's going to upset more than you think, Soolsby. Suppose he, out there in Egypt"—he pointed again to the map—"doesn't thank me for the information. Suppose he says no, and—"

"Right's right. Give him the chance, my lord. How can you know, unless you tell him the truth?"

"Do you like living, Soolsby?"

"Do you want to kill me, my lord?"

There was a dark look in Eglington's face. "But answer me, do you want to live?"

"I want to live long enough to see the Earl of Eglington in his own house."

"Well, I've made that possible. The other night when you were telling me your little story, you were near sending yourself into eternity—as near as I am knocking this ash off my cigar." His little finger almost touched the ash. "Your hand was as near touching a wire charged with death. I saw it. It would have been better for me if you had gone; but I shut off the electricity. Suppose I hadn't, could I have been blamed? It would have been an accident. Providence

"'THIS IS MY CASTLE, MY LORD—YOU LODGE YONDER'"

did not intervene; I did. You owe me something, Soolsby."

Soolsby stared at him almost blindly for a moment. A mist was before his eyes; but through the mist, though he saw nothing of this scene in which he now was, he saw the laboratory, and himself and Eglington, and Eglington's face as it peered at him, and, just before the voice called outside, Eglington's eyes fastened on his hand. It all flashed upon him now, and he saw himself starting back at the sound of the voice.

Slowly he got up now, went to the door, and opened it. "My lord, it is not true," he said. "You have not spoken like a gentleman. It was my lady's voice that saved me. This is my castle, my lord — you lodge yonder." He pointed down into the darkness where the lights of the village shone. "I owe you nothing. I pay my debts. Pay yours, my lord, to him that's beyond and away."

Eglington kept his countenance as he drew on his great-coat and slowly passed from the house.

"I ought to have let you die, Soolsby. You'll think better of this soon. But it's quite right to leave the matter to me. It may take a little time, but everything will come right. Justice shall be done. Well, good-night, Soolsby. You live too much alone, and imagination is a bad thing for the lonely. Good-night —good-night."

Going down the hill quickly, he said to himself: "A sort of second sight he had about that wire. But time is on my side, time and the Soudan—and 'The heathen in his blindness.' . . . I will keep what is mine. I will keep it!"

XXVII

THE AWAKENING

IN her heart of hearts Hylda had not greatly welcomed the Duchess of Snowdon to Hamley. There was no one whose friendship she prized more; but she was passing through a phase of her life when she felt that she was better apart, finding her own path by those intuitions and perceptions which belonged to her own personal experience. She vaguely felt, what all realize sooner or later, that we must live our dark hours alone.

Yet the frank downright nature of the once beautiful, now faded, Duchess, the humorous glimmer in the pale-blue eyes, the droll irony and dry truth of her speech, appealed to Hylda, made her smile a warm greeting when she would rather have been alone. For, a few days before, she had begun a quest which had absorbed her, fascinated her. The miner, finding his way across the gap of a reef to pick up the vein of quartz at some distant and uncertain point, could not have been more lost to the world than was the young wife searching for a family skeleton, indefinitely embodied in her imagination by the name, *James Fetherdon.*

Pile after pile of papers and letters of the late Earl and his Countess had passed through her hands from chaos to order. As she had read, hour after hour, the diaries of the cold, blue-eyed woman, Sybil Eglington, who had lived without love of either husband or son, as they, in turn, lived without love of each other, she had been overwhelmed by the revelation of a human heart, whose powers of expression were smothered by a shy and awkward temperament. The late Countess's letters were the unclothing of a heart which had never expanded to the eyes of those whose love would have broken up a natural reserve, which became at last a proud coldness, and gave her a reputation for lack of feeling that she carried to her grave.

In the diaries which Hylda unearthed—the Countess had died suddenly—was the muffled cry of a soul tortured through different degrees of misunderstanding; from the vague pain of suffered indifference, of being left out of her husband's calculations, to the blank neglect narrowing her life down to a tiny stream of duty, which was finally lost in the sands. She had died abroad, and alone, save for her faithful maid, who, knowing the chasm that lay between her mistress and her lord, had brought her letters and papers back to the Cloistered House, and locked them away with all the other papers and correspondence which the Countess had accumulated.

Among these papers was a letter to the late Lord Eglington written the day before she died. In the haste and confusion ensuing on her death, the maid had not seen it. It had never reached his hands, but lay in a pocket of the dead woman's writing-portfolio, which Hylda had explored without discovering. Only a few hours, however, before the Duchess of Snowdon came, Hylda had found again an empty envelope on which was written the name *James Fetherdon.* The writing on the envelope was that of Sybil Lady Eglington.

When she discovered the envelope, a sense of mystery and premonition possessed her. What was the association between the Countess of Eglington and James Fetherdon, the father of David Claridge? In vain she searched among the voluminous letters and papers, for it would seem that the dead woman had saved every letter she received, and kept copies of numberless letters she had written. But she had searched without avail. Even the diaries, curiously frank and without reserve, never mentioned the name, so far as she could find, though here and there were strange allusive references, hints of a trouble that weighed her down, phrases of exasperation and defiance. One phrase, or the idea in it, was, however, much repeated in the diaries during the course of years, and towards the last almost feverishly emphasized—"*Why should I bear it for one who would bear nothing for me, for his sake, who would do nothing for my sake? Is it only the mother in me, not the love in me?*"

These words were haunting Hylda's brain when the telegram from the Duchess of Snowdon came. They followed her to Heddingon, whither she went in the carriage to bring her visitor to Hamley, and kept repeating themselves at the back of her mind through the cheerful rallying of the Duchess, who spread out the wings of good-humor and motherly freedom over her.

After all, it was an agreeable thing to be taken possession of, and "put in her proper place," as the Duchess said; made to understand that her own affairs were not so important, after all; and that it was far more essential to hear the charming gossip about the new and most popular Princess of Wales, or the quarrel between Dickens and Thackeray. Yet, after dinner, in the little sitting-room, where the Duchess, in a white gown with great pink bows, fitter for a girl fresh from Confirmation, and her cheeks with their fixed color, which changed only at the discretion of her maid, babbled of nothing that mattered, Hylda's mind kept turning to the book of life an unhappy woman had left behind her.

The sitting-room had been that of the late Countess also, and on the wall was an oil-painting of her, stately and distant and not very alluring, though the mouth had a sweetness which seemed unable to break into a smile.

"What was she really like—that wasn't her quite, was it?" asked Hylda, at last, leaning her chin on the hand which held the 'cello she had been playing.

"Oh yes, it's Sybil Eglington, my dear, but done in wood; and she wasn't the graven image that makes her out to be. That's as most people saw her; as the fellow that painted her saw her; but she had another side to her. She disapproved of me rather, because I was squeezing the orange dry, and trying to find yesterday's roses in to-morrow's garden. But she didn't shut her door in my face—it's hard to do that to a Duchess; which is one of the few advantages of living naked in the street as it were, with only the strawberry leaves to clothe you. No, Sybil Eglington was a woman who never had her chance. Your husband's forbears were difficult, my dear. They didn't exactly draw you out. She needed drawing out; and her husband drove her back into her corner, where she sulked rather till she died—died alone at Wiesbaden, with a German doctor, a stray curate, and a stuttering maid to wish her *bon voyage*. Yet I fancy she went glad enough, for she had no memories, not even an *affaire* to repent of, and to cherish. La, la! she wasn't so stupid, Sybil there, and she was an ornament to her own sex and the despair of the other. His Serene Highness Heinrich of Saxe-Gunden fancied the task of breaking that ice, and he was an adept and an Apollo, but it broke his reputation instead. No doubt she is happy now. I shall probably never see!"

In spite of the poignant nature of the talk, Hylda could not but smile at the last words.

"Don't despair," she rejoined; "one star differeth from another star in glory, but that is no reason why they should not be on visiting terms."

"My dear, you may laugh—*you* may laugh, but I am sixty-five, and I am not laughing at the idea of what company I may be obliged to keep presently. In any case I'm sure I shall not be comfortable. If I'm where she is, I shall be dull; if I'm where her husband is, I'll have no reputation; and if there is one thing I want, it is a spotless reputation—sometime."

Hylda laughed—the manner and the voice were so droll—but her face saddened too, and her big eyes with the drooping lashes looked up pensively at the portrait of her husband's mother.

"Was it ever a happy family, or a lucky family?" she asked.

"It's lucky now, and it ought to be happy now," was the meaning reply.

Hylda made no answer, but caught the strings of the 'cello lightly, and shook her head reprovingly, with a smile meant to be playful. For a moment she played, humming to herself, and then the Duchess touched the hand that was drawing the bow softly across the strings. She had behind her garishness a gift for sympathy and a keen intuition, delicacy and allusiveness. She knew what to say and what to leave unsaid, when her heart was moved.

"My darling," she said now, "*you* are not quite happy; but that is because you don't allow yourself to get well. You've never recovered from your attack last summer; and you won't, until you come out into the world again and see people. This autumn you ought to have been at Homburg or at Aix, where you'd take a little cure of waters and a great deal of cure of people. You were born to bask in friendship and the sun, and to draw from the world as much as you deserve, a little from many, for all you give in return. Because, dearest, you are a very agreeable person, with enough wit and humanity to make it worth the world's while to conspire to make you do what will give it most pleasure, and let yourself get most—and that's why I've come."

"What a person of importance I am!" answered Hylda, with a laugh that was far from mirthful, though she caught the plump, wrinkled little hand of the Duchess and pressed it. "But really I'm getting well here fast. I'm very strong again. It is so restful, and one's days go by so quietly."

"Yet, I'm not sure that it's rest you want. I don't think it is. You want tonics—men and women and things. Monte Carlo would do you a world of good—I'd go with you. Eglington gambles here"—she watched Hylda closely—"why shouldn't you gamble there?"

"Eglington gambles?" Hylda's face took on a frightened look, then it cleared again, and she smiled. "Oh, of course, with international affairs, you mean. Well, I must stay here and be the *croupier*."

"Nonsense! Eglington is his own *croupier*. Besides, he is so much in London, and you so much here. You sit with the distaff; he throws the dice."

Hylda's lips tightened a little. Her own inner life, what Eglington was to her or she to Eglington, was for the ears of no human being, however friendly. She had seen little of him of late, but in one sense that had been a relief, though she would have done anything to make that feeling impossible. His rather precise courtesy and consideration, when he was with her, emphasized the distance between "the first fine careless rapture" and this gray quiet. And, strange to say, though in the first five years after the Cairo days and deeds, Egypt seemed an infinite space away, and David a distant, almost legendary figure, now Egypt seemed but beyond the door—as though, opening it, she would stand near him who represented the best of all that she might be capable of thinking. Yet all the time she longed for Eglington to come and say one word, which would be like touching the lever of the sluice-gates of her heart, to let loose the flood. As the space grew between her and Eglington, her spirit trembled, she shrank back, because she saw that sea towards which she was drifting.

As she did not answer the last words of the Duchess, the latter said presently, "When do you expect Eglington?"

"Not till the week-end; it is a busy week with him," Hylda answered; then added hastily, though she had not thought of it till this moment, "I shall probably go up to town with you to-morrow."

She did not know that Eglington was already in the house, and had given orders to the butler that she was not to be informed of his arrival for the present.

"Well, if you get that far, will you come with me to the Riviera, or to Florence, or Sicily—or Cairo?" the other asked, adjusting her gold-brown wig with her babyish hands.

Cairo! Cairo! A light shot up into Hylda's eyes. The Duchess had spoken without thought, but, as she spoke, she watched the sudden change in Hylda. What did it mean? Cairo—why should Cairo have waked her so? Suddenly she recalled certain vague references of Lord Windlehurst, and, for the first time, she associated Hylda with Claridge Pasha in a way which might mean much, account for much, in this life she was leading.

"Perhaps! Perhaps!" answered Hylda abstractedly, after a moment.

The Duchess got to her feet. She had made progress. She would let her medicine work.

"I'm going to bed, my dear. I'm sixty-five, and I take my sleep when I can get it. Think it over, Sicily —*Cairo!*"

She left the room, saying to herself that Eglington was a fool, and that danger was ahead. "But I hold a red light—poor darling!" she said aloud, as she went up the staircase. She did not know that Eglington, standing in a deep doorway, heard her, and seized upon the words eagerly and suspiciously, and turned them over in his mind.

Below, at the desk where Eglington's mother used to write, Hylda sat with a bundle of letters before her. For some moments she opened, glanced through them, and put them aside. Presently she sat back in her chair, thinking—her mind was invaded by the last words of the Duchess; and somehow they kept repeating themselves with the words in the late Countess's diary, "*Is it only the mother in me, not the love in me?*" Mechanically her hand moved over the portfolio of the late Countess, and it involuntarily felt in one of its many pockets. Her hand came upon a letter. This had remained when the others had been taken out. It was addressed to the late Earl, and was open. She hesitated a moment, then with a strange premonition and a tightening of her heart-strings, she spread it out and read it.

At first she could scarcely see because of the mist in her eyes; but presently her sight cleared, and she read quickly, her cheeks burning with excitement, her heart throbbing violently. The letter was the last expression of a disappointed and barren life. The slow, stammering tongue of an almost silent existence had found the fulness of speech. The fountains of the deep had been, broken up, and Sybil Eglington's repressed emotions, undeveloped passions, tortured by mortal sufferings, and refined and vitalized by the atmosphere blown in upon her last hours from the Hereafter, were set free, given voice and power at last.

The letter reviewed the life she had lived with her husband during twenty-odd years, reproved herself for not speaking out and telling him his faults at the beginning, and for drawing in upon herself, when she might have compelled him to a truer understanding;

and, when all that was said, called him to such an account as only the dying might make—the irrevocable, disillusionizing truth which may not be altered, the poignant record of failure and its causes.

". . . I could not talk well, I never could, as a girl," the letter ran; "and you could talk like one inspired, and so speciously, so overwhelmingly, that I felt I could say nothing in disagreement, not anything but assent; while all the time I felt how hollow was so much you said —a cloak of words to cover up the real thought behind. Before *I knew the truth*, I felt the shadow of secrecy in your life. When you talked most, I felt you most secretive, and the feeling slowly closed the door upon all frankness and sympathy and open speech between us. I was always shy and self-conscious and self-centred, and thought little of myself; and I needed deep love and confidence and encouragement to give out what was in me. I gave nothing out, nothing to you that you wanted, or sought for, or needed. You were complete, self-contained. Harry, my beloved babe Harry, helped at first; but, as the years went on, he too began to despise me for my little intellect and slow intelligence, and he grew to be like you in all things—and secretive also, though I tried so hard to be to him what a mother should be. Oh, Bobby, Bobby—I used to call you that in the days before we were married, and I will call you that now when all is over and done—why did you not tell me all? Why did you not tell me that my boy, my baby Harry, was not your only child, that there had been another wife, and that your eldest son was alive?

"I know all. I have known all for years. The clergyman who married you to Mercy Claridge was a distant relative of my mother's, and before he died he told me. When you married her, he knew you only as James Fetherdon, but, years afterwards, he saw and recognized you. He held his peace then, but at last he came to to me. And I did not speak. I was not strong enough, nor good enough, to face the trouble of it all. I could not endure the scandal, to see my own son take the second place—he is so brilliant and able and unscrupulous, like yourself; but, oh, so sure of winning a great place in the world, surer than yourself ever was, he is so calculating and determined and ambitious! And though he loves me little, as he loves you little, too, yet he is my son, and for what he is we are both responsible, one way or another; and I had not the courage to give him the second place, and the Quaker, David Claridge, the first place. Why Luke Claridge, his grandfather, chose the course he did, does not concern me, no more than why you chose secrecy, and kept your own first-born legitimate son, of whom you might well be proud, a stranger to you and his rights all these years. Ah, Eglington, you never knew what love was, you never had a heart—experiment, subterfuge, secrecy, 'reaping where you had not sowed, and gathering where you had not strawed.' Always, experiment, experiment, experiment!

"I shall be gone in a few hours—I feel it; but before I go I must try to do right, and to warn you. I have had such bad dreams about you and Harry,—they haunt me—that I am sure you will suffer terribly, will have some awful tragedy, unless you undo what was done long ago, and tell the truth to the world, and give your titles and estates where they truly belong. Near to death, seeing how little life is, and how much right is in the end, I am sure that I was wrong in holding my peace; for Harry cannot prosper with this black thing behind him, and you cannot die happy if you smother up the truth. Night after night I have dreamed of you in your laboratory, a vague, dark, terrifying dream of you in that laboratory which I have hated so. It has always seemed to me the place where some native evil and cruelty in your blood worked out its will. I know I am an ignorant woman, with no brain, but God has given me clear sight at the last, and the things I see are true things, and I must warn you. Remember that...."

The letter ended there. She had been interrupted or seized with illness, and had never finished it; and had died a few hours afterwards; and the letter was now, for the first time, read by her whom it most concerned, into whose heart and soul the words sank with an immitigable pain and agonized amazement. A few moments with this death-document had transformed Hylda's life.

Her husband and—and David, were sons of the same father; and the name she bore, the home in which she was living, the estates the title carried, were not her husband's, but another's—David's. She fell back in her chair, white and faint, but, with a great effort, she conquered the swimming weakness which blinded her. Sons of the same father! The past flashed before her, the strange likeness she had observed, the trick of the head, the laugh, the swift gesture, the something in the voice. She shuddered as she had done in reading the letter. But they were related only in name, in some distant, irreconcilable way — in a way which did not warrant the sudden scarlet flush that flooded her face. Presently she recovered herself. She — what did she suffer, compared with her who wrote this revelation of a lifetime of pain, of bitter and torturing knowledge! She looked up at the picture on the wall, at the still, proud, emotionless face, the conventional, uninspired personality, behind which no one had seen, which had agonized alone till the last. With what tender yet pitiless hand had she laid bare the lives of her husband and her son! How had the neglected mother told the bitter truth of him to whom she had given birth!—"*So brill-*

iant and able, and unscrupulous, like yourself; but, oh, so sure of winning a great place in the world, . . . so calculating and determined and ambitious. . . . That laboratory which I have hated so. It has always seemed to me the place where some native evil and cruelty in your blood worked out its will. . . ."

With a deep-drawn sigh Hylda said to herself, "If I were dying to-morrow, would I say that? She loved them so—at first must have loved them so; and yet this at the last! And I—oh, no, no, no!" She looked at a portrait of Eglington on the table near, touched it caressingly, and added, with a sob in her voice, "Oh, Harry, no, it is not true! It is not native evil and cruelty in your blood. It has all been a mistake. You will do right. *We* will do right, Harry. You will suffer, it will hurt, the lesson will be hard—to give up what has meant so much to you; but we will work it out together, you and I, my very dear. Oh, say that we shall, that . . ."

She suddenly grew silent. A tremor ran through her, she became conscious of his presence near her, and turned, as though he were behind her. There was nothing. Yet she felt him near, and, as she did so, the soul-deep feeling with which she had spoken to the portrait fled. Why was it that, so often, when absent from him, her imagination helped her to make excuses for him, inspired her to press the real truth out of sight, and to make believe that he was worthy of a love which, but through some inner fault of her own, might be his altogether, and all the love of which he was capable might be hers?

She felt him near her, and the feelings possessing her a moment before slowly chilled and sank away. Instinctively her eyes glanced towards the door. She saw the handle turn, and she slipped the letter inside the portfolio again.

The door opened briskly now, and Eglington entered with what his enemies in the newspaper press had called his "professional smile"—a criticism which had angered his wife, chiefly because it was so near the truth. He smiled, smiling was part of his equipment, and was for any one at any time that suited him.

Her eyes met his, and he noted in her something that he had never seen before. Something had happened. The Duchess of Snowdon was in the house; had it anything to do with her? Had she made trouble? There was trouble enough without her. He came forward, took Hylda's hand and kissed it, then kissed her on the cheek. As he did so, she laid a hand on his arm with a sudden impulse, and pressed it. Though his presence had chilled the high emotions of a few moments before, yet she had to break to him a truth which would hurt him, dismay him, rob his life of so much that helped it; and a sudden protective, maternal sense was roused in her, reached out to shelter him as he faced his loss and the call of duty.

"You have just come?" she said, in a voice that, to herself, seemed far away.

"I have been here some hours," he answered.

Secrecy again—always the thing that had chilled the dead woman, and laid a cold hand upon herself—"*I felt the shadow of secrecy in your life. When you talked most, I felt you most secretive, and the feeling slowly closed the door upon all frankness and sympathy and open speech between us.*"

"Why did you not see me—dine with me?" she asked. "What can the servants think?" Even in such a crisis the little things had place—habit struck its note in the presence of her tragedy.

"You had the Duchess of Snowdon, and we are not precisely congenial; besides, I had much to do in the laboratory. I'm working for that new explosive of which I told you. There's fame and fortune in it, and I'm on the way. I feel it coming"—his eyes sparkled a little. "I made it right with the servants; so don't be apprehensive."

"I have not seen you for nearly a week. It doesn't seem—friendly."

"Politics and science are stern masters," he answered gaily.

"They leave little time for your mistress," she rejoined meaningly.

"Who is my mistress?"

"Well, I am not greatly your wife," she replied. "I have the dregs of your life. I help you—I am allowed to help you—so little, to share so little in the things that matter to you."

"Now, that's imagination and misunderstanding," he rejoined. "It has helped immensely your being such a figure in society, and entertaining so much, and being so popular, at any rate until very lately."

"I do not misunderstand," she answered gravely. "I do not share your real life. I do not help you where your brain works, in the plans and purposes and hopes that lie behind all that you do—oh yes, I know your ambitions and what positions you are aiming for; but there is something more than that. There is the object of it all, the pulse of it, the machinery down, down deep in your being that drives it all. Oh, I am not a child! I have some intellect, and I want—I want that we should work it out together."

In spite of all that had come and gone, in spite of the dead mother's words and all her own convictions, seeing trouble coming upon him, she wanted to make one last effort for what might save their lives—her life—from shipwreck in the end. If she failed now, she foresaw a bitter, cynical figure working out his life with a narrowing soul, a hard spirit unrelieved by the softening influence of a great love—even yet the woman in her had a far-off hope that, where the law had made them one by book and scrip, the love which should consecrate such a union, lift it above an almost offensive relation, might be theirs. She did not know how much of her heart, of her being, was wandering over the distant sands of Egypt, looking for its oasis. Eglington had never needed or wanted more than she had given him—her fortune, her person, her charm, her ability to play an express and definite part in his career. It was this material use to which she was so largely assigned, almost involuntarily but none the less truly, that had destroyed all of the finer, dearer, more delicate intimacy invading his mind sometimes, more or less vaguely, where Faith was concerned. So extreme was his egotism that it had never occurred to him, as it had done to the Duchess of Snowdon and Lord Windlehurst, that he might lose Hylda herself as well as her fortune; that the day might come when her high spirit could bear it no longer. As the Duchess of Snowdon had said, "It would all depend upon the other man, whoever he might be."

So he answered her with superficial cheerfulness now; he had not the depth of soul to see that they were at a crisis, and that she could bear no longer the old method of treating her as though she were a child, to be humored or to be dominated.

"Oh, you see all there is," he answered; "you are so imaginative, crying for some moon there never was in any sky."

In part he had spoken the truth. He had no high objects or ends or purposes. He wanted only success somehow or another, and there was no nobility of mind or aspiration behind it. In her heart of hearts she knew it; but it was the last cry of her soul to him, seeking, though in vain, for what she had never had, could never have.

"What have you been doing?" he added, looking at the desk where she had sat, glancing round the room. "Has the Duchess left any rags on the multitude of her acquaintances? I wonder that you can make yourself contented here with nothing to do. You don't look much stronger. I'm sure you ought to have a change. My mother was never well here; though, for the matter of that, she was never very well anywhere. I suppose it's the laboratory that attracts me here, as it did my father, playing with the ancient forces of the world in these Arcadian surroundings—Arcady without beauty or Arcadians." He glanced up at his mother's picture. "No, she never liked it—a very silent woman, secretive almost."

Suddenly her eye flared up. Anger possessed her. She choked it down. Secretive—the poor bruised soul who had gone to her grave with a broken heart!

"She secretive? No, Eglington," she rejoined gravely, "she was congealed. She lived in too cold an air. She was not secretive, but yet she kept a secret—another's!"

Again Eglington had the feeling which possessed him when he entered the room. She had changed. There was something in her tone, a meaning he had never heard before. He was startled. He recalled the words of the Duchess as she went up the staircase.

What was it all about?

"Whose secrets did she keep?" he asked, calmly enough.

"Your father's, yours, mine," she replied, in a whisper almost.

"Secret? What secret? Good Lord, such mystery!" He laughed mirthlessly.

She came close to him. "I am sorry—sorry, Harry," she said with difficulty. "It will hurt you, shock you so. It will be a blow to you, but you must bear it."

She tried to speak further, but her heart was beating so

violently that she could not. She turned quickly to the portfolio on the desk, drew forth the fatal letter, and, turning to the page which contained the truth concerning David, handed it to him. "It is there," she said.

He had great self-control. Before looking at the page to which she had directed his attention, he turned the letter over slowly, fingering the pages one by one. "My mother to my father," he remarked.

Instinctively he knew what it contained. "You have been reading my mother's correspondence," he added in cold reproof.

"Do you forget that you asked me to arrange her papers?" she retorted, stung by his suggestion.

"Your imagination is vivid," he exclaimed. Then he bethought himself that, after all, he might sorely need all she could give, if things went against him, and that she was the last person he could afford to alienate; "but I do remember that I asked you that," he added—"no doubt foolishly."

"Read what is there," she broke in, "and you will see that it was not foolish, that it was meant to be."

He felt a cold, dead hand reaching out from the past to strike him; but he nerved himself, and his eyes searched the paper with assumed coolness—even with her he must still be acting. The first words he saw were, "*Why did you not tell me that my boy, my baby Harry, was not your only child, . . . and that your eldest son was alive?*"

So, that was it, after all. Even his mother knew. Master of his nerves as he was, it blinded him for a moment. Presently he read on,—the whole page—and lingered upon the words, that he might have time to think what he must say to Hylda. Nothing of the tragedy of his mother touched him, though he was faintly conscious of a revelation of a woman he had never known, whose hungering caresses had made him, as a child, rather peevish when, a fit of affection was not on him. Suddenly as he read the lines touching himself, "*Brilliant and able and unscrupulous . . . and though he loves me little, as he loves you little, too*," his eye lighted up with anger, his face became pale—yet he had borne the same truths from Faith without resentment, in the wood by the mill that other year. For a moment he stood infuriated, then, going to the fireplace, he dropped the letter on the coals, as Hylda, in horror, started forward to arrest his hand.

"Oh, Eglington—but no—no! It is not honorable. It is proof of all!"

He turned upon her slowly, his face rigid, a strange, cold light in his eyes. "If there is no more proof than that, you need not vex your mind," he said, commanding his voice to evenness.

A bitter anger was on him. His mother had read him through and through—he had not deceived her even; and she had given evidence against him to Hylda, who, he had ever thought, believed in him completely. Now there was added to the miserable tale, that first marriage, and the rights of David—David, the man who, he was convinced, had captured her imagination! Hurt vanity played a disproportionate part in this crisis.

The effect on him had been different from what Hylda had anticipated. She had pictured him stricken and dumfounded by the blow. It had never occurred to her, it did not now, that he had known the truth; for, of course, to know the truth was to speak, to restore to David his own, to step down into the second and unconsidered place. After all, to her mind, there was no disgrace. The late Earl had married secretly, but he had been duly married, and he did not marry again until Mercy Claridge was dead. The only wrong was to David, whose grandfather had been even more to blame than his own father. She had looked to help

Eglington in this moment, and now there seemed nothing for her to do. He was superior to the situation, though it was apparent in his pale face and rigid manner that he had been struck hard.

She came near to him, but there was no encouragement to her to play that part which is a woman's deepest right and joy and pain in one—to comfort her man in trouble, sorrow, or evil. Always, always, he stood alone, whatever the moment might be, leaving her nothing to do—"playing his own game with his own weapons," as he had once put it. But there was strength in it, too, and this came to her mind now, as though in excuse for whatever else there was in the situation which, against her will, repelled her.

"I am so sorry for you," she said at last.

"What do you mean?" he asked.

"To lose all that has been yours so long."

This was their great moment. The response to this must be the touchstone of their lives. A half-dozen words might alter all the future, might be the watchword to the end of all things. Involuntarily her heart fashioned the response he ought to give—"*I shall have you left, Hylda.*"

The air seemed to grow oppressive, and the instant's silence a torture, and, when he spoke, his words struck a chill to her heart—rough notes of pain. "I have not lost yet," were his words.

She shrank. "You will not hide it. You will do right by—by him," she said, with difficulty.

"Let him establish his claim to the last item of fact," he said, with savage hate.

"Luke Claridge knew. The proofs are but just across the way, no doubt," she answered, almost coldly, so had his words congealed her heart.

Their great moment had passed. It was as though a cord had snapped that held her to him, and in the recoil she had been thrown far off from him. Swift as his mind worked, it had not seen his opportunity to win her to his cause, to asphyxiate her high senses, her quixotic justice, by that old flood of eloquence and compelling persuasion of the emotions with which he had swept her to the altar—an altar of sacrifice. He had not even done what he had left London to do—make sure of her, by an alluring flattery and devotion, no difficult duty with one so beautiful and desirable; though neither love of beauty nor great desire was strong enough in him to divert him from his course for an hour, save by his own initiative. His mother's letter had changed it all. A few hours before he had had a struggle with Soolsby, and now another struggle on the same theme was here. Fate had dealt illy with him, who had ever been its spoiled child and favorite. He had not learned yet the arts of defence against adversity.

"Luke Claridge is dead," he answered sharply.

"But you will tell—him, you will write to Egypt and tell your brother?" she said, the conviction slowly coming to her that he would not.

"It is not my duty to displace myself, to furnish evidence against myself—"

"You have destroyed the evidence," she intervened, a little scornfully.

"If there were no more than that—" He shrugged his shoulders impatiently.

"Do you know there is more?" she asked searchingly.

"In whose interests are you speaking?" he rejoined, with a sneer. A sudden fury possessed him. Claridge Pasha—she was thinking of him!

"In yours—your conscience, your honor."

"There is over thirty years' possession on my side," he rejoined.

"It is not as if it were going from your family," she argued.

"Family—what is he to me!"

"What is any one to you!" she returned bitterly.

"I am not going to unravel a mystery, in order to facilitate the cutting of my own throat."

"It might be worth while to do something once for another's sake than your own — it would break the monotony," she retorted, all her sense tortured by his words, and even more so by his manner.

Long ago Faith had said in Soolsby's hut that he "blandished" all with whom he came in contact; but Hylda realized with a lacerated heart that he had ceased to blandish her. Possession had altered that. Yet how had he vowed to her in those sweet tempestuous days of his courtship, when the wind of his passion blew so hard! Had one of the vows been kept?

Even as she looked at him now, words she had read some days before flashed through her mind—they had burnt themselves into her brain:

> "Broken faith is the crown of evils,
> Broken vows are the knotted thongs
> Set in the hands of laughing devils,
> To scourge us for deep wrongs.
>
> "Broken hearts, when all is ended,
> Bear the better all after-stings;
> Bruised once, the citadel mended
> Standeth through all things."

Suddenly he turned upon her with aggrieved petulance. "Why are you so eager for proof?"

"Oh, I have," she said, with a sudden flood of tears in her voice, though her eyes were dry—"I have the feeling your mother had, that nothing will be well until you undo the wrong your father did. I know it was not your fault. I feel for you—oh, believe me, I feel as I have never felt, could never feel, for myself. It was brought on you by your father, but you must be the more innocent because he was so guilty. You have had much out of it, it has helped you on your way. It does not mean so much now. By-and-by another—an English—peerage may be yours by your own achievement. Let it go. There is so much left, Harry. It is a small thing in a world of work. It means nothing to me."

Once again, even when she had given up all hope, seeing what was the bent of his mind—once again she made essay to win him out of his selfishness. If he would only say, "I have you left," how she would strive to shut all else out of her life!

He was exasperated. His usual prescience and prudence forsook him. It angered him that she should press him to an act of sacrifice for the man who had so great an influence upon her. Perversity possessed him. Lifelong egotism was too strong for wisdom, or discretion.

Suddenly he caught her hands in both of his and said hoarsely, "Do you love me—answer me, do you love me with all your heart and soul? The truth now, as though it were your last word on earth."

Always self. She had asked, if not in so many words, for a little love, something for herself to feed on in the darkening days for him, for her, for both; and he was thinking only of himself.

She shrank, but her hands lay passive in his. "No, not with all my heart and soul—but—oh—!"

He flung her hands from him. "No, not with all your heart and soul—I know! You are willing to sacrifice me for him, and you think I do not understand."

She drew herself up, with burning cheeks and flashing eyes. "You understand nothing—nothing. If you had ever understood me, or any human being, or any human heart, you would not have ruined all that might have given you an undying love, something that would have followed you through fire and flood to the grave. You cannot love. You do not understand love. Self—self, always self. Oh, you are mad, mad, to have thrown it all away, all that might have given happiness! All that I have, all that I am, has been at your service; everything has been bent and tuned to your pleasure, for your good. All has been done for you, with thought of you and your position and your advancement, and now—now, when you have killed all that might have been yours, you cry out in anger that it is dying, and you insinuate what you should kill another for insinuating. Oh, the wicked, cruel folly of it all! You suggest—you dare!—I never heard a word from David Claridge that might not be written on the hoardings. His honor is deeper than that which might attach to the title of Earl of Eglington."

She seemed to tower above him. For an instant she looked him in the eyes with frigid dignity, but a great scorn in her face. Then she went to the door—he hastened to open it for her.

"You will be very sorry for this," he said stubbornly. He was too dumfounded to be discreet, too suddenly embarrassed by the turn affairs had taken. He realized too late that he had made a mistake, that he had lost his hold upon her.

As she passed through, there suddenly flashed before her mind the scene in the laboratory with the chairmaker. She felt the meaning of it now.

"You do not intend to tell him—perhaps Soolsby has done so," she said keenly, and moved on to the staircase.

He was thunderstruck at her intuition. "Why do you want to rob yourself?" he asked after her vaguely.

She turned back. "Think of your mother's letter that you destroyed," she rejoined solemnly and quietly. "Was it right?"

He shut the door, and threw himself into a chair. "I will put it straight with her to-morrow," he said helplessly.

He sat for a half-hour silent, planning his course. At last there came a tap at the door, and the butler appeared.

"Some one from the Foreign Office, my lord," he said.

A moment afterwards a young official, his subordinate, entered. "There's the deuce to pay in Egypt, sir; I've brought the despatch," he said.

BOOK IV

XXVIII

NAHOUM TURNS THE SCREW

Laughing to himself, Higli Pasha sat with the stem of a narghileh in his mouth. His big shoulders kept time to the quivering of his fat stomach. He was sitting in a small courtyard of Nahoum Pasha's palace, waiting for its owner to appear. Meanwhile he exercised a hilarous patience. The years had changed him little since he had been sent on that expedition against the southern tribes which followed hard on David's appointment to office. As David had expected, few of the traitorous officers returned. Diaz had ignominiously died of the bite of a tarantula before a blow had been struck, but Higli had gratefully received a slight wound in the first encounter, which enabled him to beat a safe retreat to Cairo. He alone of the chief of the old conspirators was left. Achmet was still at the Place of Lepers, and the old nest of traitors was scattered forever.

Only Nahoum and Higli were left, and between these two there had never been partnership or understanding. Nahoum was not the man to trust to confederates, and Higli Pasha was too contemptible a coadjutor. Nahoum had faith in no one save Mizraim, the Chief Eunuch, but Mizraim alone was better than a thousand; and he was secret—and terrible. Yet Higli had a conviction that Nahoum's alliance with David was a sham, and that David would pay the price of misplaced confidence one day. More than once when David's plans had had a setback, Higli had contrived a meeting with Nahoum, to judge for himself the true position.

For his visit to-day he had invented a reason—a matter of finance; but his real reason was concealed behind the malevolent merriment by which he was now seized. So absorbed was he that he did not heed the approach of another visitor down an angle of the courtyard. He was roused by a voice.

"Well, what's tickling you so, pasha?"

The voice was drawling, and quite gentle; but at the sound of it, Higli's laugh stopped short, and the muscles of his face contracted. If there was one man of whom he had a wholesome fear—why, he could not tell—it was this round-faced, abrupt, imperturbable American, Claridge Pasha's right-hand man. Legends of resourcefulness and bravery had gathered round his name.

"Who's been stroking your chin with a feather, pasha?" he continued, his eye piercing the other like a gimlet.

"It was an amusing tale I heard at Assiout, effendi," was Higli's abashed and surly reply.

"Oh, at Assiout!" rejoined Lacey. "Yes, they tell funny stories at Assiout. And when were you at Assiout, pasha?"

"Two days ago, effendi."

"And so you thought you'd tell the funny little story to Nahoum as quick as could be, eh? He likes funny stories, same as you—damn, nice, funny little stories, eh?"

There was something chilly in Lacey's voice now, which Higli did not like; something much too menacing and contemptuous for a mere man-of-all-work to the Inglesi. Higli bridled up, his eyes glared sulkily.

"It is but my own business if I laugh or if I curse,

effendi," he replied, his hand shaking a little on the stem of the narghileh.

"Precisely, my diaphanous polyandrist; but it isn't quite your own affair what you laugh at—not if I know it!"

"Does the effendi think I was laughing at him?"

"The effendi thinks not. The effendi knows that the descendant of a hundred tigers was laughing at the funny little story, of how the two cotton-mills that Claridge Pasha built were burned down all in one night, and one of his steamers sent down the cataract at Assouan. A knock-down blow for Claridge Pasha, eh? That's all you thought of, wasn't it? And it doesn't matter to you that the cotton-mills made thousands better off, and started new industries in Egypt. No, it only matters to you that Claridge Pasha loses half his fortune, and that you think his feet are in the quicksands, and 'll be sucked in, to make an Egyptian holiday. Anything to discredit him here, eh? I'm not sure what else you know; but I'll find out, my noble pasha, and if you've had your hand in it—but no, you ain't game-cock enough for that! But if you were, if you had a hand in the making of your funny little story, there's a nutcracker that 'd break the shell of that joke—"

He turned round quickly, seeing a shadow and hearing a movement. Nahoum was but a few feet away. There was a bland smile on his face, a look of innocence in his magnificent blue eye. As he met Lacey's look, the smile left his lips, a grave sympathy appeared to possess them, and he spoke softly,—

"I know the thing that burns thy heart, effendi, to whom be the flowers of hope and the fruits of merit. It is even so—a great blow has fallen. Two hours since I heard. I went at once to see Claridge Pasha, but found him not. Does he know, think you?" he added sadly.

"May your heart never be harder than it is, pasha; and when I left the Saadat an hour ago, he did not know. His messenger hadn't a steamer like Higli Pasha there. But he was coming to see you; and that's why I'm here. I've been brushing the flies off this sore on the hump of Egypt while waiting." He glanced with disdain at Higli.

A smile rose like liquid in the eye of Nahoum and subsided, then he turned to Higli inquiringly.

"I have come on business, excellency; the railway to Rosetta, and—"

"To-morrow—or the next day," responded Nahoum irritably, and turned again to Lacey.

As Higli's huge frame disappeared through a gateway, Nahoum motioned Lacey to a divan, and summoned a slave for cooling drinks. Lacey's eyes now watched him with an innocence nearly as childlike as his own. Lacey well knew that here was a foe worthy of the best steel. That he was a foe, and a malignant foe, he had no doubt whatever; he had settled the point in his mind long ago; and two letters he had received from Lady Eglington, in which she had said in so many words, "*Watch Nahoum!*" had made him vigilant and intuitive. He knew, meanwhile, that he was following the trail of a master-hunter who covered up his tracks. Lacey was as certain as though he had the book of Nahoum's mind open in his hand, that David's work had been torn down again —and this time with dire effect—by this Armenian, whom David trusted like a brother. But the black doors that closed on the truth on every side only made him more determined to unlock them; and, when he faltered as to his own powers, he trusted Mahommed Hassan, whose devotion to David had given him eyes that pierced dark places.

"Surely the God of Israel has smitten Claridge Pasha sorely. My heart will mourn to look upon his face. The day is insulting in its brightness," continued Nahoum with a sigh, his eyes bent upon Lacey, dejection in his shoulders.

Lacey started. "*The God of Israel!*" How blasphemous it sounded from the lips of Nahoum, Oriental of Orientals, Christian though he was also!

"I think, perhaps, you'll get over it, pasha. Man is born to trouble, and you've got a lot of courage. I guess you could see other people bear a pile of suffering, and never flinch."

Nahoum appeared not to notice the gibe. "It is a land of suffering, effendi," he sighed, "and one sees what one sees."

"Have you any idea, any real sensible idea, how those cotton-mills got afire?" Lacey's eyes were fixed on Nahoum's face.

The other met his gaze calmly. "Who can tell! An accident, perhaps, or—"

"Or some one set the mills on fire in several places at once—they say the buildings flamed out in every corner; and it was the only time in a month they hadn't been running night and day. Funny, isn't it?"

"It looks like the work of an enemy, effendi." Nahoum shook his head gravely. "A fortune destroyed in an hour, as it were. But we shall get the dog. We shall find him. There is no hole deep enough to hide him from us."

"Oh, I wouldn't go looking in holes for him, pasha. He isn't any cave-dweller, that incendiary; he's an artist—no palace is too unlikely for him. No, I wouldn't go poking in mud huts to find him."

"Thou dost not think that Higli Pasha—" Nahoum seemed startled out of equanimity by the thought.

Lacey eyed him meditatively, and said reflectively, "Say, you're an artist, pasha. You are a guesser of the first rank. But I'd guess again. Higli Pasha would have done it, if it had ever occurred to him; and he'd had the pluck. But it didn't, and he hadn't. What I can't understand is that the artist that did it should have done it before Claridge Pasha left for the Soudan. Here we were just about to start; and if we'd got away south, the job would have done more harm, and the Saadat would have been out of the way. No, I can't understand why the firebug didn't let us get clean away; for if the Saadat stays here, he'll be where he can stop the underground mining."

Nahoum's self-control did not desert him, though he fully realized that this man suspected him. On the surface Lacey was right. It would have seemed better to let David go, and destroy his work afterwards, but he had been moved by other considerations, and his design was deep. His own emissaries were in the Soudan, announcing David's determination to abolish slavery, secretly stirring up feeling against him, preparing for the final blow to be delivered, when he went again among the southern tribes. He had waited and waited, and now the time was come. Had he, Nahoum, not agreed with David that the time had come for the slave-trade to go? Had he not encouraged him to take this bold step, in the sure belief that it would overwhelm him, and bring him an ignominious death, embittered by total failure of all he had tried to do?

For years he had secretly loosened the foundations of David's work, and the triumph of Oriental duplicity over Western civilization and integrity was sweet in his mouth. And now there was reason to believe that, at last, Kaïd was turning against the Inglesi. Everything would come at once. If all that he had planned was successful, even this man before him should aid in his master's destruction.

"If it was all done by an enemy," he said, in answer to Lacey, at last, "would it all be reasoned out like that?

Is hatred so logical? Dost thou think Claridge Pasha will not go now? The troops are ready at Wady-Halfa, everything is in order; the last load of equipment has gone. Will not Claridge Pasha find the money somehow? I will do what I can. My heart is moved to aid him."

"Yes, you'd do what you could, pasha," Lacey rejoined enigmatically, "but whether it would set the Saadat on his expedition or not is a question. But I guess, after all, he's got to go. He willed it so. People may try to stop him, and they may tear down what he does, but he does at last what he starts to do, and no one can prevent him—not any one. Yes, he's going on this expedition; and he'll have the money, too." There was a strange abstracted look in his face, as though he saw something which held him fascinated.

Presently, as if with an effort, he rose to his feet, took the red fez from his head, and fanned himself with it for a moment. "Don't you forget it, pasha; the Saadat will win. He can't be beaten, not in a thousand years. Here he comes."

Nahoum got to his feet as David came quickly through the small gateway of the courtyard, his head erect, his lips smiling, his eyes sweeping the place. He came forward briskly to them. It was plain he had not heard the evil news.

"Peace be to thee, Saadat, and may thy life be fenced about with safety!" said Nahoum.

David laid a hand on Lacey's arm and squeezed it, smiling at him with such friendship that Lacey's eyes moistened, and he turned his head away.

There was a quiet elation in David's look. "We are ready at last," he said, looking from one to the other. "Well, well," he added, almost boyishly, "has thee nothing to say, Nahoum?"

Nahoum turned his head away as though overcome.

David's face grew instantly grave. He turned to Lacey. Never before had he seen Lacey's face with a look like this. He grasped Lacey's arm. "What is it?" he asked quietly. "What does thee want to say to me?"

But Lacey could not speak, and David turned again to Nahoum. "What is there to say to me?" he asked. "Something has happened—what is it? . . . Come, many things have happened before. This can be no worse. Do thee speak," he urged gently.

"Saadat," said Nahoum, as though under the stress of feeling, "the cotton-mills at Tashah and Mini are gone—burned to the ground."

For a moment David looked at him without sight in his eyes, and his face grew very pale. "Excellency, all in one night, the besom of destruction was abroad," he heard Nahoum say, as though from great depths below him. He slowly turned his head to look at Lacey. "Is this true?" he asked at last in an unsteady voice. Lacey could not speak, but inclined his head.

David's figure seemed to shrink for a moment, his face had a withered look, and his head fell forward in a mood of terrible dejection.

"Saadat! Oh, my God, Saadat, don't take it so!" said Lacey brokenly, and stepped between David and Nahoum. He could not bear that the stricken face and figure should be seen by Nahoum, whom he believed to be secretly gloating. "Saadat," he said brokenly, "God has always been with you; He hasn't forgotten you now."

"The work of years," David murmured, and seemed not to hear.

"When God permits, shall man despair?" interposed Nahoum, in a voice that lingered on the words.

Nahoum accomplished what Lacey had failed to do. His voice had pierced to some remote corner in David's nature, and roused him. Was it that doubt, suspicion, had been wakened at last? Was some sensitive nerve touched, that this Oriental should offer Christian comfort to him in his need—to him who had seen the greater light? Or was it that some unreality in the words struck a note which excited a new and subconscious understanding? Perhaps it was a little of all three. He did not stop to inquire. In crises such as that through which he was passing, the mind and body act without reason, rather by the primal instinct, the certain call of the things that were before reason was.

"God is with the patient," continued Nahoum; and Lacey set his teeth to bear this insult to all things.

But Nahoum accomplished what he had not anticipated. David straightened himself up, and clasped his hands behind him. By a supreme effort of the will he controlled himself, and the color came back faintly to his face. "God's will be done," he said, and looked Nahoum calmly in the eyes. "It was no accident," he added with conviction. "It was an enemy of Egypt."

Suddenly the thing rushed over him again, going through his veins like a poisonous ether, and clamping his heart as with iron. "All to do over again!" he said brokenly, and again he caught Lacey's arm.

With an uncontrollable impulse Lacey took David's hand in his own warm, human grasp.

"Once I thought I lost everything in Mexico, Saadat, and I understand what you feel. But all wasn't lost in Mexico, as I found at last, and I got something, too, that I didn't put in. Say, let us go from here. God is backing you, Saadat. Isn't it all right—same as ever?"

David was himself again. "Thee is a good man," he said, and through the sadness of his eyes there stole a smile. "Let us go," he said. Then he added in a business-like way, "To-morrow at seven, Nahoum. There is much to do."

He turned towards the gate with Lacey, where the horses waited. Mahommed Hassan met them as they prepared to mount. He handed David a letter. It was from Faith, and contained the news of Luke Claridge's death. Everything had come at once. He stumbled into the saddle with a moan.

"At last I have drawn blood," said Nahoum to himself with grim satisfaction, as they disappeared. "It is the beginning of the end. It will crush him—I saw it in his eyes. God of Israel, I shall rule again in Egypt!"

XXIX

THE RECOIL

It was a great day in the Muslim year. The Mahmal, or Sacred Carpet, was leaving Cairo on its long pilgrimage of thirty-seven days to Mecca and Mahomet's tomb. Great guns boomed from the Citadel, as the gorgeous procession, forming itself beneath the Mokattam Hills, began its slow march to where, seated in the shade of an ornate pavilion, Prince Kaïd awaited its approach to pay devout homage. Thousands looked down at the scene from the ramparts of the Citadel, from the overhanging cliffs, and from the tops of the houses that hung on the ledges of rock rising abruptly from the level ground, to which the last of the famed Mamelukes leaped to their destruction.

Now to Prince Kaïd's ears there came from hundreds of hoarse throats the cry, "*Allah! Allah! May thy journey be with safety to Arafat!*" mingling with the harsh music of the fifes and drums.

Kaïd looked upon the scene with drawn face and lowering brows. His retinue watched him with alarm. A whisper had passed that, two nights before, the Effendina had sent in haste for a famous Italian physician lately come to Cairo, and that since his visit Kaïd had been sullen and depressed. It was also the gossip of the bazaars that he had suddenly shown favor to those of the Royal House and to other reactionaries, who had been enemies to the influence of Claridge Pasha. This rumor had been followed by an official proclamation that no Europeans or Christians would be admitted to the ceremony of the Sacred Carpet.

Thus it was that Kaïd looked out on a vast multitude of Muslims, in which not one European face showed, and from lip to lip there passed the word, "Harrik—Harrik—remember Harrik! Kaïd turns from the infidel!"

They crowded near the great pavilion—as near as the mounted Nubians would permit—to see Kaïd's face; while he, with eyes wandering over the vast assemblage, was lost in dark reflections. For a year he had struggled against a growing conviction that some obscure disease was sapping his strength. He had hid it from every one, until, at last, distress and pain had overcome him. The verdict of the Italian expert was that possible, but by no means certain, cure might come from an operation which must be delayed for a month or more.

Suddenly, the world had grown unfamiliar to him; he saw it from afar; but his subconscious self involuntarily registered impressions, and he moved mechanically through the ceremonies and duties of the immediate present. Thrown back upon himself, to fight his own fight, with the instinct of primary life his mind involuntarily drew for refuge to the habits and predispositions of youth; and for two days he had shut himself away from the activities with which David and Nahoum were associated. Being deeply engaged with the details of the expedition to the Soudan, David had not gone to the Palace; and he was unaware of the turn which things had taken.

Three times, with slow and stately steps, the procession wound in a circle in the great square, before it approached the pavilion where the Effendina sat, the splendid camels carrying the embroidered tent wherein the Carpet rested, and that which bore the Emir of the Pilgrims, moving gracefully like ships at sea. Naked swordsmen, with upright and shining blades, were followed by men on camels bearing kettle-drums. After them came Arab riders with fresh green branches fastened to the saddles like plumes, while others carried flags and banners emblazoned with texts and symbols. Troops of horsemen in white woollen cloaks, sheikhs and Bedouins with flowing robes and huge turbans, religious chiefs of the great sects, imperturbable and statuesque, were in strange contrast to the shouting dervishes and camel-drivers and eager pilgrims.

At last the great camel with its sacred burden stopped in front of Kaïd for his prayer and blessing. As he held the tassels, lifted the gold-fringed curtain, and invoked Allah's blessing, a half-naked sheikh ran forward, and, raising his hand high above his head, cried shrilly, "Kaïd, Kaïd, hearken!"

Rough hands caught him away, but Kaïd commanded them to desist; and the man called a blessing on him, and cried aloud:

"Listen, O Kaïd, son of the stars and the light of day. God hath exalted thee. Thou art the Egyptian of all the Egyptians. In thy hand is power. But thou art mortal even as I. Behold, O Kaïd, in the hour that I was born thou wast born, I in the dust without thy Palace wall, thou amid the splendid things. But thy star is my star. Behold, as God ordains, the Tree of Life was shaken on the night when all men pray and cry aloud to God—even the Night of the Falling Leaves. And I watched the falling leaves; and I saw my leaf, and it was withered, but only a little withered, and so I live yet a little. But I looked for thy leaf, thou who wert born in that moment when I waked to the world. I looked long, but I found no leaf, neither green nor withered. But I looked again upon my leaf, and then I saw that thy name now was also upon my leaf, and that it was neither green nor withered; but was a leaf that drooped as when an evil wind has passed and drunk its life. Listen, O Kaïd! Upon the tomb of Mahomet I will set my lips, and it may be that the leaf of my life will come fresh and green again. But thou—wilt thou not come also to the lord Mahomet's tomb? Or"—he paused and raised his voice—"or wilt thou stay and lay thy lips upon the cross of the infidel? Wilt thou—"

He could say no more, for Kaïd's face now darkened with anger. He made a gesture, and, in an instant, the man was gagged and bound, while a sullen silence fell upon the crowd. Kaïd suddenly became aware of this change of feeling, and looked round him. Presently his old prudence and subtlety came back, his face cleared a little, and he called aloud, "Unloose the man, and let him come to me." An instant after, the man was on his knees, silent before him.

"What is thy name?" Kaïd asked.

"Kaïd Ibrahim, Effendina," was the reply.

"Thou hast misinterpreted thy dream, Kaïd Ibrahim," answered the Effendina. "The drooping leaf was token of the danger in which thy life should be, and my name upon thy leaf was token that I should save thee from death. Behold, I save thee. Inshallah, go in peace! There is no God but God, and the Cross is the sign of a false prophet. Thou art mad. God give thee a new mind. Go."

The man was presently lost in the sweltering, half-frenzied crowd; but he had done his work, and his words rang in the ears of Kaïd as he rode away.

A few hours afterwards, bitter and rebellious, murmuring to himself, Kaïd sat in a darkened room of his Nile Palace beyond the city. So few years on the throne, so young, so much on which to lay the hand of pleasure, so many millions to command; and yet the slave at his door had a surer hold on life and all its joy and lures than he, Prince Kaïd, ruler of Egypt! There was on him that barbaric despair which has taken dreadful toll of life for the decree of destiny. Across the record of this day, as across the history of many an Eastern and pagan tyrant, was written, "He would not die alone." That the world should go on when he was gone, that men should buy and sell and laugh and drink, and flaunt it in the sun, while he, Prince Kaïd, would be done with it all—

He was roused by the rustling of a robe. Before him stood the Arab physician, Sharif Bey, who had been in his father's house and his own for a lifetime. It was many a year since his ministrations to Kaïd had ceased; but he had remained on in the Palace, doing service to those who received him, and—it was said by the evil-tongued—granting certificates of death out of harmony with dark facts, a sinister and useful figure. His beard was white, his face was friendly, almost benevolent, but his eyes had a light caught from no celestial flame.

His look was confident now, as his eyes bent on Kaïd. He had lived long, he had seen much, he had heard of the peril that had been foreshadowed by the infidel physician; and, by a sure instinct, he knew that his own opportunity had come. He knew that Kaïd would snatch at any offered comfort, would cherish any alleviating lie, would steal back from science and civilization and the modern palace to the superstition of the fellah's hut. Were not all men alike when the neboot of Fate struck them down into the terrible loneliness of doom, numbing their minds? Luck would be with him that offered first succor in that dark hour. Sharif had come at the right moment for Sharif.

Kaïd looked at him with dull yet anxious eyes. "Did I not command that none should enter?" he asked presently, in a thick voice.

"Am I not thy physician, Effendina, to whom be the undying years? When the Effendina is sick, shall I not heal? Have I not waited like a dog at thy door these many years, till that the time would come when none could heal thee save Sharif?"

"What canst thou give me?"

"What the infidel physician gave thee not—I can give thee hope. Hast thou done well, O Effendina, to turn from thine own people? Did not thine own father, and did not Mehemet Ali, live to a good age? Who were their physicians? My father and I, and my father's father, and his father's father."

"Thou canst cure me altogether?" asked Kaïd hesitatingly.

"Wilt thou not have faith in one of thine own race? Will the infidel love thee as do we, who are thy children and thy brothers, who are to thee as a nail driven in the wall, not to be moved? Thou shalt live—Inshallah, thou shalt have healing and length of days!"

He paused at a gesture from Kaïd, for a slave had entered and stood waiting.

"What dost thou here? Wert thou not commanded?" asked Kaïd.

"Effendina, Claridge Pasha is waiting," was the reply.

Kaïd frowned, hesitated; then, with a sudden resolve, made a gesture of dismissal to Sharif Bey, and nodded David's admittance to the slave.

As David entered, he passed Sharif Bey, and something in the look on the Arab physician's face—a secret malignancy and triumph—struck him strangely. And now a fresh anxiety and apprehension rose in his mind as he glanced at Kaïd. The eye was heavy and gloomy, the face was clouded, the lips once so ready to smile at him were sullen and smileless now. David stood still, waiting.

"I did not expect thee till to-morrow, Saadat," said Kaïd moodily, at last. "The business is urgent?"

"Effendina," said David, with every nerve at tension, yet with outward self-control, "I have to report—" he paused, agitated; then, in a firm voice, he told of the disaster which had befallen the cotton-mills and the steamer.

As David spoke, Kaïd's face grew darker, his fingers fumbled vaguely with the linen of the loose white robe he wore. When the tale was finished he sat for a moment apparently stunned by the news, then he burst out fiercely:

"Bismillah, am I to hear only black words to-day? Hast thou naught to say but this—the fortune of Egypt burned to ashes!"

David held back the quick retort that came to his tongue.

"Half my fortune is in the ashes," he answered with dignity. "The rest came from savings never made before by this government. Is the work less worthy in thy sight, Effendina, because it has been destroyed? Would thy life be less great and useful because a blow took thee from behind?"

Kaïd's face turned black. David had bruised an open wound.

"What is my life to thee—what is thy work to me?"

"Thy life is dear to Egypt, Effendina," urged David soothingly, "and my labor for Egypt has been pleasant in thine eyes till now."

"Egypt cannot be saved against her will," was the moody response. "What has come of the Western hand upon the Eastern plough?" His face grew blacker; his heart was feeding on itself.

"*Thou*, the friend of Egypt, hast come of it, Effendina."

"Harrik was right, Harrik was right," Kaïd answered, with stubborn gloom and anger. "Better to die in our own way, if we must die, than live in the way of another. Thou wouldst make of Egypt another England; thou wouldst civilize the Soudan—bismillah, it is folly!"

"That is not the way Mehemet Ali thought, nor

Ibrahim. Nor dost thou think so, Effendina," David answered gravely. "A dark spirit is on thee. Wouldst thou have me understand that what we have done together, thou and I, was ill done, that the old bad days were better?"

"Go back to thine own land," was the surly answer. "Nation after nation ravaged Egypt, sowed their legions here, but the Egyptian has lived them down. The faces of the fellaheen are the faces of Thothmes and Seti. Go back. Egypt will travel her own path. We are of the East; we are Muslim. What is right to you is wrong to us. Ye would make us over—give us cotton beds and wooden floors and fine flour of the mill, and cleanse the cholera-hut with disinfectants, but are these things all? How many of your civilized millions would die for their prophet Christ? Yet all Egypt would rise up from the mud floor, the dourha-field and the mud hut, and would come out to die for Mahomet and Allah—ay, as Harrik knew, as Harrik knew! Ye steal into corners, and hide behind the curtains of your beds to pray; we pray where the hour of prayer finds us—in the street, in the market-place, where the house is building, the horse being shod, or the money-changers are. Ye hear the call of civilization, but we hear the Muezzin—"

He stopped, and searched mechanically for his watch.

"It is the hour the Muezzin calls," said David gently. "It is almost sunset. Shall I open the windows that the call may come to us?" he added.

While Kaïd stared at him, his breast heaving with passion, David went to a window and opened the shutters wide.

The Palace faced the Nile, which showed like a tortuous band of blue and silver a mile or so away. Nothing lay between but the brown sand, and here and there a handful of dark figures gliding towards the river, or a little train of camels making for the bare gray hills from the ghiassas which had given them their desert loads. The course of the Nile was marked by a wide fringe of palms showing blue and purple, friendly and ancient and solitary. Beyond the river and the palms lay the gray-brown desert, faintly touched with red. So clear was the sweet evening air that the irregular surface of the desert showed for a score of miles as plainly as though it were but a step away. Hummocks of sand—tombs and fallen monuments—gave a feeling as of forgotten and buried peoples; and the two vast pyramids of Sakkarah stood up in the plaintive glow of the evening skies, majestic and solemn, faithful to the dissolved and absorbed races who had built them. Curtains of mauve and saffron-red were hung behind them, and through a break of cloud fringing the horizon a yellow glow poured, to touch the tips of the pyramids with poignant splendor. But farther over to the right, where Cairo lay, there hung a bluish mist, palpable and delicate, out of which emerged the vast pyramids of Cheops; and beside it the smiling, inscrutable Sphinx faced the changeless centuries. Beyond the pyramids the mist deepened into a vast, deep cloud of blue and purple which seemed the end to some mystic highway untravelled by the sons of men.

Suddenly there swept over David a wave of feeling such as had passed over Kaïd, though of a different nature. Those who had built the pyramids were gone, Cheops and Thothmes and Amenhotep and Chefron and the rest. There had been reformers in those lost races; one age had sought to better the last, one man had toiled to save—yet there only remained offensive bundles of mummied flesh and bone and a handful of relics in tombs fifty centuries old. Was it all, then, futile? Did it matter, then, whether one man labored or a race aspired?

Only for a moment these thoughts passed through his mind; and then, as the glow through the broken cloud on the opposite horizon suddenly faded, and veils of melancholy fell over the desert and the river and the palms, there rose a call, sweetly shrill, undoubtingly insistent. Sunset had come, and, with it, the Muezzin's call to prayer from the minaret of a mosque hard by.

David was conscious of a movement behind him—that Kaïd was praying with hands uplifted; and out on the sands between the window and the river he saw kneeling figures here and there, saw the camel-drivers halt their trains, and face the East with hands uplifted. The call went on—"*Lá iláha illa-lláh!*"

It called David, too. The force and searching energy and fire in it stole through his veins, and drove from him the sense of futility and despondency which had so deeply added to his trouble. There was something for him, too, in that which held infatuated the minds of so many millions.

A moment later Kaïd and he faced each other again.

"Effendina," he said, "thou wilt not desert our work now!"

"Money—for this expedition? Thou hast it?" Kaïd asked ironically.

"I have but little money, and it must go to rebuild the mills, Effendina. I must have it of thee."

"Let them remain in their ashes."

"But thousands will have no work."

"They had work before they were built, they will have work now they are gone."

"Effendina, I stayed in Egypt at thy request. The work is thy work. Wilt thou desert it?"

"The West lured me—by things that seemed. Now I know things as they are."

"They will lure thee again to-morrow," said David firmly, but with a weight on his spirit. His eyes sought and held Kaïd's. "It is too late to go back; we must go forward, or we shall lose the Soudan, and a Mahdi and his men will be in Cairo in ten years."

For an instant Kaïd was startled. The old look of energy and purpose leaped up into his eye; but it faded quickly again. If, as the Italian physician more than hinted, his life hung by a thread, did it matter whether the barbarian came to Cairo? That was the business of those who came after. If Sharif was right, and his life was saved, there would be time enough to set things right.

"I will not pour water on the sands to make an ocean," he answered. "Will a ship sail on the Sahara? Bismillah, it is all a dream! Harrik was right. But dost thou think to do with me as thou didst with Harrik?" he sneered. "Is it in thy mind?"

David's patience broke down under the long provocation. "Know then, Effendina," he said angrily, "that I am not thy subject, nor one beholden to thee, nor thy slave. Upon terms well understood, I have labored here. I have kept my obligations, and it is thy duty to keep thy obligations, though the hand of death were on thee. I know not what has poisoned thy mind, and driven thee from reason and from justice. I know that, Prince Pasha of Egypt as thou art, thou art as bound to me as any fellah that agrees to tend my door or row my boat. Thy compact with me is a compact with England, and it shall be kept, if thou art an honest man. Thou mayst find thousands in Egypt who will serve thee at any price, and bear thee in any mood. I have but one price. It is well known to thee. I will not be the target for thy black temper. This is not the middle ages; I am an Englishman, not a helot. The bond must be kept; thou shalt not play fast and loose. Money must be found; the expedition must go. But if thy purpose is now Harrik's purpose, then Europe should know, and Egypt also should know. I have been thy right hand,

Effendina; I will not be thy old shoe, to be cast aside at thy will."

In all the days of his life, David had never flamed out as he did now. Passionate as his words were, his manner was strangely quiet, but his white and glistening face and his burning eyes showed how deep was his anger.

As he spoke, Kaïd sank upon the divan. Never had he been challenged so. With his own people he had ever been used to cringing and abasement, and he had played the tyrant, and struck hard and cruelly, and he had been feared; but here, behind David's courteous attitude, there was a scathing arraignment of his conduct which took no count of consequence. In other circumstances his vanity would have shrunk under this whip of words, but his native reason and his quick humor would have justified David. In this black distemper possessing him, however, only outraged egotism prevailed. His hands clenched and unclenched, his lips were drawn back on his teeth in rage.

When David had finished, Kaïd suddenly got to his feet and took a step forward with a malediction, but a faintness seized him and he staggered back. When he raised his head again David was gone.

XXX

LACEY MOVES

IF there was one glistening bead of sweat on the bald pate of Lacey of Chicago there were a thousand; and the smile on his face was not less shining and unlimited. He burst into the rooms of the palace where David had residence, calling, "*Oyez! Oyez!* Saadat! Oh, Pasha of the Thousand Tails! *Oyez! Oyez!*"

Getting no answer, he began to perform a dance round the room, which in modern days is known as the negro cake-walk. It was not dignified, but it would have been less dignified still performed by any other living man of forty-five with a bald head and a waistband ten inches too large. Round the room three times he went, and then he dropped on a divan. He gasped, and mopped his face and forehead, leaving a little island of moisture on the top of his head untouched. After a moment, he gained breath and settled down a little. Then he burst out:

"Are you coming to my party, O effendi?
 There'll be high jinks, there'll be welcome, there'll be room;
For to-morrow we are pulling stakes for Shendy.
 Are you coming to my party, O Nahoum?

"Say, I guess that's pretty good on the spur of the moment," he wheezed, and, taking his inseparable note-book from his pocket, wrote the impromptu down. "I guess She'll like that—it rings spontaneous. She'll be tickled, tickled to death, when she knows what's behind it." He repeated it with gusto. "She'll dote on it," he added—the person to whom he referred being the sister of the American Consul, the little widow, "cute as she can be," of whom he had written to Hylda in the letter which had brought a crisis in her life. As he returned the note-book to his pocket a door opened. Mahommed Hassan slid forward into the room, and stood still, impassive and gloomy. Lacey beckoned, and said grotesquely:

"'Come hither, come hither, my little daughter,
And do not tremble so!'"

A sort of scornful patience was in Mahommed's look, but he came nearer and waited.

"Squat on the ground, and smile a smile of mirth, Mahommed," Lacey said riotously. "'For I'm to be Queen o' the May, mother, I'm to be Queen o' the May!'"

Mahommed's face grew resentful. "O effendi, shall the camel-driver laugh when the camels are lost in the khamsin and the water-bottle is empty?"

"Certainly not, O son of the spreading palm; but this is not a desert, nor a gaudy caravan. This is a feast of all angels. This is the day when Nahoum the Nefarious is to be buckled up like a belt, and ridden in a ring. Where is the Saadat?"

"He is gone, effendi! Like a mist on the face of the running water, so was his face; like eyes that did not see, so was his look. 'Peace be to thee, Mahommed, thou art faithful as Zaida,' he said, and he mounted and rode into the desert. I ran after till he was come to the edge of the desert; but he sent me back, saying that I must wait for thee; and this word I was to say, that Prince Kaïd had turned his face darkly from him, and that the finger of Sharif—"

"That fanatical old quack—Harrik's friend!"

"—that the finger of Sharif was on his pulse. But the end of all was in the hands of God."

"Oh yes, exactly, the finger of Sharif on his pulse! The old story—the return to the mother's milk, throwing back to all the Pharaohs. Well, what then?" he added cheerfully, his smile breaking out again. "Where has he gone, our Saadat?"

"To Ebn Ezra Bey at the Coptic Monastery by the Etl Tree, where your prophet Christ slept when a child."

Lacey hummed to himself meditatively. "A sort of last powwow—Rome before the fall. Everything wrong, eh? Kaïd turned fanatic, Nahoum on the tiles watching for the Saadat to fall, things trembling for want of hard cash. That's it, isn't it, Mahommed?"

Mahommed nodded, but his look was now alert, and less sombre. He had caught at something vital and confident in Lacey's tone. He drew nearer, and listened closely.

"Well, now, my gentle gazelle, listen unto me," continued Lacey. He suddenly leaned forward, and spoke in subdued but rapid tones. "Say, Mahommed, once upon a time there was an American man, with a shock of red hair, and a nature like a spring-lock. He went down to Mexico, with a million or two of his own money got honestly by an undisputed will from an undisputed father—you don't understand that, but it doesn't matter—and with a few millions of other people's money, for to gamble in mines and railways and banks and steamship companies—all to do with Mexico what the Saadat has tried to do in Egypt with less money; but not for the love of Allah, same as him. This American was going to conquer like Cortez, but his name was Thomas Tilman Lacey, and he had a lot of gall. After years of earnest effort, he lost his hair and the millions of the Infatuated Conquistadores. And by and by he came to Cairo with a thimbleful of income, and began to live again. There was a civil war going on in his own country, but he thought that one out of forty millions would not be strictly missed. So he stayed in Egypt; and the tale of his days in Egypt, is it not written with a neboot of dom-wood in the book of Mahommed Hassan the scribe?"

He paused and beamed upon the watchful Mahommed, who, if he did not understand all that had been said, was in no difficulty as to the drift and meaning of the story.

"Aiwa, effendi," he urged impatiently. "It is a long ride to the Etl Tree, and the day is far spent!"

"Inshallah, you shall hear, my turtle-dove! One day there came to Cairo, in great haste, a man from Mexico, looking for the foolish one called T. T. Lacey, bearing glad news. And the man from Mexico blew his trumpet, and straightway T. T. Lacey fell down dismayed. The trumpet said that a million once lost in Mexico was returned, with a small flock of other millions; for a mine, in which it was sunk, had burst forth with a stony stream of silver. And behold! Thomas Tilman Lacey, the despised waster of his patrimony and of other people's treasure, is now, O son of the fig-flower, richer than Kaïd Pasha and all his eunuchs!"

Suddenly Mahommed Hassan leaned forward, then backward, and, after the fashion of desert folk, gave a shrill, sweet ululation that seemed to fill the palace.

"Say, that's A1," Lacey said, when Mahommed's voice sank to a whisper of wild harmony. "Yes, you can lick my boots, my noble sheikh of Manfaloot," he added, as Mahommed caught his feet and bent his head upon them. "I wanted to do something like that myself. Kiss 'em, honey; it'll do you good."

After a moment, Mahommed drew back and squatted before him in an attitude of peace and satisfaction. "The Saadat—you will help him? You will give him money?"

"Let's put it in this way, Mahommed: I'll invest in an expedition out of which I expect to get something worth while—concessions for mines and railways, et cetera." He winked a round, blue eye. "Business is business, and the way to get at the Saadat is to talk business; but you can make up your mind that—

'To-morrow we are pulling stakes for Shendy!
Are you coming to my party, O Nahoum?'

"By the prophet Abraham, but the news is great news," said Mahommed with a grin. "But the Effendina?"

"Well, I'll try and square the Effendina," answered Lacey. "Perhaps the days of backsheesh aren't done in Egypt, after all."

"And Nahoum Pasha?" asked Mahommed, with a sinister look.

"Well, we'll try and square him, too, but in another way."

"The money, it is in Egypt?" queried Mahommed, whose idea was that money to be real must be seen.

"Something that's as handy and as marketable," answered Lacey. "I can raise half a million to-morrow; and that will do a lot of what we want. How long will it take to ride to the monastery?"

Mahommed told him.

Lacey was about to leave the room, when he heard a voice outside. "Nahoum!" he said, and sat down again on the divan. "He has come to see the Saadat, I suppose; but it'll do him good to see me, perhaps. Open the sluices, Mahommed."

Yes, Nahoum would be glad to see the effendi, since Claridge Pasha was not in Cairo. When would Claridge Pasha return? If, then, the effendi expected to see the Saadat before his return to Cairo, perhaps he would convey a message. He could not urge his presence on the Saadat, since he had not been honored with any communication since yesterday.

"Well, that's good-mannered, anyhow, pasha," said Lacey, with cheerful nonchalance. "People don't always know when they're wanted or not wanted."

Nahoum looked at him guardedly, sighed and sat down. "Things have grown worse since yesterday," he said. "Prince Kaïd received the news badly." He shook his head. "He has not the gift of perfect friendship. That is a Christian characteristic; the Muslim does not possess it. It was too strong to last, maybe—my poor beloved friend, the Saadat."

"Oh, it will last all right," rejoined Lacey coolly. "Prince Kaïd has got a touch of jaundice, I guess. He knows a thing when he finds it, even if he hasn't the gift of 'perfect friendship,' same as Christians like you and me. But even you and me don't push our perfections too far—I haven't noticed you going out of your way to do things for your 'poor beloved friend, the Saadat'!"

"I have given him time, energy, experience—money."

Lacey nodded. "True. And I've often wondered why, when I've seen the things you didn't give, and the things you took away."

Nahoum's eyes half closed. Lacey was getting to close quarters with suspicion and allusion; but it was not his cue to resent them yet.

"I had come now to offer him help; to advance him enough to carry through his expedition."

"Well, that sounds generous, but I guess he would get on without it, pasha. He would not want to be under any more obligations to you."

"He is without money. He must be helped."

"Just so."

"He cannot go to the treasury, and Prince Kaïd has refused. Why should he decline help from his friend?"

Suddenly Lacey changed his tactics. He had caught a look in Nahoum's eyes which gave him a new thought.

"Well, if you've any proposition, pasha, I'll take it to him. I'll be seeing him to-night."

"I can give him fifty thousand pounds."

"It isn't enough to save the situation, pasha."

"It will help him over the first *zareba*."

"Are there any conditions?"

"There are no conditions, effendi."

"And interest?"

"There would be no interest in money."

"Other considerations?"

"Yes, other considerations, effendi."

"If they were granted, would there be enough still in the stocking to help him over a second zareba—or a third, perhaps?"

"That would be possible, even likely, I think. Of course we speak in confidence, effendi."

"The confidence of the 'perfect friendship.' "

"There may be difficulty, because the Saadat is sensitive; but it is the only way to help him. I can get the money from but one source; and to get it involves an agreement."

"You think his Excellency would not just jump at it—that it might hurt some of his prejudices, eh?"

"So, effendi."

"And me—where am I in it, pasha?"

"Thou hast great influence with his Excellency."

"I am his servant—I don't meddle with his prejudices, pasha."

"But if it were for his own good, to save his work here."

Lacey yawned almost ostentatiously. "I guess if he can't save it himself, it can't be saved, not even when you reach out the hand of perfect friendship. You've been reaching out for a long time, pasha, and it didn't save the steamer or the cotton-mills; and it didn't save us when we were down by Sobât a while ago, and you sent Halim Bey to teach us to be patient. We got out of that nasty corner by sleight of hand, but not your sleight of hand, pasha. Your hand is a quick hand, but a sharp eye can see the trick, and then it's no good, not worth a button."

There was something savage behind Nahoum's eyes, but they did not show it; they blinked with earnest kindness and interest. The time would come when Lacey would go as his master should go, and the occasion was not far off now; but it must not be forced. Besides, was this fat, amorous-looking factotum of Claridge Pasha's as Spartan-minded as his master? Would he be superior to the lure of gold? He would see. He spoke seriously, with apparent solicitude.

"Thou dost not understand, effendi. Claridge Pasha must have money. Prestige is everything in Egypt, it is everything with Kaïd. If Claridge Pasha rides on as though nothing has happened,—and money is the only horse that can carry him—Kaïd will not interfere, and his black mood may pass; but any halting now, and the game is done."

"And you want the game to go on right bad, don't you? Well, I guess you're right. Money is the only winner in this race. He's got to have money, sure. How much can you raise? Oh yes, you told me! Well, I don't think it's enough; he's got to have three times that; and if he can't get it from the government, or from Kaïd, it's a bad look-out. What's the bargain you have in your mind?"

"That the slave-trade continue, effendi."

Lacey did not wink, but he had a shock of surprise. On the instant he saw the trap—for the Saadat and for himself.

"He would not do it—not for money, pasha."

"He would not be doing it for money. The time is not ripe for it; it is too dangerous. There is a time for all things. If he will but wait!"

"I wouldn't like to be the man that'd name the thing to him. As you say, he's got his prejudices. They're stronger than in most men."

"It need not be named to him. Thou canst accept the money for him, and when thou art in the Soudan, and he is going to do it, thou canst prevent it."

"Tell him that I've taken the money and that he's used it, and he oughtn't to go back on the bargain I made for him? So that he'll be bound by what I did?"

"It is the best way, effendi."

"He'd be annoyed," said Lacey with a patient sigh.

"He has a great soul; but sometimes he forgets that expediency is the true policy."

"Yet he's done a lot of things without it. He's never failed in what he set out to do. What he's done has been kicked over, but he's done it all right, somehow, at last."

"He will not be able to do this, effendi, except with my help—and thine."

"He's had quite a lot of things almost finished, too," said Lacey reflectively, "and then a hand reached out in the dark and cut the wires—cut them when he was sleeping, and he didn't know; cut them when he was waking, and he wouldn't understand; cut them under his own eyes, and he wouldn't see; because the hand that cut them was the hand of the perfect friend."

He got slowly to his feet, as a cloud of color drew over the face of Nahoum and his eyes darkened with astonishment and anger. Lacey put his hands in his pockets and waited till Nahoum also rose. Then he gathered the other's eyes to his, and said with drawling scorn:

"So, you thought I didn't understand! You thought I'd got a brain like a peanut, and wouldn't drop onto to your game or the trap you've set! You'd advance money—got from the slave-dealers to prevent the slave-trade being stopped! If Claridge Pasha took it and used it, he could never stop the slave-trade. If I took it and used it for him on the same terms, he couldn't stop the slave-trade, though he might know no more about the bargain than a babe unborn. And if he didn't stand by the bargain I made, and did prohibit slave-dealing, nothing 'd stop the tribes till they marched into Cairo. He's been safe so far, because they believed in him, and because he'd rather die a million deaths than go crooked. Say, I've been among the Dagos before—down in Mexico—and I'm onto you. I've been onto you for a good while; though there was nothing I could spot certain; but now I've got you, and I'll break the 'perfect friendship' or I'll eat my shirt! I'll—"

He paused, realizing the crisis in which David was moving, and that perils were thick around their footsteps. But, even as he thought of them, he remembered David's own frank, fearless audacity in danger and difficulty, and he threw discretion to the winds. He flung his flag wide, and believed with a belief as daring as David's that all would be well.

"Well, what wilt thou do?" asked Nahoum with cool and deadly menace. "Thou wilt need to do it quickly, because, if it is a challenge, within forty-eight hours Claridge Pasha and thyself will be gone from Egypt—or I shall be in the Nile!"

"I'll take my chances, pasha," answered Lacey, with equal coolness. "You think you'll win. It's not the first time I've had to tackle men like you—they've got the breed in Mexico. They beat me there, but I learned the game, and I've learned a lot from you, too. I never knew what your game was here. I only know that the Saadat saved your life, and got you started again with Kaïd. I only know that you called yourself a Christian, and worked on him till he believed in you, and Hell might crackle round you, but he'd believe, till he saw your contract signed with the Devil—and then he'd think the signature forged. But he's got to know now. We are not going out of Egypt, though you may be going to the Nile; but we are going to the Soudan, and with Kaïd's blessing, too. You've put up the bluff, and I take it. Be sure you've got Kaïd solid, for, if you haven't, he'll be glad to know where you keep the money you got from the slave-dealers."

Nahoum shrugged his shoulders. "Who has seen the money? Where is the proof? Kaïd would know my reasons. It is not the first time virtue has been tested in Egypt, or the first time that it has fallen."

In spite of himself Lacey laughed. "Say, that's worthy of a great Christian intellect. You are a bright particular star, pasha. I take it back—they'd learn a lot from you in Mexico. But the only trouble with lying is, that the demand becomes so great you can't keep all the cards in your head, and then the one you forget does you. The man that isn't lying has the pull in the long run. You are out against us, pasha, and we'll see how we stand in forty-eight hours. You have some cards up your sleeve, I suppose; but—well, I'm taking you on. I'm taking you on with a lot of joy, and some sorrow, too, for we might have pulled off a big thing together, you and Claridge Pasha, with me to hold the stirrups. Now it's got to be war. You've made it so. It's a pity, for when we grip there'll be a heavy fall."

"For a poor man thou hast a proud stomach."

"Well, I'll admit the stomach, pasha. It's proud; and it's strong, too; it's stood a lot in Egypt; it's standing a lot to-day."

"We'll ease the strain, perhaps," sneered Nahoum. He made a perfunctory salutation and walked briskly from the room.

Mahommed Hassan crept in, a malicious grin on his face. Danger and conflict were as meat and drink to him.

"Effendi, God hath given thee a wasp's sting to thy tongue. It is well. Nahoum Pasha hath Mizraim; the Saadat hath thee and me."

"There's the Effendina," said Lacey reflectively.

"Thou saidst thou wouldst 'square' him, effendi."

"I say a lot," answered Lacey rather ruefully. "Come, Mahommed, the Saadat first, and the sooner the better."

XXXI

THE STRUGGLE IN THE DESERT

"*And His mercy is on them that fear Him throughout all generations.*"

On the clear, still evening air the words rang out over the desert, sonorous, imposing, peaceful. As the notes of the verse died away the answer came from other voices in deep, appealing antiphonal:

"*He hath showed strength with His arm; He hath scattered the proud in the imagination of their hearts.*"

Beyond the limits of the monastery there was not a sign of life; neither beast nor bird, nor blade of grass, nor any green thing; only the perfect immemorial blue, and in the East a misty moon, striving in vain to offer light which the earth as yet rejected for the brooding radiance of the descending sun. But at the great door of the monastery there grew a stately palm, and near by an ancient acacia-tree; and beyond the stone chapel there was a garden of struggling shrubs and green things, with one rose-tree which scattered its pink leaves from year to year upon the loam, since no man gathered bud or blossom.

The triumphant call of the *Magnificat*, however beautiful, seemed strangely out of place in this lonely island in a sea of sand. It was the song of a bannered army, marching over the battle-field with conquering voices, and swords as yet unsheathed and red, carrying the spoils of conquest behind the laurelled captain of the host. The crumbling and ancient walls were surrounded by a moat which a stranger's foot crossed hardly from moon to moon, which the desert wayfarer sought rarely, since it was out of the track of caravans, and because food was scant in the refectory of this Coptic brotherhood. It was scarce five hours' ride from the Palace of the Prince Pasha: but it might have been a thousand miles away, so profoundly separate was it from the world of vital things and deeds of men.

As the chant rang out, confident, majestic, and serene, carried by voices of power and shrill sweetness, which only the desert can produce, it might have seemed to any listener that this monastery was all that remained of some ancient kingdom of brimming, active cities, now lying beneath the obliterating sand, itself the monument and memorial of a breath of mercy of the Destroyer, the last refuge of a few surviving captains of a departed greatness. Hidden by the gray, massive walls, built as it were to resist the onset of a ravaging foe, the swelling voices might well have been those of some ancient order of valiant knights, whose banners hung above them, the *réclame* of their deeds. But they were voices and voices only; for they who sang were as unkempt and forceless as the lonely walls which shut them in from the insistent soul of the desert.

Desolation? The desert was not desolate. Its face was bare and burning, it slaked no man's thirst, gave no man food, save where scattered oases were like the breasts of a vast mother eluding the aching lips of her parched children; but the soul of the desert was living and inspiring, beating with vitality. It was life that burned like flame. If the water-skin was dry and the date-bag empty it smothered and destroyed; but it was life; and to those who ventured into its embrace, obeying the conditions of the sharp adventure, it gave what neither sea, nor green plain, nor high mountain, nor verdant valley could give—a consuming sense of power, which found its way to the deepest recesses of being. Out upon the vast sea of sand, where the descending sun was spreading a note of incandescent color, there floated the grateful words:

> "*He remembering His mercy hath holpen His servant Israel; as He promised to our forefathers, Abraham, and his seed forever.*"

Then the antiphonal ceased; and together the voices of all within the place swelled out in the *Gloria* and the *Amen*, and seemed to pass away in ever-receding vibrations upon the desert, till it was lost in the comforting sunset.

As the last note died away, a voice from beneath the palm-tree near the door, deeper than any that had come from within, said reverently, "*Ameen—Ameen!*"

He who spoke was a man well over sixty years, with a gray beard, lofty, benign forehead, and the eyes of a scholar and a dreamer. As he uttered the words of spiritual assent, alike to the Muslim and the Christian religion, he rose to his feet, showing the figure of a man of action, alert, well-knit, authoritative. Presently he turned towards the East and stretched a robe upon the ground, and with stately beauty of gesture he spread out his hands, standing for a moment in the attitude of aspiration. Then, kneeling, he touched his turbaned head to the ground three times, and as the sun drew down behind the sharp, bright line of sand that marked the horizon he prayed devoutly and long. It was Ebn Ezra Bey.

Muslim though he was, he had visited this monastery many times, to study the ancient Christian books which lay in disordered heaps in an ill-kept chamber, books which predated the Hegira, and were as near to the life of the Early Church as the Scriptures themselves—or were so reputed. Student and pious Muslim as he was, renowned at El Azhar and at every Muslim university in the Eastern world, he swore by the name of Christ as by that of Abraham, Isaac, and all the prophets, though to him Mahomet was the last expression of Heaven's will to mankind. At first received at the monastery with unconcealed aversion, and not without danger to himself, he had at last won to him the fanatical monks, who, in spirit, kept this ancient foundation as rigid to their faith as though it were in medieval times. And though their discipline was lax, and their daily duties orderless, this was Oriental rather than degenerate. Here Ebn Ezra had stayed for weeks at a time in the past, not without some religious scandal, long since forgotten.

His prayers ended, he rose up slowly, once more spread out his hands in ascription, and was about to enter the monastery, when, glancing towards the west, he saw a horseman approaching. An instinct told him who it was before he could clearly distinguish the figure, and his face lighted with a gentle and expectant smile. Then his look changed.

"He is in trouble," he murmured. "As it was with his uncle in Damascus, so will it be with him. Malaish, we are in the will of God!"

The hand that David laid in Ebn Ezra's was hot and nervous, the eyes that drank in the friendship of the face which had seen two Claridges emptying out their lives in the East were burning and famished by long fasting of the spirit, forced abstinence from the pleasures of success and fruition—haunting, desiring eyes, where flamed a spirit which consumed the body and the indomitable mind. Their lips, however, had their old trick of smiling, though the smile which greeted Ebn Ezra Bey had a melancholy which touched the desert-worn, life-spent old Arab as he had not been touched since a smile, just like this, flashed up at him from the weather-stained, dying face of quaint Benn Claridge in a street of Damascus. The natural duplicity of the Oriental had been abashed and inactive before the simple and astounding honesty of these two Quaker folk

He saw crisis written on every feature of the face before him. Yet the scanty meal they ate with the monks in the ancient room was enlivened by the eager yet quiet questioning of David, to whom the monks responded with more spirit than had been often seen in this arid retreat. The single torch which spluttered from the wall as they drank their coffee lighted up faces as strange, withdrawn, and unconsciously secretive as ever gathered to greet a guest. Dim tales had reached them of this Christian reformer and administrator, scraps of legend from stray camel-drivers, a letter from the Patriarch commanding them to pray blessings on his labors —who could tell what advantage might not come to the Coptic Church through him, a Christian! On the dull, torpid faces, light seemed struggling to live for a moment, as David talked. It was as though something in their meagre lives, which belonged to undeveloped feelings, was fighting for existence—a light struggling to break through murky veils of inexperience.

Later, in the still night, however—still, though air vibrated everywhere, as though the desert breathed an ether which was to fill men's veins with that which quieted the fret and fever of life's disillusions and forgeries and failures—David's speech with Ebn Ezra Bey was of a different sort. If, as it seems ever in the desert, an invisible host of beings, once mortal, now immortal, but suspensive and understanding, listened to the tale he unfolded, some glow of pity must have possessed them; for it was an Iliad of herculean struggle against absolute disaster, ending with the bitter news of his grandfather's death. It was the story of Œdipus overcome by events too strong for soul to bear. In return, as the stars wheeled on, and the moon stole to the zenith, majestic and slow, Ebn Ezra offered to his troubled friend only the philosophy of the predestinarian, mingled with the calm of the stoic. But something antagonistic to his own dejection, to the Muslim's fatalism, emerged from David's own altruism, to nerve him to hope and effort still. His unconquerable optimism rose determinedly to the surface, even as he summed up and related the forces working against him.

"They have all come at once," he said; "all the activities opposing me, just as though they had all been started long ago at different points, with a fixed course to run, and to meet and give me a fall in the hour when I could least resist. You call it Fate. I call it what it proves itself to be. But here it is a hub of danger and trouble, and the spokes of disaster are flying to it from all over the compass, to make the wheel that will grind me; and all the old troop of Palace intriguers and despoilers are waiting to heat the tire and fasten it on the machine of torture. Kaïd has involved himself in loans which press, in foolish experiments in industry without due care; and now from ill health and bad temper comes a reaction towards the old sinister rule, when the Prince shuts his eyes and his agents ruin and destroy. Three nations who have intrigued against my work see their chance, and are at Kaïd's elbow. The fate of the Soudan is in the balance. It is all as the shake of a feather. I can save it if I go; but, just as I am ready, my mills burn down, my treasury dries up, Kaïd turns his back on me, and the toil of years is swept away in a night. Thee sees it is terrible, friend?"

Ebn Ezra looked at him seriously and sadly for a moment, and then said: "Is it given one man to do all? If many men had done these things, then there had been one blow for each. Now all falls on thee, Saadat. Is it the will of God that one man should fling the lance, fire the cannon, dig the trenches, gather food for the army, drive the horses on to battle, and bury the dead? Canst thou do all?"

David's eyes brightened to the challenge. "There was the work to do, and there were not the many to do it. My hand was ready; the call came; I answered. I plunged into the river of work alone."

"Thou didst not know the strength of the currents, the eddies and the whirlpools, the hidden rocks—and the shore is far off, Saadat."

"It is not so far that, if I could but get breath to gather strength, I should reach the land in time. Money —ah, but enough for this expedition! That over, order, quiet yonder, my own chosen men as governors, and I could"—he pointed towards the southern horizon— "I could plant my foot in Cairo, and from the centre control the great machinery—with Kaïd's help; and God's help. A sixth of a million, and Kaïd's hand behind me, and the boat would lunge free of the sand-banks and churn on, and churn on! . . . Friend," he added, with the winning insistence that few found it possible to resist, "if all be well, and we go thither, wilt thou become the governor-general yonder? With thee to rule justly where there is most need of justice, the end would be sure—if it be the will of God."

Ebn Ezra Bey sat for a moment looking into the worn, eager face, indistinct in the moonlight, then answered slowly: "I am seventy, and the years smite hard as they pass, and there or here, it little matters when I go, as I must go; and whether it be to bend the lance, or bear the flag before thee, or rule a *Mudirieh*, what does it matter! I will go with thee," he added hastily; "but it is better thou shouldst not go. Within the last three days I have news from the South. All that thou hast done there is in danger now. The word for revolt has passed from tribe to tribe. A tongue hath spoken, and a hand hath signalled"—his voice lowered—"and I think I know the tongue and the hand!" He paused; then, as David did not speak, continued: "Thou, who art wise in most things, dost decline to seek for thy foe in him who eateth from the same dish with thee. Only when it is too late thou wilt defend thyself and all who keep faith with thee."

David's face clouded. "Nahoum, thou dost mean Nahoum? But thou dost not understand, and there is no proof."

"As a camel knows the coming storm while yet the sky is clear, by that which the eye does not see, so do I feel Nahoum. The evils thou hast suffered, Saadat, are from his hand, if from any hand in Egypt—"

Suddenly he leaned over and touched David's arm. "Saadat, it is of no avail. There is none in Egypt that desires good; thy task is too great. All men will deceive thee; if not now, yet in time. If Kaïd favors thee once more, and if it is made possible for thee to go to the Soudan, yet I pray thee to stay here. Better be smitten here, where thou canst get help from thine own country, if need be, than yonder, where they but wait to spoil thy work and kill thee. Thou art young; wilt thou throw thy life away? Art thou not needed here as there? For me, it is nothing whether it be now or in a few benumbing years; but for thee—is there no one whom thou lovest so well that thou wouldst not shelter thy life to spare that life sorrow? Is there none that thou lovest so, and that will love thee to mortal sorrow, if thou goest without care to thy end too soon?"

As a warm wind suddenly sweeps across the cool air of a summer evening for an instant, suffocating and unnerving, so Ebn Ezra's last words swept across David's spirit. His breath came quicker, his eyes half closed. "*Is there none that thou lovest so, and that will love thee to mortal sorrow, if—*"

As a hand secretly and swiftly slips the lever that opens the sluice-gates of a dyke, while the watchman turns away for a moment to look at the fields which the waters enrich and the homes of poor folk whom the gates defend, so, in a moment, when off his guard, worn with watching and fending, as it were, Ebn Ezra had sprung the lever, and a flood of feeling swept over David, drowned him in its impulse and pent-up force.

"*Is there none that thou lovest so—*" Of what use had been all his struggle and his pain since that last day in Hamley—his dark fighting days in the desert with Lacey and Mahommed, and his handful of faithful followers, hemmed in by dangers, the sands swarming with Arabs who feathered now to his safety, now to his doom, and his heart had hungered for what he had denied it with a will that would not be conquered. Wasted by toil and fever and the tension of danger and the care of others dependent on him, he had also fought a foe which was ever at his elbow, ever whispered its comfort and seduction in his ear, the insidious and peace-giving, exalting opiate that had tided him over some black places, and then had sought for mastery of him when he was back again in the world of normal business and duty, where it appealed not as a medicine, but as a perilous luxury. And fighting this foe, which had a voice so soothing, and words like the sound of murmuring waters, and a cool and comforting hand that sought to lead him into gardens of stillness and passive being, where he could no more hear the clangor and vexing noises of a world that angered and agonized, there had also been the lure of another passion of the heart, which was too perilously dear to contemplate. Eyes that were beautiful, and their beauty was not for him; a spirit that was bright and glowing, but the brightness and the glow might not renew his days. It was hard to fight alone. Alone he was, for only to *one* may the doors within doors be opened—only to one so dear that all else is everlastingly distant may the true tale of the life beneath life be told. And it was not for him—nothing of this; not even the thought of it; for to think of it was to desire it, and to desire it was to reach out towards it; and to reach out towards it was the end of all. There had been moments of abandonment to the alluring dream, such as when he wrote the verses which Lacey had sent to Hylda from the desert; but they were few. Oft-repeated, they would have filled him with an agitated melancholy impossible to be borne in the life which must be his.

So it had been. The deeper into life and its labors and experiences he had gone, the greater had been his temptations, born of two passions, one of the body and its craving, the other of the heart and its desires: and he had fought on—towards the morning.

"*Is there none that thou lovest so, and that will love thee to mortal sorrow, if thou goest without care to thy end too soon?*" The desert, the dark monastery, the acacia-tree, the ancient palm, the ruinous garden, disappeared. He only saw a face which smiled at him, as it had done by the brazier in the garden at Cairo, that night when she and Nahoum and himself and Mizraim had met in the room of his house by the Ezbekieh gardens, and she had gone out to her old life in England, and he had taken up the burden of the East—that long six years ago. His head dropped in his hands, and all that was beneath the Quaker life he had led so many years, packed under the crust of form and habit, and regulated thought, and controlled emotion, broke forth now, and had its way with him.

He turned away staggering and self-reproachful from the first question, only to face the other—"*And that will love thee to mortal sorrow, if thou goest without care to thy end too soon?*" It was a thought he had never let himself dwell on for an instant in all the days since they had last met. He had driven it back to its covert, even before he could recognize its face. It was disloyal to her, an offence against all that she was, an affront to his manhood to let the thought have place in his mind even for one swift moment. She was Lord Eglington's wife—there could be no sharing of soul and mind and body and the exquisite devotion of a life too dear for thought. Nothing that she was to Eglington could be divided with another, not for an hour, not by one act of impulse; or else she must be less, she that might have been, if there had been no Eglington—

An exclamation broke from him, and, as one crying out in one's sleep wakes himself, so the sharp cry of his misery woke him from the trance of memory that had been upon him, and he slowly became conscious of Ebn Ezra standing before him. Their eyes met, and Ebn Ezra spoke:

"The will of Allah be thy will, Saadat. If it be to go to the Soudan, I am thine; if it be to stay, I am thy servant and thy brother. But whether it be life or death, thou must sleep, for the young are like water without sleep. Thou canst not live in strength nor die with fortitude without it. For the old, malaish, old age is between a sleeping and a waking! Come, Saadat! Forget not, thou must ride again to Cairo at dawn."

David got slowly to his feet and turned towards the monastery. The figure of a monk stood in the doorway with a torch to light him to his room.

He turned to Ebn Ezra again. "Does thee think that I have aught of his courage—my Uncle Benn? Thou knowest me—shall I face it out as did he?"

"Saadat," the old man answered pointing, "yonder acacia, that was he, quick to grow and short to live; but thou art as this date-palm, which giveth food to the hungry, and liveth through generations. Peace be upon thee," he added at the doorway, as the torch flickered towards the room where David was to lie.

"And upon thee, peace!" answered David gently, and followed the smoky light to an inner chamber.

The room in which David found himself was lofty and large, but was furnished with only a rough wooden bed, a rug and a brazier. Left alone, he sat down on the edge of the bed, and, for a few moments, his mind strayed almost vaguely from one object to another. From two windows far up in the wall the moonlight streamed in, making bars of light aslant the darkness. Not a sound broke the stillness. Yet, to his sensitive nerves, the air seemed tingling with sensation, stirring with unseen activities. Here the spirit of the desert seemed more insistent in its piercing vitality, because it was shut in by four stone walls.

Mechanically he took off his coat, and was about to fold and lay it on the rug beside the bed, when something hard in one of the pockets knocked against his knee. Searching, he found and drew forth a small bottle which, for many a month past, had lain in the drawer of a table where he had placed it on his return from the Soudan. It was an evil spirit which sent this tiny phial to his hand at a moment when he had paid out of the full treasury of his strength and will its accumulated deposit, leaving him with a balance on which no heavy draft could be made. His pulse quickened, then his body stiffened with the effort at self-control.

Who placed this evil elixir in his pocket? What any enemy of his work had done was nothing to what might be achieved by the secret foe, who had placed this anodyne within his reach at this the most critical moment of his life. He remembered the last time he had used it —in the desert: two days of forgetfulness to the world, when it all moved by him, the swarming Arabs, the train of camels, the loads of ivory, the slimy crocodile on the sandbanks, the vultures hovering above unburied carcasses, the kourbash descending on shining black shoulders, corrugating bare brown bodies into cloven skin and lacerated flesh, a fight between champions of two tribes who clashed and smote and struggled and rained blows, and, both mortally wounded, still writhed in last conflict upon the ground—and Mahommed Hassan ever at the tent door or by his side, towering, watchful, sullen to all faces without, smiling to his own, with dog-like look waiting for any motion of his hand or any word. . . . Ah! Mahommed Hassan, it was he! Mahommed had put this phial in his pocket. His bitter secret was not hidden from Mahommed. And this was an act of supreme devotion—to put at his hand the lulling, inspiring draught. Did this fellah servant know what it meant—the sin of it, the temptation, the terrible joy, the blessed quiet; and then, the agonizing remorse, the withering self-hatred and torturing penitence? No, Mahommed only knew that when the Saadat was gone beyond his strength, when the sleepless nights and feverish days came in the past, in their great troubles, when men were dying and only the Saadat could save, that this cordial lifted him out of misery and storm into calm. Yet Mahommed must have divined that it was a thing against which his soul revolted, or he would have given it to him openly. In the heart and mind of the giant murderer, however, must have been the thought that now when trouble was upon his master again, trouble which might end all, this supreme destroyer of pain and dark memory and present misery, would give him the comfort he needed—and that he would take it!

If he had not seen it, this sudden craving would not have seized him for this eager beguiling, this soothing benevolence. Yet here it was in his hand; and even as it lay in his cold fingers—how cold they were, and his head how burning!—the desire for it surged up in him.

And, as though the thing itself had the magical power to summon up his troubles, that it might offer the apathy and stimulus in one—even as it lured him, his dangers, his anxieties, the black uncertainties massed, multiplied and aggressive rose before him, buffeted him, caught at his throat, dragged down his shoulders, clutched at his heart.

Now, with a cry of agony, he threw the phial on the ground, and, sinking on the bed, buried his face in his hands and moaned, and fought for freedom from the cords tightening round him. It was for him to realize now how deep are the depths to which the human soul can sink, even while laboring to climb. Once more the sense of awful futility was on him: of wasted toil and blenched force, veins of energy drained of their blood, hope smitten in the way, and every dear dream shattered. Was it, then, all ended? Was his work indeed fallen, and all his love undone? Was his own redemption made impossible? He had offered up his life to this land to atone for a life taken when she—when *she* first looked up with eyes of gratitude, eyes that haunted him! Was it, then, unacceptable? Was it so that he must turn his back upon this long, heart-breaking but beloved work, this panacea for his soul, without which he could not pay the price of blood?

Go back to England—to Hamley where all had changed, where the old man he loved, no longer ruled in the Red Mansion, where all that had been could be no more? Go to some other land, and there begin again another such a work? Were there not vast fields of human effort, effort such as his, where he could ease the sorrow of living by the joy of a divine altruism? Go back to Hamley? Ah, no, a million times, no! That life was dead, it was a cycle of years behind him. There could be no return. He was in a maelstrom of agony, his veins were afire, his lips were parched.

"HE HEARD A VOICE SAY, 'SPEAK—SPEAK TO ME'"

He sprang from his bed, knelt down, and felt for the little phial he had flung aside. After a moment his hand caught it, clutched it. But, even at the crest of the wave of temptation, words that he had heard one night in Hamley, that last night of all, flashed into his mind—the words of old Luke Claridge's prayer, "*And if a viper fasten on his hand, O Lord—*"

Suddenly he paused. That scene in the old Meeting-house swam before his eyes, got into his brain. He remembered the words of his own prayer, and how he had then retreated upon the Power that gave him power, for a draught of the one true tincture which braced the heart to throw itself upon the spears of trial. And now the trial had come, and that which was in him as deep as being, the habit of youth, the mother-fibre and predisposition responded to the draught he had drunk then. As a body freed from the quivering, unrelenting grasp of an electric battery subsides into a cool quiet, so, through his veins, seemed to pass an ether which stilled the tumult, the dark desire to drink the potion in his hand and escape into that irresponsible, artificial world, where he had before loosened his hold on activity.

The phial slipped from his fingers to the floor. He sank upon the side of the bed, and, placing his hands on his knees, he whispered a few broken words that none on earth was meant to hear. Then he passed into a strange and moveless quiet of mind and body. Many a time in days gone by—far-off days—had he sat as he was doing now, feeling his mind pass into a soft, comforting quiet, absorbed in a sensation of existence, as it were between waking and sleeping, where doors opened to new experience and understanding, where the mind seemed to loose itself from the bonds of human necessity and find a freer air.

Now, as he sat as still as the stone in the walls around him, he was conscious of a vision forming itself before his eyes. At first it was indefinite, vague, without clear form, but at last it became a room dimly outlined, delicately veiled, as it were. Then it seemed, not that the mist cleared, but that his eyes became stronger, and saw through the delicate haze; and now the room became wholly, concretely visible.

It was the room in which he had said good-by to Hylda. As he gazed like one entranced, he saw a figure rise from a couch, pale, agitated, and beautiful, and come forward, as it were, towards him. But suddenly the mist closed in again upon the scene, a depth of darkness passed his eyes, but he heard a voice say, "Speak—speak to me!"

He heard her voice as distinctly as though she were beside him—as, indeed, she had stood before him but an instant ago.

Getting slowly to his feet, into the night he sent an answer to the call.

Would she hear? She had said long ago that she would speak to him so. Perhaps she had tried before. But now at last he had heard and answered. Had she heard? Time might tell—if ever they met again. But how good, and quiet, and serene was the night!

He composed himself to sleep, but, as he lay waiting for that coverlet of forgetfulness to be drawn over him, he heard the sound of bells soft and clear. Just such bells he had heard upon the common at Hamley. Was it, then, the outcome of his vision, a sweet hallucination? He leaned upon his elbow and listened

XXXII

FORTY STRIPES SAVE ONE

The bells that rang were not the bells of Hamley; they were part of no vision or hallucination, and they drew David out of his chamber into the night. A little group of three stood sharply silhouetted against the moonlight, and, towering above them, was the spare, commanding form of Ebn Ezra Bey. Three camels crouched near, and beside them stood a Nubian lad singing to himself the song of the camel-driver:

> "Fleet is thy foot: thou shalt rest by the Etl tree;
> Water shalt thou drink from the blue-deep well;
> Allah send His gard'ner with the green bersim,
> For thy comfort, fleet one, by the Etl tree.
> As the stars fly, have thy footsteps flown—
> Deep is the well, drink, and be still once more;
> Till the pursuing winds panting have found thee
> And, defeated, sink still beside thee—
> By the well and the Etl tree."

For a moment David stood in the doorway listening to the low song of the camel-driver. Then he came forward. As he did so, one of the two who stood with Ebn Ezra moved towards the monastery door slowly. It was a monk with a face which, even in this dim light, showed a deathly weariness. The eyes looked straight before him, as though they saw nothing of the world, only a goal to make, an object to be accomplished. The look of the face went to David's heart—the kinship of pain was theirs.

"Peace be to thee," David said gently, as the other passed him.

There was an instant's pause, and then the monk faced him with fingers uplifted. "The grace of God be upon thee, David," he said, and his eyes, drawn back from the world where they had been exploring, met the other's keenly. Then he wheeled and entered the monastery.

"The grace of God be upon thee, David!" How strange it sounded, this Christian blessing in response to his own Oriental greeting, out in this Eastern waste! His own name, too. It was as though he had been transported to the ancient world where "Brethren" were so few that they called each other by their "Christian" names—even as they did in Hamley to-day! In Hamley to-day! He closed his eyes, a tremor running through his body; and then, with an effort which stilled him to peace again, he moved forward, and was greeted by Ebn Ezra, from whom the third member of the little group had now drawn apart nearer to the acacia-tree, and was seated on a rock that jutted from the sand.

"What is it?" David asked.

"Wouldst thou not sleep, Saadat? Sleep is more to thee now than aught thou mayst hear from any man. To all thou art kind save thyself."

"I have rested," David answered, with a measured calmness, revealing to his friend the change which had come since they parted an hour before. They seated themselves under the palm-tree, and were silent for a moment, then Ebn Ezra said:

"These come from the Place of Lepers."

David started slightly. "Zaida?" he asked, with a sigh of pity.

"The monk who passed thee but now goes every year to the Place of Lepers with the caravan, for a brother of this order stays yonder with the afflicted, seeing no more the faces of this world which he has left behind. Afar off from each other they stand—as far as eye can see—and after the manner of their faith they pray to Allah, and he who has just left us finds a paper fastened with a stone upon the sand at a certain place where he waits. He touches it not, but reads it as it lies, and, having read, heaps sand upon it. And the message which the paper gives is for me."

"For thee? Hast thou there one who—?"

"There was one, my father's son, though we were of different mothers; and in other days, so many years ago, he did great wrong to me, and not to me alone,"—the gray head bowed in sorrow—"but to one dearer to me than life. I hated him, and would have slain him, but the mind of Allah is not the mind of man; and he escaped me. Then he was stricken with leprosy, and was carried to the place from whence no leper returns. At first my heart rejoiced; then, at last, I forgave him, Saadat—was he not my father's son, and was the woman not gone to the bosom of Allah, where is peace? So I forgave and sorrowed for him—who shall say what miseries are those which, minute to minute, day after day, and year upon year, repeat themselves, till it is an endless flaying of the body and burning of the soul! Every year I send a message to him, and every year now this Christian monk—there is no Sheikh-el-Islam yonder—brings back the written message which he finds in the sand."

"And thee has had a message to-night?"

"The last that may come—God be praised, he goeth to his long home! It was written in his last hour. There was no hope; he is gone. And so, one more reason showeth why I should go where thou goest, Saadat."

Casting his eyes toward the figure by the acacia-tree, his face clouded and he pondered anxiously, looking at

David the while. Twice he essayed to speak, but paused.

David's eyes followed his look. "What is it? Who is he—yonder?"

The other rose to his feet. "Come and see, Saadat," he replied. "Seeing, thou wilt know what to do."

"Zaida—is it of Zaida?" David asked.

"The man will answer for himself, Saadat."

Coming within a few feet of the figure crouched upon the rock, Ebn Ezra paused and stretched out a hand. "A moment, Saadat. Dost thou not see, dost thou not recognize him?"

David intently studied the figure, which seemed unconscious of their presence. The shoulders were stooping and relaxed as though from great fatigue, but David could see that the figure was that of a tall man. The head was averted, but a rough beard covered the face, and, in the light of the fire, one hand that clutched it showed long and skinny and yellow and cruel. The hand fascinated David's eyes. Where had he seen it? It flashed upon him—a hand clutching a robe, in a frenzy of fear, in the courtyard of the blue tiles, in Kaïd's Palace—Achmet the Rope-maker! . . . He drew back a step.

"Achmet," he said in a low voice. The figure stirred, the hand dropped from the beard and clutched the knee; but the head was not raised, and the body remained crouching and listless.

"He escaped?" David said, turning to Ebn Ezra Bey.

"I know not by what means—a camel-driver bribed, perhaps, and a camel left behind for him. After the caravan had travelled a day's journey he joined it. None knew what to do. He was not a leper, and he was armed."

"Leave him with me," said David.

Ebn Ezra hesitated. "He is armed; he was thy foe—"

"I am armed also," David answered enigmatically, and indicated by a gesture that he wished to be left alone. Ebn Ezra drew away towards the palm-tree, and stood at this distance watching anxiously, for he knew what dark passions seize upon the Oriental—and Achmet had many things for which to take vengeance.

David stood for a moment, pondering, his eyes upon the deserter. "God greet thee as thou goest, and His goodness befriend thee," he said evenly. There was silence, and no movement. "Rise and speak," he added sternly. "Dost thou not hear? Rise, Achmet Pasha!"

Achmet *Pasha!* The head of the desolate wretch lifted, the eyes glared at David for an instant, as though to see whether he was being mocked, and then the spare figure stretched itself, and the outcast stood up. The old lank straightness was gone, the shoulders were bent, the head was thrust forward, as though the long habit of looking into dark places had bowed it out of all manhood.

"May grass spring under thy footstep, Saadat," he said, in a thick voice, and salaamed awkwardly—he had been so long absent from life's formularies.

"What dost thou here, pasha?" asked David formally. "Thy sentence had no limit."

"I could not die there," said the hollow voice, and the head sank farther forward. "Year after year I lived there, but I could not die among them. I was no leper; I am no leper. My penalty was my penalty, and I paid it to the full, piastre by piastre of my body and my mind. It was not one death, it was death every hour, every day I stayed. I had no mind. I could not think. Mummy-cloths were round my brain; but the fire burned underneath and would not die. There was the desert, but my limbs were like rushes. I had no will, and I could not flee. I was chained to the evil place. If I stayed it was death, if I went it was death."

"Thou art armed now," said David suggestively.

Achmet laid a hand fiercely upon a dagger under his robe. "I hid it. I was afraid. I could not die—my hand was like a withered leaf; it could not strike; my heart poured out like water. Once I struck a leper, that he might strike and kill me; but he lay upon the ground and wept, for all his anger, which had been great, died in him at last. There was none other given to anger there. The leper has neither anger, nor mirth, nor violence, nor peace. It is all the black, silent shame—and I was no leper."

"Why didst thou come? What is there but death for thee here, or anywhere thou goest! Kaïd's arm will find thee; a thousand hands wait to strike thee."

"I could not die there— Dost thou think that I repent?" he added with sudden fierceness. "Is it that which would make me repent? Was I worse than thousands of others? I have come out to die—to fight and die. Aiwa, I have come to thee, whom I hated, because thou canst give me death as I desire it. My mother was an Arab slave from Senaar, and she was got by war, and all her people. War and fighting were their portion—as they ate, as they drank and slept. In the black years behind me among the Unclean, there was naught to fight—could one fight the dead, and the agony of death, and the poison of the agony! Life, it is done for me—am I not accursed? But to die fighting—ay, fighting for Egypt, since it must be, and fighting for thee, since it must be; to strike, and strike, and strike, and earn death! Must the dog, because he is a dog, die in the slime? Shall he not be driven from the village to die in the clean sand? Saadat, who will see in me Achmet Pasha, who did with Egypt what he willed, and was swept away by the besom in thy hand? Is there in me aught of that Achmet that any should know?"

"None would know thee for that Achmet," answered David.

"I know, it matters not how—at last a letter found me, and the way of escape—that thou goest again to the Soudan. There will be fighting there—"

"Not by my will," interrupted David.

"Then by the will of Sheitan the accursed; but there will be fighting—am I not an Arab, do I not know? Thou hast not conquered yet. Bid me go where thou wilt, do what thou wilt, so that I may be among the fighters, and in the battle forget what I have seen. Since I am unclean, and am denied the bosom of Allah, shall I not go as a warrior to Hell, where men will fear me? Speak, Saadat, canst thou deny me this?"

Nothing of repentance, so far as he knew, moved the dark soul; but, like some evil spirit, he would choose the way to his own doom, the place and the manner of it: a sullen, cruel, evil being, unyielding in his evil, unmoved by remorse—so far as he knew. Yet he would die fighting, and for Egypt—"and for thee, if it must be so. To strike, to strike, to strike, and earn death!" What Achmet did not see, David saw, the glimmer of light breaking through the cloud of shame and evil and doom. Yonder in the Soudan more problems than one would be solved, more lives than one be put to the extreme test. He did not answer Achmet's question yet.

"Zaida—?" he said in a low voice. The pathos of her doom had been a dark memory.

Achmet's voice dropped lower as he answered. "She lived till the day her sister died. I never saw her face; but I was set to bear each day to her door the food she ate and a balass of water; and I did according to my sentence. Yet I heard her voice. And once, at last, the day she died, she spoke to me, and said from inside the hut, 'Thy work is done, Achmet. Go in peace.' And that night she lay down on her sister's grave, and in the morning she was found dead upon it."

David's eyes were blinded with tears. "It was too long," he said at last, as though to himself.

"That day," continued Achmet, "there fell ill with leprosy the Christian priest from this place who had served in that black service so long; and then a fire leapt up in me. Zaida was gone—I had brought food and a balass of water to her door those many times; there was naught to do, since she was gone—"

Suddenly David took a step nearer to him and looked into the sullen and drooping eyes. "Thou shalt go with me, Achmet. I will do this unlawful act for thee. At daybreak I will give thee orders. Thou shalt join me far from here—if I go to the Soudan," he added, with a sudden remembrance of his position; and he turned away slowly.

After a moment, with muttered words, Achmet sank down upon the stone again, drew a cake of dourha from his inner robe, and began to eat.

The camel-boy had lighted a fire, and he sat beside it warming his hands at the blaze and still singing to himself:

"The bed of my love I will sprinkle with attar of roses,
The face of my love I will touch with the balm—
With the balm of the tree from the farthermost wood,
From the wood without end, in the world without end.
My love holds the cup to my lips, and I drink of the cup,
And the attar of roses I sprinkle will soothe like the evening dew,
And the balm will be healing and sleep, and the cup I will drink,
I will drink of the cup my love holds to my lips—"

David stood listening. What power was there in desert life that could make this poor camel-driver, at the end of a long day of weariness and toil and little food and drink, sing a song of content and cheerfulness? The little needed, the little granted, and no thought beyond—save the vision of one who waited in the hut by the onion-field! He gathered himself together and tuned his mind to the scene through which he had just passed, and then to the interview he would have with Kaïd on the morrow. A few hours ago he had seen no way out of it all—he had had no real hope that Kaïd would turn to him again; but the last two hours had changed all that. Hope was alive in him. He had fought a desperate fight with himself, and he had conquered. Then had come Achmet, unrepentant, degraded still, but with the spirit of Something glowing—Achmet to die for a cause, driven by that Something deep beneath the degradation and the crime. He had hope, and, as the camel-driver's voice died away, and he lay down with a sheepskin over him and went instantly to sleep, David drew to the fire and sat down beside it. Presently Ebn Ezra came to urge him to go to bed, but he would not. He had slept, he said; he had slept and rested, and the night was good—he would wait. Then the other brought rugs and blankets, and gave David some, and lay down beside the fire, and watched and waited for he knew not what. Ever and ever his eyes were on David, and far back under the acacia-tree Achmet slept as he had not slept since his doom fell on him.

At last Ebn Ezra Bey also slept; but David was awake with the night and the benevolent moon and the marching stars. The spirit of the desert was on him, filling him with its voiceless music. From the infinite stretches of sand to the south came the irresistible call of life, as soft as the leaves in a garden of roses, as deep as the sea. This world was still, yet there seemed a low, delicate humming, as of multitudinous looms at a distance so great that the ear but faintly caught it—the sound of the weavers of life and destiny and eternal love, the hands of the toilers of all the ages spinning and spinning on; and he was part of it, not abashed or dismayed because he was but one of the illimitable throng.

The hours wore on, but still he sat there, peace in all his heart, energy tingling softly through every vein, the wings of hope fluttering at his ear.

At length the morning came, and, from the west, with the rising sun, came a traveller swiftly, making for where he was. The sleepers stirred around him and waked and rose. The little camp became alive. As the traveller neared the fresh-made fire, David saw that it was Lacey. He went eagerly to meet him.

"Thee has news," he said. "I see it is so." He held Lacey's hand in his.

"Say, you are going on that expedition, Saadat. You wanted money. Will a quarter of a million do?"

David's eyes caught fire.

From the monastery there came the voices of the monks:

"*O be joyful in the Lord, all ye lands. Serve the Lord with gladness, and come before His presence with a song.*"

XXXIII

THE DARK INDENTURE

Nahoum had forgotten one very important thing: that what affected David as a Christian in Egypt would tell equally against himself. If, in his ill health and dejection, Kaïd drank deep of the cup of Mahomet, the red eyes of fanaticism would be turned upon the Armenian, as upon the European, Christian. He had forgotten it for the moment, but when, coming into Kaïd's Palace, a little knot of loiterers spat upon the ground and snarled, "Infidel—Nazarene!" with contempt and hatred the significance of the position came home to him. He made his way to a far quarter of the Palace, thoughtfully weighing the circumstances, and was met by Mizraim.

Mizraim salaamed. "The height of thy renown be as the cedar of Lebanon, excellency."

"May thy feet tread the corn of everlasting fortune, son of Mahomet!"

They entered the room together. Nahoum looked at Mizraim curiously. He was not satisfied with what he saw. Mizraim's impassive face had little expression, but the eyes were furtively eager and sinister.

"Well, so it is, and if it is, what then?" asked Nahoum coolly.

"*Ki di*, so it is," answered Mizraim, and a ghastly smile came to his lips. This infidel pasha, Nahoum, had a mind that pierced to the meaning of words ere they were spoken. Mizraim's hand touched his forehead, his breast, his lips, and, clasping and unclasping his long, snakelike fingers, began the story he had come to tell.

"The Inglesi, whom Allah confound, the Effendina hath blackened by a look, his words have smitten him in the vital parts—"

"Mizraim, thou dove, speak to the purpose."

Mizraim showed a dark pleasure at the interruption. Nahoum was impatient, anxious; that made the tale better worth telling.

"Sharif and the discontented ones who dare not act, like the vultures, they flee the living man, but swoop upon the corpse. The consuls of those countries who love not England or Claridge Pasha, and the holy men, and the Cadi, all scatter smoldering fires. There is a spirit in the Palace and beyond which is blowing fast to a great flame."

"Then, so it is, great one, and what bodes it?"

"It may kill the Inglesi; but it will also sweep thee from the fields of life where thou dost flourish."

"It is not against the foreigner but against the Christian, Mizraim?"

"Thy tongue hath wisdom, excellency."

"Thou art a Muslim—"

"Why do I warn thee? For service done to me; and because there is none other worth serving in Egypt. Behold, it is my destiny to rule others, to serve thee!"

"Once more thy turban full of gold, Mizraim, if thou dost service now that hath meaning and is not a belching of wind and words. Thou hast a thing to say—say it, and see if Nahoum hath lost his wit, or hath a palsied arm."

"Then behold, pasha. Are not my spies in all the Palace? Is not my scourge heavier than the whip of the horned horse? *Ki di*, so it is. This I have found.

Sharif hath, with others, made a plot which hath enough powder in it to shake Egypt, and toss thee from thy high place into the depths. There is a Christian—an Armenian, as it chances; but he was chosen because he was a Christian, and for that only. His name is Rahib. He is a tent-maker. He had three sons. They did kill an effendi who had cheated them of their land. Two of them were hanged last week; the other, caught but a few days since, is to hang within three days. To-day Kaïd goes to the Mosque of Mahmoud, as is the custom at this festival. The old man hath been persuaded to attempt the life of Kaïd, upon condition that his son—his Benjamin—is set free. It will be but an attempt at Kaïd's life, no more; but the cry will go forth that a Christian did the thing; and the Muslim flame will leap high."

"And the tent-maker?" asked Nahoum musingly, though he was turning over the tale in his mind, seeing behind it and its far consequences.

"Malaish, what does it matter! But he is to escape, and they are to hang another Christian in his stead for the attempt on Kaïd. It hath no skill, but it would suffice. With the dervishes gone *malboos*, and the faithful drunk with piety—canst thou not see the issue, pasha? Blood will be shed."

"The Jews of Europe would be angry," said Nahoum grimly but evenly. "The loans have been many, and Kaïd has given a lien by the new canal at Suez. The Jews will be angry," he repeated, "and for every drop of Christian blood shed there would be a lanced vein here. But that would not bring back Nahoum Pasha," he continued cynically. "Well, this is thy story, Mizraim; this is what they would do. Now what hast thou done to stop their doing?"

"Am I not a Muslim? Shall I give Sharif to the Nile?"

Nahoum smiled darkly. "There is a simpler way. Thy mind ever runs on the bowstring and the sword. These are great, but there is a greater. It is the mocking finger. At midnight, when Kaïd goes to the Mosque Mahmoud, a finger will mock the plotters till they are buried in confusion. Thou knowest the Governor of the prisons—has he not need of something? Hath he never sought favors of thee?"

"Bismillah, but a week ago!"

"Then, listen, thou shepherd of the sheep—"

He paused, as there came a tap at the door, and a slave entered hurriedly and addressed Nahoum.

"The effendi, Ebn Ezra Bey, whom thou didst set me to watch, he hath entered the Palace, and asks for the Effendina."

Nahoum started, and his face clouded, but his eyes flashed fire. He tossed the slave a coin. "Thou hast done well. Where is he now?"

"He waits in the hall, where is the statue of Mehemet Ali and the lions."

"In an hour, Mizraim, thou shalt hear what I intend. Peace be to thee!"

"And on thee, peace!" answered Mizraim, as Nahoum passed from the room, and walked hastily towards the hall where he should find Ebn Ezra Bey. Nearing the spot, he brought his step to a deliberate slowness, and appeared not to notice the stately Arab till almost upon him.

"Salaam, effendi," he said smoothly, yet with inquisition in his eye, with malice in his tone.

"Salaam, excellency."

"Thou art come on the business of thy master?"

"Who is my master, excellency?"

"Till yesterday it was Claridge Pasha. Hast thou then forsaken him in his trouble—the rat from the sinking ship?"

A flush passed over Ebn Ezra Bey's face, and his mouth opened with a gasp of anger. Oriental though he was, he was not as astute as this Armenian Christian, who was purposely insulting him, that he might, in a moment of heat, snatch from him the business he meant to lay before Kaïd. Nahoum had not miscalculated.

"I have but one master, excellency," Ebn Ezra answered quietly at last, "and I have served him straightly. Hast thou done likewise?"

"What is straight to thee might well be crooked to me, effendi."

"Thou art crooked as the finger of a paralytic."

"Yet I have worked in peace with Claridge Pasha for these years past, even until yesterday, when thou didst leave him to his fate."

"His ship will sail when thine is crumbling on the sands, and all thou art is like a forsaken cockatrice's nest."

"Is it this thou hast come to say to the Effendina?"

"What I have come to say to the Effendina is for the world to know after it hath reached his ears. I know thee, Nahoum Pasha. Thou art a traitor. Claridge Pasha would abolish slavery, and thou dost receive great sums of gold from the slave-dealers to prevent it."

"Is it this thou wilt tell Kaïd?" Nahoum asked with a sneer. "And hast thou proofs?"

"Even this day they have come to my hands from the south."

"Yet I think the proofs thou hast will not avail; and I think that thou wilt not show them to Kaïd. The gift of second thinking is a great gift. Thou must find greater reason for seeking the Effendina."

"That, too, shall be. Gold thou hadst to pay the wages of the soldiers of the south. Thou didst keep the gold and order the slave-hunt; and the soldiers of the Effendina have been paid in human flesh and blood—ten thousand slaves since Claridge Pasha left the Soudan, and three thousand dead upon the desert sands, abandoned by those who hunted them when water grew scarce and food failed. To-day shall see thy fall."

At his first words Nahoum had felt a shock, from which his spirit reeled; but an inspiration came to him on the moment; and he listened with a saturnine coolness to the passionate words of the indignant figure towering above him. When Ebn Ezra had finished, he replied quietly:

"It is even as thou sayest, effendi. The soldiers were paid in slaves got in the slave-hunt; and I have gold from the slave-dealers. I needed it, for the hour is come when I must do more for Egypt than I have ever done."

With a gesture of contempt Ebn Ezra made to leave, seeing an official of the Palace in the distance.

Nahoum stopped him. "But, one moment ere thou dost thrust thy hand into the cockatrice's den. Thou dost measure thyself against Nahoum? In patience and with care have I trained myself for the battle. The bulls of Bashan may roar, yet my feet are shod with safety. Thou wouldst go to Kaïd and tell him thy affrighted tale. I tell thee, thou wilt not go. Thou hast reason yet, though thy blood is hot. Thou art to Claridge Pasha like a brother—as to his uncle before him, who furnished my father's palace with carpets! The carpets still soften the fall of my feet in my father's palace, as they did soften the fall of my brother's feet, the feet of Foorgat Bey."

He paused, looking at Ebn Ezra with quiet triumph, though his eyes had ever that smiling innocence which had won David in days gone by. He was turning his words over on the tongue with a relish born of long waiting.

"Come," he said presently, "come, and I will give thee reason why thou wilt not speak with Kaïd to-day. This way, effendi."

He led the other into a little room, hung about with rugs and tapestry, and, going to the wall, he touched a spring. "One moment here, effendi," he added quietly. The room was as it had been since David last stood within it.

"In this room, effendi," Nahoum said with cold deliberation, "Claridge Pasha killed my brother, Foorgat Bey."

Ebn Ezra fell back as though he had been struck. Swiftly Nahoum told him the whole truth—even to the picture of the brougham, and the rigid, upright figure passing through the night to Foorgat's palace, the gaunt Mizraim piloting the equipage of death.

"I have held my peace for my own reasons, effendi. Wilt thou then force me to speak? If thou dost still cherish Claridge Pasha, wilt thou see him ruined? Naught but ruin could follow the telling of the tale at this moment—his work, his life, all done. The scandal, the law, vengeance! But as it is now, Kaïd may turn to him again; his work may yet go on—he has had the luck of angels, and Kaïd is fickle. Who can tell?"

Abashed and overwhelmed, Ebn Ezra Bey looked at him keenly. "To tell of Foorgat Bey would ruin thee also," he said. "That thou knowest. The trick—would Kaïd forgive it? Claridge Pasha would not be ruined alone."

"Be it so. If thou goest to Kaïd with thy story, I go to Egypt with mine. Choose."

Ebn Ezra turned to go. "The high God judge between him and thee," he said, and, with bowed head, left the Palace.

XXXIV

NAHOUM DROPS THE MASK

"Claridge Pasha!"

At the sound of the words announced in a loud voice, hundreds of heads were turned towards the entrance of the vast salon, resplendent with gilded mirrors, great candelabra and chandeliers, golden hangings, and divans glowing with robes of yellow silk.

It was the anniversary of Kaïd's accession, and all entitled to come poured into the splendid chamber. The showy livery of the officials, the loose, spacious, gorgeous uniform of the officers, with the curved, jewelled scimitars and white turbans, the rich silk robes of the Ulema, robe over robe of colored silk with flowing sleeves and sumptuous silken vests, the ample dignity of noble-looking Arabs in immense white turbans, the dark, straight Stambouli coat of the officials, made a picture of striking variety and color and interest.

About the centre of the room, laying palm to palm again and yet again, touching lips and forehead and breast, speaking with slow, leisurely voices, were two Arab sheikhs from the far Soudan. One of these showed a singular interest in the movements of Nahoum Pasha as he entered the chamber, and an even greater interest in David when he was announced; but as David, in his journey up the chamber, must pass near him, he drew behind a little group of officials, who whispered to each other excitedly as David came on. More than once before this same sheikh Abdullah had seen David, and once they had met, and had made a treaty of amity, and Abdullah had agreed to deal in slaves no more; and yet within three months had sent to Cairo two hundred of the best that could be found between Khartoum and Senaar. His business, of which Ebn Ezra Bey had due knowledge, had now been with Nahoum. The business of the other Arab, a noble-looking and wiry Bedouin from the south, had been with Ebn Ezra Bey, and each hid his business from his friend. Abdullah murmured to himself as David passed—a murmur of admiration and astonishment. He had heard of the disfavor in which the Inglesi was; but, as he looked at David's face with its quiet smile, the influence which he felt in the desert long ago came over him again.

"By Allah," he said aloud abstractedly, "it is a face that will not hide when the khamsin blows! Who shall gainsay it? If he were not an infidel he would be a Mahdi."

To this his Bedouin friend replied: "As the depths of the pool at Ghebel Farik, so are his eyes. You shall dip deep and you shall not find the bottom. Bismillah, I would fight Kaïd's Nubians, but not this infidel pasha!"

Never had David appeared to such advantage. The victory over himself the night before, the message of hope that had reached him at the monastery in the desert, the coming of Lacey, had given him a certain quiet masterfulness not reassuring to his foes.

As he entered the chamber but now, there flashed into his mind the scene six years ago when, an absolute stranger, he had stepped into this Eastern salon, and had heard his name called out to the great throng, "*Claridge effendi!*"

He addressed no one, but he bowed to the group of foreign consuls-general, looking them steadily in the eyes. He knew their devices and what had been going on of late, he was aware that his fall would mean a blow to British prestige, and the calmness of his gaze expressed a fortitude which had a disconcerting effect upon the group. The British Consul-General stood near by. David advanced to him, and, as he did so, the few who surrounded the Consul-General fell back. David held out his hand. Somewhat abashed and ill at ease, the Consul-General took it.

"Have you good news from Downing Street?" asked David quietly.

The Consul-General hesitated for an instant, and then said: "There is no help to be had for you or for what you are doing in that quarter." He lowered his voice. "I fear Lord Eglington does not favor you; and he controls the Foreign Minister. I am very sorry. I have done my best, but my colleagues, the other consuls, are busy—with Lord Eglington."

David turned his head away for an instant. Strange how that name sent a thrill through him, stirred his blood! He did not answer the Consul-General, and the latter continued:

"Is there any hope? Is the breach with Kaïd complete?"

David smiled gravely. "We shall see presently. I have made no change in my plans on the basis of a breach."

At that moment he caught sight of Nahoum some distance away, and moved towards him. Out of the corner of his eye Nahoum saw David coming, and edged away towards that point where Kaïd would enter, and where the crowd was greater. As he did so, Kaïd appeared. A thrill went through the chamber. Contrary to his custom, he was dressed in the old native military dress of Mehemet Ali. At his side was a jewelled scimitar, and in his turban flashed a great diamond. In his hand he carried a snuff-box, covered with brilliants, and on his breast were glittering orders.

The eyes of the reactionaries flashed with sinister pleasure when they saw Kaïd. This outward display of Orientalism could only be a reflex of the mind. It was the outer symbol of Kaïd's return to the spirit of the old days, before the influence of the Inglesi came upon him. Every corrupt and intriguing mind had a palpitation of excitement.

In Nahoum the sight of Kaïd produced mixed feelings. If, indeed, this display meant reaction towards an *entourage* purely Arab, Egyptian, and Muslim, then it was no good omen for his Christian self. He drew near, and placed himself where Kaïd could see him. Kaïd's manner was cheerful, but his face showed the effect of suffering, physical and mental. Presently there entered behind him Sharif Bey, whose appearance was the signal for a fresh demonstration. Now, indeed, there could be no doubt as to Kaïd's reaction. Yet if Sharif had seen Mizraim's face evilly gloating near by, he would have been less confident.

David was standing where Kaïd must see him, but the Effendina gave no sign of recognition. This was so significant that the enemies of David rejoiced anew. The day of the Inglesi was over. Again and again did Kaïd's eye wander over David's head.

David remained calm and watchful, neither avoiding nor yet seeking the circle in which Kaïd moved. The spirit with which he had entered the room, however, remained with him, even when he saw Kaïd summon to him some of the most fanatical members of the court circle, and engage them in talk for a moment. But as this attention grew more marked, a cloud slowly gathered in the far skies of his mind.

There was one person in the great assembly, however, who seemed to be unduly confident. It was an ample, perspiring person in evening dress, who now and again mopped a prematurely bald head, and who said to himself, as Kaïd talked to the reactionaries,—

"Say, Kaïd's overdoing it. He's putting potted chicken on the butter. But it's working all right—r-i-g-h-t. It's worth the backsheesh!"

At this moment, Kaïd fastened David with his look, and spoke in a tone so loud that people standing at some distance were startled.

"Claridge Pasha!"

In the hush that followed, David stepped forward. "May the bounty of the years be thine, Saadat," Kaïd said, in a tone none could misunderstand.

"May no tree in thy orchard wither, Effendina," answered David in a firm voice.

Kaïd beckoned him near, and again he spoke loudly.

"I have proved thee, and found thee as gold tried seven times by the fire, Saadat. In the treasurv of my heart shall I store thee up. Thou art going to the Soudan to finish the work Mehemet Ali began. I commend thee to Allah, and will bid thee farewell at sunrise—I and all who love Egypt."

There was a sinister smile on his lips, as his eyes wandered over the faces of the foreign consuls-general. The look he turned on the intriguers of the Palace was repellent; he reserved for Sharif a moody, threatening glance and the desperate *hakim* shrank back confounded from it. His first impulse was to flee from the Palace and from Cairo; but he bethought himself of the assault to be made on Kaïd by the tent-maker, as he passed to the mosque a few hours later, and he determined to await the issue of that event. Exchanging glances with confederates, he disappeared, as Kaïd laid a hand on David's arm and drew him aside.

After viewing the great throng cynically for a moment, Kaïd said: "To-morrow thou goest. A month hence the hakim's knife will find the thing that eats away my life. It may be they will destroy it and save me; if not, we shall meet no more."

David looked into his eyes. "Not in a month shall thy work be completed, Effendina. Thou shalt live. God and thy strong will shall make it so."

A light stole over the superstitious face. "No device or hatred, or plot, has prevailed against thee," Kaïd said eagerly. "Thou hast defeated all—even when I turned against thee in the black blood of despair. Thou hast conquered me—even as thou didst Harrik."

"Thou dost live," returned David dryly. "Thou dost live for Egypt's sake, even as Harrik died for Egypt's sake and as others shall die."

"Death hath tracked thee down how often! Yet with a wave of the hand thou hast blinded him and his blow falls on the air. Thou art beset by a thousand dangers, yet thou comest safe through all. Thou art an honest man. For that I besought thee to stay with me. Never didst thou lie to me. Good luck hath followed thee. *Kismet!*—Stay with me, and it may be I shall be safe also. This thought came to me in the night, and in the morning was my reward, for Lacey effendi came to me and said, even as I say now, that thou wilt bring me good luck; and even in that hour, by the mercy of God, a loan much needed was negotiated. Allah be praised!"

A glint of humor shot into David's eyes. Lacey—a loan—he read it all! Lacey had eased the Prince Pasha's immediate and pressing financial needs—and, "*Allah be praised!*" Poor human nature—backsheesh to a Prince regnant!

"Effendina," he said presently, "thou didst speak of Harrik. One there was who saved thee then—"

"Zaida!" A change passed over Kaïd's face. "Speak! Thou hast news of her? She is gone?"

Briefly David told him how Zaida was found upon her sister's grave. Kaïd's face was turned away as he listened.

"She spoke no word of me?" Kaïd said at last.

"To whom should she speak?" David asked gently. "But the armlet thou gavest her, set with one red jewel, it was clasped in her hand in death."

Suddenly Kaïd's anger blazed. "Now shall Achmet die," he burst out. "His hands and feet shall be burned off, and he shall be thrown to the vultures."

"The Place of the Lepers is sacred even from thee, Effendina," answered David gravely. "Yet Achmet shall die even as Harrik died. He shall die for Egypt and for thee, Effendina."

Swiftly he drew the picture of Achmet at the monastery in the desert. "I have done the unlawful thing, Effendina," he said at last, "but thou wilt make it lawful. He hath died a thousand deaths—all save one."

"Be it so," answered Kaïd gloomily, after a moment; then his face lighted with cynical pleasure as he scanned once more the faces of the crowd before him. At last his eyes fastened on Nahoum. He turned to David.

"Thou dost still desire Nahoum in his office?" he asked keenly.

A troubled look came into David's eyes, then it cleared away, and he said firmly: "For six years we have worked together, Effendina. I am surety for his loyalty to thee."

"And his loyalty to thee?"

A pained look crossed over David's face again, but he said with a will that fought all suspicion down, "The years bear witness."

Kaïd shrugged his shoulders slightly. "The years have perjured themselves ere this. Yet, as thou sayest, Nahoum is a Christian," he added, with irony scarcely veiled.

Now he moved forward with David towards the waiting court. David searched the groups of faces for Nahoum in vain. There were things to be said to

Nahoum before he left on the morrow, last suggestions to be given. Nahoum could not be seen.

Nahoum was gone, as were also Sharif and his confederates; and in the lofty Mosque of Mahmoud soft lights were hovering, while the Sheikh-el-Islam waited with Koran and scimitar for the ruler of Egypt to pray to God and salute the Lord Mahomet.

At the great gateway in the Street of the Tentmakers Kaïd paused on his way to the Mosque Mahmoud. The Gate was studded with thousands of nails, which fastened to its massive timbers relics of the faithful, bits of silk and cloth, and hair and leather; and here from time immemorial a holy man had sat and prayed. At the gateway Kaïd salaamed humbly, and spoke to the holy man, who, as he passed, raised his voice shrilly in an appeal to Allah, commending Kaïd to mercy and everlasting favor. On every side eyes burned with religious zeal, and excited faces were turned towards the Effendina. At a certain point there were little groups of men with faces more set than excited. They had a look of suppressed expectancy. Kaïd neared them, passed them, and, as he did so, they looked at each other in consternation. They were Sharif's confederates, fanatics carefully chosen. The attempt on Kaïd's life should have been made opposite the spot where they stood. They craned their necks in effort to find the Christian tent-maker, but in vain.

Suddenly they heard a cry, a loud voice calling. It was Rahib the tent-maker. He was beside Kaïd's stirrups, but no weapon was in his hand; and his voice was calling blessings down on the Effendina's head for having pardoned and saved from death his one remaining son, the joy of his old age. In all the world there was no prince like Kaïd, said the tent-maker; none so bountiful and merciful and beautiful in the eyes of men.

God grant him everlasting days, the beloved friend of his people, just to all and greatly to be praised.

As the soldiers drove the old man away with kindly insistence—for Kaïd had thrown him a handful of gold—Mizraim, the Chief Eunuch, laughed wickedly. As Nahoum had said, the greatest of all weapons was the mocking finger. He and Mizraim had had their way with the Governor of the prisons, and the murderer had gone in safety, while the father stayed to bless Kaïd. Rahib the tent-maker had fooled the plotters. They were had in derision. They did not know that Kaïd was as innocent as themselves of having pardoned the tent-maker's son. Their moment had passed; they could not overtake it; the match had spluttered and gone out at the fuel laid for the fire of fanaticism.

The morning of David's departure came. While yet it was dark he had risen, and had made his last preparations. When he came into the open air and mounted, it was not yet sunrise, and in that spectral early light, which is all Egypt's own, Cairo looked like some dream-city in a forgotten world. The Mokattam Hills were like vast, dun barriers guarding and shutting in the ghostly place, and, high above all, the minarets of the huge mosque upon the lofty rocks were impalpable fingers pointing an endless flight. The very trees seemed so little real and substantial that they gave the eye the impression that they might rise and float away. The Nile was hung with mist, a trailing cloud unwound from the breast of the Nile-mother. At last the sun touched the minarets of the splendid mosque with shafts of light, and over at Ghizeh and Sakharah the great pyramids, lifting their heads from the wall of rolling blue mist below, took the morning's crimson radiance with the dignity of four thousand years.

On the deck of the little steamer which was to carry them south, David, Ebn Ezra, Lacey, and Mahommed waited. Presently Kaïd came, accompanied by his faithful Nubians, their armor glowing in the first warm light of the rising sun; and crowds of people, who had suddenly emerged, ran shrilling to the waterside behind him.

Kaïd's pale face had all last night's friendliness, as he bade David farewell with great honor and commended him to the care of Allah; and the swords of the Nubians clashed against their breasts and on their shields in salaam.

But there was another farewell to make; and it was made as David's foot touched the deck of the steamer. Once again David looked at Nahoum as he had done six years ago, in the little room where they had made their bond together. There was the same straight look in Nahoum's eyes. Was he not to be trusted? Was it not his own duty to trust? He clasped Nahoum's hand in farewell and turned away. But as he gave the signal to start, and the vessel began to move, Nahoum came back. He leaned over the widening space and said in a low tone, as David again drew near,—

"There is still an account which should be settled, Saadat. It has waited long; but God is with the patient. *There is the account of Foorgat Bey!*"

The light fled from David's eyes and his heart stopped beating for a moment. When his eyes saw the shore again Nahoum was gone with Kaïd.

BOOK V

XXXV

THE FLIGHT OF THE WOUNDED

"And Mario can soothe with a tenor note
The souls in purgatory."

"*Non ti scordar di mi!*" The voice rang out with passionate, stealthy sweetness, finding its way into far recesses of human feeling. Women of perfect poise, and with the confident look of luxury and social fame, dropped their eyes abstractedly on the opera-glasses lying in their laps, or the programmes they mechanically fingered, and recalled, they knew not why—for what had it to do with this musical narration of a tragic Italian tale!—the days when, in the first flush of their wedded life, they had set a seal of devotion and loyalty and love upon their arms, which, long ago, had gone to the limbo of lost jewels, with the chaste, fresh desires of worshipping hearts. Young egotists, supremely happy and defiant in the pride of the fact that they loved each other, and that it mattered little what the rest of the world enjoyed, suffered, and endured—these were suddenly arrested in their buoyant and solitary flight, and stirred restlessly in their seats. Old men whose days of work were over; who no longer marshalled their legions, or moved at a nod great ships upon the waters in masterful manœuvres; whose voices were heard no more in chambers of legislation, lashing partisan feeling to a height of cruelty or lulling a storm among rebellious followers; whose intellects no longer devised vast schemes of finance, or applied secrets of science to transform industry—these heard the enthralling cry of a soul with the darkness of eternal loss gathering upon it, and drew back within themselves; for they too had cried like this one time or another in their lives. Stricken, they had cried out, and ambition had fled away, leaving behind only the habit of living, and of work and duty.

As Hylda, in the Duchess of Snowdon's box, listened with a face which showed nothing of what she felt, and looking straight at the stage before her, the words of a poem she had learned but yesterday came to her mind, and wove themselves into the music thrilling from the voice in the stage prison:

> "And what is our failure here but a triumph's evidence
> For the fulness of the days? Have we withered or agonized?
> Why else was the pause prolonged but that singing might issue thence?
> Why rushed the discords in, but that harmony should be prized?"

"*And what is our failure here but a triumph's evidence?*" Was it then so?

The long weeks which had passed since that night at Hamley, when she had told Eglington the truth about so many things, had brought no peace, no understanding, no good news from anywhere. The morning after she had spoken with heart laid bare, Eglington had essayed to have a reconciliation; but he had come as the martyr, as one injured. His egotism at such a time, joined to his attempt to make light of things, of treating what had happened as a mere "moment of exasperation," as "one of those episodes inseparable from the lives of the high-spirited," only made her heart sink and grow cold, almost as insensible as the flesh under a spray of ether. He had been neither wise nor patient. She had not slept after that bitter, terrible scene, and the morning had found her like one battered by winter seas, every nerve desperately alert to pain, yet tears swimming at her heart and ready to spring to her eyes at a touch of the real thing, the true note—and she knew so well what the true thing was! Their great moment had passed, had left her withdrawn into herself, firmly, yet without heart performing the daily duties of life, gay before the world, the delightful hostess, the necessary and graceful figure at so many functions.

Even as Soolsby had done, who went no further than to tell Eglington his dark tale, and told no one else, withholding it from "Our Man"; as Sybil Lady Eglington had shrunk when she had been faced by her obvious duty, so Hylda hesitated, but from better reason than either. To do right in the matter was to strike her husband—it must be a blow now, since her voice had failed. To do right was to put in the ancient home and house of Eglington one whom he—with anger and without any apparent desire to have her altogether for himself, all the riches of her life and love—had dared to say commanded her sympathy and interest, not because he was a man dispossessed of his rights, but because he was a man possessed of that to which he had no right. The insult had stung her, had driven her back into a reserve, out of which she seemed unable to emerge. How could she compel Eglington to do right in this thing—do right by his own father's son?

Meanwhile, that father's son was once more imperilling his life, once more putting England's prestige in the balance in the Soudan, from which he had already been delivered twice as though by miracles. Since he had gone, months before, there had been little news; but there had been much public anxiety; and she knew only too well that there had been *pourparlers* with foreign ministers, from which no action came safeguarding David.

Many a human being has realized the apathy, the partial paralysis of the will, succeeding a great struggle, which has exhausted the vital forces. Many a general who has fought a desperate and victorious fight after a long campaign, and amid all the anxieties and miseries of war, has failed to follow up his advantage, from a sudden lesion of the power for action in him. He has stepped from the iron routine of daily effort into a sudden freedom, and his faculties have failed him, the iron of his will has vanished. So it was with Hylda. She waited for she knew not what. Was it some dim hope that Eglington might see the right as she saw it? That he might realize how unreal was this life they were living, outwardly peaceful and understanding, deluding the world, but inwardly a place of tears? How she dreaded the night and its recurrent tears, and the hours when she could not sleep, and waited for the joyless morning, as one lost on the moor, blanched with cold, waits for the sunrise! Night after night at a certain hour,—the hour when she went to bed at last after that poignant revelation to Eglington—she wept, as she had wept then, heart-broken tears of disappointment, disillusion, loneliness; tears for the bitter pity of it all; for the wasting and wasted opportunities, for the common aim never understood or planned together; for the precious hours lived in an air of artificial happiness and social excitement; for a perfect understanding missed; for the touch which no longer thrilled.

But the end of it all must come. She was looking frail and delicate, and her beauty, newly refined, and with a fresh charm as of mystery or pain, was touched by feverishness. An old impatience once hers was vanished, and Kate Heaver would have given a month's wages for one of those flashes of petulance of other days ever followed by a smile. Now the smile was all too often there, the patient smile which comes to those who have suffered. Hardness she felt at times, where Eglington was concerned, for he seemed to need her now not at all, to be self-contained, self-dependent—almost arro gantly so; but she did not show it; and she was outwardly patient.

In his heart of hearts Eglington believed that she loved him, that her interest in David was only part of her idealistic temperament—the admiration of a woman for a man of altruistic aims; but his hatred of David, of what David was, and of his irrefutable claims, reacted on her. Perverseness, and his unhealthy belief that he would master her in the end, that she would one day break down and come to him, willing to take his view in all things, and to be his slave—all this drove him farther and farther on a fatal, ever-broadening path.

Success had spoiled him. He applied his gifts in politics, daringly unscrupulous, superficially persuasive, intellectually insinuating, to his wife; and she, who had been captured once by all these things, was not to be captured again. She knew what alone could capture her; and, as she sat and watched the singers on the stage now, the divine notes of that searching melody still lingering in her heart, there came a sudden wonder whether Eglington's heart could not be wakened. She knew that it never had been; that he had never known love, the transfiguring and reclaiming passion. No, no, surely it could not be too late—her marriage with him had only come too soon! He had ridden over her without mercy, he had robbed her of her rightful share of the beautiful and the good; he had never loved her; but if love came to him, if he could but once realize how much there was of what he had missed! If he did not save himself—and her—what would be the end? She felt the cords drawing her elsewhere; the lure of a voice she had heard in an Egyptian garden was in her ears. One night at Hamley, in an abandonment of grief—life hurt her so—she had remembered the prophecy she had once made that she would speak to David, and that he would hear; and she had risen from her seat, impelled by a strange new feeling, and had cried, "Speak!—speak to me!" And as plainly as she had ever heard anything in her life, she had heard his voice speak to her a message that sank into the innermost recesses of her being, and she had been more patient afterwards. She had no doubt whatever; she had spoken to him, and he had answered; but the answer was one which all the world might have heard.

Down deep in her nature was an inalienable loyalty, was a simple, old-fashioned feeling that "they two," she and Eglington, should cleave unto each other till death should part. He had done much to shatter that feeling; but now, as she listened to Mario's voice, centuries of predisposition worked in her, and a great pity awoke in her heart. Could she not save him, win him, wake him, cure him of the disease of Self?

The thought brought a light to her eyes which had not been there for many a day. Out of the deeps of her soul this mist of pure selflessness rose, the spirit of that idealism which was the real cord of sympathy between her and Egypt.

Yes, she would, this once again, try to win the heart of this man; and so reach what was deeper than heart, and so also give him that, without which his life must be a failure in the end, as Sybil Eglington had said. How often had those bitter, anguished words of his mother rung in her ears,—"*So brilliant and unscrupulous, like yourself, but, oh, so sure of winning a great place in the world . . . so calculating and determined and ambitious.*" They came to her now, flashed between the eager, solicitous eyes of her mind and the scene of a perfect and everlasting reconciliation which it conjured up—flashed and was gone; for her will rose up and blurred them into mist; and other words of that true palimpsest of Sybil Eglington's broken life came instead: "*And though he loves me little, as he loves you little, too, yet he is my son, and for what he is we are both responsible one way or another.*" As the mother, so the wife. She said to herself now in sad paraphrase, "And though he loves me little, yet he is my husband, and for what he is it may be that I am in some sense responsible." *Yet he is my husband!* All that it was came to her; the closed door, the drawn blinds; the intimacy which shut them away from all the world; the things said which can only be said without desecration between two honest souls who love each other; and that sweet isolation which makes marriage a separate world, with its own sacred revelation. This she had known; this had been; and though the image of the sacred thing had been defaced, yet the shrine was not destroyed.

For she believed that each had kept the letter of the law; that, whatever his faults, he had turned his face to no other woman. If she had not made his heart captive and drawn him by an ever-shortening cord of attraction, yet she was sure that none other had any influence over him, that, as he had looked at her in those short-lived days of his first devotion, he looked at no other. The way was clear yet. There was nothing irretrievable, nothing irrevocable, which would forever stain the memory and tarnish the gold of life when the perfect love should be minted. Whatever faults of mind or disposition or character were his—or hers—there were no sins against the pledges they had made, nor the bond into which they had entered. Life would need no sponge. Memory might still live on without a wound or a cowl of shame.

It was all part of the music to which she listened, and she was almost oblivious of the brilliant throng, the crowded boxes, or of the Duchess of Snowdon sitting near her strangely still, now and again scanning the beautiful face beside her with a reflective look. The Duchess loved the girl—she was but a girl, after all—as she had never loved any of her sex; it had come to be the last real interest of her life. To her eyes, dimmed with much seeing, blurred by a garish kaleidoscope of fashionable life, there had come a look which was like the ghost of a look she had, how many decades ago!

Presently, as she saw Hylda's eyes withdraw from the stage, and look at her with a strange, soft moisture and a new light in them, she laid her fan confidently on her friend's knee, and said in her abrupt, whimsical voice, "You like it, my darling; your eyes are as big as saucers. You look as if you'd been seeing things, not things on that silly stage, but what Verdi felt when he wrote the piece, or something of more account than that."

"Yes, I've been seeing things," Hylda answered with a smile which came from a new-born purpose, the dream of an idealist. "I've been seeing things that Verdi did not see, and of more account, too. . . . Do you suppose the House is up yet?"

A strange look flashed into the Duchess's eyes, which had been watching her with as much pity as interest. Hylda had not been near the House of Commons this session, though she had read the reports with her usual care. She had shunned the place.

"Why, did you expect Eglington?" the Duchess asked idly, yet she was watchful, too, alert for every movement in this life where the footsteps of happiness were falling by the edge of a precipice, over which she would not allow herself to look. She knew that Hylda did not expect Eglington, for the decision to come to the opera was taken at the last moment.

"Of course not—he doesn't know we are here. But if it wasn't too late, I thought I'd go down and drive him home."

The Duchess veiled her look. Here was some new

development in the history which had been torturing her old eyes, which had given her and Lord Windlehurst as many anxious moments as they had known in many a day, and had formed them into a vigilance committee of two, who waited for the critical hour when they should be needed.

"We'll go at once if you like," she replied. "The opera will be over soon. We sent word to Windlehurst to join us, you remember, but he won't come now; it's too late. So, we'll go, if you like."

She half rose, but the door of the box opened, and Lord Windlehurst looked in quizzically. There was a smile on his face.

"I'm late, I know; but you'll forgive me—*you'll* forgive me, dear lady," he added to Hylda, "for I've been listening to your husband making a smashing speech for a bad cause."

Hylda smiled. "Then I must go and congratulate him," she answered, and withdrew her hand from that of Lord Windlehurst, who seemed to hold it longer than usual, and pressed it in a fatherly way.

"I'm afraid the House is up," he rejoined, as Hylda turned for her opera-cloak; "and I saw Eglington leave Palace Yard as I came away." He gave a swift, ominous glance towards the Duchess, which Hylda caught, and she looked at each keenly.

"It's seldom I sit in that Peers' Gallery," continued Windlehurst; "I don't like going back to the old place much. It seems empty and hollow. But I wouldn't have missed Eglington's fighting speech for a good deal."

"What was it about?" asked Hylda as they left the box. She had a sudden throb of the heart. Was it the one great question, that which had been like a gulf of fire between them?

"Oh, Turkey—the unpardonable Turk," answered Windlehurst. "As good a defence of a bad case as I ever heard."

"Yes, Eglington would do that well," said the Duchess enigmatically, drawing her cloak around her and adjusting her hair. Hylda looked at her sharply, and Lord Windlehurst slyly, but the Duchess seemed oblivious of having said anything out of the way, and added, "It's a gift seeing all that can be said for a bad cause, and saying it, and so making the other side make their case so strong that the verdict has to be just."

"Dear Duchess, it doesn't always work out that way," rejoined Windlehurst with a dry laugh. "Sometimes the devil's advocate wins."

"You are not very complimentary to my husband," retorted Hylda, looking him in the eyes, for she was not always sure when he was trying to baffle her.

"I'm not so sure of that. He hasn't won his case yet. He has only staved off the great attack. It's coming—soon."

"What is the great attack? What has the Government, or the Foreign Office, done, or left undone?"

"Well, my dear—" Suddenly Lord Windlehurst remembered himself, stopped, put up his eye-glass, and with great interest seemed to watch a gay group of people opposite; for the subject of attack was Egypt and the Government's conduct in not helping David, in view not alone of his present danger, but of the position of England in the country, on which depended the security of her highway to the East. Windlehurst was a good actor, and he had broken off his words as though the group he was now watching had suddenly claimed his attention. "Well, well, Duchess," he said reflectively, "I see a new nine days' wonder yonder." Then, in response to a reminder from Hylda, he continued: "Ah, yes, the attack! Oh, Persia—Persia, and our feeble diplomacy, my dear lady, though you mustn't take that as my opinion, opponent as I am. That's the charge, Persia—and her cats!"

The Duchess breathed a sigh of relief; for she knew what Windlehurst had been going to say, and she shrank from seeing what she felt she would see, if Egypt and Claridge Pasha's name were mentioned. That night at Hamley had burnt a thought into her mind which she did not like. Not that she had any pity for Eglington; her thought was all for this girl she loved. No happiness lay in the land of Egypt for her, whatever her unhappiness here; and she knew that Hylda must be more unhappy still before she was ever happy again, if that might be. There was that concerning Eglington which Hylda did not know, yet which she must know one day—and then! But why were Hylda's eyes so much brighter and softer and deeper to-night? There was something expectant, hopeful, brooding in them. They belonged not to the life moving round her, but were shining in a land of their own, a land of promise. By an instinct in each of them they stood listening for a moment to the last strains of the opera. The light leaped higher in Hylda's eyes:

"Beautiful! oh, so beautiful!" she said, her hand touching the Duchess's arm.

The Duchess gave the slim, warm fingers a spasmodic little squeeze. "Yes, darling, beautiful," she rejoined; and then the crowd began to pour out behind them. Their carriages were at the door. Lord Windlehurst put Hylda in. "The House is up," he said. "You are going on somewhere?"

"No—home," she said, and smiled into his old, kind, questioning eyes. "Home!"

"Home!" he murmured bitterly as he turned towards the Duchess and her carriage. "Home!" he repeated, and shook his head sadly.

"Shall I drive you to your house?" the Duchess asked.

"No, I'll go with you to your door, and walk back to my cell. Home!" he growled to the footman, with a sardonic note in the voice.

As they drove away, the Duchess turned to him abruptly. "What did you mean by your look when you said you had seen Eglington drive away from the House?"

"Well, my dear Betty, *she*—the fly-away—drives him home now. It has come to that."

"To *her* home—Windlehurst, oh, Windlehurst!" She sank back in the cushions, and gave what was as near a sob as she had given in many a day.

Windlehurst took her hand. "No, not so bad as that yet. She drove him to his club. Don't fret, my dear Betty!"

Home! Hylda watched the shops, the houses, the squares, as she passed westward, her mind dwelling almost happily on the new determination to which she had come. It was not love that was moving her, not love for him, but a deeper thing. He had brutally killed love—the full life of it—those months ago; but there was a deep thing working in her which was as near nobility as the human mind can feel. Not in a long time had she neared her home with such expectation and longing. Often on the door-step she had shut her eyes to the light and warmth and elegance of it, because of that which she did not see. Now, with a thrill of pleasure, she saw its doors open. It was possible Eglington might have come home already. Lord Windlehurst had said that he had left the House. She did not ask if he was in,—it had not been her custom for a long time—and servants were curious people; but she looked at the hall-table. Yes, there was a hat which had evidently just been placed there, and gloves, and a stick. He was at home, then.

She hurried to her room, dropped her opera-cloak on a chair, looked at herself in the glass, a little fluttered and critical, and then crossed the hallway to Eglington's bedroom. She listened for a moment. There was no sound. She turned the handle of the door softly, and opened it. A light was burning low, but the room was empty. It was as she thought, he was in his study, where he spent hours sometimes after he came home, reading official papers. She went up the stairs, at first swiftly, then more slowly, then with almost lagging feet. Why did she hesitate? Why should a woman falter in going to her husband—to her own one man of all the world? Was it not, should it not be, ever the open door between them? Confidence—confidence—could she not have it, could she not get it now at last? She had paused; but now she moved on with quicker step, purpose in her face, her eyes softly lighted.

Suddenly she saw on the floor an opened letter. She picked it up, and, as she did so, involuntarily observed the writing. Almost mechanically she glanced at the contents. Her heart stood still. The first words scorched her eyes.

"*Eglington—Harry, dearest,*" it said, "*you shall not go to sleep to-night without a word from me. This will make you think of me when . . .*"

Frozen, struck as by a mortal blow, Hylda looked at the signature. She knew it—the cleverest, the most beautiful adventuress which the aristocracy and society had produced. She trembled from head to foot, and for a moment it seemed that she must fall. But she steadied herself and walked firmly to Eglington's door. Turning the handle softly, she stepped inside.

He did not hear her. He was leaning over a box of papers, and they rustled loudly under his hand. He was humming to himself that song she heard an hour ago in *Il Trovatore*, that song of passion and love and tragedy. It sent a wave of fresh feeling over her. She could not go on—could not face him, and say what she must say. She turned and passed swiftly from the room, leaving the door open, and hurried down the staircase. Eglington heard now, and wheeled round. He saw the open door, listened to the rustle of her skirts, knew that she had been there. He smiled, and said to himself:

"She came to me, as I said she would. I shall master her—the full surrender, and then—life will be easy then."

Hylda hurried down the staircase to her room, saw Kate Heaver waiting, beckoned to her, caught up her opera-cloak, and together they passed down the staircase to the front door. Heaver rang a bell, a footman appeared, and, at a word, called a cab. A minute later they were ready.

"Snowdon House," Hylda said; and they passed into the night.

XXXVI

"IS IT ALWAYS SO—IN LIFE?"

THE Duchess and her brother, an ex-diplomatist, now deaf and patiently amiable and garrulous, had met on the door-step of Snowdon House, and together they insisted on Lord Windlehurst coming in for a talk. The two men had not met for a long time, and the retired official had been one of Lord Windlehurst's own best appointments in other days. The Duchess had the carriage wait in consequence.

The ex-official could hear little, but he had cultivated the habit of talking constantly and well. There were some voices, however, which he could hear more distinctly than others, and Lord Windlehurst's was one of them, clear, well-modulated, and penetrating. Sipping brandy and water, Lord Windlehurst gave his latest quip. They were all laughing heartily, when the butler entered the room and said, "Lady Eglington is here, and wishes to see your grace."

As the butler left the room, the Duchess turned despairingly to Windlehurst, who had risen, and was paler than the Duchess. "It has come," she said, "oh, it has come! I can't face it."

"Ah, it doesn't matter about you facing it," Lord Windlehurst rejoined. "Go to her and help her, Betty. You know what to do—the one thing." He took her hand and pressed it.

She dashed the tears from her eyes and drew herself

together, while her brother watched her benevolently. He had not heard what was said. Betty had always been impulsive, he thought to himself, and here was some one in trouble—they all came to her, and kept her poor.

"Go to bed, Dick," the Duchess said to him, and hurried from the room. She did not hesitate now. Windlehurst had put the matter in the right way. Her pain was nothing, mere moral cowardice; but Hylda—!

She entered the other room as quickly as rheumatic limbs would permit. Hylda stood waiting, erect, her eyes gazing blankly beforc her and rimmed by dark circles, her face haggard and despairing.

Before the Duchess could reach her, she said in a hoarse whisper: "I have left him—I have left him. I have come to you."

With a cry of pity the Duchess would have taken the stricken girl in her arms, but Hylda held out a shaking hand with the letter in it which had brought this new woe and this crisis foreseen by Lord Windlehurst. "There—there it is. He goes from me to her—to *that!*" She thrust the letter into the Duchess's fingers. "You knew—you knew! I saw the look that passed between you and Windlehurst at the opera. I understand all now. He left the House of Commons with her—and you knew, oh, you knew! All the world knows—every one knew but me!" She threw up her hands. "But I've left him—I'vc left him forever."

Now the Duchess had her in her arms, and almost forcibly drew her to a sofa. "Darling, my darling," she said, "you must not give way. It is not so bad as you think. You must let me help to make you understand."

Hylda laughed hysterically. "Not so bad as I think! Read—read it," she said, taking the letter from the Duchess's fingers and holding it before her face.

"I found it on the staircase. I could not help but read it."

She sat and clasped and unclasped her hands in utter misery. "Oh, the shame of it, the bitter shame of it! Have I not been a good wife to him? Have I not had reason to break my heart? But I waited, and I wanted to be good and to do right. And to-night I was going to try once more—I felt it in the opera. I was going to make one last effort for his sake. It was for his sake I meant to make it, for I thought him only hard and selfish, and that he had never loved; and if he only loved, I thought—"

She broke off, wringing her hands and staring into space, the ghost of the beautiful figure that had left the Opera House with shining eyes.

The Duchess caught the cold hands. "Yes, yes, darling, I know. I understand. So does Windlehurst. He loves you as much as I do. We know there isn't much to be got out of life; but we always hoped you would get more than anybody else."

Hylda shrank, then raised her head and looked at the Duchess with an infinite pathos. "Oh, is it always so—in life? Is no one true? Is every one betrayed sometime? I would die—oh, yes, a thousand times yes, I would rather die than bear this! What do I care for life?—it has cheated me! I meant well, and I tried to do well, and I was true to him in word and deed even when I suffered most, even when—"

The Duchess laid a cheek against the burning head. "I understand, my own dear. I understand—altogether."

"Oh, you cannot know," the broken girl replied; "but through everything I was true—and I have been tempted, too, when my heart was aching so, when the days were so empty, the nights so long, and my heart hurt—hurt me. But now, it is over, everything is done. You will keep me here—oh, say you will keep me here till everything can be settled, and I can go away—far away—far—!"

She stopped with a gasping cry, and her eyes suddenly strained into the distance, as though a vision of some mysterious thing hung before her. The Duchess realized that that temptation, which has come to so many disillusioned mortals, to end it all, to find quiet somehow, somewhere out in the dark, was upon her. She became resourceful and persuasively commanding.

"But no, my darling," she said, "you are going nowhere. Here in London is your place now. And you must not stay here in my house. You must go back to your home. Your place is there. For the present, at any rate, there must be no scandal. Suspicion is nothing, talk is nothing, and the world forgets—"

"Oh, I do not care for the world or its forgetting!" the wounded girl replied. "What is the world to me! I wanted my own world, the world of my four walls, quiet and happy and free from scandal and shame. I wanted love and peace there, and now . . . !"

"You must be guided by those who love you. You are too young to decide what is best for yourself. You must let Windlehurst and me think for you; and, oh, my darling, you cannot know how much I care for your best good!"

"I cannot, will not, bear the humiliation and the shame. This letter here—you see!"

"It is the letter of a woman who has had more *affaires* than any man in London. She is preternaturally clever, my dear—Windlehurst would tell you so. The brilliant and unscrupulous, the beautiful and the bad, have a great advantage in this world. Eglington was curious, that is all. It is in the breed of the Eglingtons to go exploring, to experiment."

Hylda started. Words from the letter Sybil Lady Eglington had left behind her rushed into her mind,—

"*Experiment, subterfuge, secrecy. Reaping where you had not sowed and gathering where you had not strawed. Always, experiment, experiment, experiment!*"

"I have only been married three years," she moaned.

"Yes, yes, my darling, but much may happen after three days of married life, and love may come after twenty years. The human heart is a strange thing."

"I was patient—I gave him every chance. He has been false and shameless. I will not go on."

The Duchess pressed both hands hard, and made a last effort, looking into the deep, troubled eyes with her own grown almost beautiful with feeling—the faded, world-worn eyes.

"You will go back to-night—at once," she said firmly. "To-morrow you will stay in bed till noon—at any rate, till I come. I promise you that you shall not be treated with further indignity. Your friends will stand by you, the world will be with you, if you do nothing rash, nothing that forces it to babble and scold. But you must play its game, my dearest. I'll swear that the worst has not happened. She drove him to his club, and after a man has had a triumph, a woman will not drive him to his club if—my darling, you shall trust me! If there must be the great smash, let it be done in a way that will prevent you being smashed also in the world's eyes. You can live, and you will live. Is there nothing for you to do? Is there no one for whom you would do something, who would be heart-broken if you—if you went mad now?"

Suddenly a great change passed over Hylda. "*Is there no one for whom you would do something?*" Just as in the desert a question like this had lifted a man out of a terrible and destroying apathy, so this searching appeal roused in Hylda a memory and a pledge. "*Is there no one for whom you would do something?*" Was life, then, all over? Was her own great grief all? Was her bitter shame the end?

She got to her feet tremblingly. "I will go back," she said slowly and softly. "Yes, I will go back, dear."

"Windlehurst will take you home," the Duchess rejoined eagerly. "My carriage is at the door."

A moment afterwards Lord Windlehurst took Hylda's hands in his and held them long. His old, querulous eyes were like lamps of safety; his smile had now none of that cynicism with which he had aroused and chastened the world. The pitiful understanding of life was there, and a consummate gentleness. He gave her his arm, and they stepped out into the moonlit night. "So peaceful, so bright!" he said looking round.

"I will come at noon to-morrow," called the Duchess from the doorway.

A light was still shining in Eglington's study when the carriage drove up. With a latch-key Hylda admitted herself and her maid.

The storm had broken, the flood had come. The storm was over; but the flood swept far and wide.

XXXVII

THE FLYING SHUTTLE

Hour after hour of sleeplessness. The silver-tongued clock remorselessly tinkled the quarters, and Hylda lay and waited for them with a hopeless, strained attention. In vain she tried devices to produce that monotony of thought which sometimes brings sleep. Again and again, as she felt that sleep was coming at last, the thought of the letter she had found flashed through her mind with words of fire, and it seemed as if there had been poured through every vein a subtle irritant. Just such a surging, thrilling flood she had felt in the surgeon's chair when she was a girl, and an anæsthetic had been given. But this wave of sensation led to no oblivion, no last soothing intoxication. Its current beat against her heart until she could have cried out from the mere physical pain, the clamping grip of her trouble. She withered and grew cold under the torture of it all—the ruthless spoliation of everything which made life worth while, or the past endurable.

About an hour after she had gone to bed she heard Eglington's step. It paused at her door. She trembled with apprehension lest he should enter. It was many a day since he had done so, but also she had not heard his step pause at her door for many a day. She could not bear to face it all now; she must have time to think, to plan her course—the last course of all. For she knew that the next step must be the last step in her old life and towards a new life, whatever that might be. A great sigh of relief broke from her as she heard his door open and shut, and silence fell on everything, that palpable silence which seems to press upon the night-watcher with merciless, smothering weight.

How terribly active her brain was! Pictures—it was all vivid pictures, that awful visualization of sorrow which, if it continues, breaks the heart or wrests the mind from its sanity. If only she did not *see!* But she did see Eglington and the Woman together, saw him look into her eyes, take her hands, put his arm round her, draw her face to his! Her heart seemed as if it must burst, her lips cried out. With a great effort of the will she tried to hide from these agonies of the imagination, and again she would approach those happy confines of sleep, which are the only refuge to the lacerated heart; and then the weapon of time on the mantelpiece would clash on the shield of the past, and she was wide awake again. At last, in desperation, she got out of bed, hurried to the fireplace, caught the little sharp-tongued recorder in a nervous grasp, and stopped it.

As she was about to get into bed again, she saw a pile of letters lying on the table near her pillow. In her agitation she had not noticed them, and the devoted Heaver had not drawn her attention to them. Now, however, with a strange premonition, she quickly glanced at the envelopes. The last one of all was less aristocratic-looking than the others; the paper of the envelope was of the poorest, and it had a foreign look. She caught it up with an exclamation. The handwriting was that of her cousin Lacey.

She got into bed with a mind suddenly swept into a new atmosphere, and opened the flimsy cover. Shutting her eyes, she lay still for a moment—still and vague; she was only conscious of one thing, that a curtain had dropped on the terrible pictures she had seen, and that her mind was in a comforting quiet. Presently she roused herself, and turned the letter over in her hand. It was not long—was that because its news was bad news? The first chronicles of disaster were usually brief! She smoothed the paper out,—it had been crumpled and was a little soiled—and read it swiftly. It ran:

"DEAR LADY COUSIN,—As the poet says, 'Man is born to trouble as the sparks fly upward,' and in Egypt the sparks set the stacks on fire oftener than anywhere else, I guess. She outclasses Mexico as a 'precious example' in this respect. You needn't go looking for trouble in Mexico; it's waiting for you kindly. If it doesn't find you to-day, well, *mañana*. But here it comes running like a native to his cooking-pot at sunset in Ramadan. Well, there have been 'hard trials' for the Saadat. His cotton-mills were set on fire—can't you guess who did it? And now, down in Cairo, Nahoum runs Egypt; for a messenger that got through the tribes worrying us tells us that Kaïd is sick, and Nahoum the Armenian says, You shall, and You sha'n't, now. Which is another way of saying, that between us and the front door of our happy homes there are rattlesnakes that can sting—Nahoum's arm is long, and his traitors are crawling under the canvas of our tents!

"I'm not complaining for myself. I asked for what I've got, and, dear Lady Cousin, I put up some cash for it, too, as a man should. No, I *don't* mind for myself, fond as I am of loafing, sort of pottering round where the streets are in the hands of a pure police; for I've seen more, done more, thought more, up here, than in all my life before; and I've felt a country heaving under the touch of one of God's men—it gives you minutes that lift you out of the dust and away from the crawlers. And I'd do it all over a thousand times for him, and for what I've got out of it. I've lived. But, to speak right out plain, I don't know how long this machine will run. There's been a plant of the worst kind. Tribes we left friendly under a year ago are out against us; cities that were faithful have gone under to rebels. Nahoum has sowed the land with the tale that the Saadat means to abolish slavery, to take away the powers of the great sheikhs, and to hand the country over to the Turk. Ebn Ezra Bey has proofs of the whole thing, and now at last the Saadat knows—too late—that his work has been spoiled by the only man who could spoil it. The Saadat knows it, but does he rave and tear his hair? He says nothing. He stands up like a rock before the riot of treachery and bad luck and all the terrible burden he has to carry here. If he wasn't a Quaker I'd say he had the pride of an archangel. You can bend him, but you can't break him; and it takes a lot to bend him. Men desert, but he says others will come to take their place. And so they do. It's wonderful, in spite of the holy war that's being preached, and all the lies about him sprinkled over this part of Africa, how they all fear him, and find it hard to be out on the war-path against him. We should be gorging the vultures if he wasn't the wonder he is. We need boats. Does he sit down and wring his hands? No, he organizes, and builds them—out of scraps. Hasn't he enough food for a long siege? He goes himself to the tribes that have stored food in their cities, and haven't yet declared against him, and he puts a hand on their hard hearts, and takes the sulkiness out of their eyes, and a fleet of ghiassas comes down to us loaded with dourha. The defences of this place are nothing. Does he fold his hands like a man of peace that he is, and say, 'Thy will be done'? Not the Saadat. He gets two soldier-engineers, one an Italian who murdered his wife in Italy twenty years ago, and one a British officer that cheated at cards and had to go, and we've got defences that 'll take some negotiating. That's the kind of man he is; smiling to cheer others when their hearts are in their boots, stern like a commander-in-chief when he's got to punish, and then he does it like steel; but I've seen him afterwards in his tent with a face that looks sixty, and he's got to travel a while yet before he's forty! None of us dares be as afraid as we could be, because a look at him would make us so ashamed we'd have to commit suicide. He hopes when no one else would ever hope. The other day I went to his tent to wait for him, and I saw his Bible open on the table. A passage was marked. It was this:

" '*Behold, I have taken out of thy hand the cup of trembling, even the dregs of the cup of my fury; thou shalt no more drink it again:*

" '*But I will put it into the hand of them that afflict thee; which have said to thy soul, Bow down, that we may go over; and thou hast laid thy body as the ground, and as the street, to them that went over.*'

"I'd like to see Nahoum with that cup of trembling in his hand, and I've got an idea, too, that it will be there yet. I don't know how it is, but I never can believe the worst will happen to the Saadat. Reading those verses put hope into me. That's why I'm writing to you; on the chance of this getting through by a native who is stealing down the river with a letter from the Saadat to Nahoum, and one to Kaïd, and one to the Foreign Minister in London, and one to your husband. If they reach the hands they're meant for, it may be we shall pan out here yet. But there must be display of power; an army must be sent, without delay, to show the traitors that the game is up. Five thousand men from Cairo under a good general would do it. Will Nahoum send them? Does Kaïd, the sick man, know? I'm not banking on Kaïd. I think he's on his last legs. Unless pressure is put on him, unless some one takes him by the throat and says, If you don't relieve Claridge Pasha and the people with him, you will go to the crocodiles, Nahoum won't stir. So, I am writing to you. England can do it. The lord, your husband, can do it. England will have a nasty stain on her flag if she sees this man go down without a hand lifted to save him. He is worth another Alma to her prestige. She can't afford to see him slaughtered here, where he's fighting the fight of civilization. You see right through this thing, I know, and I don't need to palaver any more about it. It doesn't matter about me. I've had a lot for my money, and I'm no use—or I wouldn't be, if anything happened to the Saadat. No one would drop a knife and fork at the breakfast-table when my *obit* was read out—well, yes, there's one, cute as she can be, but she's lost two husbands already, and you can't be hurt so bad twice in the same place! But the Saadat, back him, Hylda—I'll call you that at this distance. Make Nahoum move. Send four or five thousand men before the day comes when famine does its work, and they draw the bowstring tight.

"Salaam and salaam, and the post is going out, and there's nothing in the morning paper; and, as Aunt Melissa used to say, 'Well, so much for so much!' One thing I forgot. I'm lucky to be writing to you at all. If the Saadat was an old-fashioned overlord, I shouldn't be here. I got into a bad corner three days ago with a dozen Arabs—I'd been doing a little work with a friendly tribe all on my own, and I almost got caught by this loose lot of fanatics. I shot three, and galloped for it. I knew the way through the mines outside, and just escaped by the skin of my teeth. Did the Saadat, as a matter of discipline, have me shot for cowardice? Cousin Hylda, my heart was in my mouth as I heard them yelling behind me—and I never enjoyed a dinner so much in my life! Would the Saadat have run from them? Say, he'd have stayed and saved his life, too. Well, give my love to the girls!

"Your affectionate cousin,

"TOM LACEY.

"P.S.—There's no use writing to me. The letter service is bad. Send a few thousand men by military parcel-post, prepaid, with some red seals—majors and colonels from Aldershot will do. They'll give the step to the Gyppies!

"T."

Hylda closed her eyes. A fever had passed from her veins. Here lay her duty before her—the redemption of the pledge she had made. Whatever her own sorrow, there was work before her; a supreme effort must be made for another. Even now it might be too late. She must have strength for what she meant to do. She put the room in darkness, and resolutely banished thought from her mind.

The sun had been up for hours before she waked. Eglington had gone to the Foreign Office. The morning papers were full of sensational reports concerning Claridge Pasha and the Soudan. A *Times* leader sternly admonished the Government.

XXXVIII

JASPER KIMBER SPEAKS

THAT day the adjournment of the House of Commons was moved "to call attention to an urgent matter of public importance"—the position of Claridge Pasha in the Soudan. Flushed with the success of last night's performance, stung by the attacks of the Opposition morning papers, confident in the big majority behind, which had cheered him a few hours before, viciously resenting the letter he had received from David that morning, Eglington returned such replies to the questions put to him, that a fire of angry mutterings came from the forces against him. He might have softened the growing resentment by a change of manner, but his intellectual arrogance had control of him for the moment; and he said to himself that he had mastered the House before, and he would do so now. Apart from his deadly antipathy to his half-brother, and the gain to himself—to his credit, the latter weighed with him not so much, so set was he on a stubborn course—if David disappeared forever, there was at bottom a spirit of anti-expansion, of reaction against England's world-wide responsibilities. He had no largeness of heart or view concerning humanity. He had no inherent greatness, no breadth of policy. With less responsibility taken, there would be less trouble, national and international—that was his point of view; that had been his view long ago at the meeting at Heddington; and his weak chief had taken it, knowing nothing of the personal elements behind.

The disconcerting factor in the present bitter questioning in the House was, that it originated on his own side. It was Jasper Kimber who had launched the questions, who moved the motion for adjournment. Jasper had had a letter from Kate Heaver that morning early, which sent him to her, and he had gone to the House to do what he thought to be his duty. He did it boldly, to the joy of the Opposition, and with a somewhat sullen support from many on his own side. Now appeared Jasper's own inner disdain of the man who had turned his coat for office. It gave a lead to a latent feeling among members of the ministerial party, of distrust, and of suspicion that they were the dupes of a mind of abnormal cleverness which, at bottom, despised them.

With flashing eyes and set lips, vigilant and resourceful, Eglington listened to Jasper Kimber's opening remarks.

By unremitting industry Jasper had made a place for himself in the House. The humor and vitality of his speeches, and his convincing advocacy of the cause of the "factory folk," had gained him a hearing. Thick-set, under middle size, with an arm like a giant and a throat like a bull, he had strong common sense, and he gave the impression that he would wear his heart out for a good friend or a great cause, but that if he chose to be an enemy he would be narrow, unrelenting, and persistent. For some time the House had been aware that he had more than a gift for criticism of the Under-Secretary for Foreign Affairs.

His speech began almost stumblingly, his h's ran loose, and his grammar became involved, but it was seen that he meant business, that he had that to say which would give anxiety to the Government, that he had a case wherein were the elements of popular interest and appeal, and that he was thinking and speaking as thousands outside the House would think and speak.

He had waited for this day. Indirectly he owed to

Claridge Pasha all that he had become. The day in which David knocked him down saw the depths of his degradation reached, and, when he got up, it was to start on a new life uncertainly, vaguely at first, but a new life for all that. He knew, from a true source, of Eglington's personal hatred of Claridge Pasha, though he did not guess their relationship; and all his interest was enlisted for the man who had, as he knew, urged Kate Heaver to marry himself—and Kate was his great ambition now. Above and beyond these personal considerations was a real sense of England's duty to the man who was weaving the destiny of a new land.

"It isn't England's business?" he retorted, in answer to an interjection from a faithful soul behind the ministerial Front Bench. "Well, it wasn't the business of the Good Samaritan to help the man that had been robbed and left for dead by the wayside; but he did it. As to David Claridge's work, some have said that —I've no doubt it's been said in the Cabinet, and it is the thing the Under-Secretary would say as naturally as he would flick a fly from his boots —that it's a generation too soon. Who knows that? I suppose there was those that thought John the Baptist was baptizing too soon, that Luther preached too soon, and Savonarola was in too great a hurry, all because he met his death and his enemies triumphed —and Galileo and Hampden and Cromwell and John Howard were all too soon. Who's to be judge of that? God Almighty puts it into some men's minds to work for a thing that's a great, and maybe an impossible, thing, so far as the success of the moment is concerned. Well, for a thing that has got to be done some time, the seed has to be sown, and it's always sown by men like Claridge Pasha, who has shown millions of people —barbarians and half-civilized alike—what a true lover of the world can do. God knows, I think he might have stayed and found a cause in England, but he elected to go to the ravaging Soudan, and he is England there, the best of it. And I know Claridge Pasha—from his youth up I have seen him, and I stand here to bear witness of what the working-men of England will say to-morrow. Right well the noble lord yonder knows that what I say is true. He has known it for years. Claridge Pasha would never have been in his present position, if the noble lord had not listened to the enemies of Claridge Pasha and of this country, in preference to those who know and hold the truth as I tell it here to-day. I don't know whether the noble lord has repented or not; but I do say that his Government will rue it, if his answer is not one word—'Intervention!' Mistaken, rash or not, dreamer if you like, Claridge Pasha should be relieved now, and his policy discussed afterwards. I don't envy the man who holds a contrary opinion; he'll be ashamed of it some day. But"—he pointed towards Eglington—"but there sits the Minister in whose hands his fate has been. Let us hope that this speech of mine needn't have been made, and that I've done injustice to his patriotism and to the policy he will announce."

"A setback, a sharp setback," said Lord Windlehurst, in the Peers' Gallery, as the cheers of the Opposition and of a good number of ministerialists sounded through the Chamber. There were those on the Treasury Bench who saw danger ahead. There was an attempt at a conference, but Kimber's seconder only said a half-dozen words, and sat down, and Eglington had to rise before any definite confidences could be exchanged. One word only he heard behind him as he got up—"Temporize!" It came from the Prime Minister.

Eglington was in no mood for temporizing. Attack only nerved him. He was a good and ruthless fighter; and last night's intoxication of success was still in his brain. He did not temporize. He did not leave a way of retreat open for the Prime Minister, who would probably wind up the debate. He fought with skill, but he fought without gloves, and the House needed gentle handling. He had the gift of effective speech to a rare degree, and, when he liked, he could be insinuating and witty, but he had not genuine humor or good feeling, and the House knew it. In debate he was biting, resourceful, and unscrupulous. He made the fatal mistake of thinking that intellect and gifts of fence, followed by a brilliant peroration, in which he treated the commonplaces of experienced minds as though they were new discoveries and he was their Columbus, could accomplish anything. He had never had a political crisis, but one had come now.

In his reply he first resorted to arguments of high politics, historical, informative, and, in a sense, commanding; indeed, the House became restless under what seemed a piece of intellectual dragooning. Signs of impatience appeared on his own side; and, when he ventured on a solemn warning about hampering ministers who alone knew the difficulties of diplomacy and the danger of wounding the susceptibilities of foreign and friendly countries, the silence was broken by a voice that said sneeringly, "The kid-glove Government!"

Then he began to lose place with the Chamber. He was conscious of it, and shifted his ground, pointing out the dangers of doing what the other nations interested in Egypt were not prepared to do.

"Have you asked them? Have you pressed them?" was shouted across the House. Eglington ignored the interjections. "Answer! Answer!" was called out angrily, but he shrugged a shoulder and continued his argument. If a man insisted on using a flying-machine before the principle was fully mastered and applied —if it could be mastered and applied—it must not be surprising if he was killed. Amateurs sometimes took preposterous risks without the advice of the experts. If Claridge Pasha had asked the advice of the English Government, or of any of the chancelleries of Europe, as to his incursions into the Soudan and his premature attempts at reform, he would have received expert advice that civilization had not advanced to that stage in this portion of the world, which would warrant his experiments. It was all very well for one man to run vast risks and attempt quixotic enterprises, but neither he nor his countrymen had any right to expect Europe to embroil itself on his particular account.

At this point he was met by angry cries of dissent, which did not come from the Opposition alone. His lips set, he would not yield. The Government could not hold itself responsible for Claridge Pasha's relief, nor in any sense for his present position. However, from motives of humanity, it would make representations in the hope that the Egyptian Government would act; but it was not improbable, in view of past experiences of Claridge Pasha, that he would extricate himself from his present position, perhaps had done so already. Sympathy and sentiment were natural and proper manifestations of human society, but Governments were, of necessity, ruled by sterner considerations. The House must realize that the Government could not act as though it were wholly a free agent, or as if its every move would not be matched by another move on the part of another Power or Powers.

Then followed a brilliant and effective appeal to his own party to trust the Government, to credit it with feeling and with a due regard for English prestige and the honor brought to it by Claridge Pasha's personal qualities, whatever might be thought of his crusading enterprises. The party must not fall into the trap of playing the game of the Opposition. Then with some supercilious praise of the "worthy sentiments" of Jasper Kimber's speech and a curt depreciation of its reasoning, he declared that, "No Government can be ruled by clamor. The path to be trodden by this Government would be lighted by principles of progress and civilization, humanity and peace, the urbane power of reason, and the persuasive influence of just consideration for the rights of others, rather than the thunder and the threat of the cannon and the sword!"

He sat down amid the cheers of a large portion of his party, for the end of his speech had been full of effective if meretricious appeal. But the debate that followed showed that the speech had been a failure. He had not uttered one warm or human word concerning Claridge Pasha, and it was felt and said, that no pledge had been given to ensure the relief of the man who had caught the imagination of England.

The debate was fierce and prolonged. Eglington would not agree to any modification of his speech, to any temporizing. Arrogant and insistent, he had his way, and, on a division, the Government was saved by a mere handful of votes—votes to save the party, not to endorse Eglington's speech or policy.

Exasperated and with jaw set, but with a defiant smile, Eglington drove straight home after the House rose. He found Hylda in the library with an evening paper in her hands. She had read and reread his speech, and had steeled herself for "the inevitable hour," to this talk which would decide forever their fate and future.

Eglington entered the room smiling. He remembered the incident of the night before, when she came to his study and then hurriedly retreated. He had been defiant and proudly disdainful at the House and on the way home; but in his heart of hearts he was conscious of having failed to have his own way; and, like such men, he wanted assurance that he could not err, and he wanted sympathy. Almost any one could have given it to him, and he had a temptation to seek that society which was his the evening before; but he remembered that *she* was occupied where he could not reach her, and here was Hylda, from whom he had been estranged, but who must surely have seen by now that at Hamley she had been unreasonable, and that she must trust his judgment. So absorbed was he with self and the failure of his speech, that, for a moment, he forgot the subject of it and what that subject meant to them both.

"What do you think of my speech, Hylda?" he asked, as he threw himself into a chair. "I see you have been reading it. Is it a full report?"

She handed the paper over. "Quite full," she answered evenly.

He glanced down the columns. "Sentimentalist!" he said as his eye caught an interjection. "Cant!" he added. Then he looked at Hylda, and remembered once again on whom and what his speech had been made. He saw that her face was very pale.

"What do you think of my speech?" he repeated stubbornly.

"If you think an answer necessary, I regard it as wicked and unpatriotic," she answered firmly.

"Yes, I suppose you would," he rejoined bitingly.

She got to her feet slowly, a flush passing over her face. "If you think I would, did you not think that a great many other people would think so too, and for the same reason?" she asked, still evenly, but very slowly.

"Not for the same reason!" he rejoined in a low, savage voice.

"You do not treat me well," she said, with a voice that betrayed no hurt, no indignation. It seemed to state a fact deliberately, that was all.

"No, please," she added quickly as she saw him rise to his feet with anger trembling at his lips. "Do not say what is on your tongue to say. Let us speak quietly to-night. It is better; and I am tired of strife, spoken and unspoken. I have got beyond that. But I want to speak of what you did to-day in Parliament."

"Well, you have said it was wicked and unpatriotic," he rejoined, sitting down again and lighting a cigar, in an attempt to be composed.

"What you said was that; but I am concerned with what you did. Did your speech mean that you would not press the Egyptian government to relieve Claridge Pasha at once?"

"Is that the conclusion you draw from my words?" he asked.

"Yes; but I wish to know beyond doubt if that is what you mean the country to believe?"

"It is what I mean you to believe, my dear."

She shrank from the last two words, but still went on quietly, though her eyes burned, and she shivered. "If you mean that you will do nothing, it will ruin you and your Government," she answered. "Kimber was right, and——"

"Kimber was inspired from here," he interjected sharply.

She put her hand upon herself. "Do you think I would intrigue against you? Do you think I would stoop to intrigue?" she asked, a hand clasping and unclasping a bracelet on her wrist, her eyes averted, for very shame that he should think the thought he had uttered.

"It came from this house—the influence," he rejoined.

"I cannot say. It is possible," she answered; "but you cannot think that I connive with my maid against you. I think Kimber has reasons of his own for acting as he did to-day. He speaks for many besides himself;

and he spoke patriotically this afternoon. He did his duty."

"And I did not? Do you think I act alone?"

"You did not do your duty, and I think that you are not alone responsible. That is why I hope the Government will be influenced by public feeling." She came a step nearer to him. "I ask you to relieve Claridge Pasha at any cost. He is your father's son. If you do not, when all the truth is known, you will find no shelter from the storm that will break over you."

"You will tell—*the truth?*"

"I do not know yet what I shall do," she answered. "It will depend on you; but it is your duty to tell the truth, not mine. That does not concern me; but to save Claridge Pasha does concern me."

"So I have known."

Her heart panted for a moment with a wild indignation; but she quieted herself, and answered almost calmly: "If you refuse to do that which is honorable—and human—then I shall try to do it for you while yet I bear your name. If you will not care for your family honor, then I shall try to do so. If you will not do your duty, then I will try to do it for you." She looked him determinedly in the eyes. "Through you I have lost nearly all I cared to keep in the world. I should like to feel that in this one thing you acted honorably."

He sprang to his feet, bursting with anger, in spite of the inward admonition that much that he prized was in danger, that any breach with Hylda would be disastrous. But self-will and his native arrogance overruled the monitor within, and he said: "Don't preach to me, don't play the martyr. You will do this and you will do that! You will save my honor and the family name! You will relieve Claridge Pasha, you will do what Governments choose not to do; you will do what your husband chooses not to do— Well, I say that you will do what your husband chooses to do, or take the consequences!"

"I think I will take the consequences," she answered. "I will save Claridge Pasha, if it is possible. It is no boast. I will do it, if it can be done at all, if it is God's will that it should be done; and in doing it I shall be conscious that you and I will do nothing together again—never! But that will not stop me; it will make me do it, the last right thing, before the end."

She was so quiet, so curiously quiet. Her words had a strange solemnity, a tragic apathy. What did it mean? He had gone too far, as he had done before. He had blundered viciously, as he had blundered before. She spoke again before he could collect his thoughts and make reply.

"I did not ask for too much, I think, and I could have forgiven and forgotten all the hurts you have given me, if it were not for one thing. You have been unjust, hard, selfish, and suspicious. Suspicious—of me! No one else in all the world ever thought of me what you have thought. I have done all I could. I have honorably kept the faith. But you have spoiled it all. I have no memory that I care to keep. It is stained. My eyes can never bear to look upon the past again, the past with you—never. You have not acted like a gentleman."

She turned to leave the room. He caught her arm. "You will wait till you hear what I have to say," he cried in anger, her last words had stung him so, her manner was so pitilessly scornful. It was as though she looked down on him from a height. His old arrogance fought for mastery over his apprehension. What did she know? What did she mean? In any case he must face it out, be strong—and merciful and affectionate afterwards.

"Wait, Hylda," he said. "We must talk this out."

She freed her arm. "There is nothing to talk out," she answered. "So far as our relations are concerned, all reason for talk is gone." She drew the fatal letter from the sash at her waist. "You will think so too when you read this letter again." She laid it on the table beside him, and, as he opened and glanced at it, she left the room.

He stood with the letter in his hand, dumfounded. "Good God!" he said, and sank into a chair.

XXXIX

FAITH JOURNEYS TO LONDON

Faith withdrew her eyes from Hylda's face, and they wandered helplessly over the room. They saw, yet did not see; and even in her trouble there was some subconscious sense softly commenting on the exquisite refinement and gentle beauty which seemed to fill the room; but the only definite objects which the eyes registered at the moment were the flowers filling every corner. Hylda had been lightly adjusting a clump of roses when she entered; and she had vaguely noticed how pale was the face that bent over the flowers, how pale and yet how composed—as she had seen a Quaker face, after some sorrow had passed over it, and left it like a quiet sea in the sun, when wreck and ruin were done. It was only a swift impression, for she could think of but one thing, David and his safety. She had come to Hylda, she said, because of Lord Eglington's position, and she could not believe that the Government would see David's work undone and David killed by the slave-dealers of Central Africa.

Hylda's reply had given her no hope that Eglington would keep the promise he had made that evening long ago when her father had come upon them by the old mill, and because of which promise she had forgiven Eglington so much that was hard to forgive. Hylda had spoken with sorrowful decision, and then this pause had come, in which Faith tried to gain composure and strength. There was something strangely still in the two women. From the far past, through Quaker ancestors, there had come to Hylda now this gray mist of endurance and self-control and austere reserve. Yet behind it all, beneath it all, a wild heart was beating.

Presently, as they looked into each other's eyes, and Faith dimly apprehended something of Hylda's distress and its cause, Hylda leaned over and spasmodically pressed her hand.

"It is so, Faith," she said. "They will do nothing. International influences are too strong." She paused. "The Under-Secretary for Foreign Affairs will do nothing; but yet we must hope. Claridge Pasha has saved himself in the past; and he may do so now, even though it is all ten times worse. Then, there is another way. Nahoum Pasha can save him, if he can be saved. And I am going to Egypt—to Nahoum."

Faith's face blanched. Something of the stark truth swept into her brain. She herself had suffered—her own life had been maimed, it had had its secret bitterness. Her love for her sister's son was that of a mother, sister, friend combined, and he was all she had in life. That he lived, that she might cherish the thought of him living, was the one thing she had; and David must be saved, if that might be; but this girl—was she not a girl, ten years younger than herself?—to go to Egypt to do—what? She herself lived out of the world, but she knew the world! To go to Egypt, and——

"Thee will not go to Egypt. What can thee do?" she pleaded, something very like a sob in her voice. "Thee is but a woman, and David would not be saved at such a price, and I would not have him saved so. Thee will not go. Say thee will not. He is all God has left to me in life; but thee to go—ah, no! It is a bitter world—and what could thee do?"

Hylda looked at her reflectively. Should she tell

Faith all, and take her to Egypt? No, she could not take her without telling her all, and that was impossible now. There might come a time when this wise and tender soul might be taken into the innermost chambers, when all the truth might be known; but the secret of David's parentage was Eglington's concern most of all, and she would not speak now; and what was between Nahoum and David was David's concern; and she had kept his secret all these years. No, Faith might not know now, and might not come with her. On this mission she must go alone.

Hylda rose to her feet, still keeping hold of Faith's hand. "Go back to Hamley and wait there," she said, in a colorless voice. "You can do nothing; it may be I can do much. Whatever can be done I can do, since England will not act. Pray for his safety. It is all you can do. It is given to some to work, to others to pray. I must work now."

She led Faith towards the door; she could not endure more; she must hold herself firm for the journey and the struggle before her. If she broke down now she could not go forward; and Faith's presence roused in her an emotion almost beyond control.

At the door she took both of Faith's hands in hers, and kissed her cheek. "It is your place to stay; you will see that it is best. Good-by," she added hurriedly, and her eyes were so blurred that she could scarcely see the graceful, demure figure pass into the sunlit street.

That afternoon Lord Windlehurst entered the Duchess of Snowdon's presence hurried and excited. She started on seeing his face.

"What has happened?" she asked breathlessly.

"She is gone," he answered. "Our girl has gone to Egypt!"

The Duchess almost staggered to her feet. "Windlehurst—gone!" she gasped.

"I called to see her. Her ladyship had gone into the country, the footman said. I saw the butler, a faithful soul, who would die—or clean the area steps—for her! He was discreet; but he knew what you and I are to her. It was he got the tickets—for Marseilles and Egypt."

The Duchess began to cry silently. Big tears ran down a face from which the glow of feeling had long fled, but her eyes were sad enough.

"Gone—gone! It is the end!" was all she could say.

Lord Windlehurst frowned, though his eyes were moist. "We must act at once. You must go to Egypt, Betty. You must catch her at Marseilles. Her boat does not sail for three days. She thought it went sooner, as it was advertised to do. It is delayed—I've found that out. You can start to-night, and—and save the situation. You will do it, Betty?"

"I will do anything you say, as I have always done." She dried her eyes.

"She is a good girl. We must do all we can. I'll arrange everything for you myself. I've written this paragraph to go into the papers to-morrow morning: '*The Duchess of Snowdon, accompanied by Lady Eglington, left London last night for the Mediterranean vía Calais, to be gone for two months or more.*' That is simple and natural. I'll see Eglington. He must make no fuss. He thinks she has gone to Hamley, so the butler says. There, it's all clear. Your work is cut out, Betty, and I know you will do it as no one else can."

"Oh, Windlehurst," she answered, with a hand clutching at his arm, "if we fail, it will kill me."

"If she fails, it will kill her," he answered, "and she is very young. What is in her mind, who can tell? But she thinks she can help Claridge somehow. We must save her, Betty."

"I used to think you had no real feeling, Windlehurst. You didn't show it," she said in a low voice.

"Ah, that was because you had too much!" he answered. "I had to wait till you had less." He took out his watch.

BOOK VI

XL

HYLDA SEEKS NAHOUM

It was as though she had gone to sleep the night before, and waked again upon this scene unchanged, brilliant, full of color, a chaos of decoration—confluences of noisy, garish streams of life, eddies of petty labor. Craftsmen crowded one upon the other in dark bazaars; merchants chattered and haggled on their benches; hawkers clattered and cried their wares. It was a people that lived upon the streets, for all the houses seemed empty and forsaken. The *sais* ran before the Pasha's carriage, the donkey-boys shrieked for their right of way, a train of camels calmly forced its passage through the swirling crowds, supercilious and heavy-laden.

It seemed but yesterday since she had watched with amused eyes the sherbet-sellers clanking their brass saucers, the carriers streaming the water from the bulging goatskins into the earthen bottles, crying, "Allah be praised, here is coolness for thy throat forever!" the idle singer chanting to the soft *kánoon*, the chess-players in the shade of a high wall, lost to the world, the dancing-girls with unveiled, shameless faces, posturing for evil eyes. Nothing had changed these past six years. Yet everything had changed.

She saw it all as in a dream, for her mind had no time for reverie or retrospect; it was set on one thing only.

Yet behind the one idea possessing her there was a subconscious self taking note of all these sights and sounds, and bringing moisture to her eyes. Passing the house which David had occupied on that night when he and she and Nahoum and Mizraim had met, the mist of feeling almost blinded her; for there at the gate sat the bowáb who had admitted her then, and with apathetic eyes had watched her go, in the hour when it seemed that she and David Claridge had bidden farewell forever, two driftwood spars that touched and parted in the everlasting sea. Here again in the Palace square were Kaïd's Nubians in their glittering armor as of silver and gold, drawn up as she had seen them drawn then, to be reviewed by their overlord.

She swept swiftly through the streets and bazaars on her mission to Nahoum. "Lady Eglington" had asked for an interview, and Nahoum had granted it without delay. He did not associate her with the girl for whom David Claridge had killed Foorgat Bey, and he sent his own carriage to bring her to the Palace. No time had been lost, for it was less than twenty-four hours since she had arrived in Cairo, and very soon she would know the worst or the best. She had put her past away for the moment, and the Duchess of Snowdon had found at Marseilles a silent, determined, yet gentle-tongued woman, who refused to look back, or to discuss anything vital to herself and Eglington until what she had come to Egypt to do was accomplished. Nor would she speak of the future, until the present had been fully declared and she knew the fate of David Claridge. In Cairo there were only varying rumors: that he was still holding out; that he was lost; that he had broken through; that he was a prisoner—all without foundation upon which she could rely.

As she neared the Palace entrance, a female fortune-teller ran forward, thrusting towards her a gazelle's skin, filled with the instruments of her mystic craft, and crying out: "I divine—I reveal! What is present I manifest! What is absent I declare! What is future I show! Beautiful one, hear me. It is all written. To thee is greatness, and thy heart's desire. Hear all! See! Wait for the revealing. Thou comest from afar, but thy fortune is near. Hear and see! I divine—I reveal! Beautiful one, what is future I show."

Hylda's eyes looked at the poor creature eagerly, pathetically. If it could only be, if she could but see one step ahead! If the veil could but be lifted! She dropped some silver into the folds of the gazelle-skin and waved the Gipsy away. "There is darkness, it is all dark, beautiful one," cried the woman after her, "but it shall be light. I show—I reveal!"

Inside these Palace walls there was a revealer of more merit, as she so well and bitterly knew. He could raise the veil—a dark and dangerous necromancer, with a flinty heart and a hand that had waited long to strike. Had it struck its last blow?

Outside Nahoum's door she had a moment of utter weakness, when her knees smote together, and her throat became parched; but before the door had swung wide and her eyes swept the cool and shadowed room, she was as composed as on that night long ago when she had faced *the man who knew.*

Nahoum was standing in a waiting and respectful attitude as she entered. He advanced towards her and bowed low, but stopped dumfounded, as he saw who she was. Presently he recovered himself; but he offered no further greeting than to place a chair for her where her face was in the shadow and his in the light—time of crisis as it was, she noticed this and marvelled at him. His face was as she had seen it those years ago. It showed no change whatever. The eyes looked at her calmly, openly, with no ulterior thought behind, as it might seem. The high, smooth forehead, the full but firm lips, the brown, well-groomed beard, were all indicative of a nature benevolent and refined. Where did the duplicity lie? Her mind answered its own question on the instant: it lay in the brain and the tongue. Both were masterly weapons, an armament so complete that it controlled the face and eyes and outward man into a fair semblance of honesty. The tongue—she remembered its insinuating and adroit power, and how it had deceived the man she had come to try and save. She must not be misled by it. She felt it was to be a struggle between them, and she must be alert and persuasive, and match him word for word, move for move.

"I am happy to welcome you here, madame," he said in English. "It is years since we met; yet time has passed you by."

She flushed ever so slightly—compliment from Nahoum Pasha! Yet she must not resent anything to-day; she must get what she came for, if it was possible. What had Lacey said?—"A few thousand men by parcel-post, and some red seals—British officers."

"We meet under different circumstances," she replied meaningly. "You were asking a great favor then."

"Ah, but of you, madame?"

"I think you appealed to me when you were doubtful of the result."

"Well, madame, it may be so—but, yes, you are right; I thought you were Claridge Pasha's kinswoman, I remember."

"Excellency, you *said* you thought I was Claridge Pasha's kinswoman."

"And you are not?" he asked reflectively.

He did not understand the slight change that passed over her face. His kinswoman—Claridge Pasha's kinswoman!

"I was not his kinswoman," she answered calmly. "You came to ask a favor then of Claridge Pasha: your life-work to do under him. I remember your words,—'*I can aid thee in thy great task. Thou wouldst remake our Egypt, and my heart is with you. I would rescue, not destroy. . . . I would labor, but my master has taken away from me the anvil, the fire, and the hammer, and I sit without the door like an armless beggar.*' Those were your words, and Claridge Pasha listened and believed, and saved your life and gave you work; and now again you have power greater than all others in Egypt."

"Madame, I congratulate you on a useful memory. May it serve you as the hill-fountain the garden in the city! Those indeed were my words. I hear myself from your lips, and yet recognize myself, if that be not vanity. But, madame, why have you sought me? What is it you wish to know—to hear?"

He looked at her innocently, as though he did not know her errand; as though beyond, in the desert, there was no tragedy approaching—or come.

"Excellency, you are aware that I have come to ask for news of Claridge Pasha." She leaned forward slightly, but, apart from her tightly interlaced fingers, it would not have been possible to know that she was under any strain.

"You come to me instead of to the Effendina. May I ask why, madame? Your husband's position—I did not know you were Lord Eglington's wife—would entitle you to the highest consideration."

"I knew that Nahoum Pasha would have the whole knowledge, while the Effendina would have part only. Excellency, will you not tell me what news you have? Is Claridge Pasha alive?"

"Madame, I do not know. He is in the desert. He was surrounded. For over a month there has been no word—none. He is in danger. His way by the river was blocked. He stayed too long. He might have escaped, but he would insist on saving the loyal natives, on remaining with them, since he could not bring them across the desert; and the river and the desert are silent. Nothing comes out of that furnace yonder. Nothing comes."

He bent his eyes upon her complacently. Her own dropped. She could not bear that he should see the misery in them.

"You have come to try and save him, madame. What did you expect to do? Your Government did not strengthen my hands; your husband did nothing—nothing that could make it possible for me to act. There are many nations here, alas! Your husband does not take so great an interest in the fate of Claridge Pasha as yourself, madame."

She ignored the insult. She had determined to endure everything, if she might but induce this man to do the thing that could be done—if it was not too late. Before she could frame a reply, he said urbanely:

"But that is not to be expected. There was that between Claridge Pasha and yourself which would induce you to do all you might do for him, to be anxious for his welfare. Gratitude is a rare thing—as rare as the flower of the century-aloe; but you have it, madame."

There was no chance to misunderstand him. Foorgat Bey—he knew the truth, and had known it all these years.

"Excellency," she said, "if through me, Claridge Pasha—"

"One moment, madame," he interrupted, and, opening a drawer, took out a letter. "I think that what you would say may be found here, with much else that you will care to know. It is the last news of Claridge Pasha—a letter from him. I understand all you would say to me; but he who has most at stake has said it, and, if he failed, do you think, madame, that you could succeed?"

He handed her the letter with a respectful salutation. "In the hour he left, madame, he came to know that the name of Foorgat Bey was not blotted from the book of Time, nor from Fate's reckoning."

After all these years! Her instinct had been true, then, that night so long ago. The hand that took the letter trembled slightly in spite of her will, but it was not the disclosure Nahoum had made which caused her agitation. This letter she held was in David Claridge's hand, the first she had ever seen, and, maybe, the last that he had ever written, or that any one would ever see, a document of tears. But no, there were no tears in this letter! As Hylda read it the trembling passed from her fingers, and a great thrilling pride possessed her. If tragedy had come, then it had fallen like a fire from heaven, not like a pestilence rising from the earth. Here indeed was that which justified all she had done, what she was doing now, what she meant to do when she had read the last word of it and the firm, clear signature beneath.

"Excellency," the letter began in English, "I came into the desert and into the perils I find here, with your last words in my ear, '*There is the matter of Foorgat Bey.*' The time you chose to speak was chosen well for your purpose, but ill for me. I could not turn back, I must go on. Had I returned, of what avail? What could I do but say what I say here, that my hand killed Foorgat Bey; that I had not meant to kill him, though at the moment I struck I took no heed whether he lived or died. Since you know of my sorrowful deed, you also know why Foorgat Bey was struck down. When, as I left the bank of the Nile, your words blinded my eyes, my mind said in its misery, 'Now, I see!' The curtains fell away from between you and me, and I saw all that you have done for vengeance and revenge. You knew all on that night when you sought your life of me and the way back to Kaïd's forgiveness. I see all as though you spoke it in my ear. You had reason to hurt me, but you had no reason for hurting Egypt, as you have done. I did not value my life, as you know well, for it has been flung into the midst of dangers for Egypt's sake, how often! It was not cowardice which made me hide from you and all the world the killing of Foorgat Bey. I desired to face the penalty, for did not my act deny all that I had held fast from my youth up? But there was another concerned—a girl, but a child in years, as innocent and true a being as God has ever set among the dangers of this life, and, by her very innocence and unsuspecting nature, so much more in peril before such unscrupulous wiles as were used by Foorgat Bey.

"I have known you many years, Nahoum, and dark and cruel as your acts have been against the work I gave my life to do, yet I think that there was ever in you, too, the root of goodness. Men would call your acts treacherous if they knew what you had done; and so indeed they were; but yet I have seen you do things to others—not to me—which could rise only from the fountain of pure waters. Was it partly because I killed Foorgat and partly because I came to place and influence and power, that you used me so, and all that I did? Or was it the East at war with the West, the immemorial feud and foray?

"This last I will believe; for then it will seem to be something beyond yourself,—centuries of predisposition, the long stain of the indelible—that drove you to those acts of matricide. Ay, it is that! For, Armenian as you are, this land is your native land, and in pulling down what I have built up—with you, Nahoum, with you—you have plunged the knife into the bosom of your mother. Did it never seem to you that the work which you did with me was a good work—the reduction of the corvée, the decrease of conscription, the lessening of taxes of the fellah, the bridges built, the canals dug, the seed distributed, the plague stayed, the better dwellings for the poor in the Delta, the destruction of brigandage, the slow blotting out of exaction and tyranny under the kourbash, the quiet growth of law and justice, the new industries started—did not all these seem good to you, as you served the land with me, your great genius for finance, ay, and your own purse, helping on the things that were dear to me, for Egypt's sake? Giving with one hand freely, did your soul not misgive you when you took away with the other?"

"When you tore down my work, you were tearing down your own; for, more than the material help I thought you gave in planning and shaping reforms, ay, far more than all, was the feeling in me which helped me over many a dark place, that I had you with me, that I was not alone. I trusted you, Nahoum. A life for a life you might have had for the asking; but a long torture and a daily weaving of the web of treachery—that has taken more than my life; it has taken your own, for you have killed the best part of yourself, that which you did with me; and here in an ever-narrowing circle of death I say to you that you will die with me. Power you have, but it will wither in your grasp. Kaïd will turn against you; for with my failure will come a dark reaction in his mind, which feels the cloud of doom drawing over it. Without me, with my work falling about his ears, he will, as he did so short a time ago, turn to Sharif and Higli and the rest; and the only comfort you will have will be that you destroyed the life of him who killed your brother. Did you love your brother? Nay, not more than did I, for I sent his soul into the void, and I would gladly have gone after it to ask God for the pardon of all his sins and mine. Think: I hid the truth, but why? Because a woman would suffer an unmerited scandal and shame. Nothing could recall Foorgat Bey; but for that silence I gave my life, for the land which was his land. Do you betray it, then?

"And now, Nahoum, the gulf in which you sought to plunge me when you had ruined all I did is here before me. The long deception has nearly done its work. I know from Ebn Ezra Bey what passed between you. They are out against me—the slave-dealers—from Senaar to where I am. The dominion of Egypt is over here. Yet I could restore it with a thousand men and a handful of European officers, had I but a show of authority from Cairo, which they think has deserted me.

"I am shut up here with a handful of men who can fight and thousands who cannot fight, and food grows scarcer, and my garrison is worn and famished; but each day I hearten them with the hope that you will send me a thousand men from Cairo. One steamer pounding here from the north with men who bring commands from the Effendina, and those thousands out yonder beyond my mines and moats and guns will begin to melt away. Nahoum, think not that you shall triumph over David Claridge. If it be God's will that I shall die here, my work undone, then, smiling, I shall go with step that does not falter, to live once more; and another day the work that I began will rise again in spite of you or any man.

"Nahoum, the killing of Foorgat Bey has been like a cloud upon all my past. You know me, and you know I do not lie. Yet I do not grieve that I hid the thing—it was not mine only; and if ever you knew a good woman, and in dark moments have turned to her, glad that she was yours, think what you would have done for her, how you would have sheltered her against aught that might injure her, against those things women are not made to bear. Then think that I hid the deed for one who was a stranger to me, whose life must ever lie far from mine, and see clearly that I did it for a woman's sake, and not for this woman's sake; for I had never seen her till the moment I struck Foorgat Bey into silence and the tomb. Will you not understand, Nahoum?

"Yonder, I see the tribes that harry me. The great guns firing make the day a burden, the nights are ever fretted by the dangers of surprise, and there is scarce time to bury the dead whom sickness and the sword destroy. From the midst of it all my eyes turn to you in Cairo, whose forgiveness I ask for the one injury I did you; while I pray that you will seek pardon for all that you have done to me and to those who will pass with me, if our circle is broken. Friend, Achmet the Rope-maker is here fighting for Egypt. Art thou less, then, than Achmet? So, God be with thee.

"DAVID CLARIDGE."

Without a pause Hylda had read the letter from the first word to the last. She was too proud to let this conspirator and traitor see what David's words could do to her. When she read the lines concerning herself, she became cold from head to foot, but she knew that Nahoum never took his eyes from her face, and she gave no outward sign of what was passing within. When she had finished it, she folded it up calmly, her eyes dwelt for a moment on the address upon the envelope, and then she handed it back to Nahoum without a word.

She looked him in the eyes and spoke. "He saved your life, he gave you all you had lost. It was not his fault that Prince Kaïd chose him for his chief counsellor. You would be lying where your brother lies, were it not for Claridge Pasha."

"It may be; but the luck was with me; and I have my way."

She drew herself together to say what was hard to say. "Excellency, the man who was killed deserved to die. Only by lies, only by subterfuge, only because I was curious to see the inside of the Palace, and because I had known him in London, did I, without a thought of indiscretion, give myself to his care to come here. I was so young; I did not know life, or men—or Egyptians." The last word was uttered with low scorn.

He glanced up quickly, and for the first time she saw a gleam of malice in his eyes. She could not feel sorry she had said it, yet she must remove the impression if possible.

"What Claridge Pasha did, any man would have done, excellency. He struck, and death was an accident. Foorgat's temple struck the corner of a pedestal. His death was instant. He would have killed Claridge Pasha if it had been possible—he tried to do so. But, excellency, if you have a daughter, if you ever had a child, what would you have done if any man had——"

"In the East daughters are more discreet; they tempt men less," he answered quietly, and fingered the string of beads he carried.

"Yet you would have done as Claridge Pasha did. That it was your brother was an accident, and——"

"It was an accident that the penalty must fall on Claridge Pasha, and on you, madame. I did not choose the objects of penalty. Destiny chose them, as Destiny chose Claridge Pasha as the man who should supplant me, who should attempt to do these mad things for Egypt against the judgment of the world—against the judgment of your husband. Shall I have better judgment than the chancelleries of Europe and England—and Lord Eglington?"

"Excellency, you know what moves other nations; but it is for Egypt to act for herself. You ask me why I did not go to the Effendina. I come to you because I know that you could circumvent the Effendina, even if he sent ten thousand men. It is the way in Egypt."

"Madame, you have insight—will you not look farther still, and see that however good Claridge Pasha's work might be some day in the far future, it is not good to-day.

It is too soon. At the beginning of the twentieth century, perhaps. Men pay the penalty of their mistakes. A man's life"—he watched her closely with his wide, benevolent eyes—"is neither here nor there, nor a few thousands, in the destiny of a nation. A man who ventures into a lion's den must not be surprised if he goes as Harrik went—ah, perhaps you do not know how Harrik went! A man who tears at the foundations of a house must not be surprised if the timbers fall on him and on his workmen. It is Destiny that Claridge Pasha should be the slayer of my brother, and a danger to Egypt, and one whose life is so dear to you, madame. You would have it otherwise, and so would I, but we must take things as they are—and you see that letter! It is seven weeks since then, and it may be that the circle has been broken. Yet it may not be so. The circle may be smaller, but not broken."

She felt how he was tempting her from word to word with a merciless ingenuity; yet she kept to her purpose; and however hopeless it seemed, she would struggle on.

"Excellency," she said in a low, pleading tone, "has he not suffered enough? Has he not paid the price of that life which you would not bring back if you could? No, in those places of your mind where no one can see lies the thought that you would not bring back Foorgat Bey. It is not an eye for an eye and a tooth for a tooth that has moved you; it has not been love of Foorgat Bey; it has been the hatred of the East for the West. And yet you are a Christian! Has Claridge Pasha not suffered enough, excellency? Have you not had your fill of revenge? Have you not done enough to hurt a man whose only crime was that he killed a man to save a woman, and had not meant to kill?"

"Yet he says in his letter that the thought of killing would not have stopped him."

"Does one think at such a moment? Did he think? There was no time. It was the work of an instant. Ah,

Fate was not kind, excellency! If it had been, I should have been permitted to kill Foorgat Bey with my own hands."

"I should have found it hard to exact the penalty from you, madame."

The words were uttered in so neutral a way that they were enigmatical, and she could not take offence or be sure of his meaning.

"Think, excellency. Have you ever known one so selfless, so good, so true? For humanity's sake would you not keep alive such a man? If there were a feud as old as Adam between your race and his, would you not before this life of sacrifice lay down the sword and the bitter challenge? He gave you his hand in faith and trust, because your God was his God, your prophet and lord his prophet and lord. Such faith should melt your heart. Can you not see that he tried to make compensation for Foorgat's death, by giving you your life and setting you where you are now, with power to save or kill him?"

"You call him great; yet I am here in safety, and he is —where he is! Have you not heard of the strife of minds and wills? He represented the West, I the East. He was a Christian, so was I; the ground of our battle was a fair one, and—and I have won!"

"The ground of battle fair!" she protested bitterly. "He did not know that there was strife between you. He did not fight you. I think that he always loved you, excellency. He would have given his life for you, if it had been in danger. Is there in that letter one word that any man could wish unwritten when the world was all ended for all men? But no, there was no strife between you—there was only hatred on your part. He was so much greater than you that you should feel no rivalry, no strife. The sword he carries cuts as wide as Time. You are of a petty day in a petty land. Your mouth will soon be filled with dust, and you will be forgotten. He will live in the history of the world. Excellency, I plead for him because I owe him so much: he killed a man and brought upon himself a lifelong misery for me. It is all I can do, plead to you who know the truth about him—yes, you know the truth—to make an effort to save him. It may be too late; but yet God may be waiting for you to lift your hand. You said the circle may be smaller, but it may be unbroken still. Will you not do a great thing once, and win a woman's gratitude, and the thanks of the world, by trying to save one who makes us think better of humanity? Will you not have the name of Nahoum Pasha linked with his—with his who thought you were his friend? Will you not save him?"

He got slowly to his feet, a strange look in his eyes. "Your words are useless. I will not save him for your sake; I will not save him for the world's sake; I will not save him——"

A cry of pain and grief broke from her, and she buried her face in her hands.

"—I will not save him for any other sake than his own."

He paused. Slowly, as dazed as though she had received a blow, Hylda raised her face and her hands dropped in her lap.

"For any other sake than his own!" Her eyes gazed at him in a bewildered, piteous way. What did he mean? His voice seemed to come from afar off.

"Did you think that you could save him? That I would listen to you, if I did not listen to him? No, no, madame. Not even did he conquer me; but something greater than himself within himself, it conquered me."

She got to her feet gasping, her hands stretched out. "Oh, is it true—is it true?" she cried.

"The West has conquered," he answered.

"You will help him—you will try to save him?"

"When, a month ago, I read the letter you have read,

I tried to save him. I sent secretly four thousand men who were at Wady Halfa to relieve him—if it could be done; five hundred to push forward on the quickest of the armed steamers, the rest to follow as fast as possible. I did my best. That was a month ago, and I am waiting—waiting and hoping, madame."

Suddenly she broke down. Tears streamed from her eyes. She sank into the chair, and sobs shook her from head to foot.

"Be patient, be composed, madame," Nahoum said gently. "I have tried you greatly—forgive me. Nay, do not weep. I have hope. We may hear from him at any moment now," he added softly, and there was a new look in his wide blue eyes as they were bent on her.

XLI

IN THE LAND OF SHINAR

"Then I said to the angel that talked with me, Whither do these bear the Ephah?

"And he said unto me, To build it an house in the land of Shinar; and it shall be established, and set there upon her own base."

DAVID raised his head from the paper he was studying. He looked at Lacey sharply. "And how many rounds of ammunition?" he asked.

"Ten thousand, Saadat."

"How many shells?" he continued, making notes upon the paper before him.

"Three hundred, Saadat."

"How many hundredweight of dourha?"

"Eighty—about."

"And how many mouths to feed?"

"Five thousand."

"How many fighters go with the mouths?"

"Nine hundred and eighty—of a kind."

"And of the best?"

"Well, say, five hundred."

"Thee said six hundred three days ago, Lacey."

"Sixty were killed or wounded on Sunday, and forty I reckon in *the others*, Saadat."

The dark eyes flashed, the lips set. "The fire was sickening—they fell back?"

"Well, Saadat, they reflected—at the wrong time."

"They ran?"

"Not back—they were slow in getting on."

"But they fought it out?"

"They had to—root hog, or die. You see, Saadat, in that five hundred I'm only counting the invincibles, the up-and-at-'ems, the blind-goers that 'd open the lid of Hell and jump in after the enemy."

The pale face lighted. "So many! I would not have put the estimate half so high. Not bad for a dark race fighting for they know not what!"

"They know that all right; they are fighting for you, Saadat."

David seemed not to hear. "Five hundred—so many, and the enemy so near, the temptation so great!"

"The deserters are all gone to Ali Wad Hei, Saadat. For a month there have been only the deserted."

A hardness crept into the dark eyes. "Only the deserted!" He looked out to where the Nile lost itself in the northern distance. "I asked Nahoum for one thousand men; I asked England for the word which would send them. I asked for a thousand, but even two hundred would turn the scale—the sign that the Inglesi had behind him Cairo and London. Twenty weeks, and nothing comes!"

He got to his feet slowly and walked up and down the room for a moment, glancing out occasionally towards the clump of palms which marked the disappearance of the Nile into the desert beyond his vision. At intervals a cannon-shot crashed upon the rarefied air, as scores of thousands had done for months past, torturing to ear and sense and nerve. The confused and dulled roar of voices came from the distance also; and, looking out to the landward side, David saw a series of movements of the besieging forces, under the Arab leader, Ali Wad Hei. Here a loosely formed body of lancers and light cavalry cantered away towards the south, converging upon the Nile; there a troop of heavy cavalry in glistening mail moved nearer to the northern defences; and between, battalions of infantry took up new positions, while batteries of guns moved nearer to the river, curving upon the palace north and south. Suddenly David's eyes flashed fire. He turned to Lacey eagerly. Lacey was watching with eyes screwed up shrewdly, his forehead shining with sweat.

"Saadat," he said, suddenly, "this isn't the usual set of quadrilles. It's the real thing. They're watching the river—waiting."

"But south!" was David's laconic response. At the same moment he struck a gong. An orderly entered. Giving swift instructions, he turned to Lacey again.

"Not Cairo—Darfûr," he added.

"Ebn Ezra Bey coming! Ali Wad Hei's got word from up the Nile, I guess."

David nodded, and his face clouded. "We should have had word also," he said sharply.

There was a knock at the door, and Mahommed Hassan entered, supporting an Arab, down whose haggard face blood trickled from a wound in the head, while an arm hung limp at his side.

"Behold, Saadat—from Ebn Ezra Bey," Mahommed said. The man drooped beside him.

David caught a tin cup from a shelf, poured some liquor into it, and held it to the lips of the fainting man. "Drink," he said. The man drank greedily, and, when he had finished, gave a long sigh of satisfaction. "Let him sit," David added.

When the man was seated on a sheepskin, the huge Mahommed squatting behind like a sentinel, David questioned him. "What is thy name—thy news?" he asked in Arabic.

"I am called Feroog. I come from Ebn Ezra Bey, to whom be peace!" he answered. "Thy messenger,

Saadat, behold he died of hunger and thirst, and his work became mine! Ebn Ezra Bey came by the river. . . ."

"He is near?" asked David impatiently.

"He is twenty miles away."

"Thou camest by the desert?"

"By the desert, Saadat, as Ebn Ezra Effendi comes."

"By the desert! But thou saidst he came by the river."

"Saadat, yonder, forty miles from where we are, the river makes a great curve. There the Effendi landed in the night with four hundred men to march hither. But he commanded that the boats should come on slowly, and receive the attack in the river, while he came in from the desert."

David's eye flashed. "A great device. They will be here by midnight, then, perhaps?"

"At midnight, Saadat, by the blessing of God."

"How wert thou wounded?"

"I came upon two of the enemy. They were mounted. I fought them. Upon the horse of one I came here."

"The other?"

"God is merciful, Saadat. He is in the bosom of God."

"How many men come by the river?"

"But fifty, Saadat," was the answer, "but they have sworn by the stone in the Kaabah not to surrender."

"And those who come with the Effendi, with Ebn Ezra Bey, are they as those who will not surrender?"

"Half of them are so. They were with thee, as was I, Saadat, when the great sickness fell upon us, and were healed by thee, and afterwards fought with thee."

David nodded abstractedly, and motioned to Mahommed to take the man away; then he said to Lacey: "How long does thee think we can hold out?"

"We shall have more men, but also more rifles to fire, and more mouths to fill, if Ebn Ezra gets in, Saadat."

David nodded. "But with more rifles to fire away your ten thousand rounds"—he tapped the paper on the table—"and eat the eighty hundredweight of dourha, how long can we last?"

"If they are to fight, and with full stomachs, and to stake everything on that one fight, then we can last two days. No more, I reckon."

"I make it one day," answered David. "In three days we shall have no food, and unless help comes from Cairo, we must die or surrender. It is not well to starve on the chance of help coming, and then die fighting with weak arms and broken spirit. Therefore, we must fight to-morrow, if Ebn Ezra gets in to-night. I think we shall fight well," he added. "You think so?"

"You are a born fighter, Saadat."

A shadow fell on David's face, and his lips tightened. "I was not born a fighter, Lacey. The day we met first no man had ever died by my hand or by my will."

"There are three who must die at sunset—an hour from now—by thy will, Saadat."

A startled look came into David's face. "Who?" he asked.

"The Three Pashas, Saadat. They have been recaptured."

"Recaptured!" rejoined David mechanically.

"Achmet Pasha got them from under the very noses of the sheikhs before sunrise this morning."

"Achmet—Achmet Pasha!" A light came into David's face again.

"You will keep faith with Achmet, Saadat. He risked his life to get them. They betrayed you, and betrayed three hundred good men to death. If they do not die, those who fight for you will say that it doesn't matter whether men fight for you or betray you, they get the same stuff off the same plate. If we are going to fight to-morrow, it ought to be with a clean bill of health."

"They served me well so long—ate at my table, fought with me. But—but traitors must die, even as Harrik died." A stern look came into his face. He looked round the great room slowly. "We have done our best," he said. "I need not have failed, if there had been no treachery. . . ."

"If it hadn't been for Nahoum!"

David raised his head. Supreme purpose came into his bearing. A grave smile played at his lips, as he gave that quick toss of the head which had been a characteristic of both Eglington and himself. His eyes shone—a steady, indomitable light. "I will not give in. I still have hope. We are few and they are many, but the end of a battle has never been sure. We may not fail even now. Help may come from Cairo even to-morrow."

"Say, somehow you've always pulled through before, Saadat. When I've been most frightened I've perked up and stiffened my backbone, remembering your luck. I've seen a blue funk evaporate by thinking of how things always come your way just when the worst seems at the worst."

David smiled as he caught up a small cane and prepared to go. Looking out of a window, he stroked his thin, clean-shaven face with a lean finger. Presently a movement in the desert arrested his attention. He put a field-glass to his eyes, and scanned the field of operations closely once more.

"Good—good!" he burst out cheerfully. "Achmet has done the one thing possible. The way to the north will be still open. He has flung his men between the Nile and the enemy, and now the batteries are at work!" Opening the door, they passed out. "He has anticipated my orders," he added. "Come, Lacey, it will be an anxious night. The moon is full, and Ebn Ezra Bey has his work cut out—sharp work for all of us, and . . ."

Lacey could not hear the rest of his words in the roar of the artillery. David's steamers in the river were pouring shot into the desert where the enemy lay, and Achmet's "friendlies" and the Egyptians were making good their new position. As David and Lacey, fearlessly exposing themselves to rifle fire, and taking the shortest and most dangerous route to where Achmet fought, rode swiftly from the palace, Ebn Ezra's three steamers appeared up the river, and came slowly down to where David's gunboats lay. Their appearance was greeted by desperate discharges of artillery from the forces under Ali Wad Hei, who had received word of their coming two hours before, and had accordingly redisposed his attacking forces. But for Achmet's sharp initiative, the boldness of the attempt to cut off the way north and south would have succeeded, and the circle of fire and sword would have been complete. Achmet's new position had not been occupied before, for men were too few, and the position he had just left was now exposed to attack.

Never since the siege began had the foe shown such initiative and audacity. They had relied on the pressure of famine and decimation by sickness, the steady effects of sorties, with consequent fatalities and desertions, to bring the Liberator of the Slaves to his knees. Ebn Erza Bey had sought to keep quiet the sheikhs far south, but he had been shut up in Darfûr for months, and had been in as bad a plight as David. He had, however, broken through at last. His ruse in leaving the steamers in the night and marching across the desert was as courageous as it was perilous, for, if discovered before he reached the beleagured place, nothing could save his little force from destruction. There was one way in from the desert to the walled town, and it was through that space which Achmet and his men had occupied, and on which Ali Wad Hei might now at any moment throw his troops.

David's heart sank as he saw the danger. From the palace he had sent an orderly with a command to an officer to move forward and secure the position, but still the gap was open, and the men he had ordered to advance remained where they were. Every minute had its crisis.

As Lacey and himself left the town the misery of the place smote him in the eyes. Filth, refuse, *débris* filled the streets. Sick and dying men called to him from dark doorways, children and women begged for bread, carcasses lay unburied, vultures hovering above them—his tireless efforts had not been sufficient to cope with the daily horrors of the siege. But there was no sign of hostility to him. Voices called blessings on him from dark doorways, lips blanching in death commended him to Allah, and now and then a shrill call told of a fighter who had been laid low, but who had a spirit still unbeaten. Old men and women stood over their cooking-pots waiting for the moment of sunset; for it was Ramadan, and the faithful fasted during the day—as though every day was not a fast!

Sunset was almost come, as David left the city and galloped away to send forces to stop the gap of danger before it was filled by the foe. Sunset—the Three Pashas were to die at sunset! They were with Achmet, and in a few moments they would be dead. As David and Lacey rode hard, they suddenly saw a movement of men on foot at a distant point of the field, and then a small mounted troop, fifty at most, detach themselves from the larger force and, in close formation, gallop fiercely down on the position which Achmet had left. David felt a shiver of anxiety and apprehension as he saw this sharp, sweeping advance. Even fifty men, well entrenched, could hold the position until the main body of Ali Wad Hei's infantry came on.

They rode hard, but harder still rode Ali Wad Hei's

troop of daring Arabs. Nearer and nearer they came. Suddenly from the trenches, which they had thought deserted, David saw jets of smoke rise, and a half dozen of the advancing troop fell from their saddles, their riderless horses galloping on.

David's heart leaped: Achmet had, then, left men behind, hidden from view; and these were now defending the position. Again came the jets of smoke, and again more Arabs dropped from their saddles. But the others still came on. A thousand feet away others fell. Twenty-two of the fifty had already gone. The rest fired their rifles as they galloped. But now, to David's relief, his own forces, which should have moved half an hour before, were coming swiftly down to cut off the approach of Ali Wad Hei's infantry, and he turned his horse upon the position where a handful of men were still emptying the saddles of the impetuous enemy. But now all that were left of the fifty were upon the trenches. Then came the flash of swords, puffs of smoke, the thrust of lances, and figures falling from the screaming, rearing horses.

Lacey's pistol was in his hand, David's sword was gripped tight as they rushed upon the *mêlée*. Lacey's pistol snapped, and an Arab fell; again, and another swayed in his saddle. David's sword swept down, and a turbaned head was gashed by a mortal stroke. As he swung towards another horseman, who had struck down a defender of the trenches, an Arab raised himself in his saddle and flung a lance with a cry of terrible malice; but, even as he did so, a bullet from Lacey's pistol pierced his shoulder. The shot had been too late to stop the lance, but sufficient to divert its course. It caught David in the flesh of the body under the arm—a slight wound only. A few inches to the right, however, and his day would have been done.

The remaining Arabs turned and fled. The fight was

over. As David, dismounting, stood with his dripping sword in his hand, in imagination he heard the voice of Kaïd say to him, as it said that night when he killed Foorgat Bey, "Hast thou ever killed a man?"

For an instant it blinded him, then he was conscious that, on the ground at his feet, lay one of the Three Pashas who were to die at sunset. It was sunset now, and the man was dead. Another of the three sat upon the ground winding his thigh with the folds of a dead Arab's turban, blood streaming from his gashed face. The last of the trio stood before David, stoical and attentive. For a moment David looked at the Three, the dead man and the two living men, and then suddenly turned to where the opposing forces were advancing. His own men were now between the position and Ali Wad Hei's shouting fanatics. They would be able to reach and defend the position in time. He turned and gave orders. There were only twenty men besides the two pashas, whom his commands also comprised. Two small guns were in place. He had them trained on that portion of the advancing infantry of Ali Wad Hei not yet covered by his own forces. Years of work and responsibility had made him master of many things, and long ago he had learned the work of an artilleryman. In a moment a shot, well directed, made a gap in the ranks of the advancing foe. An instant afterwards a shot from the other gun fired by the unwounded pasha, who, in his youth, had been an officer of artillery, added to the confusion in the swerving ranks, and the force hesitated; and now from Ebn Ezra Bey's river steamers, which had just arrived, there came a flank fire. The force wavered. From David's gun another shot made havoc. They turned and fell back quickly. The situation was saved.

As if by magic the attack of the enemy all over the field ceased. By sunset they had meant to finish this enterprise, which was to put the besieged wholly in their hands, and then to feast after the day's fasting. Sunset had come, and they had been foiled; but hunger demanded the feast. The order to cease firing and retreat sounded, and three thousand men hurried back to the cooking-pot, the sack of dourha, and the prayer-mat. Malaish! If the infidel Inglesi was not conquered to-day, he should be beaten and captured, and should die to-morrow! And yet there were those among them who had a well-grounded apprehension that the "Inglesi" would win in the end.

By the trenches, where five men had died so bravely, and a traitorous pasha had paid the full penalty of crime and won a soldier's death, David spoke to his living comrades. As he prepared to return to the city, he said to the unwounded pasha, "Thou wert to die at sunset; it was thy sentence."

And the pasha answered: "Saadat, as for death—I am ready to die, Saadat; but have I not fought for thee?"

David turned to the wounded pasha.

"Why did Achmet Pasha spare thee?"

"He did not spare us, Saadat. Those who fought with us but now were to shoot us at sunset, and remain here till other troops came. Before sunset we saw the danger, since no help came. Therefore we fought to save this place for thee."

David looked them in the eyes. "Ye were traitors," he said, "and for an example it was meet that ye should die. But this that ye have done shall be told to all who fight to-morrow, and men will know why it is I pardon treachery. Ye shall fight again, if need be, betwixt this hour and morning, and ye shall die, if need be. Ye are willing?"

Both men touched their foreheads, their lips and their breasts. "Whether it be death or it be life, Inshallah, we are true to thee, Saadat!" one said, and the other repeated the words after him. As they salaamed, David left them, and rode forward to the advancing forces.

Upon the roof of the palace Mahommed Hassan watched and waited, his eyes scanning sharply the desert to the south, his ears strained to catch that stir of life which his accustomed ears had so often detected in the desert, when no footsteps, marching, or noises could be heard. Below, now in the palace, now in the defences, his master, the Saadat, planned for the last day's effort on the morrow, gave directions to the officers, sent commands to Achmet Pasha, arranged for the disposition of his forces, with as strange a band of adherents and subordinates as ever men had—adventurers, to whom adventure in their own land had brought no profit; members of that legion of the non-reputable, to whom Cairo offered no home; Levantines, who had fled from that underground world where every coin of reputation is falsely minted, refugees from the storm of the world's disapproval. There were Greeks with Austrian names; Armenians, speaking Italian as their native tongue; Italians of astonishing military skill, whose services were no longer required by their offended country; French Pizarros with a romantic outlook, even in misery, intent to find new El Dorados; Englishmen, who had cheated at cards and had left the Horse Guards for ever behind; Egyptian intriguers, who had been banished for being less successful than greater intriguers; but also a band of good gallant men of every nation.

Upon all these, during the siege, Mahommed Hassan had been a self-appointed spy, and had indirectly added to that knowledge which made David's decisive actions to circumvent intrigue and its consequences seem almost supernatural. In his way Mahommed was a great man. He knew that David would endure no spying.

and it was creditable to his subtlety and skill that he was able to warn his master, without being himself suspected of getting information by dark means. On the palace roof Mahommed was happy to-night. To-morrow would be a great day, and, since the Saadat was to control its destiny, what other end could there be but happiness? Had not the Saadat always ridden over all that had been in his way? Had not he, Mahommed, ever had plenty to eat and drink, and money to send to Manfaloot to his father there, and to bribe when bribing was needed? Truly, life was a boon! With a neboot of dom-wood across his knees he sat in the still, moonlit night, peering into that distance whence Ebn Ezra Bey and his men must come, the moon above tranquil and pleasant and alluring, and the desert beneath, covered as it was with the outrages and terrors of war, breathing softly its ancient music, that delicate vibrant humming of the latent activities. In his uncivilized soul Mahommed Hassan felt this murmur, and even as he sat waiting to know whether a little army would steal out of the south like phantoms into this circle the Saadat had drawn round him, he kept humming to himself—had he not been, was he not now, an Apollo to numberless houris who had looked down at him from behind mooshrabieh screens, or waited for him in the palm grove or the cane-field? The words of his song were not uttered aloud, but yet he sang them silently—

"Every night long and all night my spirit is moaning and
crying—
O dear gazelle, that has taken away my peace!
Ah! if my beloved come not, my eyes will be blinded with
weeping—
Moon of my joy, come to me, hark to the call of my soul!"

Over and over he kept chanting the song. Suddenly, however, he leaned farther forward and strained his ears.

Yes, at last, away to the south-east, there was life stirring, men moving—moving quickly. He got to his feet slowly, still listening, stood for a moment motionless, then with a cry of satisfaction dimly saw a moving mass in the white moonlight far over by the river. Ebn Ezra Bey and his men were coming. He started below, and met David coming up. He waited till David had mounted the roof, then he pointed. "Now, Saadat!" he said.

"They have stolen in?" David peered into the misty whiteness.

"They are almost in, Saadat. Nothing can stop them now."

"It is well done. Go and ask Ebn Ezra effendi to come hither," he said.

Suddenly a shot was fired, then a hoarse shout came over the desert, then there was silence again.

"They are in, Saadat," said Mahommed Hassan.

Day broke over a hazy plain. On both sides of the Nile the river mist spread wide, and the army of Ali Wad Hei and the defending forces were alike veiled from each other and from the desert world beyond. Down the river for scores of miles the mist was heavy, and those who moved within it and on the waters of the Nile could not see fifty feet ahead. Yet through this heavy veil there broke gently a little fleet of phantom vessels, the noise of the paddle-wheels and their propellers muffled as they moved slowly on. Never had vessels taken such risks on the Nile before, never had pilots trusted so to instinct, for there were sand-banks and ugly drifts of rock here and there. A safe journey for phantom ships; but these armed vessels, filled by men with white eager faces and others with dark Egyptian features, were no phantoms. They bristled with weapons, and armed men crowded every corner of space. For full two hours from the first streak of light they had travelled swiftly, taking chances not to be taken save in some desperate moment. The moment was desperate enough, if not for them. They were going to the relief of besieged men, with a message from Nahoum Pasha to Claridge Pasha, and with succor. They had looked for a struggle up this river as they neared the beleaguered city; but, as they came nearer and nearer, not a gun fired at them from the forts on the banks out of the mists. If they were heard they still were safe from the guns, for they could not be seen, and those on shore could not know whether they were friend or foe. Like ghostly vessels they passed on, until at last they could hear the stir and murmur of life along the banks of the stream.

Boom! Boom! Boom! Through the mist the guns of the city were pouring shot and shell out into Ali Wad Hei's camp, and Ali Wad Hei laughed contemptuously. Surely now the Inglesi was altogether mad, and to-day, this day after prayers at noon, he should be shot like a mad dog, for yesterday's defeat had turned some of his own adherent sheikhs into angry critics. He would not wait for starvation to compel the infidel to surrender. He would win freedom to deal in human flesh and blood, and make slave-markets where he willed, and win glory for the Lord Mahomet, by putting this place to the sword; and, when it was over, he would have the Inglesi's head carried on a pole through the city for the faithful to mock at, a target for the filth of the streets. So, by the will of Allah, it should be done!

Boom! Boom! Boom! The Inglesi was certainly mad, for never had there been so much firing in any long day in all the siege as in this brief hour this morning. It was the act of a fool, to fire his shells and shot into the mist without aim, without a clear target. Ali Wad Hei scorned to make any reply with his guns, but sat in desultory counsel with his sheikhs, planning what should be done when the mists had cleared away. But yesterday evening the Arab chief had offered to give the Inglesi life if he would surrender and become a Muslim, and swear by the Lord Mahomet but late in the night he had received a reply which left only one choice, and that was to disembowel the infidel, and carry his head aloft on a spear. The letter he had received ran thus in Arabic:

"To Ali Wad Hei and All with him:

"We are here to live or to die as God wills, and not as ye will. I have set my feet on the rock, and not by threats of any man shall I be moved. But I say that for all the blood that ye have shed here there will be punishment, and for the slaves which ye have slain or sold there will be high price paid. Ye have threatened the city and me—take us if ye can. Ye are seven to one. Why falter all these months! If ye will not come to us, we shall come to you, rebellious ones, who have drawn the sword against your lawful ruler, the Effendina.

"CLARIDGE PASHA."

It was a rhetorical document couched in the phraseology they best understood; and if it begat derision, it also begat anger; and the challenge David had delivered would be met when the mists had lifted from the river and the plain. But when the first thinning of the mists began, when the sun began to dissipate the rolling haze, Ali Wad Hei and his rebel sheikhs were suddenly startled by rifle-fire at close quarters, by confused noises, and the jar and roar of battle. Now the reason for the firing of the great guns was plain. The noise was meant to cover the advance of David's men. The little garrison, which had done no more than issue in sorties, was now throwing its full force on the enemy in a last desperate endeavor. It was either success or absolute destruction David was staking all, with the last of his food, the last of his ammunition, the last of his hopes. All round the circle the movement was forward, till the circle had widened to the enemy's lines; while at the old defences were only handfuls of men. With scarce a cry David's men fell on the unprepared foe; and he himself, on a gray Arab, a mark for any lance or spear and rifle, rode upon that point where Ali Wad Hei's tent was set.

But after the first onset, in which hundreds were killed, there began the real noise of battle—fierce shouting, the shrill cries of wounded and maddened horses as they struck with their feet, and bit as fiercely at the fighting foe as did their masters. The mist cleared slowly, and, when it had wholly lifted, the fight was spread over every part of the field of siege. Ali Wad Hei's men had gathered themselves together after the first deadly onslaught, and were fighting fiercely, shouting the Muslim battle-cry, "*Allah hu achbar!*" Able to bring up reinforcements, the great losses at first sustained were soon made up, and the sheer weight of numbers gave them courage and advantage. By rushes with lance and sword and rifle they were able, at last, to drive David's men back upon their old defences with loss. Then charge upon charge ensued, and each charge, if it cost them much, cost the besieged more, by reason of their fewer numbers. At one point, however, the besieged became again the attacking party. This was where Achmet Pasha had command. His men on one side of the circle, as Ebn Ezra Bey's men on the other, fought with a valor as desperate as the desert ever saw. But David, galloping here and there to order, to encourage, to prevent retreat at one point, or to urge attack at another, saw that the doom of his gallant force was certain; for the enemy were still four to one, in spite of the carnage of the first attack. Bullets hissed past him. One carried away a button, one caught the tip of his ear, one pierced the fez he wore; but he felt nothing of this, saw nothing. He was buried in the storm of battle, preparing for the end, for the final grim defence, when his men would retreat upon the one last strong fort, and there await their fate. From this absorption he was roused by Lacey, who came galloping towards him.

"They've come, Saadat, they've come at last! We're saved—oh, my God, you bet we're all right now! See! See, Saadat!"

David saw. Five steamers carrying the Egyptian flag were bearing around the point where the river curved below the town, and converging upon David's small fleet. Presently the steamers opened fire, to encourage the besieged, who replied with frenzied shouts of joy, and soon there poured upon the sands hundreds of men in the uniform of the Effendina. These came forward at the double, and, with a courage which nothing could withstand, the whole circle spread out again upon the discomfited tribes of Ali Wad Hei. Dismay, confusion, possessed the Arabs. Their river-watchers had failed them, God had hidden His face from them; and when Ali Wad Hei and three of his emirs turned and rode into the desert, their forces broke and ran also, pursued by the relentless men who had suffered the tortures of siege so long. The chase was short, however, for they were desert folk, and they returned to loot the camp which had menaced them so long.

Only the newcomers, Nahoum's men, carried the hunt far; and they brought back with them a body which their leader commanded to be brought to a great room of the palace. Towards sunset David and Ebn Ezra Bey and Lacey came together to this room. The folds of loose linen were lifted from the face, and all three looked at it long in silence. At last Lacey spoke:

"He got what he wanted; the luck was with him. It's better than Leperland."

"In the bosom of Allah there is peace," said Ebn Ezra. "It is well with Achmet."

With misty eyes David stooped and took the dead man's hand in his for a moment. Then he rose to his feet and turned away.

"And Nahoum also—and Nahoum," he said presently. "Read this," he added, and put a letter from Nahoum into Ebn Ezra's hand.

Lacey reverently covered Achmet's face. "Say, he got what he wanted," he said again.

XLII

THE LOOM OF DESTINY

It was many a day since the Duchess of Snowdon had seen a sunrise, and the one on which she now gazed from the deck of the dahabieh *Nefert*, filled her with a strange new sense of discovery and revelation. Her perceptions were arrested and a little confused, and yet the undercurrent of feeling was one of delight and rejuvenation. Why did this sunrise bring back, all at once, the day when her one lost child was born, and she looked out of the windows of Snowdon Hall, as she lay still and nerveless, and thought how wonderful and sweet and green was the world she saw and the sky that walled it round? Sunrise over the Greek Temple of Philae and the splendid ruins of a farther time towering beside it! In her sight were the wide, islanded Nile where Cleopatra loitered with Anthony, the foaming, crashing cataracts above, the great quarries from which ancient temples had been hewed, unfinished obelisks and vast blocks of stone left where bygone workmen had forsaken them, when the invader came and another dynasty disappeared into that partial oblivion from which the Egyptian still emerges triumphant over all his conquerors, unchanged in form and feature. Something of its meaning got into her mind.

"I wonder what Windlehurst would think of it, he always had an eye for things like that," she murmured;

and then caught her breath, as she added, "He always liked beauty." She looked at her wrinkled, childish hands. "But sunsets never grow old," she continued, with no apparent relevance. "La, la, we were young once!"

Her eyes were lost again in the pinkish glow spreading over the gray-brown sand of the desert, over the palm-covered island near. "And now it's others' turn, or ought to be," she murmured.

She looked to where, not far away, Hylda stood leaning over the railing of the dahabieh, her eyes fixed in reverie on the farthest horizon line of the unpeopled, untraveled plain of sand.

"No, poor thing, it's not her turn," she added, as Hylda, with a long sigh, turned and went below. Tears gathered in her pale blue eyes. "Not yet—with Eglington alive. And perhaps it would be best if the other never came back. I could have made the world better worth living in if I had had the chance—and I wouldn't have been a duchess! La! La!"

She relapsed into reverie, an uncommon experience for her; and her mind floated indefinitely from one thing to another, while she was half conscious of the smell of coffee permeating the air, and of the low resonant notes of the Nubian boys, as, with locked shoulders, they scrubbed the decks of a dahabieh near by with hemp-shod feet.

Presently, however, she was conscious of another sound—the soft clip of oars, joined to the guttural, explosive song of native rowers; and, leaning over the rail, she saw a boat draw alongside the *Nefert*. From it came the figure of Nahoum Pasha, who stepped briskly on deck, in his handsome face a light which flashed an instant meaning to her.

"I know—I know! Claridge Pasha—you have heard?" she said excitedly, as he came to her.

He smiled and nodded. "A messenger has arrived. Within a few hours he should be here."

"Then it was all false that he was wounded—ah, that horrible story of his death!"

"Bismillah, it was not all false! The night before the great battle he was slightly wounded in the side. He neglected it, and fever came on; but he survived. His first messengers to us were killed, and that is why the news of the relief came so late. But all is well at last. I have come to say so to Lady Eglington even before I went to the Effendina." He made a gesture towards a huge and gaily caparisoned dahabieh not far away. "Kaïd was right about coming here. His health is better. He never doubted Claridge Pasha's return; it was *une idée fixe*. He believes a magic hand protects the Saadat, and that, adhering to him, he himself will carry high the flower of good fortune and live forever. *Kismet!* I will not wait to see Lady Eglington. I beg to offer to her my congratulations on the triumph of her countryman."

His words had no ulterior note; but there was a shadow in his eyes which in one not an Oriental would have seemed sympathy.

"Pasha! Pasha!" the Duchess called after him, as he turned to leave; "tell me, is there any news from England—from the Government?"

"From Lord Eglington? No," Nahoum answered meaningly. "I wrote to him. Did the English Government desire to send a message to Claridge Pasha if the relief was accomplished? That is what I asked. But there is no word. Malaish, Egypt will welcome him!"

She followed his eyes. Two score of dahabiehs lay along the banks of the Nile, and on the shore were encampments of soldiers, while flags were flying everywhere. Egypt had followed the lead of the Effendina. Claridge Pasha's star was in its zenith.

As Nahoum's boat was rowed away, Hylda came on

deck again, and the Duchess hastened to her. Hylda caught the look in her face. "What has happened? Is there news? Who has been here?" she asked.

The Duchess took her hands. "Nahoum has gone to tell Prince Kaïd. He came to you with the good news first," she said with a flutter.

She felt Hylda's hands turn cold. A kind of mist filled the dark eyes, and the slim, beautiful figure swayed slightly. An instant only, and then the lips smiled and Hylda said in a quavering voice, "They will be so glad in England."

"Yes, yes, my darling, that is what Nahoum said." She gave Nahoum's message to her. "Now they'll make him a peer, I suppose, after having deserted him. So English!"

She did not understand why Hylda's hands trembled so, why so strange a look came into her face, but, in an instant, the rare and appealing eyes shone again with a light of agitated joy, and Hylda leaned suddenly over and kissed her cheek.

"Smell the coffee," she said, with assumed gaiety. "Doesn't fair-and-sixty want her breakfast? Sunrise is a splendid tonic." She laughed feverishly.

"My darling, I hadn't seen the sun rise in thirty years, not since the night I first met Windlehurst at a Foreign Office ball."

"You have always been great friends?" Hylda stole a look at her.

"That's the queer part of it; I was so stupid, and he so clever. But Windlehurst has a way of letting himself down to your level. He always called me Betty after my girl died, just as if I was his equal. La, la, but I was proud when he first called me that—the Prime Minister of England. I'm going to watch the sun rise again to-morrow, my darling. I didn't know it was so beautiful, and gave one such an appetite." She broke a piece of bread, and, not waiting to butter it, almost stuffed it into her mouth.

Hylda leaned over and pressed her arm. "What a good mother Betty it is!" she said tenderly.

Presently they were startled by the shrill screaming of a steamer whistle, followed by the churning of the paddles, as she drove past and drew to the bank near them.

"It is a steamer from Cairo, with letters, no doubt," said Hylda; and the Duchess nodded assent, and covertly noted her look, for she knew that no letters had arrived from Eglington since Hylda had left England.

A half-hour later, as the Duchess sat on deck, a great straw hat tied under her chin with pale blue ribbons, like a child of twelve, she was startled by seeing the figure of a farmer-looking person with a shock of gray-red hair, a red face, and with great blue eyes, appear before her in the charge of Hylda's dragoman.

"This has come to speak with my lady," the dragoman said, "but my lady is riding into the desert—there!" He pointed to the sands.

The Duchess motioned the dragoman away, and scanned the face of the new-comer shrewdly. Where had she seen this strange-looking English peasant, with the rolling walk of a sailor?

"What is your name, and where do you come from?" she asked, not without anxiety, for there was something ominous and suggestive in the old man's face.

"I come from Hamley, in England, and my name is Soolsby, your grace. I come to see my Lady Eglington."

Now she remembered him. She had seen him in Hamley more than once.

"You have come far; have you important news for her ladyship? Is there anything wrong?" she asked with apparent composure, but with heavy premonition.

"Ay, news that counts, I bring," answered Soolsby, "or I hadn't come this long way. 'Tis a long way at sixty-five."

"Well, yes, at our age it is a long way," rejoined the Duchess in a friendly voice, suddenly waiving away the intervening air of class, for she was half a peasant at heart.

"Ay, and we both come for the same end, I suppose," Soolsby added; "and a costly business it is. But what matters, so be that you help her ladyship and I help Our Man."

"And who is 'Our Man'?" was the rejoinder.

"Him that's coming safe here from the South—David Claridge," he answered. "Ay, 'twas the first thing I heard when I landed here, me that be come all these thousand miles to see him, if so be he was alive."

Just then he caught sight of Kate Heaver climbing the stair to the deck where they were. His face flushed; he hurried forward and gripped her by the arm, as her feet touched the upper deck. "Kate—ay, 'tis Kate!" he cried. Then he let go her arm and caught a hand in both of his and fondled it. "Ay, ay, 'tis Kate!"

"What is it brings you, Soolsby?" Kate asked anxiously.

"'Tis not Jasper, and 'tis not the drink—ay, I've been sober since, ever since, Kate, lass," he answered stoutly.

"Oh, quick, tell me what it is!" she said frowning. "You've not come here for naught, Soolsby."

Still holding her hand, he leaned over and whispered in her ear. For an instant she stood as though transfixed, and then, with a curious muffled cry, broke away from him and turned to go below.

"Keep your mouth shut, lass, till proper time," he called after her, as she descended the steps hastily again. Then he came slowly back to the Duchess.

He looked her in the face—he was so little like a peasant, so much more like a sailor here with his feet on the deck of a floating thing. "Your grace is a good friend to her ladyship," he said at last, deliberately, "and 'tis well that you tell her ladyship. As good a friend to her you've been, I doubt not, as that I've been to him that's coming from beyond and away."

"Go on, man, go on. I want to know what startled Heaver yonder, what you have come to say."

"I beg pardon, your grace. One doesn't keep good news waiting, and 'tis not good news for her ladyship I bring, even if it be for Claridge Pasha, for there was no love lost 'twixt him and second-best lordship that's gone."

"Speak, man, speak it out, and no more riddles," she interrupted sharply.

"Then, he that was my Lord Eglington is gone foreign—he is dead," he said slowly.

The Duchess fell back in her chair. For an instant the desert, the temples, the palms, the Nile waters faded, and she was in some middle world, in which Soolsby's voice seemed coming muffled and deep across a dark flood; then she recovered herself, and gave a little cry, not unlike that which Kate gave a few moments before, partly of pain, partly of relief.

"Ay, he's dead and buried, too, and in the Quaker churchyard. Miss Claridge would have it so! And none in Hamley said nay, not one."

The Duchess murmured to herself. Eglington was dead—Eglington was dead—Eglington was dead! And David Claridge was coming out of the desert, was coming to-day—now!

"How did it happen?" she asked faintly, at last.

"Things went wrong wi' him—bad wrong in Parliament and everywhere, and he didn't take it well. He stood the world off like—ay, he had no temper for black days. He shut himself up at Hamley in his chemical place, like his father, like his father before him. When the week-end came, there he was all day and night among his bottles and jars and wires. He was after summat big in experiment for explosives, so the papers said, and so he said himself before he died, to Miss Claridge — ay, 'twas her he deceived and treated cruel, that come to him when he was shattered by his experimenting. No patience, he had at last—and reckless in his chemical place, and didn't realize what his hands was doing. 'Twas so he told her, that forgave him all his deceit, and held him in her arms when he died. Not many words he had to speak; but he did say that he had never done any good to any one—ay, I was standing near behind his bed and heard all, for I was thinking of her alone with him, and so I would be with her, and she would have it so. Ay, and he said that he had misused cruel her that had loved him, her ladyship, that's here. He said he had misused her because he had never loved her truly, only pride and vain-glory being in his heart. Then he spoke summat to her that was there to forgive him and help him over the stile 'twixt this field and it that's Beyond and Away, which made her cry out in pain and say that he must fix his thoughts on other things. And she prayed out loud for him, for he would have no parson there. She prayed and prayed as never priest or parson prayed, and at last he got quiet and still, and, when she stopped praying, he did not speak or open his eyes for a longish while. But when the old clock on the stable was striking twelve, he opened his eyes wide, and when it had stopped, he said: 'It is always twelve by the clock that stops at noon. I've done no good. I've earned my end.' He looked as though he was waiting for the clock to go on striking, half raising himself up in bed, with Miss Faith's arm under his head. He whispered to her then

—he couldn't speak by this time. 'It's twelve o'clock,' he said. Then there come some words I've heard the priest say at Mass, '*Vanitas*, *Vanitatum*,'—that was what he said. And her he'd lied to, there with him, laying his head down on the pillow, as if he was her child going to sleep. So, too, she had him buried by her father, in the Quaker burying-ground—ay, she is a saint on earth, I warrant."

For a moment after he had stopped the Duchess did not speak, but kept untying and tying the blue ribbons under her chin, her faded eyes still fastened on him, burning with the flame of an emotion which made them dark and young again.

"So, it's all over," she said, as though to herself. "They were all alike, from old Broadbrim, the grandfather, down to this one, and back to William the Conqueror."

"Like as peas in a pod," exclaimed Soolsby—"all but one, all but one, and never satisfied with what was in their own garden, but peeking, peeking beyond the hedge, and climbing and getting a fall. That's what they've always been evermore."

His words aroused the Duchess, and the air became a little colder about her—after all, the division between the classes and the masses must be kept, and the Eglingtons were no upstarts. "You will say nothing about this till I give you leave to speak," she commanded. "I must tell her ladyship."

Soolsby drew himself up a little, nettled at her tone. "It is your grace's place to tell her ladyship," he responded; "but I've taken ten years' savings to come to Egypt, and not to do any one harm, but good, if so be I might."

The Duchess relented at once. She got to her feet as quickly as she could, and held out her hand to him. "You are a good man and a friend worth having, I know, and I shall like you to be my friend, Mr. Soolsby," she said impulsively.

He took her hand and shook it awkwardly, his lips working. "Your grace, I understand. I've got naught to live for except my friends. Money's naught, naught's naught, if there isn't a friend to feel a crunch at his heart when summat bad happens to you. I'd take my affydavy that there's no better friend in the world than your grace."

She smiled at him. "And so we are friends, aren't we? And I am to tell her ladyship, and you are to say 'naught.'"

"But to the Egyptian, to him, your grace, it is my place to speak—to Claridge Pasha, when he comes."

The Duchess looked at him quizzically. "How does Lord Eglington's death concern Claridge Pasha?" she asked rather anxiously. Had there been gossip about Hylda? Had the public got a hint of the true story of her flight, in spite of all Windlehurst had done? Was Hylda's name smirched, now, when all would be set right? Had everything come too late, as it were?

"There's two ways that his lordship's death concerns Claridge Pasha," answered Soolsby shrewdly, for though he guessed the truth concerning Hylda and David, his was not a leaking tongue. "There's two ways it touches him. There'll be a new man in the Foreign Office—Lord Eglington was always against Claridge Pasha; and there's matters of land betwixt the two estates—matters of land that's got to be settled now," he continued, with determined and successful evasion.

The Duchess was deceived. "But you will not tell Claridge Pasha until I have told her ladyship and I give you leave; promise that," she urged.

"I will not tell him until then," he answered. "Look, look, your grace," he added, suddenly pointing towards the southern horizon, "there he comes! Ay, 'tis Our Man, I doubt not—Our Man evermore!"

Miles away there appeared on the horizon a dozen camels being ridden towards Assouan.

"Our Man, evermore," repeated the Duchesss, with a trembling smile. "Yes, it is surely he. See, the soldiers are moving. They're going to ride out to meet him." She made a gesture towards the far shore where Kaïd's men were saddling their horses, and to Nahoum's and Kaïd's dahabiehs, where there was a great stir.

"There's one from Hamley will meet them first," Soolsby said, and pointed to where Hylda, in the desert, was riding towards the camels coming out of the south.

The Duchess threw up her hands. "Dear me, dear me," she said in distress, "if she only knew!"

"There's thousands of women that'd ride out mad to meet him," said Soolsby carefully; "women that likes to see an Englishman that's done his duty—ay, women and men, that'd ride hard to welcome him back from the grave. Her ladyship's as good a patriot as any," he added, watching the Duchess out of the corners of his eyes, his face turned to the desert.

The Duchess looked at him quizzically, and was satisfied with her scrutiny. "You're a man of sense," she replied brusquely, and gathered up her skirts. "Find me a horse or a donkey, and I'll go, too," she added whimsically. "Patriotism is such a nice sentiment!"

For David and Lacey the morning had broken upon a new earth. Whatever of toil and tribulation the future held in store, this day marked a step forward in the work to which David had set his life. A way had been cloven through the bloody palisades of barbarism, and though the dark races might seek to hold back the forces which drain the fens, and build the bridges, and make the desert blossom as the rose, which give liberty and preserve life, the good end was sure and near, whatever of rebellion and disorder and treachery intervened. This was the larger, graver issue; but they felt a spring in the blood, and their hearts were leaping, because of the thought that soon they would clasp hands again with all from which they had been exiled.

"Say, Saadat, think of it: a bed with four feet, and linen sheets, and sleeping till any time in the morning, and, 'If you please, sir, your bath is ready.' Say, it's great, and we're in it!"

David smiled. "Thee did very well, friend, without such luxuries. Thee is not skin and bone."

Lacey mopped his forehead. "Well, I've put on a layer or two since the relief. It's being scared that takes the flesh off me. I never was intended for the 'stricken field.' Poetry and the hearthstone was my real vocation—and a bit of silver mining to blow off steam with," he added with a chuckle.

David laughed and tapped his arm. "That is an old story now, thy cowardice. Thee should be more original."

"It's worth not being original, Saadat, to hear you *thee* and *thou* me as you used to do. It's like old times—the oldest, first times. You've changed a lot, Saadat."

"Not in anything that matters, I hope."

"Not in anything that matters to any one that matters. To me it's the same as it ever was, only more so. It isn't that, for you are you. But you've had disappointment, trouble, hard nuts to crack, and all you could do to escape the rocks being rolled down the Egyptian hill onto you; and it's left its mark."

"Am I grown so different?"

Lacey's face shone under the look that was turned towards him. "Say, Saadat, you're the same old red sandstone; but I missed the *thee* and *thou*. I sort of hankered after it· it gets me where I'm at home with myself."

David laughed dryly. "Well, perhaps I've missed something in you. Thee never says now—not since thee went south a year ago, 'Well, give my love to the girls.' Something has left its mark, friend," he added teasingly; for his spirits were boyish to-day; he was living in the present. There had gone from his eyes and from the lines of his figure the melancholy which Hylda had remarked when he was in England.

"Well, now, I never noticed," rejoined Lacey. "That's got me. Looks as if I wasn't as friendly as I used to be, doesn't it? But I am—I am, Saadat."

"I thought that the widow in Cairo, perhaps—"

Lacey chuckled. "Say, perhaps it was—cute as she can be, maybe, wouldn't like it, might be prejudiced."

Suddenly David turned sharply to Lacey. "Thee spoke of silver mining just now. I owe thee something like two hundred thousand pounds, I think—Egypt and I."

Lacey winked whimsically at himself under the rim of his helmet. "Are you drawing back from those railway concessions, Saadat," he asked with apparent ruefulness.

"Drawing back? No! But does thee think they are worth—"

Lacey assumed an injured air. "If a man that's made as much money as me can't be trusted to look after a business proposition—"

"Oh, well, then!"

"Say, Saadat, I don't want you to think I've taken a mean advantage of you; and if—"

David hastened to put the matter right. "No, no; thee must be the judge!" He smiled sceptically. "In any case, thee has done a good deed in a great way, and it will do thee no harm in the end. In one way the investment will pay a long interest, as long as the history of Egypt runs! Ah, see, the houses of

Assouan, the palms, the river, the masts of the dahabiehs!"

Lacey quickened his camel's steps, and stretched out a hand to the inviting distance. "My, it's great," he said, and his eyes were blinking with tears. Presently he pointed. "There's a woman riding to meet us, Saadat. Golly, can't she ride! She means to be in it—to salute the returning brave."

He did not glance at David. If he had done so, he would have seen that David's face had taken on a strange look; just such a look as it wore that night in the monastery when he saw Hylda in a vision and heard her say, "Speak—speak to me!"

There had shot into David's mind the conviction that the woman riding towards them was Hylda. Hylda, the first to welcome him back, Hylda—Lady Eglington! Suddenly his face appeared to tighten and grow thin. It was all joy and torture at once. He had fought this fight out with himself—had he not done so? Had he not closed his heart to all but duty and Egypt? Yet there she was riding out of the old life, out of Hamley, and England, and all that had happened in Cairo, to meet him. Nearer and nearer she came. He could not see the face, but yet he knew. He quickened his camel, and drew ahead of Lacey. Lacey did not understand, he did not recognize Hylda as yet; but he knew by instinct the Saadat's wishes, and he motioned the others to ride more slowly, while he and they watched horsemen coming out from Assouan towards them.

David urged his camel on. Presently he could distinguish the features of the woman riding towards him. It was Hylda. His presentiment, his instinct had been right. His heart beat tumultuously, his hand trembled, he grew suddenly weak; but he summoned up his will, and ruled himself to something like composure. This, then, was his home-coming from the far miseries and trials and battlefields—to see her face before all others, to hear her voice first. What miracle had brought this thing to pass, this beautiful, bitter, forbidden thing? Forbidden! Whatever the cause of her coming, she must not see what he felt for her. He must deal fairly by her and by Eglington; he must be true to that real self which had emerged from the fiery trial in the monastery. Bronzed as he was, his face showed no paleness; but, as he drew near her, it grew pinched and wan from the effort at self-control. He set his lips, and rode on, until he could see her eyes looking into his—eyes full of that which he had never seen in any eyes in all the world!

What had been her feelings during that ride in the desert? She had not meant to go out to meet him. After she heard that he was coming, her desire was to get away from all the rest of the world, and be alone with her thoughts. He was coming, he was safe, and her work was done. What she had set out to do was accomplished—to bring him back, if it was God's will, out of the jaws of death, for England's sake, for the world's sake, for his sake, for her own sake. For her own sake? Yes, yes, in spite of all, for her own sake. Whatever lay before, now, for this one hour, for this moment of meeting he should be hers. But meet him, where? Before all the world, with a smile of conventional welcome on her lips, with the same hand-clasp that any friend and lover of humanity would give him?

The desert air blew on her face, keen, sweet, vibrant, thrilling. What he had heard that night at the monastery, the humming life of the land of white fire—the desert, the million looms of all the weavers of the world weaving, this she heard in the sunlight, with the sand rising like surf behind her horse's heels. The misery and the tyranny and the unrequited love were all behind her, the disillusion and the loss and the undeserved insult to her womanhood—all, all were sunk away into the unredeemable past. Here, in Egypt, where she had first felt the stir of life's passion and pain and penalty, here, now, she lost herself in a beautiful, buoyant dream. She was riding out to meet the one man of all men, hero, crusader, rescuer—ah, that dreadful night in the Palace, and Foorgat's face! But he was coming, who had made her live, to whom she had called, to whom her soul had spoken in its grief and misery. Had she ever done aught to shame the best that was in herself—and had she not been sorely tempted? Had she not striven to love Eglington even when the worst was come, not alone at her own soul's command, but because she knew that this man would have it so? Broken by her own sorrow, she had left England, Eglington—all, to keep her pledge to help him in his hour of need, to try and save him to the world, if that might be. So she had come to Nahoum, who was binding him down on the bed of torture and of death. And yet, alas! not herself had conquered Nahoum, but David, as Nahoum had said. She herself had not done this one thing which would have compensated for all that she had suffered. This had not been permitted; but it remained that she had come here to do it, and perhaps he would understand when he saw her.

Yes, she knew he would understand! She flung up her head to the sun and the pulse-stirring air, and, as she did so, she saw his cavalcade approaching. She was sure it was he, even when he was far off, by the same sure instinct that convinced him. For an instant she hesitated. She would turn back, and meet him with the crowd. Then she looked around. The desert was deserted by all save herself and himself and those who were with him. No. Her mind was made up. She would ride forward. She would be the first to welcome him back to life and the world. He and she would meet alone in the desert. For one minute they would be alone, they two, with the world afar, they two, to meet, to greet—and to part. Out of all that Fate had to give of sorrow and loss, this one delectable moment, no matter what came after.

"David!" she cried with beating heart, and rode on, harder and harder.

Now she saw him ride ahead of the others. Ah, he knew that it was she, though he could not see her face! Nearer and nearer. Now they looked into each other's eyes.

She saw him stop his camel and make it kneel for the dismounting. She stopped her horse also, and slid to the ground, and stood waiting, one hand upon the horse's neck. He hastened forward, then stood still, a few feet away, his eyes on hers, his helmet off, his brown hair, brown as when she first saw it—peril and hardship had not thinned or grayed it. For a moment they stood so, for a moment of revealing and understanding, but speechless; and then, suddenly, and with a smile infinitely touching, she said, as he had heard her say in the monastery—the very words:

"Speak—speak to me!"

He took her hand in his. "There is no need—I have said all!" he answered, happiness and trouble at once in his eyes. Then his face grew calmer. "Thee has made it worth while living on," he added.

She was gaining control of herself also. "I said that I would come when I was needed," she answered less tremblingly.

"Thee came alone?" he asked gently.

"From Assouan, yes," she said in a voice still unsteady. "I was riding out to be by myself, and then I saw you coming, and I rode on. I thought I should like to be the first to say, 'Well done,' and 'God bless you!'"

He drew in a long breath, then looked at her keenly. "Lord Eglington is in Egypt also?" he asked.

Her face did not change. She looked him in the eyes. "No, Eglington would not come to help you. I came to Nahoum, as I said I would."

"Thee has a good memory," he rejoined simply.

"I am a good friend," she answered, then suddenly her face flushed up, her breast panted, her eyes shone with a brightness almost intolerable to him, and he said in a low, shaking voice:

"It is all fighting, all fighting. We have done our best; and thee has made all possible."

"David!" she said in a voice scarce above a whisper.

"Thee and me have far to go," he said in a voice not louder than her own, "but our ways may not be the same."

She understood, and a newer life leaped up in her. She knew that he loved her—that was sufficient; the rest would be easier now. Sacrifice, all, would be easier. To part, yes, and for evermore; but to know that she had been truly loved—who could rob her of that?

"See," she said lightly, "your people are waiting—and there, why, there is my cousin Lacey. Tom, oh, Cousin Tom!" she called eagerly.

Lacey rode down on them. "I swan, but I'm glad," he said, as he dismounted from his camel. "Cousin Hylda, I'm blest if I don't feel as if I could sing like Aunt Melissa in the dairy."

"You may kiss me, Cousin Tom," she said, as she took his hands in hers.

He flushed, was embarrassed, then snatched a kiss from her cheek. "Say, I'm in it, ain't I? And you were in it first, eh, Cousin Hylda? The rest are nowhere —there they come from Assouan, Kaïd, Nahoum, and the Nubians. Look at 'em glisten!

A hundred of Kaïd's Nubians in their glittering armor made three sides of a quickly moving square, in the centre of which, and a little ahead, rode Kaïd and Nahoum, while behind the square—in parade and gala dress—trooped hundreds of soldiers and Egyptians and natives.

Swiftly the two cavalcades approached each other, the desert ringing with the cries of the Bedouins, the Nubians, and the fellaheen. They met on an upland of sand, from which the wide valley of the Nile and its wild cataracts could be seen. As men meet who parted yesterday, Kaïd, Nahoum and David met, but Kaïd's first quiet words to David had behind them a world of meaning:

"I also have come back, Saadat, to whom be the bread that never moulds and the water that never stales!" he said, with a look in his face which had not been there for many a day. Superstition had set its mark on him—on Claridge Pasha's safety depended his own, that was his belief; and the look of this thin, bronzed face, with its living fire, gave him vital assurance of length of days.

And David answered, "May thy life be the nursling of Time, Effendina. I bring the tribute of the rebellious once more to thy hand. What was thine, and was lost, is thine once more. Peace and salaam!"

Between Nahoum and David there were no words at first at all. They shook hands like Englishmen, looking into each other's eyes, and with pride of what Nahoum, once, in his duplicity, had called "perfect friendship."

Lacey thought of this now as he looked on; and not without a sense of irony, he said under his breath, "Almost thou persuadest me to be a Christian!"

But in Hylda's look, as it met Nahoum's, there was no doubt—what woman doubts the convert whom she thinks she has helped to make! Meanwhile, the Nubians smote their mailed breasts with their swords in honor of David and Kaïd.

Under the gleaming moon, the exquisite temple of

"DAVID LOOKED OUT UPON IT ALL WITH EMOTIONS NOT YET WHOLLY MASTERED"

Philae perched on its high rock above the river, the fires on the shore, the masts of the dahabiehs twinkling with lights, and the barbarous songs floating across the water, gave the feeling of past centuries to the scene. From the splendid boat which Kaïd had placed at his disposal, David looked out upon it all, with emotions not yet wholly mastered by the true estimate of what this day had brought to him. With a mind unsettled he listened to the natives in the fore-part of the boat and on the shore, beating the darabukkeh and playing the *kemengeh.* Yet it was moving in a mist and on a flood of greater happiness than he had ever known.

He did not know, and Hylda did not know, that Eglington was gone forever. He did not know that the winds of time had already swept away all traces of the house of ambition which Eglington had sought to build; and that his nimble tongue and untrustworthy mind would never more delude and charm, and wanton with truth. He did not know, but within the past hour Hylda knew; and now out of the night Soolsby came to tell him.

He was roused from his reverie by Soolsby's voice saying, "Hast nowt to say to me, Egyptian?"

It startled him; sounded ghostly in the moonlight; for why should he hear Soolsby's voice on the confines of Egypt? But Soolsby came nearer, and stood where the moonlight fell upon him, hat in hand, a rustic modern figure in this Oriental world.

David sprang to his feet and grasped the old man by the shoulders. "Soolsby, Soolsby," he said, with a strange, plaintive note in his voice, yet gladly, too, "Soolsby, thee is come here to welcome me! But has she not come—Miss Claridge, Soolsby?"

He longed for that true heart which had never failed him, the simple soul whose life had been filled by thought and care of him, and whose every act had for its background the love of sister for brother,—for that was their relation in every usual meaning—who, too frail and broken to come to him now, waited for him by the old hearthstone. And so Soolsby, in his own way, made him understand; for who knew them both better than this old man, who had shared in David's destiny since the fatal day when Lord Eglington had married Mercy Claridge in secret, had set in motion a long line of tragic happenings?

"Ay, she would have come, she would have come," Soolsby answered, "but she was not fit for the journey, and there was little time, my lord."

"Why did thee come, Soolsby? Only to welcome me back?"

"I come to bring you back to England, to your duty there, my lord."

The first time Soolsby had used the words "my lord," David had scarcely noticed it, but its repetition struck him strangely.

"Here, sometimes they call me *Pasha* and *Saadat*, but I am not 'my lord,'" he said.

"Ay, but you are my lord, Egyptian, as sure as I've kept my word to you that I'd drink no more, ay, on my sacred honor. So you are my lord; you are Lord Eglington, my lord."

David stood rigid and almost unblinking as Soolsby told his tale, beginning with the story of Eglington's death, and going back all the years to the day of Mercy Claridge's marriage.

"And him that never was Lord Eglington, your own father's son, is dead and gone, my lord; and you are come into your rights at last." This was the end of the tale.

For a long time David stood looking into the sparkling night before him, speechless and unmoving, his hands clasped behind him, his head bent forward, as though in a dream.

How, all in an instant, had life changed for him! How had Soolsby's tale of Eglington's death filled him with a pity deeper than he had ever felt—the futile, bitter, unaccomplished life, the audacious, brilliant genius quenched, a genius got from the same source as his own resistless energy and imagination, from the same wild spring! Gone—all gone, with only pity to cover him, unloved, unloving, unbemoaned, save by the Quaker girl whose true spirit he had hurt, save by the wife whom he had cruelly wronged and tortured; and pity was the thing that moved them both, unfathomable and almost maternal, in that sense of motherhood which, in spite of love or passion, is behind both, behind all, in every true woman's life.

At last David spoke.

"Who knows of all this—of who I am, Soolsby?"

"Lady Eglington and myself, my lord."

"Only she and you?"

"Only us two, Egyptian."

"Then let it be so—forever."

Soolsby was startled, dumfounded.

"But you will take your title and estates, my lord; you will take the place which is your own."

"And prove my grandfather wrong? Had he not enough sorrow? And change my life, all to please thee, Soolsby?"

He took the old man's shoulders in his hands again. "Thee has done thy duty as few in this world, Soolsby, and given friendship such as few give. But thee must be content. I am David Claridge, and so shall remain ever."

"Then, since he has no male kin, the title dies, and all that's his will go to her ladyship," Soolsby rejoined sourly

"Does thee grudge her ladyship what was his?"

"I grudge her what is yours, my lord—"

Suddenly Soolsby paused, as though a new thought had come to him, and he nodded to himself in satisfaction. "Well, since you will have it so, it will be so, Egyptian; but it is a queer fuddle, all of it; and where's the way out, tell me that, my lord?"

David spoke impatiently. "Call me 'my lord' no more. . . . But I will go back to England to her that's waiting at the Red Mansion, and you will remember, Soolsby—"

Slowly the great flotilla of dahabiehs floated with the strong current down towards Cairo, the great sails swelling to the breeze that blew from the Libyan Hills. Along the bank of the Nile thousands of Arabs and fellaheen crowded to welcome "the Saadat," bringing gifts of dates and eggs and fowls and dourha and sweetmeats, and linen cloth; and even in the darkness and in the trouble that was on her, and the harrowing regret that she had not been with Eglington in his last hour,—she little knew what Eglington had said to Faith in that last hour—Hylda's heart was soothed by the long, loud tribute paid to David.

As she sat in the evening light, David and Lacey came, and were received by the Duchess of Snowdon, who could only say to David, as she held his hand, "Windlehurst sent his regards to you, his loving regards. He was sure you would come home—come home. He wished he were in power for your sake."

So, for a few moments she talked vaguely, and said at last, "But Lady Eglington, she will be glad to see you, such old friends as you are, though not so old as Windlehurst and me—thirty years, over thirty, la, la!"

They turned to go to Hylda, and came face to face with Kate Heaver.

Kate looked at David as one would look who saw a lost friend return from the dead. His eyes lighted, he held out his hand to her.

"It is good to see thee here," he said gently.

"And 'tis the cross-roads once again, sir," she rejoined.

"Thee means thee will marry Jasper?"

"Ay, I will marry Jasper now," she answered.

"It has been a long waiting."

"It could not be till now," she responded.

David looked at her reflectively, and said: "By devious ways the human heart comes home. One can only stand in the door and wait. He has been patient."

"I have been patient, too," she answered.

As the Duchess disappeared with David, a swift change came over Lacey. He spun round on one toe, and, like a boy of ten, careered around the deck, to the tune of a negro song.

"Say, things are all right in there, with them two, and it's my turn now," he said. "Cute as she can be, and knows the game! Twice a widow, and knows the game! Waiting, she is down in Cairo, where the orange blossom grows. I'm in it; we're all in it—every one of us. Cousin Hylda's free now, and I've got no past worth speaking of; and, anyhow, she'll understand, down there in Cairo. Cute as she can be—"

Suddenly he swung himself down to the deck below. "The desert's the place for me to-night," he said.

Stepping ashore, he turned to where the Duchess stood on the deck, gazing out into the night. "Well, give my love to the girls," he called, waving a hand upwards, as it were, to the wide world, and disappeared into the alluring whiteness.

"I've got to get a key-thought," he muttered to himself, as he walked swiftly on, till only faint sounds came to him from the riverside. In the letter he had written to Hylda, which was the turning-point of all for her, he had spoken of these "key-thoughts." With all the childishness he showed at times, he had felt his way into spheres where life had depth and meaning. The desert had justified him to himself and before the spirits of departed peoples, who wandered over the sands, until at last they became sand also, and were blown hither and thither, to make beds for thousands of desert wayfarers, or paths for camels' feet, or a blinding storm to overwhelm the traveller and the caravan; life giving and taking, and absorbing and destroying, and destroying and absorbing, till the circle of human existence wheel to the full, and the task of Time be accomplished.

On the gorse-grown common above Hamley, David and Faith, and David's mother Mercy, had felt the same soul of things stirring—in the green things of green England, in the arid wastes of the Libyan desert, on the bosom of the Nile, where Mahommed Hassan now lay in a *nugger* singing a song of passion, Nature, with burning voice, murmuring down the unquiet world its message of the Final Peace through the innumerable years.

[THE END.]

GLOSSARY

Aiwa, Yes.
Allah hu Achbar, God is most great.
Al'mah, female professional singer, signifying "a learned female."
Ardab, a measure equivalent to five English bushels.

Backsheesh, tip, *douceur*.
Balass, earthen vessel for carrying water.
Básha, Pasha.
Bersim, clover.
Bismillah, in the name of God.
Bowáb, a doorkeeper.

Dahabieh, a Nile houseboat with large lateen sails.
Darabukkeh, a drum made of a skin stretched over an earthenware funnel.
Dourha, maize.

Effendina, most noble.
El Azhar, the Arab university at Cairo.

Feddan, a measure of land representing about an acre.
Fellah, the Egyptian peasant.

Ghiassa, small boat.

Hakim, doctor.
Hasheesh, leaves of hemp.

Inshallah, God willing.

Kánoon, a musical instrument like a dulcimer.
Kavass, an orderly.
Kemengeh, a cocoanut fiddle.

GLOSSARY

Khamsin, a hot wind of Egypt and the Soudan.
Kourbash, a whip, often made of rhinoceros hide.

Lá iláha illa-lláh, there is no deity but God.

Malaish, no matter.
Malboos, demented.
Mastaba, a bench.
Medjidie, a Turkish order.
Moufettish, High Steward.
Mudir, the Governor of a *Mudirieh*, or province.
Muezzin, the sheikh of the mosque who calls to prayer.
Mooshrabieh, lattice window.

Neboot, a quarter-staff.
Narghileh, a Persian pipe.

Ramadan, the Mahommedan season of fasting.

Saadat-el-Básha, Excellency, Pasha.
Sáis, groom.
Sakkia, the Persian water-wheel.
Salaam, Eastern salutation.
Sheikh-el-beled, head of a village.

Tarboosh, a Turkish turban.

Ulema, learned men.

Wakf, Mahommedan court dealing with succession, etc.
Welée, a holy man, or saint.

Yashmak, a veil for the lower part of the face.
Yelek, a long vest or smock.